Dear Reader,

Both of my first two books featured gray wolf packs—although I did have a gray wolf and red wolf fall for each other. In the third book, I wrote about Arctic wolves. For the fourth book, I was back to the gray wolves. Next, I wanted to write about a red wolf pack, and that became *Seduced by the Wolf*.

Now, where to set the story? I used to live in Oregon, and I loved it there. I went to both Portland Community College and Portland State University, and we lived in Tigard. I loved hiking on the forested trails, rambling near the rugged coastline, visits to Mount Hood to climb and to sled when the snows fell. I experienced the adventures of trying to make my way home from college in blizzard conditions. I loved the rainy weather and the month of summer sun we had. It was so green there—just beautiful. I wore waffle stompers and a rain parka and reveled in the great outdoors. It was so different from Florida where we had lived previously.

So yes: woods, wolf sightings, rugged coastline—a perfect setting for the red wolf pack.

I often incorporate true human stories and real-life wolf stories in my books. In this case, I used a story about a wolf biologist who was trying to save a she-wolf and her pups. My heroine, Cassie Roux, is a biologist who studies wolf ecology and is on a mission to rescue a she-wolf and her pups after the wolf's mate has been killed. Although Cassie is a red wolf shifter, she is not looking for entanglements with the red wolf pack in the area. It is her job to teach others about how important wolves are to the ecosystem.

Cassie doesn't need a wolf in her life, and she certainly doesn't need to be tied down to a pack. But there's a hot male red wolf who is seriously cramping her style.

With a shortage of female red wolves in his pack and the way Leidolf Wildhaven already feels about Cassie, he's on a mission to convince her she needs to be with him. Forevermore. After having taken over the pack from a group of rogue wolves and dealing with some newly turned wolves, Leidolf has his hands full. But no matter what, he wants Cassie in his life. He never anticipated how much trouble that could stir up! But there's a reason he's a pack leader. He gets things done. And when he makes up his mind that he wants something, he gets it.

Red wolves are beautiful, but unfortunately the population of pure red wolves is dwindling. Gray wolves and coyotes have been known to mate with red wolves, and while it might seem awful to have other species' DNA mixed with theirs, inbreeding among red wolves could be an even worse problem.

On the East Coast, there are known to be a few red wolves in North Carolina. For years, people have reported sighting red wolves on Galveston Island and along the Gulf Coast. The biologist who tracked them down said he knew they weren't coyotes because of the way they interact with one another—and their unique voices. This pack of wild canines have extinct red wolf DNA as well as coyote DNA.

Sounds like an idea for another story!

I hope you are enjoying the wolf saga, and I look forward to sharing more about their world with you in coming books! Thanks for reading and loving my wolves!

Terry Spear

Praise for Terry Spear

"This action-packed story crackles with mystery, adventure...and passion; a worthy addition to Spear's beautifully imagined werewolf world."

— *Library Journal* for *Seduced by the Wolf*

"Ms. Spear has produced another winner with her wonderful wolfish world...mystery, death-defying action, sizzling sensuality, humor, romance, as well as a bit of the paranormal make this a book you won't want to miss."

— *Romance Junkies* for *Alpha Wolf Need Not Apply*

"Ms. Spear has written another wonderful story that illustrates the best of holiday romances... A howling good time and a recommended read."

— *Long and Short Reviews* for *A Silver Wolf Christmas*

"A page turner that had everything...plenty of exciting action, suspense, and steamy passion... A highly recommended read."

— *The Romance Reviews* Reviewer Top Pick for *SEAL Wolf Hunting*

"*A Highland Werewolf Wedding* is another shining example of exactly why Terry Spear is the Queen of the shifter romance."

— *Night Owl Reviews*, 5 Stars, Reviewer Top Pick for *A Highland Werewolf Wedding*

Also by Terry Spear

SEDUCED
BY THE
WOLF

TERRY
SPEAR

sourcebooks
casablanca

Published by Sourcebooks Casablanca, an imprint of Sourcebooks
P.O. Box 4410, Naperville, Illinois 60567-4410
(630) 961-3900
sourcebooks.com

Originally published as *Seduced by the Wolf* in 2010 in the United States of
America by Sourcebooks Casablanca, an imprint of Sourcebooks.

Printed and bound in Canada.
MBP 10 9 8 7 6 5 4 3 2 1

I dedicate Seduced by the Wolf *to my son and daughter, who are always behind me 100 percent and who are as proud of me for my accomplishments as I am of them.*

CHAPTER 1

EXCEPT FOR A COUPLE OF CARS PARKED OUTSIDE THE town hall, the lot was empty, and it appeared the wolf biologist speaking here tonight wouldn't have much of an audience to lecture to.

The Oregon air surrounding him felt damp and cool, not like the drier, much sunnier weather Leidolf Wildhaven had left behind in Colorado. He kept telling himself he'd get used to it. Old-time brass lanterns cast a golden glow over the sidewalk. A steady breeze stirred the spring leaves of the massive white oaks that lined the brick walk leading to the two-story building. An antiquated clock chimed seven times in the center of the tower on top, announcing to everyone in the listening area that the time had arrived for the lecture to begin.

He let out his breath and headed for the building. Anything to do with wolves concerned him, and even though the "doctor" couldn't say anything he didn't already know, he wanted to see how others reacted to her talk concerning them. At this rate, it looked as though no one was going to show.

He took two steps at a time up the brick stairs and strode into the building, his gaze focusing on the empty chairs and the speakerless podium.

Dressed in a gray suit, Millie Meekle, the woman in charge of tourism and special events in the area, wrung her hands nearby and shook her head, her stiff, glued-together silver hair not moving a fraction out of place.

"Oh, Mr. Wildhaven, this is a disaster. Dr. Roux had a flat tire at the place she's staying, and my husband dropped me off here, so I haven't any vehicle to go get her." She waved at the empty seats. "And no one has even shown up yet."

"Where's she staying?"

Several men sauntered into the town hall, their boots tromping on the wooden floor, their expressions annoyed. "Where's the doc?" one of the men asked gruffly.

Millie quickly spoke up. "She's stuck at the Cranberry Top Bed and Breakfast. Mr. Wildhaven's kind enough to offer to get her. She's staying in the Blue Room, first door on the left down the hall from the entryway," she directed Leidolf.

The man snorted. "We don't need no damned wolf biologist telling us how we should reintroduce wolves into the wild out here."

"Now, Mr. Hollis," Millie said.

"Don't 'Now, Mr. Hollis' me, Millie. You know I raise sheep, and if any damn wolf slinks onto my land, I'll kill him dead. That's what I'll do."

"I'll go get her," Leidolf said. He stalked out of the building with its oppressive heat and back into the cool out-of-doors. He hadn't figured any of the livestock owners would bother to come to the meeting, but after seeing the burly men, he was afraid the professor was bound for trouble.

Climbing into his Humvee, he assumed the woman probably wouldn't get a whole lot of lecturing done but instead would be faced with a barrage of condemning remarks. He still couldn't figure out why in the world she'd come here instead of lecturing to a more intellectual crowd in the city of Portland, two hours away.

Putting the vehicle in drive, he headed to the Cranberry Top, a quaint little red-roofed home with white siding and a white picket fence. Like many of the homes in the area, the place had been turned into a bed-and-breakfast inn because it was situated on a creek perfect for fishing and picturesque Mount Hood could be seen way off in the distance. Great for a Portland getaway.

When Leidolf arrived at the inn, he saw the vehicle in question, a green pickup with California plates that was tilting to one side. *Women.* Probably didn't know how to change a tire or call for someone to come and fix a flat.

He'd barely opened the door to his Humvee when a woman hurried out, red hair in curls down to her shoulders and bouncing with her every step, eyes sea green and wide and hopeful, brow furrowed as she clutched a leather satchel tightly against her chest and headed straight for him. *Dr. Roux?* At least he presumed that was who she was, only he'd expected someone a lot less leggy and less stunning to look at.

What he'd figured he'd see was a gray-haired older woman, her hair swept back in a bun, with oval gold-rimmed glasses perched on her nose. Instead, this woman looked to be in her midtwenties and in terrific form, with shapely legs and a body to match. He envisioned her hiking through woods on wilderness treks to observe wolves, dispelling the notion that she was strictly a classroom lecturer.

"Dr. Roux?" he asked, feeling more like a knight in shining armor now.

She didn't smile but looked worried as hell as she chewed a glossy lip and then gave a stiff nod. "Did Millie send you for me?" She didn't wait for him to answer and motioned to the truck. "I changed the tire already."

He frowned and glanced back at the flat tire.

"Someone was nice enough to ruin the spare also when I ran inside to clean up," she added, her tone peeved. "It was too late to have the spare fixed before the meeting."

Irritated that any of the townspeople would treat her that way, he bit back a curse. Yet he couldn't help being surprised for a second time. First, by her appearance. Now, by how capable the little woman was.

He motioned to his Humvee. "I'm Leidolf Wildhaven, rancher south of town. I'll take you to the meeting and have one of my men fix the tires while you're lecturing."

"A rancher," she said softly, her voice slightly condemning.

He cast her a smidgeon of a smile. "Yeah, but cougars are the only animals that bother me of late. Wolves? They're my kind of animal. Protective, loyal—you know, like a dog, man's best friend."

"They're wild, Mr.—"

"I'd prefer you call me Leidolf."

"I'm Cassie. Never met a rancher before who liked wolves." She sounded as though she didn't believe he would care for wolves. Maybe even worried that he might cause her trouble when she lectured.

She climbed into his vehicle and took a deep breath, and her eyes widened again. He swore if he hadn't blocked her in as he held the door ready to shut it for her, she would have escaped. He heard her slight intake of breath and her heartbeat accelerate. Her gaze swiftly swept over him as if he was suddenly someone of more importance. She swallowed hard and smoothed her skirt over her lap, drawing his eye, and then she pulled away from him as much as possible.

She took another deep breath and met his gaze. "Wolves

are wild and unpredictable. But you're right. They're also protective and loyal. Thanks for coming to get me."

He smiled in response, appreciating that she was a wolf advocate yet understood wolves well enough to realize how dangerous they could be, and felt a slight connection to her right away. Before he could shut her door, she quickly added, "You...*are* taking me to the town hall, right?"

"Yeah. Millie Meekle said you needed a lift."

Cassie still looked a little alarmed when Leidolf climbed into the vehicle, and he supposed he could understand her wariness. Millie should have called to let Cassie know he was coming to get her.

"I never figured I'd have trouble out here." She snapped her seat belt in place and pressed herself against the passenger door, almost as if she was attempting to keep as far away from him as she could.

For someone who studied wolves, she seemed a tad skittish. Which made him wonder if she'd had trouble with men before. Instantly, that thought gnawed at him, no matter that he'd just met her.

Leidolf glanced at her as he drove back to the meeting place. "Why not lecture in Portland? You'd have had much more of a draw."

A long silence filled the air.

"People need to be educated in places like this," she finally said.

Leidolf didn't respond, but he was already bothered by where this was leading. And he had a sneaking suspicion it was the very reason she had come here.

She looked out the window and didn't say anything further.

He cleared his throat. "Why in places like this?"

A prolonged silence filled the space between them, elevating his concern. Turning her head in his direction, she gave him a sad kind of smile. "Because unless the wolf is in the Oregon Zoo, the people of Portland are unlikely to see any wolves running around their fair city."

"Out here?"

He felt her observing him while he concentrated on the road. Like she studied wolves? Wouldn't she be surprised to learn he was one also, whenever he had the urge to shift.

"They might be out here, some day."

"You don't seem the type who wastes time talking about future events. Have you seen a wolf in this area?" he asked, very much to the point. He had to know. Had she seen one of his pack members running in his or her fur coat in the woods around here?

She looked back out the window.

Hell. "Cassie, have you seen a wolf in these parts?"

"They've been spotted in several different locations all over Oregon. People everywhere need to be educated. That's what I do," she said evasively.

Concerned about what she'd observed, Leidolf pulled into a parking space at the town hall. Several vehicles now filled the lot. He hoped that most of the good citizens of the area would behave themselves. And if she'd seen what he suspected she had, he hoped the hell she didn't mention it in the lecture. He suspected that she was worried he might want the wolf eliminated if she told him she'd actually witnessed it—because he was a rancher, despite saying he liked wolves.

Before he could climb out of his Humvee to get her

door, she hopped out, thanked him, and hurried up the brick walk. "Sorry," she said, in a rush to get to the front door. "I'm fifteen minutes late."

He thought she hurried to stay away from him for some other reason. He couldn't fathom what that reason was. He had brought her here safe and sound and would have one of his men fix her tires. So why would she fear him?

The fact that he was a rancher? Or maybe she was so used to being around wolves—the real kind—that she wasn't equipped to deal with the wolfish human kind. On the other hand, maybe he was making something out of nothing. Maybe she was just anxious because of being late to her own speaking engagement. That was all.

He stalked after her and opened the door before she reached it. "It looks like most everyone just arrived, so I'd say you were right on time."

She gave him a tight smile, but the attempt at a friendly response didn't reach her eyes. She hurried inside, her heels clicking on the wooden floor, and the conversation died to absolute silence. Leidolf took a seat in back where he could observe everyone. As attractive as the woman was, he'd have preferred watching her, the way she slid her hands gently over her notes, the way her full, glossy lips parted as she spoke, the sweet tone of her voice, even when she was worried about being late or annoyed that someone had ruined her tires.

He forced his gaze from her and glanced at several kids, who appeared to be high-school students, seated to one side of the room with pens and notepads in hand. Probably would receive some kind of special credit for coming here tonight. Even a couple of twin girls from his pack were in the audience, although pack members homeschooled their own. Their father must have made them come. Alice and Sarah glanced back at Leidolf and smiled. He bowed his head in acknowledgment.

On the other side of the hall, he recognized most of the men, ranchers all of them. One man raised pygmy goats; six others, cattle like him; and the sheepherder. The man who really caught his attention was a blond who also garnered Cassie's. Her eyes widened, and she fussed over her notes, but she looked back at him as he grinned broadly. Someone she definitely knew but apparently wasn't overly happy to see. She didn't seem to be from the area. In fact, her bio said she was from California, and Leidolf didn't remember seeing either of them here before. So had the man followed her here?

Leidolf studied the man again. Tall, thin, wearing hiking boots, jeans, and a camouflage jacket. He looked like a hunter. Leidolf already didn't like him.

Pulling his cell phone out, Leidolf texted his second-in-command, Elgin, telling him which vehicle to have repaired, what needed to be accomplished, and to take his time in getting it done. And then Leidolf sat back to listen to the little lady's speech.

After she finished her talk, he meant to speak to her again and learn the truth. What kind of wolf had she seen, and where?

—∾—

Cassie couldn't believe all her rotten, bad luck. First, the idiot or idiots had to ruin not one but two of her tires. Then the absolute hunk who comes to rescue her was one of her kind. How could she get so lucky? And to top all that off? Fellow wolf biologist Alex Wellington had to track her down again. What was his problem? What part of *I work alone* did he not get? Not that he wasn't cute or good at his job, but sometimes she liked to shift while she was working, and she sure as hell didn't want him studying *her* as one of his wolf projects.

Avoiding looking at Leidolf, his handsome features rugged, his eyes penetrating and insightful, she knew he could be even worse trouble for her. She'd been so upset about the tires and being late to the lecture that when he gave his name, it hadn't registered at first. *Leidolf* was Norse for *wolf descendant*! And the last name, Wildhaven, was typical of a red *lupus garou* name.

The fact that he said he was a rancher had also thrown her off. No way would she have thought a wolf would be in the ranching business. Once she'd gotten a whiff of his *lupus garou* scent, she'd known the truth. She fought a smile. His comment about wolves, like dogs, being man's best friend made sense. From a wolf's standpoint anyway.

She had barely begun to talk about wolves—their history and their future—when one of the men seated near the front said, "Sure, we used to kill 'em for money. The only good wolf is a dead wolf."

Wondering if the scruffy-looking, bearded man was the one who had taken care of her tires, she bit her tongue and clenched her teeth. Her gaze riveted on Leidolf. He was giving the man a look like he'd better watch what he said, and all of a sudden, she realized something more about the werewolf in her midst.

He said he'd have one of his men see to her tires. She blinked. He couldn't be the pack leader here, could he? Or maybe he was a subleader. Not that it would make much difference, since he would report back to the head honcho that he had located a female red in their territory.

She groaned inwardly at her rotten luck.

"Mr. Hollis," Millie said, her voice pleading, breaking into Cassie's distressing ruminations. "Dr. Roux will take questions at the end of her lecture. For now, we'll just let her present her case." She smiled a little nervously and motioned for Cassie to begin again.

Cassie gave her a tight smile. She'd never had this many problems lecturing before and certainly had never expected to find a red wolf in the area. Once she had learned of the wolf, she felt it her duty to make the people aware that wolves were not a threat for the most part and that it was illegal to shoot them.

Alex nodded, as if approving her every word.

Leidolf was busy texting someone. Thankfully, he hadn't seemed to smell her scent. The hunter's spray had appeared to hide what she was from him. She still had worried that if he'd gotten too close, he might have detected she was a red wolf like himself.

She continued with her speech, wanting to get this over with, while she normally loved pleading the wolves' case. She usually wasn't in a werewolf's territory either. And that could mean trouble. Especially because she was an unmated red, and packs were always looking for unmated females.

She'd barely made it to page two of her notes when Mr. Hollis interrupted her again, his voice reproachful. "Last year, a woman broke into the zoo and set a wolf free. Or at least that was the story the newspapers gave. Naked woman in zoo frees red wolf. So do you advocate freeing wolves from the zoo too?"

Cassie set her papers aside. The man was referring to Bella Wilder, red werewolf, who had shifted while in captivity from her wolf form to her human form during the new moon. Unless the werewolf was a royal with very few human roots in its bloodline, like Cassie happened to be, it could not remain as a wolf or change into one during the new moon. Cassie couldn't imagine how terrifying that change had to have been for the woman.

Leidolf studied Cassie, his brows slightly raised, waiting to see how she would respond to the question. If only he'd known what she truly was and how she cherished the wolf kind as much as her own werewolf kind. Alex still wore his silly smile, cheering her on.

Attempting not to become antagonistic in response to Mr. Hollis's question, Cassie stood taller and maintained a cool but professional tone.

"The woman was the victim of a crime, Mr. Hollis. She was left naked in the wolves' pen, and the red wolf was stolen. She was never found guilty of the crime of aiding anyone in setting the wolf free. And the red wolf was never found."

Mr. Hollis harrumphed and folded his arms across his broad chest. "You didn't answer my question, Doc. Do you believe the wolves in the zoo should be released into the wild? You said yourself that they don't have the same kind of life in the zoo as they do living in the wide, open spaces. You know." He motioned to the other ranchers. "Where they can kill our sheep and goats and cattle."

"Most animals in the zoo are born and bred there. So they're more suited to a zoo environment. Many haven't ever lived in the wild."

"So you're saying no, they shouldn't be released?" Mr. Hollis persisted.

"That's what she's saying," Alex said, as if he was talking to someone who was a little slow to understand.

While she appreciated that Alex stuck up for her, Cassie preferred to fight her own battles.

Mr. Hollis turned around and glowered at Alex. "She's the wolf expert here. If I want your opinion, Sonny, I'll ask for it. Otherwise, mind your own business."

Alex arched a brow and offered a little smile. He was almost as much of an expert on wolves as Cassie was, although being one part time, she did have the advantage. She was glad he kept his mouth shut and didn't say anything further.

A student raised his hand, and Hollis shut up while she answered the students' questions. Cassie was relieved to see most of the ranchers quit the place. Not Mr. Hollis. She hoped she didn't have to deal with him afterward. And Alex. How in the world was she going to lose him as she attempted to slip into the wilds to study the rare red in the woods?

Of course, Leidolf was the other major problem. He already suspected she'd seen a wolf. She frowned. It couldn't have been one of his people, could it? She sure hoped not. And now because of the tire situation, she was stuck dealing with him a little while longer. At least until she paid one of his men for repairing her tires and thanked him for the gesture. She definitely didn't want Leidolf learning she was one of his kind. The sooner she was as far away from him and any members of his pack as she could get, the better.

Another girl's hand shot up, and she proposed her question. Cassie loved educating students, since they were more eager to learn than adults. But right now, she was ready to slip away before anything else went wrong tonight. And she was afraid it would—as soon as she tried to get away from Leidolf without telling him about the wolf she'd actually seen.

CHAPTER 2

As soon as Cassie finished responding to questions, Hollis moved in to harass her at the podium. Leidolf intercepted him, not intending to let him bother Cassie further, while the students gathered around her to ask about her chosen career field. Dividing Leidolf's attention, the blond guy also inched closer to get a word with Cassie.

The other ranchers shook their heads and left.

"What?" Hollis said to Leidolf as he blocked the sheepherder's path. "Don't tell me you love wolves too. You raise cattle!"

"She's just an educator. That's all."

Hollis shifted his glower from Leidolf to Cassie. "She ought to be in some other kind of business, the way she looks. If she starts advocating that we allow Oregon to be a safe haven for wolves..." He gave Leidolf another scowl. "A lot of ranchers will turn into hunters is all I got to say." He stalked out of the building.

Glad Hollis had left, Leidolf folded his arms and looked at Cassie. He was surprised how much she understood about wolves. She truly was an expert, knowing them inside and out. His admiration of her went even deeper. The love she had for them was what really struck him.

"Have you ever slept with real wolves?" a wide-eyed girl asked. "My German shepherd sleeps with me on campouts. Would the wolves you've studied in the wild let you get that close?"

Cassie glanced at Leidolf.

He was used to reading people, and yet he was getting mixed feelings from her expression. Worry that she might say the wrong thing to the older teen girl maybe? He wasn't certain. What got to him was the way her eyes suddenly became glazed with tears.

Cassie quickly looked back at the girl and said, "Uhm, no. They're wild, and even though I grew close to the packs, even howling so they would gather around me as if I were one of the pack, I didn't... didn't sleep with them."

The hitch in her voice, the change in her tone, the tension in her posture made Leidolf think she *had* slept with them. Why would she be upset about it? Why not tell the truth?

"Did you ever miss the pack when you left them?" another girl asked.

Cassie smiled, but the look was sad. She swallowed hard. "Of course."

"Any that were really special? I mean, weren't they like all the same to you?" the first girl asked.

Cassie shook her head. "No. All wolves are different. Ever have dogs?"

The girl nodded.

The other said, "Yeah, two cockapoos. You know, cocker spaniel–poodles. And they're really different from each other. One's really friendly with everyone. The other just with us."

"The same with wolves," Cassie said. "One I called Crooked Tail. He had fur that stood up every which way, no matter if he went swimming with us or..."

"You swam with the wolves?" one of the boys asked.

Her gaze flicked back to Leidolf as if she wanted to know

what he thought of the matter. Her swimming with the wolves did surprise him. He'd expected she'd sit back with notepad and pen, journaling everything that the wolves did. He hadn't expected her to howl to gather them or swim with them.

He smiled. She didn't. She seemed uptight about having mentioned it at all. She nodded to the boy. "Yes. Anyway, no matter what he did, his fur always stuck out every which way."

"And he had a crooked tail," one of the girls said.

"Yes. And he was kind of a clown. Seemed to go along with everything else." Cassie sounded more lighthearted now.

She waited patiently for the next question, but one of the boys looked at his watch and said, "I gotta go to work. Thanks for all the cool stuff."

"You're welcome." Cassie seemed relieved when the questioning drew to a close and began gathering her notes.

The teens all headed outside, talking about school ending in a few weeks for summer break, and Millie thanked Cassie and then handed her an envelope.

"Cassie, imagine my surprise to see you here," the blond guy said, taking Millie's place as she tidied up the room.

Cassie immediately rolled her eyes at the man and slipped her lecture notes into her leather case along with the envelope from Millie. "Alex, as many times as you've *found* me, you'd think you'd come up with something more original to say."

"Cassie," Leidolf said, coming to her rescue. At least she seemed to need rescuing, and he was the one to do it. "I'll take you back to your place."

"I'll take her," the blond said. "We're old friends."

She seemed torn, and that puzzled Leidolf. She'd been fairly obvious about not wanting to be in Alex's company, but why was she reluctant to be in Leidolf's when all he had done was offer her assistance?

The fact that Alex called himself an old friend also bothered Leidolf, although he had no business caring one way or another concerning her relationship with the man.

"Cassie?" Leidolf motioned to the door. He still intended to ask her about the wolf she'd seen, and the blond guy wasn't going to interfere.

"Alex, one of Mr. Wildhaven's men is taking care of a couple of flat tires for me. We'll have to have a rain check."

Mr. Wildhaven was it now?

Alex's face fell. Leidolf almost felt some compassion for the man. *Almost.* He gave Cassie a smile, but she quickly looked away from his gaze, and her cheeks colored slightly. His smile broadened. Was she embarrassed at turning down Alex, someone she was better acquainted with, to spend more time with a man she barely knew?

"I'm sure one of my men has fixed your tires by now," he assured her. He hoped Elgin would ensure that whoever repaired the tires took his time without making anything of the request. Leidolf hoped they'd assume his reasoning was that the woman would talk for quite a while during her lecture and his men had no need to rush the job.

He walked Cassie out of the building and down the steps. Time to question the little lady further and hope she wasn't as evasive as before.

Alex waved at her as he got into a black truck and waited. She shook her head.

"I heard what you said back there to him. Is this Alex stalking you?" Leidolf asked her as he got in the Humvee, trying to keep his voice light.

"No, just an admirer of my work."

"And he followed you here from…?"

"He's a wolf biologist from California also," she finally said with a huff.

Hell. Had this guy seen one of Leidolf's people in his or her wolf coat? "So you work together?"

"No." She shook her head to emphasize the point. "He just wants to."

For whatever insane reason, Leidolf was glad she didn't want to work with the guy, but he didn't like that Alex ignored Cassie's wishes.

When Leidolf and Cassie arrived back at the Cranberry Top B&B, they discovered a tire jack elevating Cassie's truck on the passenger's side, and the ruined spare was gone. Cassie frowned. Leidolf quickly hid his relief and pulled out his phone.

"I'll see how long this is going to take." He texted Elgin, mentioning that if repairing the doctor's tires was going to take a while, he'd have time to question the woman about some urgent business.

Elgin's response was immediate. *"Take ur time. 7 cars ahead of her. Good luck."*

No way were that many vehicles waiting to be repaired ahead of hers at this time of night, and besides, his men would have gotten priority, considering how much business his pack members gave the auto-repair shop. Elgin came through for him as usual.

Leidolf shut off his phone, let out his breath as if he regretted the news, and then turned to speak to Cassie. She was watching him, her large eyes expressive.

"I'm sorry to say seven vehicles are ahead of you," he said with just the right apology coating his words.

Instantly, she narrowed her eyes.

He spread his hands. "My foreman will let me know as soon as the tires are fixed. Would you care for a cup of coffee?"

Cassie sat rigid against the seat again, leaning against the door as far as she could get from him.

"Hot tea? Dinner?" he suddenly asked. "I haven't had anything to eat, come to think of it. Great little Italian place if you like pastas and such."

Her lips parted, and then she clamped them shut and pursed them again. She tilted her chin up and seemed even warier than before, if that were possible. "Can you drive me to the shop?"

"Pardon?"

"The shop. Where your men have taken my tires. Maybe I can get the repairmen to expedite matters. I'm on a tight schedule and need to leave…" She hesitated.

He raised his brows. "Surely you don't plan to drive out tonight. If the Cranberry Top won't accommodate you for another night because of your delay…" On one hand, he had the sneaking suspicion she was attempting to call his bluff about the repair shop. He didn't know what gave him away. On the other hand, he assumed she had another night booked at the B&B and didn't want him checking her story out further either.

"Dinner?" he asked.

"Fast food," she said with a cute little frown, and she folded her arms across her waist.

He squelched a chuckle, loving the way she had so graciously capitulated. He wasn't about to tell her the small town had no fast-food places he'd be willing to take her to. And he decided the Italian place wouldn't suit her as much as the Forest Club, where tables sat under fake trees covered in real bark that looked about as real as the ones in the woods surrounding his ranch. The club's "sky" was black velvet sprinkled with twinkling white lights, and dance music beat a rhythm made for hot dance numbers on a chilly night. The only real drawback was that one of the mated couples in his pack owned the place, and many of his pack members frequented it too.

Still, it was the perfect place for questioning the doc about her wolf sighting. Nice table situated in the dark forest, massive trunks hiding them from most of the other guests. And she probably had never seen anything quite as unique.

He drove her to the place a mile away, and when they reached the expansive building where giant maples towered over the gravel parking lot at irregular intervals like a forest, she frowned at him. He thought she'd be pleased because of the kind of work she did. Or maybe she lectured a lot and didn't really live among the wolves as he thought.

She opened her door, and he hurried out of the vehicle to reach her before she shut the passenger door. "It's not a fast-food restaurant," she said matter-of-factly.

"None of them are very appealing around here. I thought you might enjoy something kind of unusual. Since you're a wolf biologist and all." He reached behind her, and with a whisper of a touch on her back, guided her to the building, which looked like a hobbit's home, with a thatched roof for quaint appeal. The composite roof shingles underneath protected the occupants during frequent rains or the occasional snowstorm.

Cassie wasn't smiling yet, and her step slowed the closer they got to the entrance as they walked on the pine-needle-covered pathway as if they were strolling through piney woods. He reached for the door, but one of his men pushed it open, heading out with his mate. As soon as he saw Leidolf with Cassie, the man and his mate grinned, backed out of Leidolf and Cassie's way, and followed them back inside.

Leidolf sighed. He should have figured that no matter where he took the attractive redhead, his people would be curious as to what might develop. He guessed they still didn't know him well enough to realize that except for a one-night stand or two with a willing human, he wasn't ever taking one as a mate.

Cassie suddenly shrank away from Leidolf and even groaned. He glanced down at her. "Are you all right?"

She looked a little pale.

"Cassie?"

—◆◆—

What else could go wrong tonight? Cassie didn't even want to pose such a question in her head for fear she'd get an answer she didn't like. The Forest Club was the most interesting eatery she'd been to in a very long time, and if she hadn't been worried about Leidolf and his people discovering what she was, she would have loved it. The problem was the place was filled with his...well, *their* kind.

She took a deep, fortifying breath. Okay, she could do this. She was used to pretending to her colleagues that she was only a human wolf biologist. She could pretend she was a human wolf biologist to this crowd of werewolves. As long as the hunter spray didn't give out on her. Or she didn't give herself away in some other manner.

Leidolf guided her to a secluded booth that formed their own little forest hideaway. The only other tables nearby were empty.

She could do this.

Thankfully, Leidolf escorted her to one side of the booth and then sat opposite her, like the perfect gentleman. She supposed he was looking for a little nighttime diversion. He must not be mated.

"Like it?" he asked, handing her a menu already placed on the table against a tree trunk.

She finally gave him a genuine smile. "Thanks. I love it. Feels like home. Except for the music." She motioned in the direction of the beat.

He smiled broadly back, looking relieved she'd changed her tune. "Maybe you'd like to dance later."

"Uhm, no. Thanks. Don't dance." She quickly looked at the menu and fought the blush that rose to her cheeks.

"Ever?" He sounded disappointed.

She gave him a quick smile meant to appease but faked to high heaven. "Sorry, never."

"I can teach you—"

"No."

He watched her. She didn't have to look up to know he was studying her, trying to figure her out.

"You're not a hard-shell Baptist, no drinking, no dancing, are you?"

She smiled, only this time it was for real. "No. I'll have the…" She frowned as she studied the menu. "Forest Urchin Special."

"A vegetarian's dish."

She nodded. "Red meat's not good for you, you know." She figured that would throw him off track if he had any inkling she was a wolf, although she was dying to have the chicken or beef added for substance. A little bit of meat would give her more energy to sustain her for longer. And she'd need it for her trek through the woods tonight. As soon as she could have her truck in working order and leave.

"I'll have the roast tenderloin." He closed up the menu and motioned to one of the waiters, who hurried to bring them glasses of water.

The man had been staying clear of them, trying to give them privacy, Cassie thought, as she'd seen him attempting not to be noticed but glancing often in their direction. Probably all Leidolf's pack members were dying to know where this would lead. Which most likely meant Leidolf *was* their pack leader. *Great. Just great.*

All of a sudden, Alex stalked into the club, spied her in their little hidden part of the forest, smiled, and headed for one of the empty booths across from them. She wondered how he'd found her this time. Must have followed them from a distance.

The waiter glanced in Alex's direction, but after Leidolf ordered for them, he cast the waiter a look, turned his head toward Alex, and then gave a very subtle nod to the waiter.

She knew what it meant. Alex was encroaching on Leidolf's territory. Even if Leidolf only wanted to be with her for one evening, he wasn't about to let Alex interfere. The waiter smiled at Cassie in a knowing way and then hurried to speak to Alex.

He spoke low, but with her enhanced wolf hearing,

she overheard him say, "I'm sorry, sir. These two tables are reserved. And the rest of the place has been booked until closing. Perhaps you'd like to make reservations to dine here another night."

Leidolf hadn't had to make reservations. And she predicted no one would sit in the tables across from them while she and Leidolf remained here tonight.

Leidolf opened the wine menu. "Want a glass of wine?"

"Uh, no, thanks." She sure didn't need to drink before she started her long trek later tonight, trying to hunt the wolf down.

He closed the menu. "All right. So where did you see the wolf?"

—◆◆◆—

Leidolf couldn't figure out Cassie's mixed messages. One minute, she seemed resigned—like when she agreed to eat with him. She was skittish again when she entered the club and then panicky when he mentioned the wolf.

He knew for sure she'd seen one then. But where? And was it one of his reds? Or was it a plain old gray wolf, nothing to really worry about?

He waited for her to answer his query: where had she seen the wolf? She hesitated, took a sip of water, and glanced over at their waiter, George, as he brought their meals. She smiled at him and placed the napkin on her lap, totally ignoring Leidolf's question.

As soon as George put the food down, asked if they needed anything else, and then hurried off, she eyed Leidolf's tenderloin. If he hadn't thought she was a vegetarian because of the dish she'd ordered and because of her comment about red meat not being good for him, he would have sworn she wanted some of his roast.

He cut up a portion of it, slid his plate over, and smiled. "Won't kill you. I promise."

Her gaze switched from him to his meat again, and she began to shake her head and decline, but he insisted. She wanted it. Probably concerned about her figure. She had nothing to worry about in that regard from what he could tell.

"Go ahead, Cassie."

She looked up at him. "You said you hadn't eaten and you're hungry."

He chuckled. "Pass over some of your rabbit food. We can share."

Still, she hesitated.

He eyed her mushrooms sautéed in a spicy sauce along with spinach and broccoli, carrots, and potatoes. "Looks a lot better than my plain old baked potato."

She twisted her mouth a little and considered his tenderloin again. "Are you sure?"

"Absolutely. We can always get more if we want."

He didn't know why it pleased him so much, but he wanted her to like this place as much as he did. He wanted her to enjoy her meal as much as he would, and he really wished she'd dance with him. Maybe it would make up for the way some bastard had given her so much trouble in the form of two flat tires, or the way Hollis had interrupted her when she was lecturing about the wolves. Or the annoyance she had felt about Alex following her around. Maybe it had to do with how much she truly loved wolves.

She seemed to enjoy the meat like he did, almost as

much as he enjoyed watching her savor every bite of the tenderloin. As if it was her first good meal in ages and would be the last for even longer.

"Are you sure you don't want a glass of wine?" he asked.

She shook her head no and sighed deeply. "Thank you for bringing me here. I'll never forget it."

He could tell she meant it, but a tinge of regret slipped into her words. Which made him hopeful she'd want to stay with him longer. Dinner, drinks, and then an intimate tryst with a human woman was the usual fare for him when he felt the need and found a woman who wished it as much as he did. Except he hadn't felt the need since taking over the pack several months ago. Not with any other woman.

He really wanted to be with Cassie for the night, although he felt her pulling away again. Since she was human and he couldn't develop a long-lasting relationship with her, it shouldn't have bothered him that she was leaving soon, but strangely it did.

"You said you slept with the wolves. Didn't this domesticate them somewhat? I thought wolf biologists didn't interact much with the wolves they studied for fear the wolves wouldn't be afraid of man anymore. Which could put them in a world of hurt if hunters came across them."

She shrugged. "We study them to help educate people about the wolves' true natures. They're wary of humans until those of us who study them show we're not to be feared."

Leidolf raised his brows. "I see. I was curious about your calling to wolves. I've never heard of someone howling so that a wolf would understand." A human anyway. He hadn't ever met a wolf biologist before, so what she really did was still a mystery in part.

"That would be understandable since you're a rancher and I doubt you'd be running around with a pack of wolves." She almost seemed to smile at the mention. *Almost.*

He sat back in his chair and smiled at her. If only she knew. "I'd love to hear you howl. You should have done so for the teens. They would have gotten a kick out of it."

"I don't normally demonstrate for human audiences. I really don't think that Mr. Hollis would have appreciated it. I don't believe some of the other men in the audience would have either. If you'd like to experience such a thing, they have howling outings for people at the International Wolf Center near Ely, Minnesota. Or howl-ins at Wolf Haven International where they take in captive-born wolves or Wolf Park where they have howl night programs."

"Really," he said with surprise. "So I take it you've been there?"

"Of course. Wolves everywhere and anywhere interest me." She motioned to the treed booths. "You and I are in a restaurant with civilized folk. I'm sure no one would appreciate it if I suddenly let out a howl."

He motioned to the forest surrounding them. "We're in the woods."

"What if I attract a bunch of wolves?" She lifted her water glass, and her lips curved up slightly.

"I'll assure them that you're with me," he said.

The same amused expression lit her eyes, entrancing, mysterious, like looking into darkened green windows, a hint of something just beyond.

She shook her head. "I'm sure the management wouldn't like it."

"I'm friends with the management."

This time, she smiled broadly.

"Come on. Just once." He really didn't believe she could manage a good howl, being human, although his own kind could. He was curious how she'd sound.

"All right. You get us kicked out of here, you remember I told you so." She took two deep breaths, held it, cupped her hands over her mouth, and tilted her face up to the black velvet ceiling mimicking the night sky. She let loose a howl, rising up and slowly tapering off in perfect cadence, just like a wolf would.

And she was beautiful.

Four of his people walked by, looked them over, smiled, and went on their way.

She chuckled. "Guess there aren't any wolves around here."

Yeah, except the ones that just inspected them, maybe now thinking she was a *lupus garou* and not a human. Hell, half his people here tonight were probably dying to see her but were cautious, not wanting to annoy him. "Very nice howl. I imagine you can gather an entire pack."

"I do pretty well."

When she was talking about wolves, she seemed in her element. He was curious what else she did in her spare time beyond studying wolves. He envisioned her collecting stuffed ones and paintings of them. Maybe she had some statues collecting dust around her place. "Have any hobbies?"

She paused and sipped her tea, looked at him thoughtfully, and then said, "No, not really. I'm pretty busy with my job. What about you?"

She sounded a little sad, and he realized his situation mirrored hers.

He shrugged. "Ranching tends to take a lot of my time." And chasing down wayward newbie werewolves, not to mention trying to heal a pack scarred by past leadership. Which probably had something to do with his interest in Cassie. He was always so busy taking care of others that he didn't much cater to his own needs. And for the first time in eons, he really wanted to enjoy a woman's company.

"Are you sure you don't want to dance?" he coaxed. "A quick one?" He almost said to work off some of the extra calories she'd just eaten, figuring that would convince her, but then decided that might not be such a good idea. He rose from his seat and reached out his hand.

She looked from his hand to his eyes. She wasn't saying no. She was considering it.

"Just one. I promise. You pick the music. We can sit by the dance floor and have water to drink, and when you get in the mood…"

"My tires are probably already fixed by now."

He noted she didn't wear a watch. In fact, she didn't clutter her natural beauty with jewels and baubles of any kind. No earrings, no bracelets, or anything, which reminded him of his own kind. "I'm sure they are. One dance, and I'll take you back to your place."

He couldn't believe how desperate he sounded. He could see in her eyes that the desire was there and yet fear too. Not of him exactly though, or she wouldn't be considering dancing with him. Maybe fear of letting go. He wasn't certain.

"Come on," he cajoled, taking her hand and pulling her gently from the bench. "Just one dance."

Her heart was beating hard. So was his, as if both were preparing to synchronize the rhythm of their blood with the beat of the music. As he escorted her to the bar and dance floor, conversations at booths where some of his people were sitting died down, gazes following him and his date, while small smiles accompanied expressions. No one would say anything to his face when he returned to the ranch, but he could hear the buzz behind his back now. Leidolf had found a redheaded beauty to make his mate.

Not in this lifetime. Not with all the stuff he'd had to deal with recently pertaining to newly turned *lupus garous*. Or maybe they were glad to see *him* finally live a little.

"Just one dance," she said, "and then I have to go."

"Just one dance," he agreed, a little too eagerly, and hoped he could keep on dancing until the club closed at three the next morning.

All the drink tables by the dance floor were filled, and the sprinkling of disco lights overhead made it appear as though a rainbow of fairy lights illuminated a forest. One of the couples seated nearest to them quickly vacated their table, smiling at him and at Cassie. She didn't look at them, as if she was embarrassed to let down her hair like this with a perfect stranger. Yet when he motioned for George to bring them water and the waiter hurried to follow them, Cassie kept walking toward the dance floor.

"Two waters," Leidolf mouthed to George, hoping Cassie hadn't planned to dance to only one song that was half over as he hurried after her.

The bandleader cast Leidolf a knowing wink, and Leidolf gave him a wry smile back, then took Cassie's hand and pulled her gently into his arms. She danced like a fairy, her heels gliding across the floor with ease, never faltering, always in step, her body soft and light and graceful. Why had she resisted dancing to such a degree? She was a superb dancer, and he could have stayed with her like this through the night. Then again, he wondered how she could dance so well if she was so busy observing wolves and hadn't time for much else.

The music played on and on, and he rested his head lightly against the top of hers. He noted amusement on his peoples' faces, glances at the band as they didn't end the song when it should have finished, smiles from other dancers just as tickled.

"Hmm," Cassie murmured as she rested her head against Leidolf's chest, "the band forgot to end the song." She sounded perfectly content, though, to continue the dance, and not in the least bit surprised.

And then the band finally ended the song. He expected her to pull away, to say she wanted to return to the B&B, but instead the band whipped up another slow beat, and she didn't make any move to quit the dance floor. Just softly clung to him as if there was no tomorrow.

He hadn't been with a woman who had felt this good ever. Until she called it a night, he should have been content to dance with her as long as he could. Instead, he was already trying to figure out how to get her to stay with him the rest of the evening. Maybe it was her honest, simple love of wolves that made him cherish being with her so. He wasn't sure. All he knew was that he didn't want to let her go. Not anytime soon.

And hell, he still hadn't gotten her to tell him about the wolf she'd seen!

—◊◊◊—

Cassie knew better than to dance with Leidolf. She knew better, so why was she willing to risk detection? If he learned why she was really here and what she intended to do and that she was one of them, he wouldn't allow it, if he was truly the pack leader. And the way everyone rabidly watched them on the dance floor, the way they smiled and looked hopeful, he had to be their leader and needed a mate.

God, he felt good. Not to mention he smelled delightful, of the fresh spring air, masculine, his body warm and strong. And he made her feel feminine and wanted. She hadn't danced with one of her kind in a very long time, not like this. She hadn't expected it, not his gentleness. Probably figured as a human, she'd break. Especially as nervous as she'd been to come here in the first place.

Dancing with him like this felt so right, while she knew it was a big mistake. Ignoring that little voice that told her to thank him nicely and return to her place and say goodbye, she continued to dance with him. Song after song.

The band was kind enough not to pause in between songs. They never took a break either; they just kept on playing while Leidolf and she kept on dancing. She could have danced until the sun came up, and she thought if Leidolf had asked it, the club would have stayed open until then.

Despite trying to block the feeling, deep down she realized a part of her was missing out on life because of her obsession with studying wolves and lecturing about them. It was easier in some ways to work all the time than to deal with her past.

Even so, she knew this had to end. She finally lifted her head and with a faked sleepy voice said, "They're probably ready to close about now, don't you think?"

At a quarter past three, she noted no one had left, everyone wanting to please their leader, probably dying to tell the rest of the pack what he'd been up to with the redheaded wolf biologist all night.

"Maybe another half hour," Leidolf said.

She smiled and kissed his cheek. He returned the smile and dipped his head to kiss her lips, but she quickly pulled away and took his hand. "Everyone needs to go home. I need to get my sleep. My tires have to be fixed by now."

She swore she heard him groan, but she caught him bowing his head slightly to the band and to some of his people as he walked her out of the dance room.

"Thanks for asking me to dance," she said softly.

"I thought you couldn't dance." He pulled her under his arm and held her close as they walked outside into the brisk chilly air.

"Just didn't want to." More to the point, she didn't want anyone like Leidolf to sidetrack her from her life's work, although he'd had more of an effect on her already than she wanted to admit.

He gave her a light squeeze. "Glad you changed your mind."

She could tell from his husky tone of voice that he was more than glad. Now for the tough part. Sleeping at the B&B was not part of the plan. She had planned on going straight to where she spied the wolf, parking her truck, and tracking her. How was she going to get rid of Leidolf when he took her back there without clueing him in to what she was up to?

CHAPTER 3

As soon as Leidolf drove Cassie back to her place from the Forest Club, he knew something was wrong. She was quiet on the way there, which could have been due to the late hour, but it was more than that. She seemed apprehensive, chewing on her bottom lip, sighing, concentrating on the passenger window. At least she wasn't sitting rigidly against the door like she'd done previously. He guessed sharing a meal and dancing the night away with him had cured her of whatever fears she had of getting close to him.

He really wanted to stay the rest of the night with her. And he had hoped that as much of a connection as they'd made, she'd want the same thing. Instead, she was distancing herself from him again.

"Here we are, Cassie," he said, parking beside her truck.

She jerked her head up, and he realized she'd fallen asleep. He guessed she wasn't a night owl and was just overly tired.

"Want me to carry you inside?"

She yawned and stretched, then pulled a key card out of her satchel. "No. Thanks for everything, Leidolf. What do I owe you?"

He frowned at her, not comprehending. He hadn't intended for her to pay for the meal at the club.

"The tires." She cast him a tired smile.

"Nothing. They shouldn't have been flattened in the first place." He hesitated to open his door, not wanting her to flee into the inn. "Can I see you tomorrow? For breakfast before you leave?"

"I don't eat breakfast, and I'll be long gone by then. If you have a business card and I'm in town again later, I'll give you a call."

The brush-off. It shouldn't have mattered. She was human. He couldn't have had any kind of long-term commitment with her. It did bother him. He didn't know why. Maybe because he hadn't been with a woman in so long, and she seemed so perfect. Just to spend the rest of the night with.

He noted one of his men watching the truck from the distance, hidden in the woods. Good. Elgin had given the word to make sure no one ruined her tires again while she remained here.

"Night, Leidolf." She seemed to want to kiss him, her gaze shifting to his mouth, her tongue sweeping over her lips as if in preparation, but when he leaned over to kiss her the way he really wanted to, she opened her door and headed for the inn.

Watching her hurry up the flagstone walk, he knew he should leave it be. Let her go. Then again, he could come by in a couple of hours and try to see her one last time before she left for good. Maybe she'd change her mind and share a bite of breakfast with him anyway.

He rubbed the whiskers appearing on his chin. Hell, he needed to give her his number in the event she left before he could see her again in the morning, just in case she did return to the area and wanted to visit him. He opened his door, slammed it shut, and hurried toward the inn, telling himself he had the most honorable of intentions. Even though he was dying to kiss the vixen good night, no sweet and unassuming peck on the cheek like she'd given him. Truly, that simple sign of affection had stirred him up all over again.

Like a wolf on the hunt, he picked up his pace as the door to the inn closed shut behind her.

—∼∼—

Cassie's heart raced as she ran through the hallway, heading for the kitchen and the back door that led out to the herb garden. As soon as she reached the kitchen, she heard the front door open. *Leidolf.* Had to be him. Coming to say good night? Hoping for an invitation to stay the rest of the evening maybe. At least, she figured, he wanted a kiss. And she would have given it to him, if she hadn't worried she was getting herself in deeper trouble.

She opened the kitchen door with a squeak, just about giving herself a heart attack as he stopped before the door of her room and called out in a low voice, "Cassie? It's me, Leidolf." He didn't say anything for a moment. "I forgot to give you my number."

Feeling bad that she had to leave him without further word this way, she exited the house, shut the door, and slipped behind some shrubs in the event he heard the squeaking door and came to investigate. He didn't. Yet she had a job to do, and being with Leidolf or any other *lupus garou* wasn't going to help her get it done.

She waited until the front door shut. When Leidolf's Humvee roared to life, she remained where she was until he drove off. Then she raced around to her truck, unlocked the door, and threw in her briefcase. She'd change out of her dressy clothes after she parked in the woods. Now was the time to find the little red wolf.

As soon as she got on the road, she thought she was being followed. She glowered at the headlights behind her. She'd picked them up close to the B&B. Surely, Leidolf hadn't been watching and waiting for her to sneak off.

She considered the height of the headlights. Looked like a pickup truck. She tapped her thumbs on the steering wheel. Someone was probably guarding her truck so no one else tore up her tires. Either that, or it was Alex. She groaned.

Without any other choice, she drove two hours out of her way in the direction of California until the truck finally turned off. And then after driving another fifteen minutes to ensure she didn't pick him up again, she returned to the location where she'd seen the red wolf from the road.

At the turnout for the trailhead, Cassie parked, changed clothes, and slept for a couple of hours. Then she grabbed her field pack and took off into the woods to locate the red wolf. After three hours of hiking up and down the hills and valleys and crossing two rocky creeks, she was sure she was closing in on the elusive wolf.

In hot pursuit of her goal, she slipped through the dappled forest, the filtered sunlight giving it a ghostly appearance. Her boots barely made a sound on ground cushioned with years of accumulated composting leaves, the earthy smell mixed with that of the ancient Douglas firs in the Mount Hood National Forest. She lifted her nose and sniffed the chilly spring air again, trying to locate the female wolf's scent that she'd smelled after tracking her into the area.

Was it a regular *lupus* or a *lupus garou*?

Had to be a wolf. A werewolf wouldn't be running around in its fur coat in broad daylight. Or shouldn't be. Unless she was in trouble. Then that would put a different spin on the whole scenario.

As a wolf biologist, Cassie was normally interested in only one thing: a plain old wolf and its pack that she could study to dispel the myths and legends about the big, bad wolves—and get paid so she could continue to devote her life to their cause. She swallowed a lump in her throat. She owed their kind.

Her shoulders growing weary, she shifted her backpack and crouched down to observe the ground, looking for signs of wolf prints. The water lapping at a bank some distance through the trees caught her attention. Maybe the wolf had left tracks on a muddy bank while she paused to drink there. Unless the bank was rocky...

Cassie headed in that direction to check it out.

What sounded like light footfalls on crunchy dried-out leaves caught her attention. Abruptly, she stopped in the heavily wooded area, smelled the air again, and listened. Just the breeze caressing the leaves and pine needles surrounding her, and hidden in the thick foliage, birds twittering with one another or scolding her for being too close to their nest, the babies peeping for another meal. Yet for the last couple of hours, she had felt as if someone was following her, tracking her every move. So what...or *who* would be trailing her?

Taking a deep breath of the cool air, she didn't catch the scent of anyone or anything else. Either she was imagining things, or whatever it was knew to keep downwind of her.

She hoped it wasn't Alex Wellington, trying to track her down again. Letting out an exasperated sigh, she swore she'd never convince him she strictly worked alone. And then she thought of Leidolf and those of his pack. She stood very still, listening, not hearing anything further. That was all she needed. Leidolf or one of his people tracking her.

She brushed aside the soft, needle-covered branches of a hemlock blocking her view of the source of water and... *gasped*.

Not at the spectacular sight of the dark blue lake, still closed for visitor day use until May, but at the naked man standing midthigh in the cold water, his back to her as he stared out across the region.

She didn't see anything to garner his attention but the beauty and serenity of the vista. Picturesque Mount Hood, the snow-covered volcanic mountain in the distance, the focal point of the whole landscape, so prominent that it could be seen from a hundred miles away.

Well, it would have been the prominent feature if a naked man hadn't been standing in the lake in front of the view, taking center stage instead.

Chestnut hair curled about the nape of his neck, shorter than she thought a reclusive mountain man would wear it. His backside was pure delight to look at, from his broad and muscled back down to his narrow waist and a toned butt a girl could die for. Muscular legs disappeared into water that rippled in the slight breeze.

She sniffed the air but couldn't catch his scent. Being a *lupus garou*, she could smell the mood of an individual like any wolf could—whether he was fearful, aggressive, cowed, or sexually aroused. The way the man was standing so peacefully, she assumed his scent would be a mixture of woods, water, musky male, and blissful serenity.

Before she could back up and leave, he dove into the lake with a splash and, with a powerful momentum, began swimming freestyle. Fascinated, she watched his compelling overarm strokes and legs slicing the water, wondering how he could stomach the cold. Unexpectedly, he plunged beneath the surface. Forever, it seemed, she watched the dark blue waters, the building clouds making them appear blacker. And no sign of the man. He remained under so long that she finally took a step forward in rescue mode when he suddenly rose up like Poseidon, Greek god of the sea, took a deep breath, and dove under again. She half expected him to be wielding a trident while porpoises swam alongside him.

Frozen in place, she continued to watch where he'd disappeared, when he abruptly shot up again. Only this time, he headed for the beach. She frowned. Leidolf? She couldn't be sure with the way he dove in and out of the water so quickly and the distance between her and the beach. Waiting for him to dive again, she didn't move. This time, he remained on the surface and kicked vigorously with his legs, his arms plying the water, his head mostly submersed under water as he swam toward the shore and a pile of clothes she hadn't noticed before.

To her relief, his focus remained on the beach whenever he turned his head to take a breath of air. She was afraid that if she backed into the woods, he would notice her movement and, *God forbid*, realize she'd been a voyeur spying on him. Not that spying on him bothered her overly much. If he was going to run around naked at a closed park, it was *his* fault that she caught him at it. She still didn't want him catching *her* spying on him. Especially if the man *was* Leidolf.

So the plan was that as soon as he concentrated on dressing, she'd slip away.

Upon reaching the shallows, he stood, and she swallowed hard. He looked different naked, his hair dripping wet. It *was* Leidolf.

His strong legs plowing through the water, he waded toward the shore. The lake rippled at his navel, water droplets raised like translucent pearls all over his golden skin, his nipples crisply pebbled. *Beautiful, powerful, tantalizing.* Poseidon in the flesh, just as masculine and intriguing to women as the god who had exerted his power over them, just like his brother Zeus.

At least that was the effect Leidolf had on her. And she wasn't easily swayed by men's appearances. In or out of their clothes.

While he was looking in the direction of his clothes, she took a step back into the shadows of the hemlocks, the soft needles brushing her arms. Without watching where she was going, she stepped on a branch, snapping the dead wood in two. *Big mistake.* With her sensitive hearing, she thought it sounded like the noise echoed across the lake, reaching faraway Mount Hood and even Portland two hours away. Heart racing, she didn't move, afraid to make any further noise, hoping he hadn't heard her.

Leidolf whipped his head around. She should have known he'd hear her. His olive-colored eyes widened when he saw her standing half hidden in the hemlocks. Stiff and motionless like a damned scared doe not moving an inch, she waited to see what happened next. Yet she was every bit the predator as her wolf kind were.

Except for a slight smattering of stubble, lightly reddish in color, Leidolf's face was chiseled perfection that matched the rest of his physique from his sculpted abs and muscular arms down his torso to a trim waist. A red thatch of hair framed his staff already stirring with her perusal. Water droplets slid provocatively down every inch of his skin, caressing like a silky delicate touch.

She swallowed hard and looked up. He was male excellence. At least in the physical department. And to think she'd had that body next to hers at the club half the night, dancing nice and slow.

At first, his expression revealed his surprise to see her standing there, but then he quickly switched his attention from her to the surrounding woods as if he was looking for her hiking companions. Maybe thinking she was with Alex or someone else. His relaxed stance turning rigid, he coiled his fingers into fists and tightened his jaw. The way he hastily reacted indicated he was searching for danger, ensuring she was alone. Probably any man would have done the same thing in the event she had companions with her who were trouble. Especially when he was naked without any weapons for defense.

Apparently reassured no one of a threatening nature was in the immediate vicinity, he shifted his heated gaze back to her and took in her whole appearance.

"Are you lost, Cassie?" he asked, his expression still serious as he lifted his chin slightly and inhaled a deep breath, like any self-respecting *lupus garou* would do.

In answer to his question, she shook her head, but the adrenaline already flooding her bloodstream kicked her heart into a more frantic pace. She hadn't smelled him on her trek through the woods, but then she probably hadn't come across his trail, and the way the breeze was blowing, she hadn't gotten a whiff of him that way either. Plus, if he had never been through this area as a wolf, he wouldn't have left scent markings. With the hunter spray she was wearing so she could catch up to the she-wolf without detection, he still couldn't smell her either.

"I thought you had returned to California." He sounded a little bit perturbed, yet he schooled his expression. "Just hiking then?" He didn't sound as though he thought she was just hiking. He had to have figured she was looking for the wolf she'd seen—that he knew she'd seen.

She didn't answer his question, not wanting to get into a full-blown conversation with him and certainly not to explain her business here. She figured it wouldn't hurt to offer an apology. "I didn't mean to disturb your solitude."

She took another step back and bumped into a branch, nearly giving her a heart attack, until she came to grips with her fear that it was only a branch and not another man behind her, this one blocking her escape path. As much as she wanted to turn and leave, she couldn't, wouldn't back down, tuck tail, and race off.

His stern expression shifted from a look like he was somewhat irritated that she had intruded on his privacy when he'd thought she'd left town and wouldn't see him further to a slight upward curve of his lips, his eyes darkening, and his brows lifting and lowering quickly—signaling both amusement and further *interest*. As if maybe he had another chance to be with her for longer.

"No problem. *Stay*, enjoy the *view*. I'll just slip on some clothes." He wore the most devilishly sinful expression when he said the words, emphasizing that *he*, and not Mount Hood, was the view she was so enjoying. She feared he had another agenda. One that meant he wanted to learn more about this wolf she was most likely searching for. She figured now he worried she'd seen one of his own people.

"Thanks, but I need to be on my way." Yet despite admonishing herself for it, she wasn't in any real hurry to leave. She hadn't had such a good time in forever as she'd had with him last night. Living with real wolves certainly hadn't been the same. And quick romps with human males hadn't either.

God, Leidolf was hot, and her body was burning up with his perusal. She took another step around the branches, still backing up, her gaze holding his. He didn't make a move toward her, but the look in his intensely intrigued gaze said he wanted to. That if she made a sudden movement, that if she ran, he'd hunt her down. Like a wolf would instinctively do if something suddenly dashed away from him.

Some darkly wolfish part of her wanted him to, wished to be hungered after like he seemed to desire her, which was more than ludicrous. She had to find the female wolf, locate the she-wolf's pack, and befriend them. Frolicking with a *lupus garou*—alpha leader type—wouldn't pay the bills and, most importantly, wouldn't help the wolf kind.

"Are you sure? That you really want to leave?" His lips lifted a little more, smug, arrogant.

"I'm sure," she finally said, but her hesitation to say so proved she wasn't all that sure. Her wolf nature was the problem, wanting a say in what she should do, how she should feel. Despite trying to keep it in abeyance.

"Are you looking for a spot to…*camp* for the night?" he

asked, his voice dark and seductively entrancing and a lot more enticing than she was willing to admit.

Before she could catch herself, her lips parted slightly, his gaze riveting to them.

"No," she said, not sounding as stern as she should have. Way too wishy-washy instead. Like she'd been about sharing his tenderloin with him and dancing also.

The gleam in his eyes said he knew he'd hooked her in part.

He still didn't make a move toward her though. He probably thought he might scare her away. Maybe thinking like he had last night. He looked like it was killing him to stay where he was and not advance on her, his hands still clenched, the muscles in his thighs taut. As an alpha *lupus garou*, he'd want to shorten the distance between them, move in real close, and check her out further. Smell her, touch her if she would allow it, like an alpha wolf would inspect another he wanted to befriend or chase off.

The sensible side of her was trying to convince herself to leave, pronto, to do the job she'd come here for. But the wickedly curious part of her that he had awakened—

"Plenty of fresh water, fishing even, steelhead, salmon, though both are somewhat elusive, hiding, difficult to catch," he said.

"Thanks, but—"

He waved his arm at the lake, his hand opening palm up, inviting her to stay and fish. "Crawdads are easier to come by. And soft earth to bed down on is perfect for whatever you have in mind to do, plus...*other* conveniences are available."

"You?" popped out of her mouth before she could halt

the word. He was so overconfident in the way he came across, although she imagined most women would have melted at his suggestion—like she was nearly doing when she knew damned well she could never tangle with a *lupus garou* in that manner, not unless she wanted him for a mate—so she guessed it wasn't really a case of overconfidence on his part but just the way things were where he was concerned.

He chuckled, the darkly humorous tone rippling through her like a beacon warning of delectable danger. He tilted his head slightly to the side and toward her as if saying yes, which sent another unnerving chill down her spine. If he'd been human, he could have been giving her a subtle, very cool nod of his head, but his action was an alpha *lupus garou*'s declaration.

She should have taken heed and left right then and there. But Leidolf intrigued her like no man had ever done. Not only that, but she really had a problem with backing down. Long ago, she had learned that taking that stance could be as treacherous as facing the trouble. She didn't have to be a genius to know Leidolf definitely was trouble.

She folded her arms and tilted her chin up a hair. "The campgrounds aren't open yet. And this one's not for overnight use even if it was open." Not that she didn't bend the rules herself when the situation warranted.

"Don't tell me you've never enjoyed nature in a more natural way," he said.

If only he knew. "I don't believe in breaking the law."

He raised his brows. "I don't either. Some things shouldn't be regulated though." He sighed. "If you'd rather stay with me at a more private place, I own a cabin in the woods not far from here."

She shook her head.

Without any indication he was going to move, Leidolf suddenly waded toward the shore, shoving the water aside with his powerful legs as if the very waters would part for him, startling her. His leg muscles moved fluidly, exquisitely as his belly tightened and his jaw clenched, his whole demeanor determined and focused. And then? He gave her a suave and smoky kind of wink that said she was his. And that she knew it.

Yet she was frozen with indecision. How could she explain what she was doing here without him coming after her, watching what she did, when she knew in part he would be there to protect his own kind? Also, she was sure he'd keep trying to wear her down, to capitulate, and have a tryst with him. Worse, she didn't trust the way she felt when she was with him. Even throughout the day, she had chided herself for giving in to dance with him like she did. Yet it had felt so right, so good.

He left the water and stalked toward his clothes, and she knew before he dressed, it was now or never.

Then everything was decided for her.

She smelled a whiff of the female red wolf, and her work ethic kicked back in.

She whipped around in the direction she sensed the wolf, took another sniff, and analyzed the scent. It *was* the she-wolf Cassie had been chasing for so many hours!

Without a backward glance at Leidolf, who would inspire the world's greatest artists to create a marble likeness and could get her into really hot water if she'd fooled around with him, she raced off on the hunt again.

"Cassie!" he yelled, almost desperate, but she ignored the urge to slow down and wait for him.

Her field pack pounded against her back as she left the hunk of red *lupus garou* to further ponder the lake's beauty and his surroundings in solitude. Although now he wouldn't think of anything other than her and what she was doing here. She hoped she'd find the she-wolf and her pack before it grew dark and that they were the kind she could write up in her latest journal on wolf behaviors. Also that Leidolf Wildhaven wouldn't locate her before she was done.

She wished he hadn't been a *lupus garou*, just a hunk of a man, who she could have spent some time with in a brief pursuit of pleasure.

What had Leidolf planned anyway? To take her in his arms? Kiss her senseless? Before he knew what she was, of course. If he'd been human, she envisioned taking *him* into her embrace and kissing him speechless.

Running through the woods, tracking the female's scent the best she could, she was unable to fathom why she found Leidolf so irresistibly appealing. Maybe his gallantry last night—taking her to the town hall and having her tires fixed. Or the way he stood up to Hollis, who was determined to bully her further after she finished her lecture.

But what she really loved was the way Leidolf had shared his meal with her when he knew she was dying to have some of that juicy roast tenderloin. And dancing so divinely with her when he figured she wanted to despite her initial reluctance.

Or was it something more basic—the onset of spring, the rebirth of flowers, and the time for wild animals to have their babies. The natural drive for wolves to mate, to procreate, to have their own offspring?

She realized then she'd been spending *way* too much time with regular wolves and had not taken enough of a break to satisfy a more primal need—quickly rectified with a romp with a strictly human type.

Her heart beating wildly, the sense of the chase renewed, she caught the female red's scent drifting from the west and paused to get her bearing. And then, the instinct to hunt filling her blood, she raced off again to locate the red wolf.

Without her express permission, her thoughts returned to the hot, naked *lupus garou* she'd left behind next to the ice-cold water, wishing just an inkling that he would chase after her and attempt to track her down, just like she was doing with the she-wolf. Which was just plain insane.

So when she thought she heard a branch snap close by, why did she glance over her shoulder, thinking he was coming for her? And hoping she would see that wicked gleam in Leidolf's eyes again that said he wanted her and if she was agreeable, she *would* be his. She envisioned his powerful body, still naked, chasing after her, formidably like a wolf on the run, ready to take her down.

In an attempt to shake loose of sinful fantasies that would only thwart her mission if she gave into them, she sprinted even faster away from the scene of temptation.

Surprised as hell Cassie had appeared here at his lake and then charged off and left him behind again, Leidolf grabbed his trousers and began jerking them on while he studied the forest where the woodland nymph had disappeared. He hadn't been able to believe it when one of his men told him she was headed back to California last night after he assumed she was staying the night at the B&B.

Thinking he'd be alone in his isolation for the day, enjoying his lake, his refuge from leading the Portland pack for a few hours, pondering how much Cassie had affected him last night, he'd never expected to see her again. Ever. If she was back, had she stayed somewhere else, or had she returned as soon as his tracker had stopped following her? And if that was so, had she spied him following her and waited to return after he did, or had she just changed her mind and come back?

If she had returned last night and not stayed overnight somewhere else, had she been in the woods for the rest of the night? Hell. What if someone else from his pack had come into this area wearing his or her fur coat and she caught the werewolf at it?

He rubbed the stubble on his chin, unable to quit watching the trees where she had vanished, feeling as though by some miracle, she'd suddenly reappear. He knew she had been struggling with the notion of staying with him. If something hadn't triggered her to leave, a damnable conscience maybe or something else, perhaps the need to seek out the wolf—they could have shared a few hours of bliss or more. And then he could have learned her business.

He yanked on his shirt and breathed deeply, but the breeze was blowing the wrong way, and he couldn't smell her. Couldn't sense whether there'd been a hint of fear in her stance or not. Although he didn't think so. But more than wanting to sense what she'd been feeling, he craved her, which was a dangerous notion for a *lupus garou* who desired to have a mate and, even worse, was leaning toward the disagreeable notion of turning a human.

Grinding his teeth, he scowled. Hell, how could he

think of doing such a thing? He'd dealt with enough newly turned *lupus garous* lately to know how much of a problem one could be. And here he was a royal with very few human roots in his bloodline.

Then he realized he hadn't noticed any scent on her last night either. Nothing that would clue him in as to where she was if he found her again. She had to have been using a hunter's spray. Sure, so she could track a wolf. Most likely one of his people. He growled inwardly.

He sat down on a log and pulled on his socks and then his boots.

Her olive eyes had taken in every inch of him, no matter that he was naked, maybe especially because he was naked. Which had stirred a raging fire deep inside him, despite the frigid water. If she'd stared at his body much more, he was sure the water would have begun to boil. Yet she had not been in the least bit embarrassed by the way his body had reacted to her fascination.

Then her expressive eyes had challenged him—*an alpha leader!*—to leave her alone as if she was too proud to become some man's conquest. Yet another more fleeting look had flickered across her face...a look of desire, as if she welcomed his interest, just as much as he craved hers in return.

Or was it just wishful thinking on his part?

He shook his head. If there was one thing he was good at, it was reading people. His own and others. Cassie Roux wanted him, even if she was fighting with herself to live a little. Just like last night when they had danced.

He laced his boots in a rush.

Where was she bound in such a hurry? To locate the

wolf she'd seen. Had to be. He didn't like that she was doing so, nor that she was alone. Predators in the form of bears and cougars, not to mention an unscrupulous hunter or two, could make mincemeat of the woman.

Hell, if she was searching for evidence his people had been in the woods, thinking that they were wolves, it was his duty to ensure she didn't find anything or anyone she shouldn't. He'd become her guide, since he knew these woods so well. And if she wanted a place to stay, his cabin on a creek across the river was perfect for getting out of the weather. Perfect for a rendezvous. He might even make her forget all about wolves of the furry persuasion.

In hunting mode, he bolted in the direction Cassie had dashed off.

CHAPTER 4

IN HER WOLF FORM, AIMÉE ROUX TRIED TO KEEP UP WITH the woman she thought might be her cousin, Cassie—the Greek name meaning *she entangles men*. And yep, right there, seducing a naked man in a lake, was Cassie—if it was her—enticing the man to come to her. Without any effort, she was doing a great job of it too, suckering him right in. Aimée admired her, wishing she could be just like her.

So what did Aimée's name stand for? French for *loved*. Loved all right. Every relationship ended in disaster. But worse than that, she swore she was always at the wrong place at the wrong time when bad things were going down.

Aimée had to chase after Cassie, had to know the truth. No longer was she solely focused on keeping out of a would-be murderer's path. She had a new goal: to discover if the woman was truly Cassie.

The truth, though, could kill Cassie. When she learned her cousin hadn't died but had caused their family's deaths. Aimée groaned. She had made a royal mess of everything.

The man from the lake grew closer to her hiding place, and when he sprinted past, she lifted her nose out of habit and took a sniff of his scent. Her heart nearly quit beating. He smelled like one aroused hunk of a *lupus garou*.

She planned to skirt way around his trail so she could catch up to Cassie without running into him, when he suddenly stopped and lifted his nose and sampled the air.

An icy wave of recognition washed over her. The man

probably captured her scent. What if he was a member of the same pack as the men who intended to kill her? One of their friends?

She bolted into the woods away from him and Cassie and hoped like hell he wouldn't take chase, because he'd catch her for sure.

———

Leidolf had every intention of catching up to Cassie, convincing her to stay with him for a while longer, and learning more about what she had seen. If she thought she was tracking a wolf and it was someone from his pack, he had to convince her to move on before the situation got out of hand. When he reached the place where she had dashed off, he paused and smelled the air to sense her mood.

But what he sensed astounded him. A female wolf?

He sniffed the air some more. The feminine fragrance of arousal scented the air also, but coming from the direction his woodland nymph had dashed. Turning his head, he sampled the air again. Hell. He'd wished by some miracle Cassie was a *lupus garou*. He couldn't smell a *lupus garou* in the direction she had run. The unfamiliar wolf smell came from the area he had just passed.

Torn with indecision, he wanted to go after the woman who challenged him like an alpha female would and looked him over like she wanted to ravish him right then and there, who had danced with him like she wished to never let go... that was who he *wanted*. But a *lupus garou* female was what he *needed*.

He switched direction and headed for the wolf's scent

when someone stomped through the crisp fall leaves blanketing the ground, coming from the direction that Cassie had run and headed his way. Was she returning to speak further to him?

Instead of Cassie, one nearly out of breath, red-faced subleader, Elgin, materialized out of the thick woods and headed straight for him. *To Leidolf's profound disappointment.* Then three more of his men soon followed. Fergus, his other subleader, looked just as reluctant to give him any bad news.

Hell. No way would Elgin and the others come here to speak to him unless something was wrong with the pack. Talk about lousy damn timing.

After a brief hesitation, Elgin stroked his beard and then hurried to join Leidolf. He seemed resigned to share whatever ill tidings he had, and damn the consequences. Which Leidolf was grateful for, hoping the pack he'd taken over last fall would soon heal.

He started to ask if Elgin or any of the other men had seen Cassie. She'd been dressed as though she was hunting lions in the jungles of Africa, and the notion intrigued him. A huntress at heart, not just a wolf observer. He sure as hell wished she was a *lupus garou* too.

He shook his head at himself. The red hair and the olive green eyes caught his imagination—the built-in triggers for wanting to see a red *lupus garou* in every redheaded female he came across. And the urge to race after her still lingered in his blood.

He took a settling breath. "What's wrong, Elgin?"

Elgin cleared his throat. "Quincy, Pierce, and Sarge took off in their wolf coats across the valley and are headed in this direction. I've sent our men out searching for them, and any who spy them are to report back. Since no cell-phone contact is available this far out, I came to warn you. They had a good head start, and at a wolf's run, they could be anywhere by now."

Leidolf growled under his breath, "Any indication why the three of them took off?" Way too early for the cover of darkness to help shield the wolves from human sight.

Elgin's frown deepened. "We assumed Sarge was antsy from being newly turned and couldn't stop the change."

Giving a dark and disgruntled sigh, Leidolf took off in the direction of his Humvee, hiking at a vigorous pace through the forest, while Elgin and the other men hurried to catch up. Ensuring the men didn't get caught in their wolf coats was tantamount to their secrecy and safety. But as soon as he finished this little task, he was determined to learn the truth about the wolf he'd smelled. He just had to set aside the unfathomable urge to locate Cassie. And given the circumstances, she could become even more of a problem now.

"Sarge is another story. Fergus, you were supposed to have someone watching him at all times," Leidolf said, climbing over a fallen tree in their path.

He truly didn't blame Fergus, considering how much responsibility he'd given his second subleader. Anything to try and make his people feel needed and well respected, to turn around the ill feelings they had about themselves due to Alfred's maniacal rule.

"Sorry, Leidolf." Fergus hung his head a little. "Sarge was helping Quincy and Pierce clean out the loafing shed when I saw the brothers take off after Sarge, all in their wolf coats."

"Hell. The brothers ought to know better than to change and run in the woods or anywhere else during daylight hours. Especially now that we have a wolf biologist searching for wolves in the area."

Elgin frowned. "The woman who gave the lecture last night? Carver said she'd left for California."

"Yeah? Well, Cassie Roux gave him the slip and returned here." Leidolf ducked under a tree branch. "I don't envy our neighbor on the coast. Hunter Greymere's got his hands full of newly turned wolves. And all we have is one, but he's… something else." *Sarge was a case and a half.*

"Quincy and Pierce aren't much better, and they were *born lupus garous*. I know you wanted to take them in since they needed a pack to provide them guidance, *but…*" Elgin didn't have any patience for *lupus garous* who were twenty, had been ousted from a pack in Southern California, and hadn't learned to follow pack rules.

In truth, the twin brothers had been kicked out of three packs already, no one wanting to deal with men that old who seemed untrainable. In Elgin and Leidolf's own pack, teens were another story. Elgin had the patience of a wise old wolf when dealing with them, even though he and his mate, Laney, had never had any children of their own.

But Leidolf felt the brothers were still salvageable. "Someone should have given them more guidance when they were younger. When their parents died, they were foisted off on another pack, and the leader there didn't have the balls to make them mind. I have high hopes we'll teach them to be model *lupus garous*."

Elgin grunted.

Well, maybe not *model lupus garous*. Some never learned

how to exist in a pack and became loners. But Leidolf didn't believe the brothers were hopeless.

"I suppose you don't want to shift." Elgin sounded disinterested in the proposition, despite bringing it up.

His other men appeared more hopeful that Leidolf would give them permission to shift. "No. It would probably take a fraction of the time for us to track them down, but I don't advocate running in the woods in broad daylight. If we came across hunters, we'd have a hell of a lot more to worry about." Not to mention if Cassie saw them.

Elgin cleared his throat. Leidolf pushed aside a hemlock branch and waited for him to propose his question.

Elgin cleared his throat again.

Leidolf glanced back at him, his other men remaining silent.

Elgin's concerned gaze met Leidolf's, and he blurted out, "I saw a beautiful redheaded woman running through the woods wearing khaki shorts and shirt, big lion-tamer hat, carrying a backpack, and I worried she might have seen something that had frightened her. Like three red wolves."

Fergus nodded.

Leidolf's woodland nymph. "Did you smell her?"

At the puzzled look on his men's faces, Leidolf wished he hadn't asked.

Then Elgin frowned. "No, she was downwind of us. Why?"

"I smelled a female red wolf."

Elgin's eyes widened. "Hell." He glanced back in the direction they'd come. "Oh, hell. You wanted to go after her."

Despite his genetics commanding him to go after the wolf, Leidolf wanted Cassie, but he didn't want to let his people know that. Hair the color of copper, thick and curly, was bound except for the tendrils that had escaped their confinement, and begging to be caressed. He would have loved to have tossed her safari adventurer's hat aside and released her tresses, allowing them to fall carelessly over her shoulders. And plunged his hands into the silky strands, then pulled her close to delight in the feel of her, the smell of her, and to kiss her like she deserved to be kissed, just like he craved to last night, the redheaded woodland nymph.

Skin shimmering with perspiration had flushed beautifully with his perusal. Her nipples had puckered against the tank top she wore, the luscious crowns straining for release. Given the chance, he would have freed the hostages and stroked them with his tongue to appease them.

Elgin rubbed his whiskered chin. "Do you think she saw our men in their wolf coats?"

"She didn't encounter our men, just one red wolf. Me."

Elgin stared at Leidolf. "Oh."

"I wasn't wearing my wolf coat." Leidolf's rules were the same for him as they were for his people, something the previous leader and his select cronies hadn't been interested in abiding by.

"Oh."

Leidolf raised a brow at him. "She seemed intrigued."

Elgin managed a small smile, his look hopeful that Leidolf had finally found a woman he was interested in. Fergus and his other men quickly hid smiles.

"Then she changed her mind and ran off," Leidolf explained.

"Oh."

Leidolf laughed. "Yeah, well, if she'd wanted to ravish

me, and she looked like she had half a mind to, I would have given myself to her willingly."

Elgin's lips lifted slowly.

Poor guy. He still wasn't used to Leidolf's leadership and wry sense of humor, but he and the rest of their people would eventually learn his ways were totally different from Alfred's. And infinitely saner.

"She was the red wolf then?"

He wasn't about to tell Elgin how desperately interested he'd been in chasing after Cassie and how he wouldn't have hesitated if his second-in-command hadn't come to him with urgent pack business, even though Cassie was the *wrong* object of his desire.

Elgin was still smiling, and Leidolf hoped his subleader wouldn't spread the word about his interest in the woman. Everything a leader did was important to the pack. He didn't feel this tidbit of news needed to be shared, but he figured it would be anyway. Still, he had to let Elgin know the woman wasn't a wolf of *any* variety. Thankfully, not a soul had said a word about her when he returned to his ranch, and none of the men here with him now had been at the club last night, so they wouldn't have recognized her.

"The wolf I smelled wasn't the woman."

Elgin's smile faded, and he frowned deeply. "Oh. Was the one you smelled one of us?"

"Possibly."

Elgin didn't say anything for several seconds and then finally said, "Do you want me to go after her?"

Hell no. Leidolf tried to curb the disagreeable expression he cast Elgin, but from the concerned look on his subleader's face, he didn't veil it well enough.

"I can't make Sarge mind me. You're the only one who can," Elgin warned.

As if Leidolf would neglect his leadership duties when it could mean exposing their kind to the world just to chase down a *possible* female *lupus garou*. "I'll track her down later, *after* I've taken care of this business."

Appearing relieved, Elgin nodded. "There's...well... another situation that needs to be addressed. Irving and Tynan are off somewhere again without telling me or Fergus. God knows where. I seriously think they're pulling something, and not anything that's good.

"When you first came to lead our pack, we got rid of the four who were really running things. Unfortunately, there were a few more who went along with Alfred's rule. The rest of us couldn't fight against them. But some holdouts from the old regime who received Alfred's favors for...well, bringing women to him may very well still exist in the pack."

"You think Irving and Tynan might have been some of Alfred's henchmen?"

"Possibly. Alfred's henchmen were secretive. We were always looking over our shoulders, wondering who might tell Alfred what we were saying about him and his thugs. Five men took off immediately after Alfred and his cohorts died, so we figured that they were part of his network and thought that was the end of it. Now I think these two men were also involved."

"What's their background?"

"Part of the pack in the beginning. They were bitten and turned in California a couple of hundred years ago. They're cousins."

Hell if Leidolf didn't already have a truckload of

problems to deal with. "They know the rules. If they work for me, they have to let you know if they're going to be out of the area."

Elgin gave a stiff nod.

"When they return, have them report to me."

An eerie howl reverberated through the vicinity, originating more than five miles away.

"Satros," Leidolf said under his breath. The oldest member of the pack and the least agile, Satros should never have been wearing his wolf coat in broad daylight in the woods.

Hell, what now?

CHAPTER 5

HER HEART RACING WITH EXCITEMENT, CASSIE HID IN the thick brush, watching the highly agitated, scrawny female red wolf pace back and forth in front of a tangle of blackberry brambles. What was she doing? With her back to Cassie, the wolf stopped, her ears twitching, listening to the sounds in the breeze.

The air was thick with moisture, and suddenly a mist of rain began to pitter-patter on the leaves around Cassie.

Then she heard a noise that made her heart nearly quit beating. The sound of wolf pups mewling. The wolf was a mother. And protecting her litter. No wonder she'd been on the move so much.

In wolf heaven, Cassie watched the mother sniff the air. Cassie strained to hear any sound of the pups again, but they were quiet now.

Then the awful realization hit her. The mother appeared to be alone. Cassie hadn't seen a sign of any other wolves in the area. Alone, the mother and her pups couldn't fend for themselves.

Even though it was broad daylight, and her *lupus garou* instincts warned her not to shift, Cassie had no other choice. Not when she had to protect the mother and her brood and also bring them food so the mother could stay near her litter and feed them.

Cassie listened again, this time for any sounds of humans

in the area. She lifted her nose and sampled the breeze. No human scent either.

Reasonably assured she could shift without anyone spying her, she pulled off her backpack and her Indiana Jones hat. Then she freed her hair, bound in a ponytail, and shook it out. After sitting on her butt on the cold, damp earth, she removed her boots and socks, observing the wolf the whole time.

She couldn't help wondering about Leidolf, the image of a sea god still imprinted in her thoughts, and what *he* would think if he spied her stripping before she shifted. If she hadn't been wearing hunter's spray, would he have tried to track her down? Most likely.

The wolf's back was still turned to Cassie, so the female didn't notice her. Cassie continued to strip, then stuffed her clothes into the backpack, at least keeping them dry from the light rain drizzling down on her, and buried the water-proof pack underneath leaves and a labyrinth of branches. Naked, Cassie shivered. Then she began the shift, stretching her muscles.

Luxuriating in the feel of the change, she trembled as the cool air swept over her nakedness until the heat of the shift warmed her thoroughly and fur covered her skin, her body transforming into the shape of a red wolf instantly. She dropped to all fours, her black claws digging into the fertile soil. And instantly felt even more at home in the woods.

The sound of a long, low howl suddenly pierced the air, maybe a half mile away in the direction directly behind her. That was when the she-wolf turned fully around and looked Cassie's way. The two locked gazes, the wolf mother standing stock still, half hidden in the undergrowth beneath the trees. Her amber eyes stared at Cassie's eyes, watching her for her reaction. Hell, if Cassie spooked the mother, she might abandon her pups. Cassie wasn't equipped to move the whole kit and caboodle to a safe place by herself at this point and then capture the mother so that she could join her brood.

Even though the howl—the call for a gathering of wolves by an older male—had disturbed Cassie, she concentrated on the she-wolf in front of her, who likewise continued to observe Cassie, the closer threat.

Another wolf howled, this one a lot closer to them than the other, and Leidolf frowned at Elgin. "It's Quincy returning Satros's call. Hopefully, Pierce—"

Pierce let out a companion call. He wasn't in close proximity to his twin, though, when the two were usually joined at the hip.

"Now where the hell is Sarge?" Leidolf asked.

"Most likely he won't howl. At least he hasn't before when he's changed into his wolf coat," Fergus said.

"All right. You search in the direction Quincy and Pierce called from. Tell them I'm out here and expect them to mind you, and they will. I'm going after Satros. He's a crafty old wolf, and if anyone can track Sarge down, it'll be him."

Elgin tried to hide a look of disbelief, but then he quickly nodded. Despite Satros's age, he still could smell and hear almost as well as anyone. Although he had discovered a coyote and a couple of red-furred dogs he mistakenly thought were red wolves off in the distance. No one would let the old fellow live the mistakes down either. But Leidolf couldn't help respect him for all that he had contributed to the pack in the past and the stability he provided to them now. Leidolf didn't want him or anyone else running in their wolf forms during the day. Not unless they were in a secure place.

"In our human forms, right?" Elgin asked.

"Yes." Leidolf wanted to run as a wolf so he could move faster and sniff the ground for the scent left by wolf paws. And he would, as soon as his men were out of sight. He didn't want them sharing the danger, nor did he want them knowing that their pack leader was going against his own rules.

"I'll have Satros howl a message when I've reached him. When you find Quincy and Pierce, guide them to where I am. We'll gather the pack and then search as a group for Sarge if he doesn't join us voluntarily."

"All right. Hook up with you shortly." Elgin stalked off with the other men in the direction they'd heard Quincy howl.

Leidolf headed straight for the sound of Satros's communication, concentrating on a good location to ditch his clothes, intending to shift to locate Satros but to return with the old wolf and change before letting the others know to join them. Before he could find a good location to hide his clothes, he smelled a woman's aroused scent. Cassie. But something was wrong with the scenario. She wasn't anywhere nearby.

Unsure why he could smell her, he paced around the area. The closer he grew to a pile of branches and leaves, the stronger her beckoning fragrance. He poked around at debris and discovered a backpack. For a second, he just stared at it. He didn't doubt for an instant that it was Cassie's olive-green backpack. But why would she leave it behind?

He jerked it free from the branches and unzipped the bag. Inside, he found the clothes she'd been wearing, so she must have changed into something else. But why leave her backpack behind? A couple of water bottles jostled around in the bottom along with several energy bars, but underneath everything, he discovered hunter's concealing spray.

He glanced around the area. Her boot treads had stopped right here where she'd changed clothes. And then? Wolf tracks led away from the site. Wolf prints smaller than his own would make. And...

He leaned over to touch a few strands of fur snagged on a branch...a red wolf's fur. If Cassie was one of them, why couldn't he smell...

He yanked the can of hunter's spray out of the bag. She had to be one of *them*. No other tracks were located anywhere near the site. Only her boot prints walking to this point and wolf prints leading away. No *wonder* she'd fascinated him so. And why she had been so concerned he might learn the truth about her. Yet her natural inclination to be with one of her kind must have led her to dance with him anyway all night long.

With his wolf's nose to the ground, he could detect the scent her paws had left on the ground and follow her trail much more easily. Even hunter's spray wouldn't stop the natural secretion of a wolf's scent while walking. And Leidolf could move a hell of a lot faster. But the instinct for self-preservation ran high also, and he knew the danger he could be in if he shifted and a hunter caught him in his sights. Which made him wonder why she was running in her wolf coat during daylight. Unless she had no other choice.

That was when he heard another wolf's howl in the distance. Maybe five miles away. The wolf sounded as though she was pleading for help. Wolves called to others to gather them together when they were separated. So were other wolves in the area? *Lupus* only? Was she searching for a mate? The other wolf he'd smelled? His woodland nymph?

He tore off his clothes, decided Cassie's backpack was as good a place as any to hide his things, and shoved them inside. Then he hid the backpack again, all his senses on higher alert as he surveyed the area, making sure no one was about. Once assured he was alone, he stretched his arms heavenward, welcoming the warmth in his muscles as if he had just immersed himself in a steamy bath designed to loosen up the tension in every cell. Then with super *lupus garou* speed, he shifted, his muscles and bones reshaping wondrously, effortlessly, so fast he was human, then wolf the next instant. Adrenaline coursed through his bloodstream as the exhilaration of hunting down the red wolf filled him with urgency.

He dashed off with a twist, heading straight for the wolf in need, hoping he'd find Cassie.

—◊◊◊—

In the instances where Cassie had observed litters as a wolf biologist, the wolf packs had allowed her to watch the pups, even play with them as they grew older and began to leave the den, usually in her human form.

In the case of the wolf pack she'd lived with after her family died, she'd stayed with the pack in mostly her wolf form because of her youth and having no one else's protection.

This situation was different. The female was warier and had every right to be. She didn't have anyone to protect her litter of pups if Cassie turned out to be bad news. Unless the males she heard calling were from the she-wolf's pack. Then Cassie would have a whole pack to observe. It didn't make any sense that they wouldn't be near the she-wolf, protecting her and the pups.

A peace offering and a much needed meal for the she-wolf and her pups might help the mother accept Cassie. Sniffing the wet air, she smelled a rabbit nearby. Ready to hunt, Cassie turned and loped off, despite having hunted only for the sake of survival when she'd been a teen, too many years ago. How hard could it be?

She was a wolf, and hunting had to be instinctive. Like riding a bicycle was for a human.

Cassie poked her nose around and spied the elusive brown rabbit, half hidden in the dripping wet brush, his eyes wide. Cassie dodged for it, but with his big back feet, he shoved away from the ground and fled. Before she could reach him, he dove into a burrow. She poked her nose into the damp hole, her hope to provide a meal for the half-starved wolf and pups her overriding incentive.

The rabbit hopped out of another tunnel entrance to the den a few feet away and into a thicket of blackberries. Cassie thrust her nose into the brambles attempting to reach him, but he disappeared into another rabbit hole in the middle of the thorny shrubs. No matter how hard Cassie dug with her front paws, trying to reach him, and shoved her snout through the arching, twisting blackberry vines, scratching her nose on the barbed thicket, she could not reach the fur ball. Which made her think of *Alice in Wonderland* and the Mad Hatter and how futile her efforts were. Exasperated with herself, Cassie smelled...water. And when she listened hard...the sound of running water. A creek or river nearby. Fish maybe?

With the rain still lightly falling, she ran in the direction of the water and soon came upon a rushing creek splashing over boulders. A fallen tree limb ambushed the creek's path on one side. Fifteen Mile Creek, if she recalled the map she had of the area. Dorsal fins surfaced all over the place! Salmon. And lots of them.

Nearer the center of the creek, the boulders were bigger, the water deeper, swifter, and darker. Entering the creek in her red-wolf form, her eyes glued to the salmon, Cassie watched them swim closer to her, and she began stalking them in the shallows. Clouds hung low in the sky, and the water was snow-chilled. The raindrops increased in volume and frequency, striking the water with a loud slushing sound, but Cassie's outer guard hairs kept her from getting soaked and prevented her from freezing. The salmon swam nearer over the water-rounded stones, some drawing close to her legs, immersed in the flowing stream, and bumping her a time or two.

Just a minute or two more, patience being a great wolf virtue, she waited, panting, her jaws readied. Almost smiling. Then spying the biggest, fattest salmon headed in her direction, perfect for a wolf-litter feast, she lunged. Her paws spread wide, her footing sure even on the slippery moss-covered rocks, she snapped up what must have been about a ten-pounder.

The salmon struggled to get loose. She gripped him tighter, her mouth dripping with water, her outer dense coat of fur wet. She clambered over the rocks and left the stream, shook, and headed back toward the wolves' den, her head held high.

With a loping gait, Cassie raced back to the area where she had discovered the wolf and her pups, the Chinook salmon held tight in her jaws. When she reached the site where she'd seen the wolf, the female had vanished. Her stomach flip-flopping, Cassie hurried to the location where she thought the pups had been. She dropped the fish and poked around at the blackberry brambles.

Smelling the pups and the meat and milk the mother had fed to them, which meant they were around two weeks or older to be eating meat, but not hearing any sound from them, Cassie lifted her nose. She tried to get a whiff of the scent of the red wolf or her litter of pups and which direction she'd moved. Cassie headed away from the den, pausing to poke her snout into a hole that a badger had hastily dug. No scent of the wolf or her pups. She woofed low, attempting to get them to respond to her if they were nearby but hidden from sight.

A spotted owl hooted from a tree, and Cassie twisted her head in his direction, listening for sounds of the wolf pups mewling. Screeching its arrival, a peregrine falcon flew high above the coniferous treetops. But Cassie could detect no sounds of the wolf litter.

She retrieved the salmon and then brushed by a red cedar, the branches giving off an aromatic smell, momentarily adding spice to the fishy smell of the salmon in her mouth. She slipped through the lush ferns, ended up back on a hiking trail where humans traveled, and edged off it again through more ferns, rain droplets clinging to the feathery fronds as the rain grew heavier. Her heart beating harder, Cassie frantically searched the area for the new wolf's den and the pups that needed their mother close by. But where had the female red moved them?

Hell, Cassie knew she'd taken too long to reach the creek and fish. Not that fishing was the problem, she soon realized, but going after the blasted rabbit earlier had taken precious time when she should have found the creek first and gone fishing instead. Hunting for prey wasn't her usual job, nor did it interest her when she ran in her wolf coat, but she hadn't thought she could be that inept at it. Or that a cotton-tailed rabbit could outwit her so easily.

She reached a high point on a hill and stood still, listening, sniffing the air. *Come on, where have you gone to now?*

And then something moved in the distance through a clearing. *A red wolf.* Instantly, she froze. The wolf was bigger, not the she-wolf. It didn't see her yet.

Cassie remained frozen in the downpour, a sheet of gray coming straight down from the same-colored sky, the salmon the only other thing moving its tail and head jerking slightly in her mouth. And she knew if the wolf looked in her direction, he'd see her. His head suddenly swiveled her way. The wolf's amber eyes caught sight of the movement, of her and the fish.

The wolf was a male—had to be, as large as he was. And a beautiful red. Was he the one that had called for a gathering? She hadn't seen any sign of other wolves anywhere near the female and her pups. She couldn't believe the mother wolf was on her own. Was he with her then? Protecting her? That would be good news.

But what if he was a *lupus garou*? Yet…he shouldn't be out here running in daylight in his wolf coat, just like she shouldn't be. Maybe he was just a *lupus*.

Like her, the male wolf didn't move, his gaze focused on hers. She stayed put, waiting to see what he did. She didn't want to try to locate the pups while another wolf watched. Most wolves adored young ones, played, fed, and taught them how to survive, but she'd read of a group of phantom wolves who killed off another wolf pack, leaving their pups to starve in a cave. And then the phantom wolves had disappeared from the area.

In another case, a rabid wolf had killed a whole pack he'd come across. Not that this wolf was anything like either case, but as much as she'd studied wolves' behavior, any of them could be unpredictable. In any event, she had no plan to lead him to the she-wolf's new den, if she could locate it herself.

The wolf continued to observe her, and then he gave a wolf's version of a smile as if he'd made a decision and headed straight for her.

Her heart took a dive. She was an intruder in their territory, and he was part of a pack. She damn well bet it was Leidolf's red *lupus garou* pack. And if she didn't find the female and her pups and soon, she was sure a whole gang of *lupus garous*—mate-hungry bachelor male types—would be in the area, searching for her.

Adrenaline flooding her veins, she ran down the other side of the ridge, her jaws growing tired of carrying the salmon. She had to lose the red male, find the she-wolf, give her the fish for the pups, and figure out a way to take care of the pups and the she-wolf somewhere beyond the vicinity of a *lupus garou* pack's territory.

But where was the blasted new den? And how was she going to lose the red male in the meantime?

—⁓—

She was too far away to reach quickly, but Leidolf hoped the red wolf on top of the ridge, carrying a salmon in her mouth, was Cassie. As soon as he reached the peak of the ridge, he sniffed the ground and caught her scent. And then raced off again. He was torn between locating his men and finding the little red female, but she could be in as much danger as his men. He reminded himself he had others looking for them but no one else to look after her.

It was the oddest thing though. Just when he thought he was within inches of locating her, Cassie's scent would disappear. Back and forth, he continued to track her, and then he'd get another whiff and take off again. Almost as if she knew he was tracking her, and she was trying to avoid capture.

His spirits soared when he believed he would soon catch her. When he came to the river, he lost her scent. Not liking that he was exposed to prying hunter eyes on the naked bank, Leidolf ran downstream anyway in a rush but, not locating her scent, tried upstream. Same thing. He couldn't sense her at all. He stopped and stared at the river. She *had* to have crossed it.

Hell. He dove in and wolf paddled through the choppy currents. When he finally reached the other side, he shook the excess water off his fur and then sniffed at the ground. No sign of her scent here either. He ran upstream. Nothing. Then downstream. He found no smell of her there. He stared at the river. Had she been caught by an undercurrent, being not as strong as he was and unable to swim straight across?

"Hey, Joe," someone whispered, hidden in the woods on his side of the riverbank. "Do you see what I see?"

Leidolf's heart beat even harder.

"Hot damn, a red wolf, but it's too big to be Rosa, Thompson. You want to get the male or should..."

That's all Leidolf had to overhear. He darted into the river, swimming as fast as a wolf could, which he swore was a hell of a lot slower than he could swim as a human. Despite the sound of the flowing water muffling the noise, he heard the men scrambling across the riverbank, their boots scattering rocks. He just hoped their guns didn't have the range to shoot him across the river. And thankfully, they didn't fire at him while he was swimming.

As soon as he reached the other side, his natural instinct was to shake the water from his fur coat, but his human half compelled him to forget the ritual and head for the forest. A gunshot rang out, and Leidolf dodged into the woods, but not before he felt a prick in the meat of his left flank. Damn it. Which reminded him why he and his pack members were never to risk changing in broad daylight and run around as wolves unless they had no choice.

He continued to race through the woods, intending to reach his clothes and shift and then hide his wound. But whatever the men had shot him with wasn't causing him to bleed. He glanced back at his hip. A tranquilizer dart dangled from his flank. Hell.

Pushing himself to reach the location where his clothes were stashed, Leidolf stumbled but caught himself and kept running. He felt as though he'd had a ton of beers to drink and the alcohol was slipping through his bloodstream at a phenomenal rate. Thoughts of the redheaded wood nymph flashed through his mind until he envisioned in his fading consciousness that he could actually see her shift.

He didn't remember collapsing or that he lay still, panting, buried under cool lacy ferns. He barely remembered Joe or a guy named Thompson who had fired the dart that was buried in his flank. Instead, his thoughts drifted to the river, to Cassie's scent, her mournful howl, if it was hers, and the river that had swallowed her up.

What the hell had happened to her? It was as if she just simply vanished.

All he knew was he had to find her before the hunters caught her too.

CHAPTER 6

CASSIE DIDN'T THINK THE SITUATION COULD GET ANY worse. First, the she-wolf took off with her pups and hid them somewhere else. Then the she-wolf howled, but she was way too far away for Cassie to reach her quickly. Not only that, but a whole slew of male wolves were prowling the forest.

Then? Cassie discovered Leidolf tracking her, doggedly trying to locate her. But the worst-case scenario? A gunshot rang out from the direction where the wolf had been. What if Leidolf got shot because of her? She'd let the river carry her downstream for a couple of miles so he wouldn't find her scent anytime soon, and that had worked well for her. But now it seemed to have caused more problems than she ever thought possible.

Leidolf was a powerful runner and a much-too-thorough hunter. She'd had a head start when she caught him following her scent, and she'd quickly buried the fish. If she hadn't backtracked in a few places, quickly shifting and climbing a tree once to watch him—totally confusing him—he would have caught her. As soon as he had run off, she'd climbed down the tree, shifted, and raced off in a different direction. He was really, really good at tracking her, and she hadn't lost him for long. The river trick worked though, only she sure hadn't meant for the poor guy to get shot. *If* he got shot.

Her breathing quickened from all the running and swimming, she panted in the thick of the forest, looking upstream in the direction he had to be. She'd recrossed the river again and was on the same side she was originally on. Was he on this side with her? Or was he on the other side now?

She knew she should look for Leidolf, one of her own kind, and make sure he wasn't injured. It wouldn't do for hunters to get hold of him. While normally she wasn't afraid of much of anything, hunters terrified her. Her heart pounding in her dry throat, she thought of her adopted wolf pack members all dead, solely because of hunters, and the old guilt came into play—she had survived. And worse, what if she'd been the reason for their deaths?

But this time, she knew *she* had caused the wolf to come under fire.

She glanced back in the direction that the female wolf had howled. *Hell.* No matter that she was a wolf biologist, dedicated to studying wolves and educating people about them, or that she needed to help the mother in need, she had to ensure her own kind weren't found out.

Then again, maybe he wasn't shot. She paced some more. Damn, she couldn't risk not going to his aid. And if she had to protect him against hunters, she was ready. At least she thought she was. If she didn't locate him, that meant he was fine and she could go back to her she-wolf business.

Taking a deep breath, she bounded through the woods.

She barely heard the sound of the river not far away. Mostly she heard the blood rushing through her ears as she raced to locate the wolf, in the event he was injured, before the hunters could reach him.

As she drew closer to the location where she'd entered

the river the first time, she heard two men's voices across the water, and she froze in place in the woods.

"I hit him. He was a big male and was running so fast, I'm sure he'll get some distance before we can locate him. Want to swim across?"

"Hell, Joe, I don't swim well, and in this frigid water, we'd both suffer from hypothermia before we knew it. We'll have to return to the truck, and the first bridge we come to, drive across to the other side, and hike in to find him."

Silence.

Her heart pounding, the blood still rushing through every artery, Cassie waited.

"Okay, Joe, let's go before it gets dark. We'll never find him then."

Kicking stones, they tromped across the bank and disappeared into the woods.

I hit him, echoed through her brain. She didn't want the trouble she could get into with dealing with a local *lupus garou* pack. She sure as hell didn't want to be the cause of a *lupus garou*'s death. Past experience haunted her with the knowledge, and that was what sent chills racing through her.

She knew she shouldn't advertise her location if others of his pack were out here searching for her too. If she could, she'd alert them he needed help and then vanish, like she'd done with him. And if he was alone, maybe he still had the strength to communicate with her so she could locate him. After that, she didn't know what she could do. She had to get him to safety somehow.

She sniffed the breeze, and if it had been blowing in the right direction, she could have smelled him up to a mile and a half away. She didn't smell any sign of him.

In the lowest, deepest, most woeful lonely wolf howl she could manage, she called to him, begging him to respond, praying no other hunters were in the area or that Leidolf's men would locate her.

In his foggy brain, Leidolf heard the red female wolf calling to him, her howl the most winsome he'd ever heard, just the right resonance, the right tempo, sexy and powerfully stirring, if he wasn't so damned drugged, he would stir. It wasn't the same as the howl he'd heard earlier. That first had not been as deeply seductive or half as close by. Was it Cassie?

He tried to respond but only managed a feeble woof. *Hell.* How could he howl with his head plastered to the moss-covered forest floor?

Instead, he listened for her to repeat her call, hoping in his not-so-clear mind that she'd grow closer to him and smell him when he couldn't vocalize his location.

She didn't make another sound, and he tried to lift his head again. Without success. Cursing himself for the predicament he was in, he thought briefly about his pack and what they would say if they could see him now. Not only that but what his sister would say if she knew what had become of her brother, who never made a mistake.

And then the darkness overcame his thoughts, like a heavy mist forming in his brain, disguising his mental notes and thickening until everything blanked out.

When Leidolf didn't respond, Cassie figured he was passed out and unable to call to her. Frantically, she kept crisscrossing the area, searching for his location. Finally smelling the scent from his footpads on the path through the forest headed away from the river, she ran after him with her nose to the soil. Not far from the river, she located the large red male lying on his side, half-buried in ferns and dead to the world. A beautiful big red, his fur dark and shiny, his body powerful and sturdy. She needed to get him some place safe where the hunters couldn't locate him.

She moved in closer and nudged his nose with hers. He didn't respond. Not good. She tried again, this time licking his face, rubbed her muzzle against his, and then she pawed at his legs. She woofed low next to his ear, trying to stir him. How far away had the hunters parked their vehicle? How far to the nearest bridge where they would cross over and be on this side of the river? And how long would it take them to locate the male wolf from the trailhead near where they would have to park?

Maybe hours. Darkness would come soon. She couldn't wait. She shifted from a wolf to a human. Then, in her chilled and naked form, she crouched in front of the wolf's head and lifted it, talking to Leidolf, trying to get him to wake. He didn't move. She laid his head back down and then ran her hand over his body, sifting through his fur, searching for any kind of wound, unable to see where he'd been hit. Which meant he'd probably been shot on the other side.

Only one way to do this.

"Sorry," she apologized beforehand, not wanting to hurt him but needing to see the damage. She took hold of his legs and used them as a lever to turn him over. He didn't groan or growl or anything, which concerned her even more.

She gingerly swept her fingers through his fur, looking for an injury. No blood on his fur and no wound anywhere, but a dart was lying on the ground where he had been resting. She picked up the dart. Tranquilizer? She didn't know what the drug smelled like, so that didn't help. Crouching at his back, she rested her head on his side and listened. His heart beat slowly, tired, drugged.

She let out her breath in relief. He wasn't wounded. If hunters found him, he could still be in real trouble.

"You need to get up," she whispered in his ear, one hand stroking his neck, the other the crown of his head. "Leidolf, you've got to get up before the hunters come for you."

Still, he didn't respond. Figuring more roughness was required to wake him, she growled and shoved at his back. "Get up! Now!" Which didn't work either.

Hell.

Okay, fine. She stepped around him and knelt down in front of his snout, intending to offer him what she assumed he really wanted and hope that he would stir enough to get on his way while she took off in another direction as a decoy for the hunters. Kneeling before him, she stroked the top of his head between his ears and whispered in one of them, "You chased me, and now that I'm all yours, you're too tired to come out and play?"

His eyes opened, but he didn't seem focused on anything. She rubbed her cheek against his and scratched some more between his ears. "Hmm, the big, bad wolf isn't so big and bad anymore."

She swore he smiled in a big, bad wolf way.

Naked, the redheaded woman of his lakeside fantasies, the same little wolf biologist who had stirred his interest earlier, stroked Leidolf's back and rubbed her cheek against his, a throwback to their wolf ways, not only a form of endearment but something deeper. Her brows furrowed, her expression remained concerned. When she was in her wolf form and had nuzzled his muzzle with her own, the wolf scent glands in her skin had rubbed against his, indicating she had claimed him as part of her pack. Whether she had done so consciously or as a way to get him on his feet and hadn't meant anything by it, he wasn't sure.

He took another deep breath of her scent, memorizing it, and managed a feeble wolf smile. Her swim in the river had washed off the hunter's spray, and now he could smell her delectable scent just fine.

Hell, if he hadn't been so dead to the world, he would have responded to her touching him and claimed her right back, tenfold. Her fingers swept over his fur, examining every inch of him, sensually like a lover would in the wolf's courtship phase. Or like a pack member would groom an injured wolf, comforting him both physically and mentally. He would have been in heaven, if he hadn't been so out of it. *Damn it.*

Her breath tickled his ear as she whispered into it and stirred his need to have her as she pressed her heavy breasts against his shoulder. Then she moved her fingers to his head between his ears and began to scratch. Her touch wouldn't scratch the itch she'd started. The scent of her stirred-up feminine pheromones was an enticing concoction as she leaned in close to him.

He should have had a raging hard-on. Why was he too tired to respond to her loving ministrations? He couldn't fathom why his body didn't react to her shoving at him or her whispered words in his ear. Or even earlier, when she was a wolf, licking his face, kissing him wolf style. He sure as hell wanted to show her just what her attentions meant to him and give her back so much more in return.

The couple of times he'd managed to get his eyes open, he'd seen the woman of his dreams kneeling before him, the red curly thatch of hair between her legs teasing him, her delectable breasts tantalizing him.

But the last words she spoke really got his attention. Something clicked in his tired brain—"Hmm," she'd said in such a sultry, heated way—and he was ready to flip her on her back and take her, forgetting for the moment he was a wolf and she was a redheaded woodland nymph taunting him with her sexual prowess, urging him to do wicked things with that sweet naked body of hers.

He tried to pry an eye open again as her body pressed heavily again against him. He swore nerve endings in every hair follicle in his fur coat responded to her touch, sending an urgent message to his brain. *Get up, shift, and show the woman just how wickedly bad you can be.*

The rest of her words were purred in his ear, and if he hadn't learned she was a wolf shifter, he might have mistaken her for a big beautiful cat, a sleek panther type.

...*The big, bad wolf isn't so big and bad anymore,* she had said, the words hauntingly seductive, encouraging him to take her.

He smiled. Oh yes, he could be very bad. If he just wasn't so damned tired. Had she kept him up all night? Had his way with her for hours? He couldn't remember.

His thoughts drifted again, and he didn't remember anything until she shook him hard. "Get up, you lazy lout."

He managed to peel one eye open again and blinked. He sensed that the position of the sun had slipped a few notches in the sky. The air had grown colder. Her brow furrowed, Cassie kneeled before him. *Lazy lout*, she'd called him, he finally realized. He lifted his head slightly and looked at her.

The scowl remained fixed in place, her lips pursed, her red brows furrowed, her hair drifting in red curls over her shoulders. He stared at her hair, wanting to sift his fingers through the silky strands in the worst way. His gaze refocused on her eyes, sea green, heated... God, she was beautiful.

He had to shift. Show her what he could do with her after she had so blatantly called him out. He could barely lift his head. He tried to lie on his stomach but couldn't get the strength to lift his body in that direction.

Frowning, she looked worried and then leaned over, dangling her breasts in front of his nose as she tried to push him so he was lying on his stomach. He licked a breast, unable to help himself, wishing he was in his human form. She shook her head, rose to stand beside him, and folded her arms across her breasts, which left the rest of her bared for his viewing pleasure: long legs, the red thatch of hair covering her mound, pink feminine lips peeking out, teasing him to come and play.

"The hunters could be here any minute now, and you'd be in real trouble."

He refocused on her face. She spoke angrily, but no matter how much she growled at him, he loved the sound of her voice, her narrowed green eyes spitting fire, her full lips turned down. Which triggered the craving to hug her tight and kiss her into submission.

As soon as she said the words, they heard someone coming. The redhead's eyes grew big. Then she crouched next to Leidolf, her enticing breasts at eye level and his focal point as she whispered, "Lie down, and I'll bury you. Then I'll lead them away. Just stay here and sleep off the tranquilizer. Then go home. And *leave* me alone."

His gaze shifted back to hers, her expressive eyes showing a mixture of worry and pleading. He wouldn't lie down on his side again, not when he was finally lying on his stomach and felt more in control. But more than that, he was going to protect her, not the other way around.

Before he could tell her no in a wolf's growling way, she pushed him back on his side and started burying him with leaves—*him*, an alpha leader! *Damn it.* Then she shifted into the prettiest little red wolf he'd ever seen, her coat a rich red, a slightly lighter mask on her face highlighting her almond-shaped eyes, her ears perked, listening for danger, her tail tipped in black ink sticking straight out…an alpha female for sure. Before he could lift his head to tell her what to do in his wolf's commanding way, she dashed off. And if he could have, he would have cursed out loud.

***

Cassie started to run off in an attempt to lead the hunters away from Leidolf in his drugged state, until she smelled more *lupus garous*. Men, all of them, four or five, she thought. She stopped, hidden in the mosaic of evergreens and listened to their movement, no one saying a word. They had to be Leidolf's pack members. Thank God, for his sake.

She hoped they would find him without her having to give herself away. And if they located him, she was out of here.

"Elgin, do you smell what I smell?" one of the men asked, his voice hushed and a little nervous.

Crap. She figured they must have smelled her. Why wasn't the hunter's spray... Oh hell, the swim across the river must have washed it away. Having believed they were hunters to begin with, she knew she hadn't anything to worry about them smelling her, until they turned out to be *lupus garous.*

"In addition to Leidolf's scent? A red female. That one he said he smelled earlier, most likely. Maybe we shouldn't have come this way looking for him. He'll be pissed if he rendezvoused with that female and didn't want us to know about it yet," Elgin said, his voice a whisper.

"The female wolf howled, and we had to make sure she was all right," one of the men said.

"All right, Fergus. But I still say if we find him humping a redhead, we leave before he sees us, or you do all the talking."

The other two men, silent up until now, chuckled. One said, "Glad the two of you are his subleaders."

"Here, oh crap. Leidolf's..." Fergus said, shuffling through leaves. "Hell, he's alive. Heartbeat's really slow though."

Lots more rustling of leaves. "No bloody wound," Elgin said, sounding relieved. "He's...damn, he's been tranquilized. Let's get him out of here, now."

"What's he doing in a wolf coat?" one of the other men asked.

"You have to ask?" Elgin said.

They thought he was rendezvousing with her as a wolf in broad daylight? What kind of an alpha leader was he?

"He changed into his wolf form to track her more easily," Elgin added, in case the others hadn't figured it out. "I know he said he wouldn't, but if she was in need and called out to him, he would have found her more easily as a wolf."

Oh. Well they'd sure had her going for a second. She sighed. Good. She hated believing they thought she was fooling around with a *lupus garou* as a wolf before she'd even made his acquaintance as a human. Not that she intended to see any of these people again, but still, she did have some pride.

"What about the female?" Fergus asked.

Cassie could envision the man's raised brows at the question, waiting for Elgin's response.

For what seemed like an eternity, although she was certain only a few seconds passed, no one said anything. Which didn't bode well. Then Elgin said, "We've got to get Leidolf back to the ranch. And we've got to send more of our men out here to search for Sarge and the twin brothers."

For a second, she breathed a sigh of relief.

Leidolf must have fallen asleep, because he didn't make a peep. She was sure he would have thrown a fit when he learned his men planned to spirit him away from the woman who had been seducing him right before his groggy eyes and no one went looking for her.

No other words were spoken, but as the men began moving, they didn't all head in the same direction. Some returned the way they had come, but others began stalking her way.

Hell, they had to have used hand signals, figuring she might be nearby and didn't want to scare her off. Which meant? Some were trying to track her down. To give them the benefit of the doubt, maybe they worried she'd been tranquilized nearby also.

Still in her wolf form, she dashed off. The river trick could work again.

————

Omigod, Aimée thought as she caught sight of the scrawny red wolf moving her pups into a new den. Her fur-covered skin clung to her ribs, and she was way too gaunt to be able to nurse her pups well. Aimée had heard her howl and knew it wasn't Cassie's, but she'd lost Cassie some hours ago, if she was the woman in the safari outfit she'd tried to track. And the howl probably meant the female was in trouble. Aimée wanted to help her. But a real wolf? I mean, Aimée was a real wolf too at the moment, but this one was an honest-to-God *lupus*-only kind of wolf. The pups began crying.

Aimée quickly went in search of food. Was this what her cousin was trying to do? Take care of the female wolf? Sounded like something Cassie would get involved in.

Aimée had heard the other wolves howling but didn't believe they were part of this wolf's pack, or they would have been here with her now. Which meant?

She shuddered. Irving and Tynan, her would-be murderers, could be the ones calling to each other.

CHAPTER 7

As soon as Alex Wellington spied Cassie Roux's green pickup parked in the Mount Hood National Forest, twenty miles east of Portland and the northern Willamette Valley, he thought the area was just her kind of place.

With sixty square miles of forest and numerous streams, creeks, several lakes, more than a million acres of land, and a thousand-plus hiking trails, the national forest was perfect for a pack of wolves. He figured Cassie must have come across wolves somewhere out here or she wouldn't have been in the small town lecturing about them.

Wedging his pickup behind hers, Alex effectively blocked her truck between the oaks and Douglas firs so she couldn't steal away if she returned before he located her. Before meeting her, work had been just that…work, a job. But not with Cassie in the picture. She made it a game. Something fun.

Glad that the rain had died down to a thick mist, Alex grabbed his backpack, locked his door, and circled around her truck, searching for where her tracks would lead. She was a damned good wolf biologist; he had to give her that. And he wanted to know what made her so damned good. Well, more than that. He wanted them to be good *together*, a wolf biologist team. The perfect scenario. If that rich rancher hadn't kept him from visiting with her socially after her lecture…

He frowned and jerked his backpack straps over his

shoulders, then looked around at the woods for a footpath she might have taken. Spying one, he started down it, the spongy ground cushioning his every step, while green leafy branches and ferns stretched out to the foot-and-a-half-wide trail and brushed the sides of his boots from time to time.

A mosaic of leaves and pine needles shed the previous autumn covered the earth, masking the ground and the tracks of anyone who'd walked this way recently. Eyes to the ground, Alex continued down the path, searching for an elusive hiking-boot tread, Cassie's small size-six footprint, or any other indication that she'd headed in this direction. No broken twigs, no crushed ferns off the main trail.

He knew she wasn't bound to manmade trails like the average Joe. Even when she hiked through pristine forests, she left the wilds of nature undisturbed as if she were a woodland fairy who melted into the scenery. He'd always admired her for that, but it meant tracking her was all the more time-consuming and difficult. As much as it was for him when he was tracking wolf packs.

He paused and looked back at her truck, which merged with the greenery. She always seemed to find the packs as if she had a divining rod for wolves. Hell, he could go months before he finally spotted one. And even then, getting to know them took a meticulously long time.

But Cassie Roux could blend in with a pack and form attachments, as if she had been one of the gang forever, within such a short time that it was unnatural. He swore she had to have been a wolf in a former life. When he'd said so to her once after she'd given a lecture at UCLA, she'd given him a quick smile and his stomach had flip-flopped, and in that instant, he'd fallen hard for the woman.

His step less sure, he backtracked down the path to return to her truck. When he reached her pickup, he peered inside. Spotlessly clean as usual. No sign of anything left behind so that anyone who might be tempted to break into her vehicle to steal possessions, like they did at trailheads sometimes, wouldn't be bothered.

Finally spying the faint tread mark of one of her hiking boots where she had slipped off the leaves from autumns past and made several small cuts in the muddy earth in between two grand oaks, he smiled.

"Got you."

But after four hours of hiking up and down hillsides through dense forest, he observed a set of boot prints. He measured his foot against them. Size ten like he wore. And they were following Cassie's.

Had she hooked up with another man? Another wolf biologist? His heart sank with the notion, but then a fresh worry plagued him. Was someone stalking her?

Then a set of wolf prints caught his attention, and he elatedly knelt down to examine them. Glancing around, he noted several more, crisscrossing the area as if frantically searching for something. And another wolf's prints, the tracks indicating a longer gait, the prints a little larger.

Another concern overshadowed his excitement at finding the wolf prints though. Perplexed, he glanced around the area and studied the soil closer.

The wolves' prints were all over the place, but the trail of Cassie's boot prints and the man's tread markings had abruptly ended.

—⁓—

"Since he shifted, we've already poured two pots of coffee—*full caffeine strength*—into Leidolf," Laney said to someone in the great room down the hall at Leidolf's ranch house while he reclined in his bed, the tranquilizer the hunter shot him with still stirring in his bloodstream. "And you've already brought Quincy and Pierce home. Sarge...well, Satros said he'd find him and make him return to the ranch, Elgin. We need to find the woman Leidolf was with before she gets hurt. If she's not already."

Leidolf sat up in bed, so groggy that all he knew was he had to pee really badly, and he had to get to the forest as soon as humanly possible to rescue Cassie.

"He keeps rambling about her being in danger," Laney added, her words couched in concern, her voice lowered but not low enough that Leidolf couldn't hear her.

Alone in the bedroom, Leidolf growled to himself, "I do not ramble."

"We already have two men on it. And I've talked to him about more of us going back for her, but he says no, that he has to be the one to rescue her. He's not making any sense. He can't go anywhere in the shape he's in. If she needs our help, we need to give it to her," Elgin said, agreeing with his mate wholeheartedly in the great room.

"Nothing is wrong with the shape I'm in," Leidolf groused in a mumble.

"Well, go do it, Elgin. You and Fergus. Go get her and bring her back to him. Don't listen to him. He's too drugged to make any sense. You're both great trackers and his subleaders, which means if he's incapable of leading the pack, the two of you run it."

"No!" Leidolf shouted.

Damn if he could barely remember what had happened except that hunters had shot him when he was trying to track Cassie down, and then she had attempted to rouse him. Roughly at some point, tenderly at another. And with neither working, she resorted to the words he wanted to hear. *Hmm, the big, bad wolf isn't so big and bad anymore* rumbled around in his brain, the minx mouthing the words so sweetly even now in his half-tranquilized state, he was becoming aroused. And then? She had called him a lazy lout.

He snorted, then tried to climb out of bed but fell back against the pillows and swore under his breath.

The great hall remained silent, not a word spoken or a body moving around. He envisioned his pack members waiting in horrified silence until he gave them permission to speak. He groaned.

Hell, the nymph's last words to him were *Leave me alone*, and those three little words ricocheted around his tired brain. She was damned good at evasion, as much as he was damned good at tracking one of his kind down. So he was certain that if half his men were chasing her in the woods, they'd scare her off, and she'd leave the area pronto for good.

He reached up to run his hands through his tangled hair. He had to do something, even if he couldn't do much of anything.

"Elgin!" He tried to curb his anger, but he was afraid he didn't quite manage it.

Someone hurried down the hall and then poked his head in the bedroom.

"You wanted me?"

Leidolf ground his teeth and glowered at Elgin. "We need a damn nurse or doctor in our pack. Now! *Damn it.*

If we had one, she could most likely give me something to counteract the drug in my system."

"Yes, sir, but we don't know any."

"Help me get dressed."

Elgin didn't move an inch into the room. "You can't stand."

Leidolf took an exasperated breath. "I have to make sure she's all right."

"Why didn't she stay with you until we arrived?" The accusation was right out front. Cassie didn't want him; *that* was why.

"She thought you were hunters. So she was trying to lead you away from me, only..."

Elgin's eyes widened a little.

Yeah, Leidolf knew just what Elgin suspected, that the woman realized the men were part of his wolf pack and had taken off instead of coming home with them.

"She may already have a mate and a wolf pack," Elgin offered.

Not the way she tried to seduce Leidolf. Or had it only been an act, an attempt to protect him, get him on his feet, and on his way to a safer place? Sure, she'd said so. Then again, she smelled too provocative not to have been intrigued by him. And the fact that she danced with him... She was more interested than she wished to let on.

He smiled wryly.

Elgin stood taller. "Fergus and I are personally searching for the little lady."

Leidolf frowned. "No, she—"

His face flushed, cell phone in hand, Fergus rushed into the room. "All hell's broken loose. Sorry, Leidolf. Quincy and Pierce are determined to make up for all their mistakes, so as soon as they learned you found a red in Mount Hood National Forest, they took off to get her and bring her back to you...wearing their wolf coats—*again*."

"Holy hell. Gather our men, Fergus. And, Elgin, tell Laney to make me some coffee to go—"

"I'll fix a couple of thermoses," Laney promised, her voice raised so he could hear her from where she was hidden in the hallway, eavesdropping. She hadn't needed to raise her voice. As close as she was to the door, he heard her just fine.

Leidolf shook his head.

Fergus punched in numbers on his phone and headed down the hallway. "Boss said it's a go, Carver. Spread the word to your group."

"Elgin, help me get dressed," Leidolf demanded.

"But you can barely—"

Leidolf gave him a look that said he wouldn't argue about this, and Elgin headed straight for the closet. So much for trying to ensure he kept on an even keel where his people were concerned.

Hell, it was bad enough that Cassie was racing through the woods on her own in danger of being tranquilized by the same men who shot him, but once Pierce and Quincy joined her, it could turn into a total disaster. And Sarge? He didn't totally trust that Satros could locate Sarge on his own if he hadn't by now.

Cassie had successfully evaded Leidolf's men and hadn't run into any signs of the men with the tranquilizer guns.

So she was back to her goal of finding the she-wolf and her litter. After she returned to the place a mile away where she had left the buried salmon, she uncovered it and then seized the fish and took off.

The advantage of being a wolf biologist was that federal and state grants and even magazines paid Cassie to do what she loved best—mingle with feral wolves to study them and document their behavior. If these people saw her now as she raced through the ancient Douglas firs, flourishing beside the creek in her red wolf coat, fish in mouth, they'd think she was one of those she was paid to research. She just had to be very careful she didn't provide the people who paid her all the money with clues about wolves that sounded like they had a lot of human characteristics, thereby giving anything away about her own wolf genetics.

Plus, she was an oddity in her field, beyond the obvious wolf difference. When other researchers studied wolves, they'd often go as teams. And many had asked to accompany her on her searches since she was so successful at winning wolves over. What techniques did she use? How was she able to get so close and document so much?

A smug smile touched her lips. Wouldn't they like to know why she had such a special rapport with the feral animals? She hadn't expected to find a female wolf in a dire situation that needed her help. Or a *lupus garou* she'd put in harm's way.

She stopped and listened for sounds of anyone following her again. No one seemed to have tracked her *yet*. Or they were being awfully quiet about it.

She had to hurry more now, had to find the wolf before Leidolf woke wherever his pack was taking him, regained his strength, and came back to locate her, insisting she taunt him with her attempts at seduction when he was fully awake.

She dove through the woods, searching again for the she-wolf, and hoped this didn't take the rest of the day and night. She had to sleep sometime. Definitely not during the day.

But after several hours, she brushed through the branches of a Douglas fir and stopped dead in her tracks.

Only a few hundred yards away, a man crouched over a patch of ferns. Nearly having a stroke, she stood still. *Alex Wellington*. The blond, blue-eyed wolf biologist was easy on the eyes and a nice enough guy. He thought he was a real ladies' man, and if she'd been interested in the type, she might have fallen for him herself. But although he loved wolves, she was sure he wouldn't be able to cope with what she truly was. And she wasn't interested in settling down with either a human or a *lupus garou*.

Alex's hand clutched a stick as he poked around at leaves and pushed aside fern fronds, his backpack most likely containing gear for a hike of several days. He was tracking her, damn it. Or the mother wolf. In some of the areas she had traversed, she was sure she'd left a few muddy wolf prints, enough to give her away to someone like him who could track a wolf.

A couple of Douglas firs screened her in part, so she half blended in the woods. With her heart pounding double time, she hoped he wouldn't look up and spy her before she could back out of here, traverse the creek, and head to another area. As if he'd read her thoughts, he raised his head and looked in her direction. His lips parted slightly, and his eyes grew wide.

He'd never seen her in her wolf form, but he had the same look of admiration on his face as he did when she caught him studying her as she lectured on wolves. He really did love wolves, and if she had been in her human form, she might have enlisted his help at this point with the mother wolf and her brood.

He didn't move, and she knew he was afraid of frightening her off. She also knew he wouldn't hurt her, but then again, she feared he might have spooked the mother worse if she could have solicited his help.

Then men's voices carried to them, and she looked in their direction. Angry voices. Dangerous voices. "I told you, damn it. All you had to do was hide the body out here until I could get the proper tools to bury her. So where the hell *is* her body?"

Alex's tanned face paled as he remained crouched, unmoving, his head turned in the direction of the men's voices.

"And I told you," another man said, his tone as dark and threatening, "this is where I put it. Right here, damn it. Maybe a cougar dragged it off."

"Then start searching for her. We have to bury her, or she'll bury me if someone runs across the body. And believe me, if I get caught, so will you."

The two men headed in Cassie and Alex's direction. She could outrun them, avoid them, but Alex was at too much of a disadvantage. Heart in her throat, she dropped the salmon and covered it with leaves with her paw.

Alex wasn't moving, as if he was worried about her safety. She was worried about his! *Move it, Alex!*

She dodged into the woods away from the menace.

Someone ran in her direction. She glanced back. Alex was hot on her trail. She could lead him away from the men for a while, and she'd have soon outrun Alex and the men, but one of them fired a shot in their direction. The bullet made a cracking noise as it hit a nearby tree trunk.

"Someone was spying on us," one of the men shouted. "He's gone this way!"

Oh God, no. Alex was the kind of man who might scatter broken hearts all over the place because of his easy way with women and his inability to stick with a girl for the long term, but he was a nice enough guy as men went. She slowed down her run. Barely breathing hard, Alex was running toward her, his face not even sweating, a fine blond stubble just appearing on his taut jaw, his blue eyes full of worry.

When she paused, he waved at her to keep going as if she should know human signals. But the men were running straight after them, finding the trail of stomped-on ferns and broken twigs, hearing Alex's crashing through underbrush and heavy footfalls. And they were gaining. Maybe she could delay them. Or sidetrack them so Alex could get away. She couldn't communicate with him to let him know what she had in mind to do. She had to factor in that an injury could put her in peril.

When she stopped, so did Alex. She shook her head. He would try to protect her. He pulled out a hunting knife, and she stared at it and then looked into his eyes. He had a desperate look in his expression.

She hadn't thought to kill the men, but Alex was right. They were in danger of being murdered. Or at least Alex was. The men drew closer. Alex couldn't survive when the men carried guns and he was only armed with a knife.

Before she could change her mind or think about the wolf pups and what would become of them if she didn't help the mother or worry about facing down a pair of hunters, she focused on Alex. Her only thought was saving a human's life. A human she respected in the field of wolf biology. A friend, not close, but close enough.

She charged off in the direction of the men.

"No!" Alex shouted.

Damn it! Stay hidden and be quiet. He ran after her. He'd get himself killed.

"Over here," the one man said and switched direction, coming straight for her.

She circled around a ponderosa pine and came face-to-face with one of the devils himself, Blackbeard, his black hair long and curly, his beard just as black and scruffy, his clothes Army-issue olive-drab that blended into the new green leaves of the forest. She couldn't get a hint of his scent. Since she was downwind of him, she should have sensed something. What he'd eaten, garlic, beef, his male human scent, sweat, fear. Something. Hunter's elimination spray.

She narrowed her eyes at the menace. As a wolf, her instincts would be for self-preservation. As a *lupus garou*, she had to be concerned with secrecy at all costs. As a human and fellow wolf biologist, she had to save Alex. Yet what she was about to do was not only dangerous but also went against her better *lupus garou* judgment.

The hunter aimed his rifle at her. She leapt at him, noticing his brown eyes were nearly black as he regarded her with shock and surprise. A distressed cry pealed from his lips.

Her action so startled him that he didn't shoot. But the cocking of a rifle to the left of her forced the fur to bristle

along Cassie's back to the tip of her tail. Half-hidden in
the shadows of the woods, the man's companion in crime
pulled the trigger.

The shot rang out across the forest, the sound deafening
to her sensitive ears. The bullet hit her in the shoulder, like
a rock striking her, but she didn't feel any pain. Not yet. Her
lunge had knocked the first man flat on his back, and she
figured the other would shoot her again.

She had no choice but to run and hope like hell Alex took
care of himself. She bolted for the woods, and the man fired
again two more times but missed her both times, the bullets
splintering bark off two nearby trees. She ran straight past
Alex, who was crouching in the ferns, knife still in hand.

"Hell, man, you all right?" one of the murdering bastards
said to his companion.

The other just groaned.

Good. Maybe Alex would still have a chance to get away.
But new gunfire rang out from somewhere in the distance.
Three shots in rapid succession. She zigzagged away from
the new gunfire, the adrenaline in her system running so
high that she didn't feel the pain yet. She knew when it hit,
she'd better be somewhere safe or she'd be in a hell of a lot
more trouble.

Despite pushing herself, Cassie felt her run slowing,
but she didn't hear any sound of the men following her.
Was Alex all right? Staying hidden? With her wolf speed,
she'd managed to put a good deal of distance between her
and them. Which in part was good—maybe they wouldn't
catch up to her, although she was sure they'd be more interested in killing the human who had overheard them than a
wounded wolf that would probably die anyway, to their way

of thinking. But that meant they would probably continue to look for Alex.

Cassie stumbled, her loping run slowing to a trot now. A cold wetness matted her fur. Her heart beat too hard, and her breathing was labored, making her lungs ache. She stumbled again and swore at herself. She couldn't save anyone if she didn't keep moving, didn't stay on her feet…

She fell. Just collapsed against her will, the strength gone, unable to move an inch in any direction, the pain now streaking through her wound. Sprawled on the woodland floor half-buried by new spring ferns, she lay panting on her side while purple trillium wildflowers pointed at her muzzle as if identifying her hiding place. A few hours and she hoped she'd heal enough to make her way back to check on Alex.

The sound of two people running through the underbrush in her direction fed into her worst nightmares. She held her breath. The murderers would kill her if they found her. Then the footfalls abruptly stopped. For several seconds, they were quiet, which heightened her sense of fear.

Had they lost her trail?

CHAPTER 8

DESPITE LEIDOLF'S INSISTENCE THAT *HE* DRIVE, ELGIN wouldn't let him, and Fergus and Carver backed his subleader up. Who the hell was the pack leader around here *anyway*?

Elgin kept defending his actions. "You could barely dress without my help."

Leidolf gave him a look warning him not to say another word about it. Carver and Fergus tried to appear serious, but he noted the slight humor in their expressions. He ignored the other men, not wanting to see the same kind of smirks on the rest of his people's faces.

Not once had Leidolf ever shown a "drunken" side of himself, and they wouldn't *ever* see him like this again, if he had anything to say about it. "That was dressing. I can *drive* just fine."

His men looked half worried that he'd give them hell when he was feeling more like himself, but he could see they were proud of themselves for sticking up for what they felt was right. All of them stood taller, their chins raised, their expressions determined, their brows slightly furrowed.

Even in his fog-clouded mind, he knew that their standing up to him when they thought it was the correct action to take was a positive step in the right direction. If only he hadn't been so mad that they overrode his every order.

He growled at them when Fergus and Carver carried him out to the Suburban and helped him into the middle seat. He snarled at them when Carver had the nerve to fasten his seat belt for him. And damn if Elgin didn't drive like a little old man when he finally hit the main road.

"Drive faster, damn it, Elgin. I could trot out there as a wolf and make it there a hell of a lot faster."

He glanced at the rifles they'd brought with them, and Fergus said, "We brought tranquilizer guns in the event we run into the hunters who are armed in that manner. Figured you didn't want us to shoot anyone with bullets."

"Good thinking."

Carver handed Leidolf the first of the thermoses of hot, black coffee that Laney had made for him. He seized the damned thing and began drinking. Taking a pause after swallowing another mouthful, he said, "Elgin...drive... faster!"

Then his cell phone rang, and Carver hurried to take the thermos from him while Leidolf fumbled to get the cell phone off his belt, nearly dropping it in the process. Carver raised his brows at him as if to point out that Leidolf couldn't have managed driving in the shape he was in. Leidolf gave him another hard scowl back.

When Leidolf answered the phone, expecting news from Laney or the other men in the truck following them, he heard his sister's too sweet voice. Mated to a gray and living in Silver Town, Colorado, his sister, Lelandi, would not have believed it to learn her stern brother was pampering a pack of psychologically and physically abused werewolves. But only within his pack. Elsewhere, he would take on the best of them if any threatened trouble for his kind.

"Laney called and said you found a mate. When would be a good time for me to visit?" Lelandi asked.

"Laney was mistaken." Hell, he might want Cassie for a mate, and she certainly seemed interested in him, although somewhat apprehensive to let on, but where women were concerned, he could never be certain. And what had possessed Laney to tell his sister what was going on anyway? Hell, she'd better not call his mother.

"You sound drunk, dear brother. Which is totally uncharacteristic for you. In fact, I don't remember you ever drinking anything alcoholic. What's wrong?"

"I've got—" He almost said pack problems. Not the thing to say. Hell, what if his brother-in-law felt the urge to come out and rescue him? Or worse, his sister? He sure wasn't going to tell her a hunter had tranquilized him. He growled. "I'm in the middle of...hell, *nothing's* wrong."

"Let me talk to Elgin."

"He's driving." As soon as the words slipped out, he knew it had been the wrong thing to say.

Such a long pause followed that he swore he could hear his sister's thoughts churning. If he went anywhere, he always drove. Even once he turned thirteen and was tall enough to reach the gas pedal because of their dad being wheelchair-bound. Well, more than that. He didn't trust women drivers. Or men.

"What's wrong?" she asked again, sounding worried this time.

"Lelandi, nothing. And don't try to psychoanalyze me with that coursework you're taking. Your mate should know better than to let you try to become a psychiatrist."

"Psychologist."

"Same thing. Both think they can read your mind." Static began to fill the airwaves. "You're breaking up. I'll talk to you later." He hung up on his sister and saw Carver observing him.

Fergus quickly turned around to watch out the front windshield. None of his pack members had met his sister, so he was sure they were curious about his relationship with her. It was strained. Not only had she mated a gray against his wishes, which was a sticking point between them, but she resented him for leaving their pack when his family had needed him.

And considering what could have happened to his family and how their other sister had died, he would forever wear the guilt. He'd had his reasons for leaving, but Larissa's death made none of them count for anything.

Then something else occurred to him. "Elgin, why did you come looking for me in the woods? You were supposed to be searching for Quincy and Pierce."

"We had found them, and Carver took them back to the ranch. We were still trying to track Sarge down when we heard the female howl and located you," Elgin said.

"Did Elgin tell you a cougar killed two of our newborn calves?" Fergus asked. "Did you want us to hunt him down?"

The ranch had already lost a ton of money, but Leidolf couldn't figure out why. They certainly couldn't afford to lose a bunch of their livestock.

An accountant he was not. None of his pack members would volunteer for the job of keeping track of financial matters either, and he wasn't ready to force someone to do the tedious work. Not when he feared that whoever did the job would be afraid to own up to him that something was wrong with the finances or wouldn't know how to figure out the discrepancies, just as he couldn't.

"Might be a female with cubs. What about that zoo man who likes to rescue wild animals?" Leidolf suggested.

"The one who put the red female, Bella Wilder, in the zoo? Henry Thompson?"

"Yeah, that's the one." Feeling overwhelmingly groggy, as though he'd worked a week straight without any sleep, Leidolf shut his eyes for a moment. Damn the tranquilizer still clouding his blood. When he opened his eyes, everyone was watching him. Including Elgin, who slipped his gaze to the rearview mirror to check up on Leidolf. He was not sleeping, damn it!

"Maybe Thompson will take the cougar into the zoo. I'd like to get to know the man a little better. Apparently, he's still looking for the 'missing' red wolf, and I'd hate to think he might grab one of our pack members some day, thinking it's her," Leidolf said.

"Alfred said he should have eliminated him when he had the chance after the man put Bella in the zoo," Elgin said.

"Alfred said and did a lot of things he shouldn't have. And look where it got him."

Everyone was silent.

Leidolf let out his breath. "We'll hunt the cougar down and turn her over to Thompson, along with her cubs, if she has any. If the zoo staff would rather, they can relocate her to some other location where she won't endanger livestock. Halfway monitoring Thompson's activities might preclude one of our people getting picked up in their wolf forms in the future."

Elgin grunted under his breath. "And stick him or her in the zoo."

"It helps to know your...well, not exactly enemy.

Thompson has the best intentions for keeping the wolf kind safe."

"Confined," Elgin sourly said.

Leidolf sighed, figuring it was going to take a devil of an effort to get this pack turned around. He reached his hand out for the thermos of coffee, and when Carver gave it to him, he began drinking the hot, black stuff again. He just hoped he could walk on his own when he got to where they were going.

He glanced out the window. Hell, was Elgin driving even slower now?

"Elgin!"

He felt the vehicle surge forward and smiled.

Between drinking the second thermos of coffee and the time it took to drive back to the Mount Hood National Forest, Leidolf felt almost normal again when they arrived. Maybe not quite. He felt half drugged and half hyped-up on caffeine. But Leidolf wasn't about to slow down. Not when his people and Cassie could be in danger.

In a rush to locate his wayward pack members and the woman of his dreams, Leidolf and his men finally reached the place where he had fallen after being drugged and where she had run off.

"Spread out," he told the ten men with him. "Pass the word along if you see a sign of any of them."

Elgin and the rest of Leidolf's men quickly spread out in a long line through the woods.

Within minutes, shots rang out, and Leidolf feared the worst. Maybe Quincy or Pierce, who had gone in search of the female in their wolf coats, had been shot. Or maybe Sarge or Satros or his woodland nymph had. But perhaps none of that had happened. Maybe hunters had killed a deer or some other unfortunate creature.

Praying his men were safe and Cassie was also, Leidolf hurried toward the sound of the last shots fired, while five of his men, led by Fergus, took off for the area where the first gunfire had sounded. Elgin, Carver, and three other men followed Leidolf, searching for any clues.

"Female red," Elgin soon warned, pointing to drops of blood and wisps of red fur snagged on a couple of branches.

His heart hammering, Leidolf lifted the soft fur to his nose and smelled. It was hers. Cassie's. His blood pounded as he quickly studied the ground for the trail of blood she would leave behind. "This way."

"It's the female who was with you, watching over you, isn't it?" Elgin asked, keeping close by, searching for any evidence of her trail. "We'll find her, Leidolf. We'll take her back to the ranch with us. No damned hunters are going to kill her."

Leidolf barely heard him, his temper ready to explode. If he found the man who had shot her, he'd have to rein in the darker side of his personality, or he would rip him to shreds.

Hurting like hell from the bullet in her shoulder now, lying on the ground in no condition to run or fight back, Cassie felt as if whoever had been following her had turned into a couple of wraiths that would suddenly appear before her, their expressions grisly as they condemned her to death.

She had watched too many horror movies. The men stood quietly some distance from her, hidden in the woods from her view.

"Blood trail leads this way," a man's gruff voice finally said. "Damned hunters. They're wolf tracks too, Joe."

Oh hell. Whoever they were, they'd tracked her.

Again, silence. Then the man spoke again. "Red fur, red wolf."

Great. They even knew what she was. More wolf biologists? That would be highly unlikely. Were they Leidolf's men then? Still searching for her after they had taken their pack leader home?

"You think it's her, don't you, Thompson? Rosa? The wolf we caught and put in the zoo last year?"

Her heart skipped a beat. *Zoo?* Not Leidolf's men then.

"She's a red wolf all right. This is definitely some of her fur. Got to be Rosa."

Rosa? Was that the name of the she-wolf with the pups Cassie had discovered?

She lay very still as the men headed for her again, closing in. She didn't know who they were, but at least they didn't seem to be hunters intent on killing her. But the mention of zoos put a terrifying new spin on her situation.

Their heavy boots tromped the ground, growing closer and closer.

"There! Hell, she's been hit," Thompson said, stopping suddenly, his blue eyes wide, his brow furrowed. He stretched his hands out as if to show he wouldn't shoot her, while a rifle hung ominously from a strap over his shoulder. His clothes were a mottled green and black in an attempt to blend in with his surroundings, but his blue eyes caught her attention the most. If he was peering out of a hunter's blind, his eyes would easily have given him away.

She stirred, or at least attempted to, but a stabbing pain streaked through her shoulder, and she moaned.

"Easy, girl. I'm not going to hurt you," he said quietly, reassuringly as if he picked up injured feral wolves all the time.

She lifted her head to growl, to warn the two men to stay away, but she didn't have the strength.

"She's in bad shape. Should we tranquilize her?" Joe asked, drawing closer. He was not quite as tall as Thompson. He looked like an army guy in camouflage fatigues, except that his clothes were so wrinkled and baggy that she figured he would have failed an inspection in a military formation.

"Use a lighter dose on her. It'll help ease her pain."

No, damn it, not a drug. She tried to rally and lifted her head but dropped it back down in exasperation, her strength zapped.

Joe readied his rifle and fired. A stab in her flank followed. She jerked a little in response. So much for the dart helping her fight the pain. She thought she growled at them, but she wasn't sure. Now she knew how Leidolf had to have felt. Well, not from the pain, but from the tranquilizer. She almost wished he was kneeling over *her*, naked, coaxing her to take him on, nuzzling her face, and shoving her limp body, anything to get her lazy butt off the ground and in wolf motion again. Strong, agile, quick, and out of here.

Thompson walked around her, taking in her appearance. "Must be Rosa. But what of the other we shot? He has to be her mate."

Other wolf? So these were the guys who shot Leidolf!

With a tranquilizer dart. Sure. Hell. Here she had saved his butt, not that she hadn't been the one to get him into the perilous situation in the first place, but where was he when *she* needed rescuing? Probably happily sleeping it off in a soft bed at home, while she ended up in a wolf pen with a concrete floor and a trough of water, caged in!

Thompson took a deep breath and crouched close to her back, running his hand over her like she was his pet dog. "We've got to get her to the vet, have her patched up, and save her life."

A vet? Her wolf genetics would appear perfectly normal to the vet, so no problem there. She just didn't need an animal doctor poking around at her insides.

"Grab her muzzle, will you, Joe?"

Whatever Thompson planned on doing, she assumed she wasn't going to like it. She tried to twist her head away, but she couldn't move it an inch any which way. Joe took hold of her muzzle and held on tight. She growled low from the throat.

Thompson examined her belly, running his hand over her teats, and then lifted her leg. "She hasn't had a litter of pups, but she's in heat."

Yeah, not as a human, of course, but anytime between January and April, the wolf side of her was in heat, her wolf half-ready for a *lupus garou* mate. She sighed. No wonder Leidolf had sent her pheromone levels racing to the moon. Poor tired wolf. If he had been awake enough when she located him sleeping in the ferns to smell her elevated estrogen levels and felt the way she touched him so intimately like a lover would, he wouldn't have given her a chance to escape him. And she wasn't sure she would have wanted to either.

"Just wanted to make sure we didn't leave a litter behind in a den somewhere nearby when we pack her out of here. But the big male we shot might have already serviced her."

Gently, Thompson let go of her leg and moved away from her. Joe quickly released her muzzle and stepped back. She didn't have the strength to snap at him for confining her anyway, so he needn't have worried.

"Call it in, if you can get some reception way out here. We really need to find the male too," Thompson said.

She closed her eyes. At least Leidolf would be safe. And for that, she was grateful.

The sun was diminishing fast. The smell of the sweaty men and the feel of the cool breeze against her face disappeared. A strange heat pumped through her veins until her mind could no longer focus on what her mission was. Her thoughts about wolf pups and the she-wolf, about murderers and these men and the blond, blue-eyed wolf biologist, about vets and zoos, and Leidolf standing naked in the lake, his green eyes willing her to spend the night with him, about the way she taunted him to take her when he was a drugged wolf, and the way he smiled devilishly back, and any other thought she managed to grab onto all faded into oblivion.

CHAPTER 9

LEIDOLF AND HIS MEN HAD TRAVELED OVER A MILE, finding the red's blood trail in spots to help them track her, when he heard two men talking. He motioned for Elgin and the rest of his men to stop in place. They were too far away to see what was going on, but they could hear the men's conversation just fine.

"I can't get any reception on the phone way out here either, Thompson. I tried closer to the highway while I was looking for the male wolf."

"Hell, we've got to get her to the vet. At least the bleeding's stopped. We can use this between us to carry her to the truck. Here, help me roll it out. But I'd hoped we could get some more men out here to search for her mate, and we could take them both to the zoo at the same time, Joe."

Mate? Hell, these were the two men across the river who had shot him! And planned to take him to the zoo?

Elgin looked at Leidolf and smiled as if Thompson's words were an indication of things to come—as far as the mate comment went. He better not be smiling about the fact that Leidolf could have ended up in the zoo.

Thompson? Henry Thompson? Hell, the zoo man. This was not the way Leidolf had in mind to get to know the man better.

"I couldn't find any sign of the male after looking for him for the last few hours. The drug in his system might have worn off," Joe said. "He could be anywhere by now. But I guess if she's got a mate, this means we can't hook Rosa up with Big Red once she's sufficiently healed."

"Never know," Thompson said. "We might not ever find the male out here to pair them up again, so Big Red might have a chance. As soon as we get her to the zoo, we'd better ensure some additional security measures are in place in case someone tries to free her again."

No way was his woodland nymph going to be stuck in a pen with a horny wolf.

"Should we shoot them and rescue her?" Elgin whispered to Leidolf.

Moving as quietly as a wolf, Leidolf nodded, stepped closer to get a visual on the men, and raised his rifle, but before he could give the final order, all hell broke loose. In their wolf coats, his *lupus garou* upstarts raced toward Thompson and Joe, their hackles raised, their teeth bared, both fiercely growling and prepared to lunge.

Holy crap! Pierce and Quincy!

Leidolf would kill them.

<hr />

Alex hid in the woods, desperate to chase after the wounded red wolf and take care of her, but he didn't dare move. The black-bearded man had fallen hard, hit his head on the edge of a rock, and wasn't moving. Dead maybe? At least Alex could hope. Even though he believed in justice by trial, in a case like this where the murderer had just shot a wolf and was ready to kill him too, he hoped the rock had done the guy in.

His companion paced, called to him, tried to get him to his feet, but the guy was too big. The other man was a sawed-off reddish-blond with a butch haircut, a tough-looking little dude, but despite his determined scowl, he couldn't budge the bigger man.

The blood in Alex's veins ran like ice as he worried about the fate of the wolf. He had to find her. He couldn't fail her after she had protected him.

He gripped his knife tighter. Normally a pacifist at heart, he wanted to kill the shooter himself for wounding the rare red wolf.

But what he couldn't get over was the way the wolf had attacked the hunter. Not attacked him exactly though. Leapt at him, and at once, Alex had expected to see a torn jugular. But instead of hurting him, she'd just stopped him from shooting her, as if she had human instincts. As if she had been someone's pet.

As a wolf, she should have continued to run away. She should have left Alex behind to fend for himself. Her actions didn't make any sense.

"Can you hear me?" The short guy paced some more. "Hell, you just stay here then. I'll look for the guy who was listening to us." He cocked his rifle and stalked into the woods to the left of where Alex was hiding.

As soon as the man disappeared from sight, Alex headed for the wolf's trail as quietly as he could, hoping like hell the shooter wouldn't find it too. He suspected the shooter would only go after him, not a wounded wolf. He scrambled over tree roots, tripping through ferns and wildflowers after the wolf, trying to locate the trail of blood she was leaving on leaves and branches before the shooter discovered it. This was not the kind of study Alex had had in mind when he began his wolf research eight years earlier.

As a weird afterthought, he wondered what Cassie would do for the wolf if she were in his shoes. Then a new concern flooded his thoughts. What if she was nearby and ran into this maniac on her own? And the shooter thought she also had overheard their conversation?

She would be in terrible peril.

—⁓—

Hidden in the woods, Leidolf cursed his impulsive new red *lupus garous* right before they attacked Thompson and Joe as they were laying out a makeshift canvas stretcher while the wolf lay still on the ground. Leidolf immediately fired a shot.

Both of his wolves fled from the sound of the gunfire, and the dart made its target. Thompson reached for the dart in his left buttock and tried to stand but stumbled. Before a stunned Joe could react, Elgin took a shot at him, and the man parroted Thompson's actions.

"We've...we've been tranqed," Joe slurred and then passed out next to the wolf.

"Hell." Thompson fell beside him, his eyes shut tight in sleep, and he began to snore.

Leidolf and his men hurried forth to check on Cassie, while his wayward *lupus garous* licked her face, whimpered, and pawed at her feet, trying to get her to stir. Then the sound of crashing through the woods garnered all their attention. Leidolf readied his rifle, but it was only Fergus, his face red with exertion.

"Got trouble..." Fergus stopped speaking and stared at the red wolf. "Is she one of us?"

"Yeah." Leidolf jerked off his coat, then tugged his shirt free and tied it against the wound on her shoulder as best as he could manage. "What's the trouble, Fergus?"

"The hunters who shot her, I suspect, are on their way here."

"All right. Let's get her out of here." Leidolf yanked his jacket back on and then lifted Cassie off the damp earth. He gave his new pack members a scowl that said he'd deal with them later. He had to get his pack members to work together as a bona fide pack. It was the only way they'd ever survive and flourish.

"What are you going to do with her?" Elgin asked, looking hopeful that he'd keep her.

Leidolf's wolf half said that he rescued her while she was in his territory and that she as much as attempted to seduce him when he wasn't able to respond, which meant she wanted to be his. His human half warned him to get used to disappointment. "She stays at the ranch until we learn why she was out here."

"But are you going to make her one of us?" Elgin asked.

Leidolf raised a brow at him. Everyone in the pack had to know he would be interested in Cassie if she was free to mate. But did they think he'd stoop so low as to force her to join them?

"What about them?" Fergus asked, motioning to Thompson and Joe as Leidolf carried the injured wolf away from the zoo men.

"The hunters can take care of them. Just be thankful that Thompson and Joe didn't see us. But how is anyone going to explain the appearance of two male reds and the female in the area?"

Not to mention Leidolf's own run-in with the men from the zoo.

Leidolf let out his breath. "They'll think a whole pack of reds have moved into the woods around here. No more hunting in our wolf coats here now for a long damn time. But something else concerns me. The wolf I smelled earlier was a different one. Had Cassie been alone? Or had she been with another?"

Elgin rubbed his chin and frowned. "If another unattached *lupus garou* female is in the area, you'll have a fight on your hands for sure."

Over only one of them. This one for damned sure was *his* to pursue.

As they stalked in the direction of the turnout where they'd parked the SUV about four miles from there, Cassie slept soundly in Leidolf's arms, and he held her closer. Then she stirred. He'd expected she would remain asleep until after they got her in the SUV, or even better, until they got her back to his ranch, but she wriggled a little more.

Leidolf shifted his hold on her, tightening his grip in case she became combative. A wolf was a wolf, whether it was a feral *lupus* or a *lupus garou*, and either could be a handful if it took exception to being transported in this manner, especially one that was wounded.

Elgin frowned. "She's waking."

No shit.

And she was waking fast. Again she squirmed, struggling to get free, as if she didn't like being confined by him. She hadn't opened her eyes yet and appeared to be sleeping still.

Fergus drew closer. "Want me to hold her muzzle so she doesn't try to bite you?"

Before Leidolf could respond, Cassie shifted. Right in his arms. She barely gave any warning, just growled low and jerked her head up as if she was going to bite him. She didn't bare her canines, but her green eyes narrowed as she looked up at him, a strange flicker of recognition, and then...she shape-shifted...

...into a soft, naked, beautiful woman.

"Holy cow," Fergus said, jerking off his coat.

Elgin was shedding his too and quickly draped it over her nude body. He lifted his brows and his lips slightly. "Hot damn, she truly is the woman I saw running through the woods yesterday. No wonder you danced with her until way past closing this morning."

Leidolf ducked his head underneath a tree branch and hid a smile. His look would have been pure wickedness had he allowed his pack members to see it as he tightened his hold on the curvaceous woman. One hot, red *lupus garou* in the flesh. He took a deep breath of her sweet, sexy scent, all woman and wolf, and enjoyed the softness of her body, her heat pressing against him.

"Everyone said she pulled you onto the dance floor and wouldn't let go until the wee hours of the morning. And you did say she approached you yesterday at the lake, right? And she acted real interested in you?" Elgin continued, a twinkle in his eye.

It was the first time Leidolf had seen this side of Elgin, more at ease, the conversation more lighthearted.

His expression neutral, Fergus watched Leidolf to see his reaction. Leidolf refused to react in front of his men.

"Since she hung around you when you were drugged until we arrived, I'd say there's something there." Elgin

seemed coolly amused. "We'll have to ensure she sticks around this time and doesn't run off again."

"I'll do whatever I can to help," Fergus said, serious-like, but Leidolf noted a slight lift to his lips.

Tightening his hold on her, Leidolf didn't reply. Hell, this was *his* business, not pack business. He took a deep breath of her scent. He was more than ready to win over the little red wolf who seemed more interested in real wolves than her own kind.

He meant to win.

Following the wounded wolf's trail, Alex paused when he heard men's voices. Then they faded. He continued looking for signs of the wolf until he shoved aside a pine branch and stopped dead. Two hunters lay deathly still on the ground, blood soaking the leaves beside them.

He hurried to the two men, hoping he'd find them still alive. That was when he spied the dart in the buttocks of the one man. Tranquilizers? What the hell?

Alex crouched over the smaller of the two men and grasped his wrist. A tired pulse. He checked the other man and found the same result. Relieved they weren't dead, he examined their rifles, outfitted with tranquilizer darts also. One recently fired. At each other? But only one had been fired.

Before he checked for identification, Alex searched the area, looking for signs of where the wounded wolf had managed to limp off to, assuming that the blood was hers. All he found were snapped twigs, men-sized boot imprints

in the muddier areas from the recent rain, men's tracks leading to the scene from several directions, and men's footprints leading away from the scene all in one direction. And wolves' tracks. Two sets of wolves' paw prints running beside the men's boot treads.

Staring at the trail left behind, Alex rubbed his stubbly chin. It appeared other men had shot the now sleeping men with tranquilizers and taken off with the wolves. Probably the same men he'd just overheard talking. From the distance they'd been from him, he hadn't heard their conversation. Thank God he hadn't arrived at the scene a few minutes earlier, or he imagined he would have been sleeping beside these men.

Again, he considered the wolf paw prints. The wounded female wolf and one other that hadn't been shot appeared to have moved through the area. He examined the muddy soil further. *No.* Two wolves had come in from a different direction than the one the wounded female had traversed, as evidenced from the trail of blood she'd left behind. So one of the men was carrying the wounded female?

Animal rights activists?

Alex walked in the direction they had taken for several yards and discovered patches of guard hairs. The wolves were still wearing heavy winter coats, and they were also red wolves, not grays. Three red wolves together in a pack? In Oregon? My God, what a find!

If the tracks had been of one woman's smaller-sized prints, he would have sworn Cassie had hooked up with a wolf pack and had herself carried the red female off to safety. She couldn't have lifted a female and carried her any distance, and there were no signs of her tracks at all.

Which was more than bizarre, since he'd pursued her tracks for hours headed away from her pickup and then lost them. To wolf tracks. And those led him to the one female red wolf. At least the shooter who had wounded her didn't seem to be venturing in this direction. Probably afraid he'd be facing hunters with bullets. Still, he worried about Cassie and where she'd disappeared to. And that the men who had shot the wolf might run across Cassie and shoot her also.

Alex searched through the men's pockets and found the bigger man's driver's license. Henry Lee Thompson of Portland. And the other, Joe Smith, also of Portland. And ID cards for the Oregon Zoo. Hunters, but the kind who put wild animals in a zoo.

Alex leaned over and tried to wake the men. "Henry," he called out, shaking the bigger man's shoulder. "Henry Lee Thompson." No success. Then he tried with Joe, first attempting to pull him to a sitting position and then shaking him a little, but the guy's head fell back, his mouth dropped open, and his eyes remained closed. "Joe, wake up."

Having no luck with either of the men, Alex pulled out his cell phone to call 911.

But what the hell was he supposed to say? Two men down, tranquilized. One wounded red wolf missing. Two more wolves—red wolves, of all things—running through the area with a pack of men. One female biologist had vanished. Two murderers on the loose, one in bad shape, maybe suffering a concussion. And a woman's body was somewhere out in this location, maybe hauled off by a cougar? Or some very abbreviated version.

Alex knew one thing. His report wouldn't include his name.

CHAPTER 10

SNAPPING HER EYES SHUT, CASSIE GROANED, FEELING like crap. Her shoulder hurt like the blazes, and Leidolf's carrying her was jarring her way too much to be appreciated. The tranquilizer was still making her brain fuzzy, and her thoughts drifted from memories of studying Arctic wolves in the frozen Canadian Arctic to checking out the red wolves in hot, muggy Florida. And then a flicker of memory that she'd so longed to suppress—her home and her uncles' homes all ablaze, choking smoke filling the air, as she hid in the woods nearby, unable to save them, unable to do anything but save herself. And the horrible guilt she always felt that she'd lived and they'd died.

She blinked away tears and closed her eyes again, the drug making her feel loopy, out of control. She breathed in the masculinity of the virile *lupus garou* carrying her. She had to know where she stood with this pack and how much trouble she would have with having invaded their territory.

Yet it was their own damned fault. No one had been in the area in eons. No one had left scent markings to claim these particular woods. That much she remembered. Why was she running through the woods as a wolf during the day? Too dangerous: it wasn't like her.

Her thoughts drifted again, back to Leidolf who held her tightly against his chest, as if already claiming her. Possession was nine-tenths of the law, right?

He squeezed her tighter against his hard body as if he

was afraid he wasn't holding her close enough. Any closer and she'd be joined to him permanently. Even now, she could smell he had the hots for her. His pheromones had kicked in, screaming he wanted her.

The aroma was so tantalizingly seductive that he triggered her own hormones to give her biological drives away. Which, for her, was just too bizarre to consider. She hadn't felt like that toward any male *lupus garou* ever. Probably because she tended to stay clear of their kind of packs. Much safer to… Her thoughts drifted again like a slip of scent in the breeze that scattered and disappeared.

He glanced down at her, his expression dark as he stalked through the woods, his men pulling branches away so he could walk unimpeded with his head held high, like the king. But his olive-green eyes caught her attention, and his lips curved up a hint. He knew, damn it. She couldn't hide her physical reaction to him, not with them both being *lupus garous*. Not with their all too sensitive sense of smell.

He took in a deep breath, and his smile broadened, a killer smile that could entice any woman to strip off her clothes and scream, "Take me, oh godly one."

And she was ready to do just that, no matter what she stood for. For now, she hadn't a clue what that was. She didn't think she wanted to become any male's mate. But the memory of dancing with Leidolf returned with a vengeance, loving the way he felt, the physical closeness she hadn't shared with anyone in eons. And emotionally, it had felt just as satisfying. But staying with him didn't fit in with her…plans.

Her gaze focused on his bare chest, sculpted abs begging her to explore every inch, to a light smattering of hair trailing down his chest and disappearing into…she couldn't see. Exposing his torso, he wore a leather jacket left open. His stubborn chin, proud and set high, with a light stubble of reddish hair covering it, made him appear sinfully roguish. He looked down at her and smiled, slyly this time. Yeah, he'd caught her ogling him again, showing too much interest.

She moaned and shut her eyes, trying to block out the sight of him, the smell of him, the feel of him holding her close, the heat of his body, the hardness, the firm hold he had on her. *His.* That was what his whole posture shouted. And for an instant, she enjoyed the feeling, even though she fought against it.

She tried to recall what had happened earlier, before she found herself in his arms. Why was Leidolf carrying her, where was he taking her, and what the hell had happened?

Her mind kept drifting, preventing her from focusing on anything for long. She caught only scattered fragments that didn't make a whole lot of sense—something about hunters and tranquilizers, zoos and veterinary clinics—and then the thoughts faded again, the streaks of pain the only thing that kept her thoughts from shutting down completely. And the smell and heat of him. He exuded danger, although she believed he meant to keep her safe. It was a different kind of peril. Somewhere in the recesses of her mind, she recognized the threat for what it was—her freedom, not her life, was at risk.

She glanced at the two red wolves running ahead of them and at the two older men keeping pace with the macho wolf who carried her. Every once in a while, the two men with him would look at her, smiles on their faces. They thought their leader had found his mate and were mightily pleased.

A big, black Suburban came into view, and two men hurriedly opened the doors. The wolves jumped into the very back seat. The other men waited, looking her over, smiling appreciably.

Elgin hurried around to the driver's side of the vehicle. "Guess old Satros was right when he told us about her fishing for salmon earlier in her red wolf form."

Leidolf laid her gently on the seat. "Head for the ranch." He climbed in and pulled her into his arms so the other men could get to the back seat while the last one climbed into the front passenger seat. Leidolf's embrace was warm and comforting.

"Why didn't anyone tell me Satros learned about her earlier?" Leidolf finally said, his voice irritated.

"I figured that she was just a wolf," Elgin said.

Fergus cleared his throat. "Ever since you became pack leader, Satros has made it his mission to locate a mate for you."

Leidolf raised his brows at Fergus. The man smiled back and shrugged. "He's quiet, doesn't ever say much, but he's always had the pack's best interests at heart. And that means making sure you're well satisfied staying with the pack and having a mate to ensure we have offspring to carry the pack forward a generation or two."

"He wasn't wearing his wolf coat when he was trying to track down *my* mate earlier then, was he?" Leidolf gave Cassie a devilish smile.

She closed her eyes. The old wolf must have been watching her when she was at the creek fishing, but she'd never caught sight of him. And she had news for Mr. Overly Confident One… She was *not* his mate. She sighed. Just because she danced with him all night long, and just because she couldn't quit gawking at him at the lake or said what she did to get him on his feet when he was drugged didn't mean she wanted Leidolf for a mate now.

"Old Satros didn't say," Fergus said. "He and five of our men are still looking for Sarge."

Leidolf ground his teeth, and Cassie was sure he figured the old man had been wearing his wolf coat earlier today and didn't like it. Or maybe Leidolf's annoyance had something to do with whoever this Sarge was, most likely a real troublemaker.

"Did you see the female red? Had she been with you?" Leidolf asked Cassie, his tone gentle. She still heard the hint of command in his voice, as if he was so used to being in charge that he was having difficulty switching roles to being a concerned male. On the other hand, he probably didn't want his men seeing him in the role of besotted male.

She rested her cheek against his bare chest, his skin warm and his muscles hard, and she vaguely wondered why on this cold spring day his chest would be naked, while his arms were covered in leather. He wrapped his arms around her in a comforting way.

She lifted her head to take another look at him, but the movement sent another sharp pain digging into her shoulder. The last thing she remembered was dropping her head hard against his firm chest and hearing him curse under his breath.

⁓⁓⁓

Seeing the number of vehicles at his ranch house as Elgin drove up to the front walk, Leidolf suspected all his pack members had arrived to see Cassie. Wanting to be alone with her until she was better, he growled, "Who called the pack meeting?"

In the Suburban, no one said a word as Fergus hurried to get Leidolf's door for him and Elgin let Pierce and Quincy out of the back of the vehicle. Both jumped out and bounded to greet Leidolf as if they hadn't seen him in ages, maybe attempting to get into his good graces again after this latest fiasco.

Leidolf carried a sleeping Cassie to the house, but Elgin's and Fergus's jackets exposed too much of her long, shapely legs in front of the rest of his men to his liking, despite the fact that they were used to the nudity issue when shifting. But changing form occurred quickly as a means to prevent humans from catching them in the middle of a shift. This wasn't at all the same. At least that was how he rationalized his not liking his men seeing Cassie so exposed.

Then this business of Elgin calling the pack together irked him. Leidolf cast him a harsh look.

Elgin didn't look cowed. He should have, for once! In fact, if Leidolf had to describe his expression, he'd say his subleader looked rather pleased with the turnout. He couldn't help but be satisfied that Elgin was showing some real leadership qualities.

Leidolf wasn't about to let Elgin know it, though, in the event his subleader entertained the notion of pulling another stunt like this. "Elgin?"

"I told Laney we were bringing in the injured woman, the wolf biologist you took to the club last night. She must have called the alert roster."

"Why? This isn't an emergency where all our pack

members need to be present. It's like crying wolf." Leidolf raised both brows to emphasize the importance of his comment.

"Laney must have misinterpreted what I told her." Elgin shrugged, not looking in the least bit worried.

Leidolf glanced at a smiling Fergus as he got the door, but the man quickly hid the expression. No one came out of the house to greet them as Leidolf headed toward the front door with his precious bundle of soft and supple woman. But Leidolf noticed some movement in at least three of the windows.

He buried an exasperated sigh. The woman wasn't his. *Yet.* He certainly intended for her to be. He didn't need his whole pack to coerce her to stay; he planned to do his very best in that regard.

Fergus moved out of Leidolf's path. To Leidolf's relief, only a couple of the men greeted him in the great room with serious expressions, nods of heads, and nothing more. Everyone else stayed out of sight. Probably afraid he'd really be pissed if they crowded him when the woman was injured.

Laney hurried out of the kitchen. Elgin quickly shook his head at her as if to warn her Leidolf wasn't pleased with what they had done. She ignored her husband's warning and hurried after Leidolf.

"Is she still bleeding?"

"No. She's lost some blood though."

"We need to get her a transfusion. Can't we take her to the hospital?" Laney asked, hurrying behind him as he stalked toward his bedroom.

"She'll build it back up. We have no medical staff at the

hospital, as you're well aware. And we can't explain the bullet wound." He glanced back at Laney, who was wringing her hands, and he realized that for the first time since he'd known her, she was rattled. He softened his tone. "She'll be all right in our care." Then he frowned. "You didn't need to call the alert roster for this."

Laney had the nerve to look innocent. "Elgin said it really was important. That the whole pack needed to know."

Leidolf looked in Elgin's direction. This time, Elgin appeared sheepish.

"Uh-huh," Leidolf said, then strode into the bedroom.

"I'll help you tape up her wound, but then I have to see to Felicity." Laney hurried to pull his covers back on the bed, and he smelled the fresh scent of spring.

She must have washed his sheets in a hurry, just in time to bring his little red wolf home with him. At least he approved of her doing that.

"The babies aren't on their way yet, are they?" he asked.

He laid Cassie in his bed and then set Elgin's and Fergus's jackets aside. Her skin was pale, and she seemed so much more demure while sleeping under the influence of the drug. He took her hand and ran his thumb over the delicate bones in her fingers, so small compared to his large hands. Yet despite how fragile she seemed at times, she showed strength of character—like when she'd tried to rescue him instead of running off to save her own skin from the hunters who'd shot him. Not many werewolves would have done so when they weren't even a member of the pack.

After rummaging through drawers in the bathroom, Laney hurried back into the bedroom. "Yes, the babies are on their way. Here." She handed him the tape and sterile gauze. "I'll get something to clean up the dried blood." She hurried back to the master bathroom.

Leidolf pulled the covers up to Cassie's waist and then brushed a wisp of silky hair away from her cheek. Now in peaceful sleep, she seemed so different. As if it had been eons ago that he was in the same situation, drugged, although the caffeine seemed to be wearing off, and all the running around he'd been doing seemed to be catching up to him.

But no longer did he see her as the woman who had leaned close to him, tantalizing him with taunting words and her seductive scent and body, whispering to him with a hot and sexy voice, touching him as if she were already his lover. Nor did he see her as the woman who had scowled at him, worried, attempting to help him to stand, trying to get him to safety.

Now she was at peace, content and angelic, and wounded. He hoped the injury wouldn't cause her too much discomfort later when the tranquilizer wore off. He did have something that would aid her sleep to keep her from feeling any pain during the night.

So what mood would she wear when she woke?

He didn't want to think about it. Combative? Maybe. Ready to bolt? Probably, if the way she took off when his men found him was any indication. Or the way she'd given him the slip at the B&B, and Carver also when he had followed her out of town. And Leidolf wouldn't forget her last words to him when he'd been drugged, pointed and commanding, *Leave me alone.*

If he'd been just any man or she just any woman, he might have done just that, left her alone. But no matter what she said, her actions and, hell, her pheromones spoke much louder and clearer than words. She wanted him. He just had to ensure she saw her feelings for what they truly were.

Laney hurried back into the bedroom and handed Leidolf a couple of warm, wet washcloths and a dry towel. "Here, I'll let you do this," she said. "I'll return later."

"To be with Felicity?" he asked, crouching beside the bed and washing away the dried blood on the nymph's arm, her skin golden and silky.

"Yes, yes. The babies are due soon."

Leidolf looked up at her, noting her anxiousness. "The other women?" Surely Felicity wasn't alone.

"Ready to help her. I think Felicity has pretty much decided to birth them as a wolf. Easier that way."

So then why the anxiousness? The women rarely had trouble with multiple births because of their *lupus garou* strength.

Leidolf ran the warm washcloth over Cassie's shoulder blade and lower, where drips of blood had trailed down her breast, careful not to touch her wound. She was beautiful. Every inch of her.

"When will you return?" He again looked at Laney's expression, suspecting she had darker motives. Six other women in the pack could watch Felicity and help her take care of her babies. Why would Laney need to be there too?

He realized then how much he relied on her help, as much as he did her mate's.

"I'll return as soon as I can. Elgin says you were with Cassie at the club until it closed. That she's that wolf biologist you listened to earlier in the night. Since you know her somewhat, it would probably be better if you stayed with her until I returned. Unless you want Elgin to."

Leidolf gave her a look like she had to be joking. Laney gave a wry smile.

"Is Felicity's mate with her?"

Laney chuckled. "Of course. I swear you'd think Harvey is having the babies. He's been complaining of severe stomach pains all afternoon. Says it was food poisoning, but we all know better. And you know how it is when the female of our species has babies. The woman is finally in charge. Every time she snaps at him—for getting her in this way in the first place—he jumps. And after the babies come, she'll still be in charge." Laney gave an evil smile and nodded at Cassie. "Remember that when the time comes."

Taping the gauze over Cassie's wound, Leidolf shook his head. Harvey was a beta. Leidolf would never be like that, although the notion of getting to that stage in his relationship with Cassie sure appealed. "Let me know how everything turns out for Felicity."

"I will. Elgin told everyone no one is to disturb you. I'll return as soon as I can." Laney headed out of the room, faster than he had ever seen her move, and shut the door behind her.

He assumed it was a calculating matchmaking scheme on her part. As soon as she shut the door and the house was quiet, the adrenaline that had built up in his system drained off. Now he felt like a tired, old wolf, needing a well-deserved nap. He covered Cassie with the comforter and then walked across the room to the recliner Laney had picked out for him, saying he needed it for relaxation. Going to the forest, to the lake where he'd seen his nymph, was his place to relax. It would never be the same after finding her there. And he wished they could return some day and take up where they'd left off.

At first, he sat down in the recliner, pulled out the footrest, and stretched out. He tried to keep his eyes open while he watched Cassie sleeping soundly. She turned over, and the comforter slipped down, exposing her breasts. He groaned, remembering how as a wolf he'd licked the left one. Except he'd been a lot groggier then. Sighing, he hoped she'd heal quickly and didn't suffer from her injury for long.

He rubbed his chin and stared at the sleeping beauty. What if she woke after he fell asleep? What if she tried to slip away without him or any one of his pack members knowing it?

He wouldn't put it past her.

Hell. He rubbed his eyes. He couldn't stay awake. She had taunted him, saying he wasn't such a big, bad wolf after all. Smiling, he thought he wouldn't be *too* awfully bad, but she'd asked for it.

He left the chair, stalked over to the bed, and studied her sleeping face. She was beautiful in a wild wolf way. And just as radiant as a human. And his. Once he *convinced* her of it.

He climbed into bed, slipped under the covers, and gathered her gently into his arms. She snuggled up against him as if she belonged there. Which she did. If he didn't hold her, he told himself, she could still wake and leave him while he slept without his knowing it.

Her satiny skin against his, the heat of her body, and her scent made him want her all the more, but he set aside his cravings to mate and closed his eyes, his one hand caressing her back, the other resting on a soft buttock. Her cheek was against his chest, her warm breath tickling his skin. She was the embodiment of everything magical.

And woman and wolf—*all* his.

~~~

Poseidon rose from the sea as a veritable hunk of a god, droplets of water clinging to him like translucent pearls, as if the clams had given up their claim to their hidden treasures for the god they adored. Poseidon was the seducer of women, just like his brother Zeus, god of all the gods. It was the god of the sea who held her attention now, wove a spell of compliance over her, encouraged her to stay right where she was, standing next to the hemlocks.

Half wanting to remain with him, half wanting to leave before it was too late, she stood in awe. Eyes the color of the sea, green and expressive, gazed into hers as if reading every wickedly sinful thought she had—from the notion of licking each water droplet off his golden body to kissing his rigid nipples and his full lips born to seduce.

And she was... Artemis, goddess of the hunt and of the moon. The goddess was supposed to be chaste, but Cassie didn't feel the least bit innocent as she smiled a little at the sea god. Looking as though he couldn't wait another second to have her in his arms, he advanced on her, taking great strides through the water.

Suddenly, she, who was supposed to be the hunter, felt hunted and fought taking a step back. Go to him, a little voice goaded her. Show him how much you really want him. Be the one in charge.

Which suited her fine. In response, she moved toward him, not in a stalking way like he did, her stride shorter, but she walked with as much purpose, her gaze willing him to back

down now. But of course, he didn't. And in fact, his lips twitched
upward, his eyes sparkling with mirth.

So much for her being in charge. He had her right where he
wanted her. As far as she was concerned, she felt the same way
about him.

Then before she knew what was happening, he was peeling
her huntress clothes off her, the safari hat, her backpack, shirt,
and tank top. She didn't remember the rest, only that he was
lying naked beneath her as if she'd tackled him, his body heated
and musky and masculine. Her own body naked against his felt
sexy and aroused.

The hair of his chest tickled her breasts, his nipples stand-
ing at attention, waiting for her kisses, and his erection poked
her in the belly. It was the way his hand stroked her back with
a sensual caress and his other that rested on her buttock that
really got her attention. Even now the heat and ache pervaded
her loins, and she spread her legs, opening herself up to him,
welcoming him in.

Unable to sleep just yet, Leidolf held Cassie in his arms and
continued to lightly stroke her back, loving the feel of her silky
skin, thinking about everything she'd said and done when he'd
first met her. He still couldn't believe she'd been one of his
kind all along, hiding the fact from him and everyone else.

No wonder she knew so much about wolves. He couldn't
fathom why she'd be so attached to wolves of the *lupus*-only
persuasion. That she'd work as a wolf biologist studying them
and championing their cause. Yet the way she spoke about
wolves and her obvious love of them endeared her to him.

He threaded his fingers through her satiny hair, recalling the conversation they'd had at the restaurant. She'd teased about attracting wolves if she howled, knowing full well the place was filled with their kind. He smiled at her deviousness. He understood why she kept her secret from them. She was in his territory, under his jurisdiction. Running around in her wolf form wasn't allowed unless *he* said so, or she was at risk for *not* doing so. He didn't believe for an instant that she'd been at risk until she'd become a wolf.

Shaking him loose of his thoughts, the vixen spread her legs in an open invitation to sex. Her scent was an aphrodisiac as it was, keeping him fully hard and wanting. She was awake and wanting him in return?

He stilled his hand on her back and opened his eyes. And frowned at the top of her head, her cheek resting soundly on his chest. She seemed to be fully asleep. *Hell.* What was he thinking? He'd hoped she was offering herself to him. That was what he was thinking. He sighed. Her pheromones were telling him a different story, and if he reached down and touched her between her legs, he was sure he'd find her wet and ready for his penetration. Was she dreaming of having sex with him?

When she was ready, he'd be all too willing to oblige. For now, he needed to spend time with her, show her what he was capable of, if she gave him half a chance. With the gentlest of touches, he caressed her back, hoping he'd help to fulfill her fantasies even if she was only dreaming.

His real hope was she would wake and want what he was willing to offer her: a pack to preside over, a family, but most of all—*him.*

CHAPTER 11

CASSIE LUXURIATED IN THE FEEL OF POSEIDON, THE WAY HE *touched her lower and lower down her backside, but then he suddenly stopped the sexy onslaught at the tip of her tailbone, his fingers poised as if ready to continue any second. Carry on, she wanted to command him.*

"Cassie? Cassie, are you awake?" he whispered. His voice was rough and husky and pleasingly seductive.

She wanted to murmur her approval, but she couldn't summon the energy to respond.

"I imagine all my bachelor males are wishing they were the pack leader about now," he said, his voice still hushed.

Pack leader? Poseidon?

She was still trying to sort his words out when he kissed the top of her head. She wanted to lift her face and kiss his lips, but she couldn't gather the strength to move her head. Then…she managed to skim her fingertips over the bare skin at his waist, and he sucked in his breath, his fingers renewing their softly sensuous strokes on her backside.

Hmm, she had power over the Mighty One. She liked his possessiveness, protectiveness, the way he was wary yet desired her.

"Cassie," he said again, his voice tight with need.

He hesitated to speak any further for so long that she thought he'd changed his mind.

He ground his teeth and let out his breath. "Cassie, if you're awake, I want you to know that we have a lot of eligible bachelors in the pack. Carver is one, and his daughters are lovely girls and could use a mother." His hand stilled on Cassie's back.

He was giving her up, just like that?

"What I mean to say is that since you don't have a pack, we'd love for you to join ours. No strings attached. And if you have a friend you left behind in the woods, she can join us also."

How did he know she didn't have a pack? And what friend was he referring to?

She snuggled closer to him, slipped her hand around his waist, and sighed. He was hers, and she wasn't going to be any other man's...conquest. Well, not...not...

She lifted her head slightly and looked into his eyes. *Leidolf.* In the flesh. She wasn't dreaming after all.

He gave her a worried smile, and she closed her eyes and rested her head against his chest again. "Hmm, not interested in anyone else in your pack," she mumbled, unbelievably tired. "*Anyone*," she amended. "In your pack."

He resumed stroking her back, sending delicious spikes of interest through her willing body. Her mind wasn't falling for the deal.

"I meant to say the other bachelor males might be interested in the other woman, and the both of you could join our pack." He gathered her tighter into his embrace as if claiming her for his very own. No matter what her groggy mind thought of the situation, she felt right at home with the wicked hunk of a *lupus garou.*

Why couldn't he be just a cute human good for a quick fling? He was so much more, and that was what scared her.

"I assume you figured out that I'm the pack leader in Portland and the surrounding areas. So why didn't you let me in on your little secret that you were one of us? Did you think I'd bite?" He sighed deeply, and for an instant, she felt badly she'd kept her true nature hidden. Except that she had a job to do, and she was sure Leidolf wouldn't let her do it. "Who is the other woman, Cassie?"

"A female red wolf," she whispered and then licked her dry lips, so, so tired.

"A *lupus garou*, you mean?"

"No."

He renewed his gentle, sweeping caress. "She's not one of my pack. You have to realize the danger she's in while wearing her wolf coat and running through the woods."

"I've never seen her before." Cassie yawned.

"Sorry, Cassie. You must be pretty tired still. I'm used to coaxing answers from my pack members, mistreated under an earlier *lupus garou*'s leadership."

"Mistreated," she whispered, the thought of hunters killing wolves coming to mind. She couldn't imagine a werewolf pack mistreating each other. Maybe because the only one she'd ever truly known was her extended family's.

"Badly mistreated, yes. So you spotted a red wolf in our woods around here, lectured at the town hall about wolves and their importance, and then went to the forest to locate her? Why go alone? Why not tell me about it? You recognized I was a *lupus garou*. That I'd have to look into the matter. If she's another *lupus garou*, she—"

"Needs to know who's boss?"

He smiled.

Cassie closed her eyes. "She's a wolf. Not one of us."

His hand stilled on her back. "Why are you so interested

in the wolf kind? If she's just a wolf and not one of us, you put yourself at risk for what reason?"

"They...they killed them. All. No more killing. I...I have to...to educate people about them."

"Who killed whom?"

Hunters. Slaughtered wolves. Gunfire. Pop! Pop! Pop! Whimpers and groans and death. Her adopted family. No more.

Leidolf didn't ask any more questions. He began to stroke her hair as if he was comforting her, and he was. He knew all the right touches, the kind that could make her melt against him and want everything he was offering... for the moment. As soon as she was more alert, she'd be off doing what she knew best how to do. Not be a pack leader's mate, not live with a pack, but continue to go it alone, helping those who needed her.

His hands slipped down to rest on her back, and she waited for him to begin stroking her again...until he softly snored.

Snored? She shook her head against his broad chest and sighed deeply, vaguely thinking she needed to leave, to return to the forest, to renew her search for the she-wolf and her pups until everything—the hard contours of his muscles, his once rigid erection, the warmth of his body, the feel of his arms wrapped tightly around her in a lover's embrace—faded completely away.

Several hours later, the darkness gripped the bedroom Cassie rested in. With her wolf's night vision, she could see an older woman, her strawberry curls streaked with strands of silver, as she sat dozing in an overstuffed chair, her round face peaceful in sleep. She wore jeans and a sweater, a blanket over her lap, as if she was staying the night—and would act as the pack's first warning when Cassie woke.

That was when Cassie's mind snapped to, her thoughts instantly clearing. The realization that a murderer had shot her near where she had been searching for the she-wolf and her den—and Alex's predicament—came back to her in a flood of memories.

And now? She was a guest in Leidolf's home. How far from the woods was she? How was she going to return there?

She'd parked her pickup a couple of miles from the site where she'd hiked in to locate the she-wolf. Once she could get to it, she'd have the two bags of clothes that were hidden under the seats. She groaned and ran her hands through her disheveled hair, but a shock of pain stabbed the bullet wound on her shoulder. She realized that except for a bulky bandage, she was lying naked in the bed. It was the usual way for most of them to sleep, but she wasn't like the normal *lupus garous* and instead did her own thing.

Being naked felt way too sensual, particularly when she was lying in… She sniffed the freshly laundered sheets. *His* scent flooded her with a warm, tingling feeling. *Leidolf's* bed. And hell, she'd dreamed she'd had her wicked way with him while he was Poseidon and she was Artemis. She shook her head at her silly fantasies. In the old days, her mother would have said it was a sign Cassie was burying deeper feelings, which she didn't want to consider.

The woman guarding Cassie jerked awake and stared at her for a minute, then smiled warmly. "I'm Laney, and now that you're up, I'll tell Leidolf."

Cassie took another deep breath and smelled his woodsy scent on the ultrasoft cotton sheets again, the same as she'd smelled when he'd carried her, except that the added aroma of his sexual pheromones when he had held her were now imprinted on her brain.

"He'll be glad you're looking so much better. He brought you here because it's the nicest of all the bedrooms. He stayed with you until I was able to watch over you for a while so that he could dress down a couple of our people for going after you in their wolf coats. Now the local news station is reporting that a pack of red wolves is running through the area. All hell's broken loose."

Cassie suspected Leidolf hadn't brought her here *just* because it was the nicest bedroom, but because it was *his* bedroom. The news about the reporters and hunters couldn't have been worse. Cassie *had* to get to the she-wolf and pups and Alex. "I need some clothes, and I have to go back there, pronto."

The woman hurriedly rose and headed for the door as if to block it or warn Leidolf that the little red wolf was ready to make her escape. "You can't return there. Not now. A slew of hunters… Thompson and his friend, that Joe character, who are philanthropists for the zoo…reporters… you name it…will be all over the area. If that isn't bad enough, some guy called 911 and reported that two men had murdered a woman and dumped the body in the woods. And that someone had tranquilized Thompson and Joe."

Laney smiled. "Of course, Leidolf and my Elgin were the ones responsible for that once they found you with them. Well, in part because Quincy and Pierce went to attack the men—the two new members of our pack I mentioned before who were wearing their wolf coats during the day while searching for you—and Leidolf had to act quickly. So none of our people can visit the forest for a good long while until Leidolf okays it. Besides, you're wounded, for heaven's sake."

"Did they mention any name? Of the one who called 911?" Cassie prayed it was Alex and he had made it out all right. Although thinking further on the situation, she figured since he and she were the only two there when they overheard the murderers speaking, it had to be him.

"No. The sheriff's office is trying to sort it all out. They said that a man had called from the highway and reported the two tranquilized men from the zoo. Then he gave directions to where they were located because he couldn't get reception where the men had been drugged. Two more men were involved in some kind of murder scheme that he'd overheard while hiking in the forest. And one of the men had shot a rare red wolf, illegally hunting, and tried to shoot him for overhearing them.

"To top that all off, some wolf biologist is running around the area, and he's worried she's lost or come to harm. Until the police know what they're up against, I'm sure they're not saying who the man was who called 911. He's probably considered a suspect in some of the goings-on. You know how it is, since he seems to know so much. He reported the descriptions of the men, both wearing camouflaged clothes, one a short strawberry blond with a butch haircut, and the other with long, black curly hair."

"Blackbeard," Cassie said under her breath.

"What?" Laney asked, her eyes widening.

"Sounds like the guy looked like Blackbeard. The pirate. You know."

"I didn't mention that he wore a beard. No one said anything about that."

Cassie clamped her mouth shut.

Laney frowned. "Did you see the men?" She clapped a hand over her mouth and then dropped her hand away. "Of course you did. One of *those* men shot you. You're the wolf biologist the man had mentioned. Oh, oh, Leidolf won't like this at all."

Quickly, Cassie changed the subject. "I'm surprised, the way reporters get hold of a story, that they haven't discovered who the 911 caller was and are reporting the guy's name all over the place."

Unless he was afraid for his life. Sure. He was a witness, and hell, so was she. At least the men didn't get a look at her in her human form, and she hoped they hadn't gotten hold of Alex either. She did get a good look at both men, and she should have known their scent if they hadn't been hiding it with hunter's spray. She assumed that was what was covering up their smell. But *lupus garous* didn't interfere in strictly human affairs. Too much could go wrong.

Hell, if she had smelled them, she could see the police asking her to stand behind one of those two-way mirrors and point out the two men in a lineup. She'd want to be sure she got the right men by sniffing them first since her sense of smell was the best identifier there was. If she insisted on checking them out that way, the police would think she was a nutcase for sure.

Laney studied Cassie in a thoughtful wolf way. "If a man called 911, saying he knew you'd been shot and that he'd heard the murderers' conversation, had you also? Do you know the man who called 911? Is he your mate?"

"No," Cassie said, not about to reveal who he was or anything about him or what she'd been doing there. *Lupus garous* would not appreciate that she'd been in her wolf form with a human or that she'd behaved uncharacteristically as a wolf in front of him. "It's dark out. Surely they wouldn't all be out there in the middle of the night. Even if they were, they couldn't see where they were going."

The pause between them was heavy with speculation.

Laney's gray brows pinched together. "You're probably right. I've heard some hunters have binoculars that allow them to see in the half-light of dawn and dusk, but it would be too dark for them unless they're wearing night-vision goggles. Leidolf is worried that they would want to kill the wolves, despite the fact that red wolves are rare. The reporters and the others probably wouldn't be in the woods this late." Then Laney switched topics and said, "Leidolf is a royal, by the way. You wouldn't happen to be one too, would you?" She looked hopeful.

For a heart-wrenching moment, Cassie thought of her own family—royals too. She hadn't considered what it might be like being with a *lupus garou* family, a pack, again. The way that pack members all looked after one another appealed on some level. Maneuvering was always tantamount in a pack, wanting to please the leader, always trying to be on top, but she missed the closeness with others. She'd been fighting those feelings for years. Never wanting to replace her own family, as if it would hurt her memory of them. Never wanting to fear losing her family to some new lethal threat if she joined a new one.

She couldn't deceive the woman who reminded her of her mother, caring, kind, but also not someone who was easily deceived.

The desire to have hearth and home and a family pack

was starting to get on Cassie's nerves. She attributed it to the need to settle down and have children of her own, which she'd been effectively squashing. Spring and the rebirth of trees and flowers had something to do with it. Oddly, the she-wolf and her pups had stirred that need all over again to an even greater degree. Well, and being with that alpha male, Leidolf, and the way his nearness triggered estrogen levels she didn't know she had. She didn't want to desire a man like that. *Ever*. Although her feelings for Leidolf already ran deep, she had no intention of giving in to such needs.

"I need clothes," Cassie reiterated, avoiding Laney's question about being a royal. When few humans diluted the lineage, the biggest advantage was being able to shift when the new moon was out or not having to shift when the other phases of the moon came into play.

She yanked aside the covers and climbed out of bed but winced when the pain in her bandaged shoulder sent a message straight to her brain—she wasn't perfectly healed yet. She felt a lot better than she had earlier though. Probably sleeping for several hours had helped.

"If you were recently turned, where's the pack that took you in?" Laney asked.

"In the redwoods in California."

"Northern California, oh." Then Laney frowned, and instantly, Cassie worried that frown meant she knew Cassie wasn't from there. Then the woman gave a pleasant smile, one that said she'd lived too many years for a younger *lupus garou* to attempt to deceive her with tall tales. "You can't leave yet."

Cassie raised her brows at the lady, not liking that Leidolf would dictate to her. She headed for the closet. "I'm doing some research, which I'm being paid for, and I'm on a deadline. So I want to thank Leidolf and all of you for taking care of me, but I need to return to the woods, finish my work, and return home to my pack pronto."

"No women's clothes in there," Laney warned.

Cassie stopped in the middle of the floor, knowing that would probably be the case, but she didn't care. Any clothes would do. Even the pack leader's. Then again, she probably should wait until Laney left the room. Which meant Cassie wasn't thinking very clearly, and if she hadn't needed so badly to go to Alex and the she-wolf's aid, she would rest a while longer until her brain was functioning more properly and her shoulder didn't hurt so much.

She'd considered telling Laney about the wolf pups, but not all *lupus garous* had the same sympathies for real wolves that she did. As long as the wolves didn't interfere with *lupus garous'* own pack dynamics, they tolerated them. She couldn't risk telling them if they thought her safety more important than that of the she-wolf and her litter. She was certain Leidolf wouldn't like it if he knew she planned risking her neck to return to the woods to check on a human wolf biologist either.

Without knowing Leidolf's politics, she wasn't about to let him know what she had in mind to do. Only this time, she'd have to risk looking for the pups and Alex as a human. She didn't think that zoo man and his friend or any hunter would mess with her, but could she find the wolf before someone killed her? And the puppies were left to fend for themselves? They'd never last.

Laney considered the bandage on Cassie's shoulder. "Is your shoulder hurting a lot?"

"No, it's fine." No way did Cassie want Laney or anyone else thinking she needed further medical care. And her shoulder really was much better.

"Hmm. I'll let Leidolf know you're awake." Laney turned, opened the door, and let out a squeak, her hand flying to her breast.

CHAPTER 12

CASSIE'S OWN HEART SKIPPED A COUPLE OF BEATS AS SHE stared at Leidolf standing in the open doorway of his bedroom, his fist raised, ready to rap on the door. He looked from Laney to Cassie, who still stood in the middle of his bedroom floor—totally aware she was naked except for the bandage over her shoulder and feeling way too vulnerable. Too late to hide her nakedness or her unnatural reaction. Which would be a sure indication she was a loner...and didn't live with a pack.

Wearing a pair of jeans, rugged hiking boots, and a soft, fuzzy flannel shirt, Leidolf was gorgeous in a dangerous, feral sort of way and taller than most red males she'd encountered. His chestnut hair, tinged red, had been ruffled by the wind, making him look wild and untamable. His darkened eyes held hers captive for a moment, like a wolf would challenge her, watching to see if she'd back down. The same way he had when he saw her at the lake.

Was she alpha enough? That was what he was trying to determine. Or at least she thought so. She'd lived longer with real wolves than with her own kind, so she wasn't really experienced in dealing with a lusty alpha male *lupus garou* who was interested in her. Still, he had the same alpha male posturing.

His gaze roamed lower, all the way down her naked body, as if he was looking over his ultimate conquest. She glared at him and folded her arms across her chest, which sent another stab of pain into her shoulder. She winced, although she attempted to hide her discomfort. "I'm not looking for a mate, if you want to know my status."

His eyes flicked back to hers. She had a job to do—and mixing it up with a red *lupus garou* alpha leader and joining a pack were not in the plans.

Then his stern expression softened. "Where is your family, Cassie?"

"My family was killed," she said, not having told anyone the truth for many years. Saying it still hurt.

His expression turned sympathetic; she'd rather he was scowling at her. Much easier to deal with someone who was annoyed with her than someone who was tugging at her heartstrings.

"You said they had died. Did you mean your family?" he ventured.

Died? She frowned at him. She was certain she hadn't told him her life's story when she'd been out of it. "I don't remember what I said to you. It must have been the drugs."

He looked skeptical. Then he cocked a brow heavenward. "You don't have a mate." She'd stated she wasn't looking for one, but that wouldn't make any difference to him as long as she didn't already have one.

"No, I don't. Like I said, I'm not looking for one." She reiterated her stance because he seemed to need to hear it again, although she didn't sound as firm in her resolve as she meant to.

He smiled deeply, his eyes devilishly speculating. He bowed his head slightly, his tone nurturing when he said, "If you're feeling well enough and desire something to eat, you can join us in the den." The way he spoke wasn't an offer but rather a command. His gaze slid over her again, this time in a languorous manner, as if she was there for his viewing pleasure. "I recommend you dress first. My bachelor males might get a little restless at the sight of you."

As if *he* wasn't the one who was restless at the sight of her!

"She said she's from a pack in the redwoods of California," Laney offered, her brows raised a little.

Did Laney know something about the pack living there, or was she just suspicious of Cassie's story?

Leidolf's eyes rounded as he looked from Laney to Cassie. "The California redwoods? *Really.* And your pack leader's name?"

Cassie ground her teeth and then attempted a smile. Leidolf probably didn't know a pack that far away from his own territory. Most leaders wouldn't. So it was a bluff on his part, she was certain. "Harold Wilden."

"Really. I thought the leader of the redwood area was a gray pack leader."

Her lips parted in surprise. "Uhm, yes, a gray." Hell, a gray pack lived there?

"Wilden's a red's last name. Hunter Greymere was the leader in that area until a fire forced his pack to move north. He took over his uncle's cabin resort along the Oregon coast. One of his grays actually joined my pack."

Oh, that was how Leidolf knew about them. Great. "Well, a little more south of the redwoods," Cassie amended.

"Ah. A red pack."

"Yes."

"The leader by the name of Wilden." His eyes sparkled in the low light of the room, and he shifted his attention to

Laney. "We'll see you both in a few minutes." He spoke as if he was leaving Cassie in Laney's charge, and Cassie stiffened a bit.

No one was in charge of her. Not when she'd been a loner all these years and did just fine on her own.

"She's hurting," Laney said, telling on her.

Cassie wasn't about to take anything for the pain. Not when it would make it more difficult for her to return to the forest.

Leidolf frowned. "We have pain medication."

"No, I'm fine." Cassie tried to sound convincing, but she saw the look in Leidolf's eyes. He knew she needed something for the pain, but she wasn't going for it. And he knew why.

Then he inclined his head toward Cassie, his eyes spearing her with a look that said he wanted her and she was already his, so get used to the idea. "Just to let you know *my* status, I *am* looking for a mate." He bowed his head a little, punctuating his remark.

The way he said it, he acted as though she was available just for him anyway. He was so arrogant! The last time she had put up with a male that had wanted her like that, he hadn't been half as egotistical, or half as hot either. And she definitely hadn't felt anything for him. Leidolf? He was real trouble, triggering needs she didn't even want to consider. More than just feeling the physical needs, though, she didn't want to deal with the emotional baggage. She'd always worked extra hard to avoid feeling anything for her kind because it brought back memories of what she'd lost.

Leidolf was undoing that resolve.

And then the physical side of the equation created more punishment. Her nipples tingled beneath her arms, traitors, and she had the unfathomable urge to either throw him on the bed and make him show her just what he had in mind to do with her—or strangle him. She tried to convince herself that strangling him was preferable. It wasn't working.

He seemed a little hesitant to leave and shoved his hands into his pockets, the all-powerful alpha male now appearing a little unsure of himself, which made her feel somewhat uptight. Even Laney looked a little apprehensive, as if she didn't know what to do.

Then Leidolf directed his question at Laney. "Can you leave us alone for a moment?"

She glanced back at Cassie, almost as if she wanted to stay and chaperone, but she quickly bowed her head to Leidolf and left the room, closing the door behind her. Leidolf pulled the fuzzy, brown blanket off the recliner and wrapped it around Cassie in such a protective, endearing way that tears formed in her eyes. Damn it.

He led her to the bed and sat her down, then knelt beside her and took her hands in his. "Cassie, you were pretty out of it when I talked with you earlier. I asked if you would like to stay with our pack. No strings attached. Just join us. Get to know us. And—"

She attempted a sincere smile when she was really trying to hide her true feelings. Hell, she ought to just come clean. Although if she did, he would think he had more leverage.

"But I have a pack." Which, in a way, she did. Although not just one, several. Except the wolves couldn't shift. "I want to thank you and your people for your generosity in taking care of me, but I really have business to attend to. So if Laney could drive me back to the forest and drop me off, I'd be forever grateful."

Leidolf gave a conceited half smile, not buying into her story or her request. "Laney must have told you what's happening in the forest right now. With hunters crawling all over the place? The police? Reporters? Not only that, but you're still injured. And it wouldn't do to let you return there and get yourself into more trouble." He swept away a curl of hair tickling her cheek and tucked it behind her ear. His gaze shifted from her eyes to her lips, and she knew he wanted to kiss her.

And damn it, she wanted him to!

A little voice nagged at her to do it, just because she was dying to feel what it would be like to be kissed by the alpha pack leader. It wouldn't mean anything, she assured herself. Just a kiss. Her lips feeling dry as sand, she licked them. His mouth curved up a hint, and his gaze refocused on hers. Then he took her hand and kissed it, as if he were a proper English gentleman coming to call.

That wasn't what she had in mind! He rose, continued to watch her, and hollered, "Laney!"

The door immediately opened. Cassie figured the woman had been glued to it while trying to hear what was going on.

"Yes?" Laney asked, as if she were completely above suspicion.

"Get Cassie something to wear so she can join us for dinner." Then he bowed his head slightly to Cassie, turned around, and left the room.

Cassie immediately got up from the bed, the blanket still wrapped around her as she stared at the departing alpha leader.

That was it? That was the only kind of a kiss he was going to bestow upon her?

As soon as he shut the door behind him, Cassie switched her attention to Laney, whose expression was one of refrained amusement.

"Clothes?" Cassie asked in a sweetly innocent voice that sounded way too calculating to her ears. *And keys to a fast getaway car?* Before she changed her mind and decided to stay.

Laney's smile grew. "Sure. My things might be a bit big for you, but I may have something that's a little snug on me. My home is across the compound, but it shouldn't take me too long to drive over there, grab a couple of items, and return."

Cassie gave her a camera smile back, but she recognized that the woman wanted her to stay with the pack. Probably to satisfy the alpha leader's needs. A cold beer and a good woman could do wonders for an alpha male's disposition. So much the better for his pack members. And with fewer females in most packs, she imagined Laney would have loved another woman to talk to.

While she waited for Laney, Cassie quickly noted a messy pile of papers sitting on a desk next to a computer on the other side of the room, a brown leather couch in a sitting area, and an empty bookshelf. She raised her brows. Not a reader? Then she saw a book opened on top of the desk. Wondering what would appeal to Leidolf when he had no other books, she peered a little closer and saw the biographical page of Julia Wildthorn, the red *lupus garou* romance writer, and a colorful photo of the pretty redhead. Probably doctored with the miracles of photo-reworking programs.

She scowled. Hell, here he was acting like he wanted Cassie, while he had been ogling the picture of a romance author? And as evidenced by no other books in the room, he didn't even read? Maybe he had read Julia Wildthorn's book. Probably all her books, so he could tell her how much he loved her work, whether he did or not.

Then Cassie saw his desktop calendar and edged a little closer to take a peek. A cleanly handwritten note on Saturday boldly proclaimed: *Book signing, 2–4 p.m., Julia, Powell's.*

Cassie scowled even further. Julia: first-name basis. So how many red females was he chasing? He'd acted like Cassie was the only one for him, and in reality, he had a bevy of red females waiting in the wings? Then she growled under her breath, more peeved at herself for caring than for being irritated with him. He was a male *lupus garou* after all. So what was *her* excuse?

Her attention switched to the velvet comforter on the king-sized bed, rumpled now after she'd tossed and turned there, and the patio doors leading outside where the sky was dark. She glanced at the bedside clock. Half past ten. A good time to search for the she-wolf and her pups and learn what happened to Alex.

Laney cleared her throat, and Cassie's heart skipped a beat. She'd thought the woman had already left. Paused at the door, Laney had been watching her the whole time, cataloging everything she did. Cassie was used to being the one who did the observing, although wolves watched her every move while she was with a pack, curious about her, intrigued. For a different reason. A shiver ran up her spine, and she felt totally exposed that a *lupus garou* had been analyzing her actions and would no doubt report every move she'd made to Leidolf. And he'd be damned amused.

"Leidolf hasn't wanted anyone to help him redecorate the place, so he just had some things removed, and the bed and linens are all new. He had Elgin, my mate, get rid of the old bed, because it reminded him of the former pack leader."

Former pack leader. Had Leidolf ousted him? As curious as Cassie was, she figured the less she knew about Leidolf and his pack, the better.

"Then again, he really needs a mate to help him decorate the place." Laney smiled again. "Maybe you should lie down until I return." She motioned to Cassie's injured shoulder. "You know how it is. Rest helps us recuperate even faster. I'll be right back, Cassie. And, dear, welcome to the pack." She waited for Cassie to comply.

Peeved but trying not to show it, Cassie climbed back into bed and pulled the covers over her in an attempt to play the game.

"Be right back," Laney said again, smiling slightly as if she knew what Cassie was planning. Then she hurried out of the room and shut the door.

As soon as it clunked closed, Cassie planned to snatch some of Leidolf's clothes and make her escape. When she grabbed the comforter to yank it aside, the bedroom door squeaked open. Her heart drumming with anxiety at nearly being caught trying to leave the bed again, she whipped her head around. She figured she must look guilty as charged, and she hadn't even done anything, *yet.*

"I want you to learn who the woman is and where she's from, Elgin," Leidolf said, pacing across the great room in front of several of his pack members, all of them wanting to know just where this was leading.

He couldn't hide how captivated he was, more than he had ever been with any woman. Apart from their phero-mones kicking each other's into high gear, he wanted her—the way she challenged him and hid her *lupus garou* identity from him, the way she was as intrigued with him as he was with her and focused on her own wishes, his be damned. Still, he could read in her actions that she was having a hard time sticking to whatever her own plans were.

Hell, when he'd wrapped the blanket around her, she'd come to tears. Which, to him, meant she hadn't had anyone take care of her in a long damned time. She needed what he had to offer, and he sure needed her.

Yeah, he desired her body and soul, and he knew that buried deep in her psyche, she wanted him. Now he just had to help her see it both their ways. From the way she reacted to him, he knew she wasn't a loner at heart, but she'd become one out of necessity. Her family was dead, she said. That had to be the reason for her fear of being with another pack.

Elgin pulled at his red beard thoughtfully, the streaks of gray giving him added character. "Laney says the woman told you she has a pack."

"I doubt she has. They wouldn't want one of their unmated females running around the world without someone watching out for her."

Elgin's face brightened, but then he frowned. "Laney warned me the little lady wants to return to the woods."

Leidolf snorted. "She isn't going anywhere. The bullet hole in her shoulder won't heal that quickly, and with all the riffraff sure to be searching out there," he said, giving Quincy and Pierce a pointed look, "it's not safe for anyone, least of all a lone female." He looked around the room for the other major source of contention—Sarge, who was being monitored closely by three of his men.

Satros was sleeping soundly in an overstuffed chair, his romp to locate Sarge and, earlier, the search for a red wolf mate for Leidolf having taken their toll on his stamina.

Leidolf considered the twin brothers again. If Quincy and Pierce hadn't needed a pack to keep them in line and if the trouble they had been getting into wasn't due to poor judgment, Leidolf would have made them leave. That was just what had happened to them before, and he couldn't help feeling that some leader needed to make sure they fit into a pack.

He noticed Evan, one of his male teens, watching him, and Carver observing the teen, irritation evident on the middle-aged widower's face. Seemed Leidolf couldn't ever resolve one problem without six more taking its place. He might as well have a word in private with the boy. Leidolf motioned for everyone but Evan to leave the room. Once the door was shut and they were alone, he waved to a chair.

"Evan, I want you to stay out of trouble."

Evan let out his breath, sat on the chair hard, and then spread his hands palm up. "I'm not doing anything. Really."

Leidolf raised his brow. "Stay away from Carver's daughters."

"One of them constantly chases after me." Evan shrugged. "Whenever her father and sister aren't around, she's coming on to me. What am I supposed to do?"

"Stay away from her. Gently tell her you're not interested."

His look defiant, Evan shoved his hands in his pockets.

"Evan?"

"Of all the girls in the pack, she's the only one who's really an alpha. I like that she comes after me."

"Yeah, and if her father learns of it, *he'll* come after you…and then what?"

"I'm not afraid of him."

"You should be. Her father has the final say about who she sees until she's an adult."

"He doesn't want her to see *anyone*, least of all me. I'm not going to lie to you. If Alice wants to see me, I'll be there for her."

"Alice, the quiet one?" Leidolf frowned at Evan. "Hell, as your pack leader, I highly recommend against it."

"But?"

"As a teen in your situation, I wouldn't listen to anyone who had a lick of sense either. So do us both a favor. No sneaking around to be with her. Let Carver know face-to-face that you want to see his daughter."

Evan's defiance continued to shine through. Then he gave a sharp nod. "All right. It won't work, you know."

"Won't know for sure unless you try."

"Did it work for you?"

Leidolf gave him a small smile. "Hopefully better for you than it did for me."

Footfalls stalked toward the room, and Leidolf said, "Have everyone come back in. Just remember what I said."

"Yes, sir," Evan said and hurried to tell everyone to rejoin them.

When the men reentered the room, Leidolf was surprised to see Irving and Tynan. Sporting a head bandage,

Tynan had as big a scowl as Irving. They should have looked guilty as hell for not doing their ranching duties and leaving without a word to anyone, again.

"Where have the two of you been?" Leidolf growled. "And what the hell happened to you, Tynan?"

"We were hunting for that cougar," Irving said, his steely eyes focused on Leidolf's, not backing down. He jerked a thumb in Tynan's direction. "Because of the rain, he slipped on some rocks and hit his head hard against a boulder. Hard head, though, nothing damaged. Much."

At least the twin brothers didn't give Leidolf new headaches maliciously. And Sarge was just a major nuisance. But Irving and Tynan? Leidolf was beginning to suspect they were real trouble.

He wished Elgin hadn't been so reluctant to make him aware of them months earlier when Leidolf first arrived in the pack. Leidolf's complacency could be seen as a weakness. Further, not realizing the problem was also an indication that he didn't have what it took to lead the pack. At least anyone who had half a notion to challenge him might think so.

Leidolf narrowed his eyes at Tynan and Irving. "I didn't give you permission to leave and neglect your duties, and you haven't let Elgin or Fergus know your whereabouts for several days."

The look on the two men's faces remained frozen in stone. No regret for what they had been up to. Just as arrogant as Alfred's cronies had been.

Leidolf scowled at the men, his voice low and menacing. "Did you kill any of the human girls like Alfred and his henchmen did?"

Tynan glanced at Irving, which told Leidolf that Irving was running the show and also that they were involved somehow in what Alfred had done.

"Did you?" Leidolf growled. He knew if they had, they wouldn't admit to it. They would have signed their death warrants by doing so. But their reactions would reveal the truth in part.

Tynan quickly shook his head.

Irving said, "No." But the way he spoke was a challenge. *Prove it.*

And Leidolf would do just that. He lifted his nose and smelled the air, but he couldn't capture any scent from the two men. "Why are you wearing hunter's spray?"

"I told you we went hunting for the cougar," Irving said, with a snide twist to his words.

"Your guns were armed with regular bullets?"

A flutter of concern crossed Tynan's face.

"Of course," Irving said, as if the question was idiotic.

Leidolf stood taller like an alpha wolf leader would, his posture and voice threatening mayhem if the men didn't take heed. "The cougar will be tranquilized, not killed. Do you understand?"

"Alfred would have killed the cat and been done with it," Irving said, challenging Leidolf's authority.

A couple of the men grumbled something Leidolf couldn't make out. Elgin snorted but held his tongue. Fergus and Carver both scowled at Irving, fists tightening and appearing as though they were ready to tear Irving apart.

Although Irving and his cousin weren't born *lupus garous*, they'd been werewolves for a long time. But a pecking order still existed, and Irving would be no match for Leidolf.

"And you know where Alfred is now." Leidolf gave him a look that said if he didn't mind pack rules, he could join his former pack leader, six feet under.

If these men had murdered innocent women, they would be dealt with in the only way their kind dealt with pack members who committed such atrocities. Wolf to wolf in the ancient way. And Irving and Tynan had to realize that.

So what was making them hang around and not tuck tail and run before they met their fate? The only reason Leidolf hadn't torn into them before this was that before he did so, he had to learn beyond a shadow of a doubt that the men were guilty of a crime.

CHAPTER 13

WITH ONLY A PENLIGHT TO ILLUMINATE HIS WAY, HIS lantern having given out hours earlier, Alex reached his truck and leaned against it. He hesitated to return to the thick of the woods close to where he might still encounter the men who had tried to shoot him and who had shot the red wolf. He assumed the wolf was in good hands now with the men who had rescued her from the zoo staff, if only because wolves had been running with them. They probably belonged to the men, which would explain the female's unnatural protective behavior around Alex.

So much for observing red wolves in the wild. He should have known that finding a pack of red wolves living out here was too good to be true.

Police officers and an ambulance crew had already rescued the drugged men who worked for the zoo. Alex had kept a low profile, watching from the woods to ensure they would be all right, never revealing himself or his identity. But what kept him from leaving the area was Cassie's truck. He peered inside it again. She hadn't been here since she left it yesterday sometime, and he couldn't help worrying about her. No matter how much he told himself she was a capable woman when roaming through the wilderness, he couldn't help the concern that nagged at him. What if she'd run afoul of the murderers? Or she ran into some other trouble? An injury? A wild-animal attack? Other hunters mistaking her for a deer?

Then he recalled the man's footprints that had followed Cassie's. Had he been with her or stalking her?

He let out his breath in exasperation, threw his backpack over his shoulders, and headed into the woods again, determined to stay in the national forest until he could locate her.

―⁓―

As soon as Leidolf stepped inside the bedroom, Cassie yanked the covers back over her body, trying to pretend she hadn't intended to run off. She was sure he could hear her heart beating too fast. He smiled at Cassie in a way that said he knew just what she'd been planning. As hot as her cheeks felt, they were probably flushed.

"Two young ladies in our pack would like to visit with you," Leidolf said, but instead of anyone else coming into the room as she expected, he shut the door. "But first, I wanted to talk to you further."

Oh brother, more of his trying to convince her she needed to join his pack. Not about to be swayed but to be polite for their caring for her, she took a deep breath, sat back against the pillows with the covers tucked up under her arms, and motioned to the recliner. "Go ahead."

She had no intention of saying anything further about herself though. The less said, the better.

He gave her a shadow of a smile, his expression saying that there was no way he was putting that much distance between them, and then sat on the mattress next to her, his hip pressed against hers. He was the personification of seduction.

She would not look at his lips again, calculating how

they would feel pressed against hers. Instead, she tilted her chin up, and when he didn't say anything, she prompted again, "Proceed."

She didn't know if his need to talk was a delaying tactic to give Laney more time to arrive, or if he wanted to stay close to Cassie longer, but whatever it was, the more she was with him, the more she couldn't see Leidolf as just a one-night-stand kind of guy. That wasn't helping her remain objective in the least.

He finally reached down and took hold of her hand and massaged the top with his thumb using a gentle stroke, which again wasn't helping her objectivity one iota.

"I left my pack a couple of years ago because of problems with the leadership, but it was a dangerous situation for my family," Leidolf began, his voice dark.

Already she didn't like the tone of this talk. She kept her eyes focused on his when she wanted to turn away, bury her feelings deep, and not speak about families or danger or what had become of them.

"Because I left them, my sister died."

Cassie swallowed hard and this time looked away. What if she had been the reason her family died? Because she'd run off to be with the wolf pack that day? What if she had been home instead, and she could have warned her family before they were murdered?

"I tried to get my family to move away, but they wouldn't. My father owned the territory before he was injured permanently in an avalanche, and he was bound and determined to stay. It had been his family's home for generations," Leidolf continued.

Cassie looked back at him. He still watched her and

analyzed her expression to learn whatever he could from her reactions. She'd never met a man who was so attuned to watching people's actions and reactions while attempting to understand them.

"I tried to get my sisters to come with me at least. But I didn't have any luck, and one of my sisters died."

"It wasn't your fault," Cassie said. She knew it wasn't. Even if Leidolf thought he was responsible. He couldn't be, not the way he had taken over this pack, one that, in his own words, had been abused. She swallowed hard. Although she was sure it couldn't have been his fault, she still couldn't come to grips with the way she felt about her own family.

"You're right, Cassie, but for a long time, I felt it was my fault, that I was the cause of my sister's death. My remaining sister blamed me. What's worse, she was the one who tried to uncover what had happened to our sister when I should have been the one to do so. But I didn't know that Larissa had run off or mated with a gray and then was murdered. Even so, she was my responsibility."

"Your father's, since he was still alive," Cassie said.

"My father was disabled."

"Yet she listened to him, not you. What if your father had moved the family?"

Leidolf nodded, but the pain was still reflected in his expression.

"It wasn't your fault," Cassie said again, softly, with feeling.

"I came here to live, away from my home in Colorado, the life of a loner in the wilderness, a mountain man."

"Poseidon," she said under her breath.

"What?"

She took a deep breath and shook her head. "A mountain

man. Or nature lover. That's what I thought you were when I saw you at the lake." *And Poseidon, godlike, seductive, edible.*

"I *had been* a mountain man, scruffy, scraggly beard, long hair."

She smiled.

He chuckled. "I looked like a wolf even without my fur coat on."

"Not when I saw you. I figured you were just…" She shrugged.

"Sexy as hell?" He leaned over, kissed her forehead, and then leaned back and gave her one of those unbelievably devilish winks that said he knew her too damned well. "I thought that about you too."

She folded her arms and tilted her chin up. "What had you intended to do when you came stalking out of the lake after me?"

"See your reaction. See if you stayed, ran away, or stalked in my direction, intending to have your way with me, like you sure seemed intent on."

She smiled and touched the top button on his shirt, her gaze switching to his. Her lips curved up a little.

He sighed and removed her hand from his shirt and then kissed it again. "We are a lot more alike than you think, Cassie. A lot more." He rose from the bed. "The girls wanted to meet you."

More of the "let's see which pack member can convince you to stay" routine.

Leidolf opened the door and motioned for the girls to enter the room. "They're to keep you company until Laney returns with clothes for you."

The auburn-haired teen girls entered Leidolf's bedroom,

both smiling like rays of sunshine on a gray, foggy day, their amber eyes just as gleeful as they greeted Cassie. She remembered them attending her lecture. Neither of the girls had asked her a question. And why should they have? They probably knew as much about wolves as she did.

The way Leidolf gave them each a stern look, the unspoken message meant, *Guard our guest, and don't let her get away.*

He bowed his head to Cassie and left the girls alone with her, keeping the door wide open.

Just in case they had to cry out for help if Cassie tried to steal away anyway.

"I'm Alice, and this is my twin sister, Sarah. Leidolf told us to keep you company while Laney went to fetch clothes for you. We live next door to Forest Park in Portland. When Leidolf went in search of you in the Mount Hood National Forest, the whole pack, even those scattered in nearby towns around Portland, heard about it. They gathered here while you were sleeping. Everyone was dying to see you. Even though Leidolf hadn't called for a pack meeting."

"Yeah, I think he was a little bit surprised at first to see everyone here," Sarah chirped. "He figured he had you mostly to himself." She grinned. "But I think he's enjoying showing you off."

"He'd been searching for a mate even before he took over the pack." Sarah twisted a long curl of hair around her finger and looked at her sister as if seeking confirmation.

Alice caught her eye and smiled, then faced Cassie. "Yes. He tries not to let on, but everyone gossips about it. We all know you're the one he wants."

"To be his mate." Cassie figured the pack had to have

made the assumption, not that Leidolf himself had already told them so. No alpha male could be *that* arrogant.

"Absolutely." Sarah released the stranglehold she had on her hair, leaned against the dresser, and folded her arms. "You're the one. Of course, Dad was peeved you were already spoken for, because he wants a mate. He says it's because we need a mother, but we're old enough that we really don't. If it makes him happy…" She shrugged. "We'd be happy."

"We know he's just lonely. He misses Mom terribly," Alice said.

"Your mom died?"

"Yes, in a bad car accident five years ago."

"I'm so sorry to hear it." Cassie figured she had been about the same age as the girls when she lost her extended family, and a wave of memories of profound grief and loss swept over her. Of being alone in the wilderness. Of returning to her family's cabins while flames consumed them and never again being able to smell her family's unique scents…remembering her mother cooking at the iron stove, her father bringing in the wood, her sister darning socks, something Cassie could never get the hang of…and their cousin, Aimée, who was like their sister, fun to be with, hiking, swimming, and sharing their dreams. She recalled losing her uncles and aunts too, and their lighthearted banter, except for her unmated uncle who could be quite stern. Then their three homes were in ashes, the sound of nature encroaching on the otherwise deathly silence.

She took a deep breath and looked at the girls. "Well, Leidolf will have to find someone else. I have a pack."

The girls' eyes rounded, and then they shared a glance. They smiled broadly and both said, "Sure you do."

Cassie was glad she wasn't interviewing for a job as these girls' mother. She'd never be able to put anything past them. In fact, she was beginning to think she couldn't hide anything from anyone. She hadn't realized how well a pack of *lupus garous* could read her. Of course, when she'd been with her own family, she hadn't had to be that devious. Except for when it came to studying the wolves. Maybe her family knew about it all along and were just allowing her to get it out of her system.

Before she could think further about it, Alice nodded. "Yep, Leidolf said you're afraid to join us."

Afraid. That was a fighting word. Cassie didn't like to think of herself as afraid of anything. Not after her family was murdered. Not after she'd fended for herself before going to live with the wolf pack she'd befriended. Not when they were killed also. And not when she'd become a loner for good. Except that she was afraid of wolf hunters. In that regard, she had a healthy fear.

Sarah added, "Yeah, while you were sleeping, Leidolf said you're a loner, and they can be difficult to draw into a pack. He was a loner too, so he knows all about it. At first, our elders had a hard time convincing him we needed him, since Elgin was the one who killed the last of the bad wolves in our pack. Elgin only did what he had to do. He knew Leidolf was on his way to save the pack. And everyone wanted him to be the pack leader."

Alice quickly spoke up. "If he hadn't tangled with this really bad dude, a gray from Colorado, Leidolf would have killed the last of the bad reds instead of Elgin. Leidolf was too injured to fight the murderous reds in our pack then. Or he *would* have. Elgin didn't want to lead, and he's happy to be Leidolf's second in command. We're all going to help Leidolf keep you. Then he'll never want to leave us."

Although Cassie couldn't see Leidolf as the kind of man who would abandon his adopted pack, whether he had a mate or not, she envisioned being clapped in irons because that was the only way anyone could ensure she stayed in one place.

Sarah nodded. "Oh yes. If he has you to get mad at, he'll be happier with the pack. That's what *Evan* says."

Both girls' eyes sparkled when Alice added, "Evan's really cute, but Dad won't let us get near him if he can help it."

"He's your age?"

"Yeah, well, a little older." Sarah put a hand to her heart and sighed. "He leaves us alone on account of Dad. I don't think he's afraid of him… Evan's pretty alpha. He doesn't want to stir things up too much in the pack and make Leidolf mad. Being that he's the leader, no one wants to anger him."

Cassie stifled a groan. All she needed was to get tied down with a pack leader whose temper got away from him at the least provocation and who took it out on his pack members.

On the other hand, why had the pack wanted him to lead so badly? Maybe because the others had been so rotten that Leidolf seemed like an angel in comparison. She laughed to herself. He definitely wasn't angelic in the least bit. Not the way he judged her with that sinfully seductive expression he had. An enticing devil was more like it.

"Well, except for Sarge," Alice said. "He's newly turned and angers Leidolf all the time. Dad said Sarge should never have been allowed to live."

"Oh?"

"He was a Dark Angel," Sarah hurried to say.

"Dark Angel?"

Alice spoke low. "Werewolf killer. No one likes him. He's an omega wolf, skulking around the outskirts of the pack. A total loser. Dad said he did drugs. Not any longer though. If he did, Dad would terminate him."

"Oh."

"Yeah, well, he's bad news." Sarah pointed to her arm. "And he had this tattoo on his arm right here… *Dark Angel,* Dad said. We weren't allowed to see it. I mean, for one, no werewolf could safely wear a tattoo. Also it was what the—"

"Words represented," Alice said, stealing Sarah's words. "A little laser surgery and the words were history. The *reason* for the tattoo still turns most of the pack members off, no matter that it's gone and only a slight scar remains. Sarge doesn't care. Keeps wearing short-sleeved shirts to show it off like a badge of honor, Evan says. No one likes Sarge for that reason and because he keeps causing so much trouble."

"Then there's Irving and Tynan. Dad says they're up to no good." Sarah nodded her head once, emphasizing her point.

Alice's eyes grew big as she added more of the pack news. "Oh yeah, and Pierce and—"

Hurried footsteps sounded down the hall, and everyone turned to see who was coming. Cassie gave up on thinking she might get out of the ranch house anytime soon.

Half out of breath, Laney rushed into the room with an armful of bright and flowery clothes. She gave the girls a stern look. "I hope you've been only telling Cassie about all the nice people we have in the pack."

Both bit their lips and glanced at Cassie. She smiled. She wouldn't give them away.

"These are not the latest fashion, but they should fit. And one of the ladies wants to meet you. She's bedridden for the time being. Would you mind seeing her? She's at the other end of the house and will be for a few days."

No, Cassie didn't want to be drawn any further into the pack's problems for fear she'd end up feeling more for them than was wise to, but if the woman was bedridden and would be cheered by seeing Cassie, it was the least she could do.

She raised her brows at the floral fabrics that looked like they were from the tie-dye, peace sign era...silky bell-bottom pants covered in bright pink roses, a blue tulip shirt, neither of the colors or the flowers matching, and a tie-dyed bandanna. The combination of brilliant colors made her eyes ache. She'd look like a mixed-up bouquet of flowers when she went to dinner. Worse? She'd really stand out if she tried to blend into the woods once she returned there. Maybe that was Laney's devious way of making sure she didn't leave anytime soon. It wouldn't be enough to stop Cassie.

"Leidolf will let me go shopping with you to buy you some more things, once you've healed up a bit more."

She had to have permission? Cassie harrumphed. That would be the day. Although she had to give him credit: his reasoning was sound, as he knew she wouldn't stay put. Hmm, what if she went to the army-navy store? Got some nice camouflage clothes like the hunters wore? Although she knew that wasn't a possibility, it sure appealed.

"Do you need help dressing?" Laney motioned to Cassie's injury.

"No, thank you. I just need some..." Privacy, that was what Cassie nearly said. But *lupus garous* who lived in packs didn't need privacy when dressing. "… uhm, shoes?" Cassie managed to say without blowing her tenuous cover.

"Mine are probably a couple of sizes too big," Laney apologized.

Alice pointed at her small feet. "I'm probably more your size. And Sarah too, since we wear the same size shoes."

"We didn't think to bring any with us, and we live two hours from here," Sarah said. Then her eyes widened. "You weren't the red wolf our dad smelled in the park, were you? Dad would have a fit if he learned you were the one he had smelled earlier. Although he knew he'd have to give the wolf up to Leidolf if he found her."

Alice added, "He hoped he could locate her and befriend her, and Leidolf would take pity on him and let him have her for a mate if she was agreeable. He looked for the red wolf for days while Leidolf was in Maine, taking care of important pack business. Dad even had us help him search. We never could find any sign of where she slipped off to. And she didn't seem to return."

Before Cassie could respond, Sarah cleared her throat. "Leidolf looked for her yesterday, and we were afraid he was going to be mad that Dad didn't tell him about her."

"Yeah, and he really wanted to go with Leidolf to see if he found her this time."

"Why, we didn't know." Sarah tucked her hair behind her ear. "I guess he thought he still might have a chance with her."

"Leidolf wouldn't let Dad go with him. Dad was really not happy about it."

"Which park?" Cassie asked.

Alice offered, "Forest Park in the city of Portland."

"No, it wasn't me." Cassie suspected it might be the wolf with the pups. The girls' father would be disappointed to hear she was a real wolf. Cassie got out of bed and pulled the shirt on, then the pants. They might have been a little snug on Laney, but they were way too loose on Cassie. If she let go of the hip-hugger pants, they would be puddled at her feet. "You didn't happen to bring a belt, did you?"

Laney shook her head. "Oh my, no."

Alice lifted up her own shirt and shook her head. No belt. "I meant to put one on, but we were in such a rush to get here that I forgot."

"I never wear belts," Sarah said. "Too cumbersome if I want to shift quickly. Not that we do that very often, except when we have to. Leidolf's very strict about when and where we shift. Unless it's in the privacy of our home. A belt is just one less thing to have to remove."

"Maybe Leidolf has one." Cassie headed for the closet.

Everyone was dead silent, and she figured they were afraid he wouldn't like it if she came to the meal wearing one of his belts without his permission. She was sure he wouldn't want to see her wearing only a short, cropped shirt that rested high above her belly button and hip-huggers that gathered around her feet.

She grabbed a black leather belt off a rack, hurried back out of the closet, and nearly laughed to see the girls and Laney, their mouths gaping. Then the three smiled.

"Well, if she lives through this, we know he's got a mate," Sarah said and giggled.

"Absolutely," Alice said.

Laney shook her head. "Why didn't I think of that?"

Then the problem was that Laney's floral pants had no belt loops. Trying to make do, Cassie fastened the too-big belt around the pants. "No one happens to have anything I can use to make another hole in the belt, does anyone?"

"Uhm," Alice said. "That might be going a little too far."

Cassie looked around at the dresser and desk, but she didn't see a sharp instrument she could use. Just as she reached for a desk drawer, Elgin poked his head into the bedroom. "Food's on the table. Is everyone ready to eat?"

The girls and Laney looked really relieved for the interruption to what Cassie was about to do.

Giving up her quest to make another hole in the belt, Cassie buckled it, but the black leather slipped down low on her hips and made her feel more exposed than when she wasn't wearing anything. She hoped the feast wouldn't take too long before she could return to bed, pretend to sleep, and then slip out into the night, but she was afraid the pants would never stay up if she was on the run. And the fabric was so silky that it would be way too cold to wear in the wilderness. Not to mention way too bright.

"I'm taking her to see Felicity first," Laney said and directed Cassie down the hall.

"We want to go too," the girls both said at once.

Cassie thought it odd, figuring the bedridden wolf probably wouldn't want all the attention at once.

When she walked into the bedroom after Laney, she found a wolf sound asleep in a bed with wolf pups sleeping beside her or on top of her, their eyes squeezed shut, their tiny paws pink, their fur slick and dark. Passed out in a comfy chair near the bed was a snoring, bearded man with dark circles beneath his eyes.

Cassie slowly approached the mother, who opened her eyes and watched her.

"This is Cassie," Laney explained. "And, Cassie, meet Felicity and her brood. She chose to have wolf pups instead of babies, easier to birth and easier to take care of when they're that many. And that is her mate, Harvey." She motioned to the sleeping man.

He looked like his mate's ordeal had worn him out also.

"Felicity," Cassie said, motioning to the pups. "May I?"

Felicity bowed her head.

Cassie walked over to the bed and picked up one of the pups, who wrinkled his nose and licked his lips but continued to sleep.

"Oscar. He's the alpha male so far. Firstborn, first to suckle," Laney said, sounding like a proud grandmother.

Sarah and Alice stood at the footboard and smiled at the pups.

Cassie picked up another pup, and it cried out, startled. Cassie rubbed her face against it. She loved wolf pups. She couldn't help it, but she felt a kinship to all the wolf kind, whether they were *lupus* or *lupus garous*.

"That one's Melissa. She's sweet and quiet and better learn to take charge or she'll be at the bottom of the heap," Laney said.

Cassie stroked the back of the next pup, also a male.

"Keith, next in charge. And the other female is Pamela, and she's a real fighter. No bossy brother is going to steal her place at her mother's teat at feeding time."

Cassie smiled. She'd heard that was exactly the way she was when she was a young wolf pup. "They're beautiful," Cassie told the mother, and she swore the wolf breathed a sigh of relief.

The wolf's gaze shifted toward the door, and Cassie turned to see what caught her attention. Leidolf stood in the doorway watching Cassie. Not what she wanted to see. All at once, she felt maneuvered into the matchmaking bit again. Come see what you can have if you give Leidolf a chance. Her face felt hot first, and then the uncomfortable sensation spread all over her body.

Despite not wanting to feed into Leidolf's delusions, Cassie didn't want to hurt Felicity's feelings, so she said, "If I *ever* settle down for good, I'll be lucky to have offspring as beautiful as yours."

Felicity gave her a wolf smile. Even though Cassie had never had children of her own, she still always felt connected to mothers. Maybe because she had a caregiver personality. Or maybe because she had always loved pups and kids, and they seemed to adore her just as much.

When she turned around, Leidolf was still waiting for her. She got the distinct impression he wanted her company again.

She sighed. No way to avoid the issue.

CHAPTER 14

CASSIE JOINED LEIDOLF, AND HE WALKED HER DOWN THE
hall, not leaving an inch of free space between them, just like
wolves who were courting or mated would stick close together.
Trying to ignore their close proximity, she peeked into five
more bedrooms, all well furnished, each having sitting areas
and patio doors. The ranch must have cost a fortune.

When they reached the living room, the place was just as
elegant with leather couches, Persian rugs, crystal chande-
liers, and oil paintings of the Oregon coastline. All around
the room, brass wolf sculptures were displayed in various
poses—from resting in packs to nuzzling each other or
snarling at one another.

Why then was Leidolf's bedroom so austere? It almost
seemed he preferred to live in the most primitive of settings.
A cave if he could have managed, she imagined. Ah, a loner,
the girls had said. Kind of like Cassie, living out of a suitcase
half the time or out of a backpack. No place was home
anymore.

"We didn't want to be real formal," Laney said, motioning
to a table set up as a buffet with tons of food—beef tenderloin, chicken, ham slices, mashed potatoes, and chunks of
cheese, as well as tomatoes, salad, melons, and grapes.

Leidolf stood apart from Cassie, giving her some room
to maneuver around the table. She didn't notice the spread
of food as much as she did the way Leidolf watched her
in the crowd of people, probably twenty to thirty pack

members. He stood out among them, his shoulders straight, his dark gaze fixed on hers, his head lifted high, in charge, the dominant male. No matter that the room was filled with tension as everyone watched them, his gaze was steady and unaffected.

He was a calming presence, although she had never felt as self-conscious when she was speaking to an auditorium full of people as she did now. Maybe because that was impersonal. She lectured, answered questions, then disappeared again into the wilderness, looking for another wolf pack to observe and grow attached to.

This was different. These people expected her to stay. And they expected Leidolf to make it happen. Every eye was on her, and she figured they all had every intention of making her welcome and would aid Leidolf in any way to ensure she stayed.

Except for one of the men. He was blonder than the rest of the people and skulking on the outskirts. He appeared sullen and unhappy to be here. The two men standing on either side of him looked like twin brothers and appeared to be guarding him.

Newly turned… Sarge? The Dark Angel? Had to be him the way no one else stood near him. He steadily observed her, and she didn't like the calculating look in his expression.

Leidolf stole her attention again, the way he watched her, his gaze finally taking in her appearance, the short cropped top, the low-slung pants, and *his* belt.

He offered a small smile and motioned to the table. "Cassie."

Everyone waited for her to do something, anything. She was the honored guest. She sighed. This might be the last good meal she had in a while. Might as well make the most of it before she took off.

When she reached for a plate, Laney hurried to get her one. "Rest your shoulder, dear. I'll carry it to where you decide to sit afterward."

"Thank you, but I really can manage."

"The honor is all mine," Laney said, smiling.

They were treating her like a long-lost princess of the realm—which again stirred her longing to belong to a pack. Well, not any pack. If she'd been a different woman, someone who needed a man, Leidolf and his pack might have done nicely.

Cassie filled her plate with slices of ham and roast beef, mashed potatoes and gravy, and spinach salad and tomatoes, topped with blue-cheese dressing. All of it looked scrumptious and smelled heavenly. Her stomach grumbled, and she was sure the whole group heard it.

Leidolf raised his brows a little. Yeah, he had heard. She couldn't seem to keep much secret from him.

Then a couple of men passed out glasses of wine while the pack members began filling their plates full of food. Everyone drifted to chairs and couches, finding a spot to perch while they ate and conversed. Leidolf extended his hand and pressed it against the small of her back, guiding Cassie to a conspicuously empty velour couch. His hand on her skin stirred all over again the craving for something more than the life she had. She tried to ignore what his touch did to her until his hand shifted around her hip, pulling her close as he moved her around a couple of his men. His action was loving and gentle and possessive. Some part of her liked that possessiveness, as if she belonged with him and with this pack.

Even so, her whole body heated several degrees while everyone watched their progression, and she didn't remember a time when she had felt this exposed. When they reached the couch, Leidolf motioned with his free hand for her to sit, still possessively embracing her hip. As soon as she sat, she missed the warmth of his touch, which was plain crazy.

Laney handed Cassie's plate to her, and raising a glass, Leidolf said, "I propose a toast for our pack members returning safely."

She drank some of her wine, delighted in the rich bouquet, and felt a buzz right away, probably because she hadn't had anything alcoholic to drink since the previous Christmas when she had joined some fellow researchers in a little holiday cheer. And got blitzed. Luckily, she had managed to slip away before she did anything really stupid.

Leidolf sat down beside her, way too close, way too possessively, when the couch had ample room for them to spread out. On the one hand, the way his leg touched hers annoyed her. He was in her space, and she fought moving away from him. Again the issue of running away made her stand her ground. On the other hand, some part of her wanted more of his touch. Craved it, as if she were a wolf in heat. Which technically, damn it, she was. And he was making all the right moves on her, which she was having a damn hard time ignoring.

Until now, her wolf urges had never troubled her. Damn if his pheromones weren't triggering hers again.

If she could just have her way with him, would that resolve the craving she had for him? Then she'd be mated with him for life, and she didn't want anything permanent with a guy. Any guy. Not when she knew just where it would lead. No more running off to study wolves. Not without her mate's permission. And she assumed a pack leader wouldn't give it. Not when he wanted her with him to run a pack. And not when he would worry about her being alone in the wilderness facing who knew what. Maybe another naked man in a lake somewhere. Or maybe another hunter.

He reached across her leg to grab a saltshaker off the coffee table, his arm brushing the borrowed silky, floral pants against her skin, heating her to the core all over again. When she shot him a look to cool it, his eyes sparkled with mischief. Even if she at first thought he had touched her innocently, his expression said otherwise. She figured Leidolf was the kind of man who was always in control of his actions. Planning, making every move count for something, leaving nothing to chance.

As he returned the salt to the very same spot on the table instead of just leaving it on his side, his arm rested unnecessarily against her thigh. She shoved his arm off her leg and smiled when he raised his brows at her, while he wore a devilish smile of his own. She had every intention of proving the point that she wasn't his. Which was what this was all about. The mating game. Werewolf style.

The great room grew completely silent, and she looked up and found every eye on them.

One of the men, tall like Leidolf, broke the silence. "My girls say you weren't the one roaming through Forest Park."

Responding before Cassie could, Leidolf shook his head and lifted his glass of wine. "No, Carver. The wolf had a different scent. Not the same one at all."

Cassie figured Carver had to know that, since his

daughters said he'd been searching for the other wolf. So what was this really all about?

Several of the men stood a little taller, interest reflected in their intrigued expressions. If the wolf Carver and Leidolf had smelled was the mother with the pups, the bachelors were sure to be disappointed. Cassie wasn't about to mention the she-wolf had pups. She probably had made a big mistake mentioning to Laney that she intended to return to the forest at all.

"Is she related to you?" Carver asked, his voice serious, as if he were already letting the other men know his interest in the woman, but a hint of hopefulness made her sympathize with him.

"No," Cassie said, hating to disappoint him, but she wouldn't expound on the wolf any further than that. Not that she knew any more about the wolf in Forest Park than what she suspected.

Carver didn't look dissuaded. He stuck fairly close to the couch and her while he sipped a glass of wine and watched her. Did he think that if the wolf was related to Cassie, she would put in a good word with her? She would, if it meant the twin girls would have a mother.

She glanced over at Alice and…she and her sister, Sarah, weren't together as she expected. Cassie surveyed the room full of people and saw Alice inching her way over to a boy around her age, tall with sparkling amber eyes and lifted lips as he watched the girl slip closer to him. He had the devil in his expression, every bit as enticing as Leidolf himself. No wonder Carver didn't want his daughters near the boy. It had to be Evan, the boy they had described as a real alpha. She sighed. The girls needed a mother to ensure boys like him didn't get the best of them and that a father like Carver didn't kill the boy in the interim if he went a little too far.

While she attempted to ignore everyone around her, Cassie enthusiastically forked up some more gravy and mashed potatoes but flinched when a twinge of pain spiraled through her shoulder. She breathed through the pain and then ate the bite of potatoes. She hadn't had a home-cooked meal like this in ages, and it sure was good. Although the dinner she shared with Leidolf at the Forest Club sure had been delicious. Eating freeze-dried stuff on the trail got really tiresome after a while. And she had every intention of getting another plateful of the home cooking as soon as she was done with this one.

Conversations renewed in hushed voices, too many of them speaking for her to catch any one topic in particular, although she heard snippets of conversation—*She's perfect...right for him...have to keep her...won't be easy.*

She tried to ignore them and enjoy the food instead. Leidolf stuck close to her, his leg pressed against hers, showing her just how much he wanted her, which was triggering her own cravings. No man had ever turned her on with such a gentle, unimposing touch. She still wondered what it would be like to experience his kisses.

Her gaze wandered to his lips as he spoke to Elgin. Leidolf had manly lips that she imagined would be darned pleasurable pressed against her own. Elgin glanced at her, which triggered Leidolf to look also. Her face heated, and she looked back at her food, the remainder almost gone.

She clenched her hands, trying to stop the tingling in her nipples. "You could give me a little more room," she said to Leidolf. She spoke in her normal voice, which shouldn't have garnered any notice.

It did. Every conversation in the room instantly died.

Some out and out watched for Leidolf's reaction. Others just smiled and were less obvious about it.

"I could," Leidolf said smoothly. He didn't move. His steady gaze challenged her to do something about it.

She let out a heavy breath in exasperation. *Choose your battles wisely*, her father had always warned her when she was a kid and wouldn't take any guff from others in the nearby town.

Was it worth it to take the alpha leader down a notch or two?

She wouldn't have hesitated if they'd been alone. Every pack member watched to see how she would react to the leader's challenge. Fine. She drew close to Leidolf, pressing her breasts against his shoulder, tilting her chin up to speak with him privately. He leaned over so she could whisper into his ear.

"Give me some breathing space, or you can wear the rest of my glass of wine." She tilted the glass a little from side to side, warning him, her expression deadly serious.

He tsked and leaned down to whisper in her ear, which felt way too sensuous. "What a waste that would be." His warm breath and silky words did a number on her already heightened senses.

She leaned away from him, waiting for him to comply, armed and ready if he didn't.

His eyes focused on hers, Leidolf smiled broadly and then slapped his thighs. "Cassie's getting a little too hot."

She could kill him! And gave him a look that showed

him so. She swore a couple of muffled chuckles erupted deeper in the crowd.

He slid a few inches away from her and continued to speak to Elgin as if nothing had happened.

Her face still flushed, she was hot all right. Stirred up in the beginning, embarrassed in the end. She couldn't tell from the pack members' smiling faces if they thought she had won the confrontation or Leidolf had.

She shook her head at herself. No sense in rationalizing the outcome. Leidolf had won, hands down. Although she should have been irritated, she couldn't help but admire the crafty wolf. Never had anyone bested her in a situation like this. He definitely was her match.

Nearly finished with her meal, she set her fork on the plate. Leidolf motioned for a bottle of wine, and when Fergus brought it to him, he poured Cassie another glass. Alice and Sarah hurried over to the couch, eager to please her too.

Sarah stretched out her hands. "Would you like some more of anything to eat? We'll get it for you."

The two girls reminded her of herself and her twin sister when they'd been about their age. Nearly always together, except for when Cassie visited the wolf pack a few times. Recalling the last time she'd been with her sister and cousin while they were still alive, swimming in the river near their cabin one hot summer day, she blinked away the mist of tears forming in her eyes. "Mashed potatoes and gravy and another slice of beef. Thanks, girls."

The girls were too eager. Everyone smiled a little too much. The room seemed to tilt some. Leidolf still talked to Elgin, something about getting a nurse and an accountant in their pack. He'd seen the tears form in her eyes, probably heard the slight hitch in her voice when she spoke to the girls. He seemed more aware of her struggle to keep her emotions in check than anyone else she'd ever known. More than that, he appeared concerned. No one had ever worried about how she felt, and his expression disconcerted her. Much easier to deal with her past regrets when no one else cared a whit about what she was feeling.

He watched her now, and she worried he'd put his arm around her shoulder and pull her close. She didn't need his comfort or his strength. She could deal with her issues on her own just fine, like she'd always done.

Her strength sliding away, she couldn't seem to garner the strength to do much of anything. Against her will, her body leaned back into the couch cushions, her head dropping onto them. The cushions were soft, like pillows filled with fairy dust. Leidolf and Elgin looked at her. And smiled.

Calculating smiles. Traitorous smiles.

The girls returned with another plate full of food, but Cassie couldn't seem to lift her head and sit up or raise her hands to take the plate. And sometime or another, the refilled wineglass had disappeared from her grasp.

She wasn't hungry either anymore. Rather, she felt like her whole being was slipping, slipping, slipping away.

Leidolf's words were muffled as he spoke about all that Cassie had been through and how she couldn't eat any more right now. The girls looked disappointed, but then their sweet expressions faded away.

"She's tired," Leidolf said close to her ear, his words faint, the world swirling in her head, the darkness descending.

"The wound, the tranquilizer, the run, the fear of being hunted…she needs to rest."

The wine…too…much…wine…to…drink…or…

She narrowed her eyes at Leidolf, his steady gaze focused on her.

…the…wine…was…drugged.

CHAPTER 15

LEIDOLF SLIPPED HIS ARMS UNDERNEATH CASSIE'S LEGS and back and lifted her. Déjà vu, just like earlier in the day. Except she was dressed this time in silk, her belly and back exposed.

The minx was hurting more than she was letting on. Laney had warned him earlier, and he'd seen the way Cassie had winced a number of times, subtly a couple of times, not so subtly once, even when they were eating and drinking. In part, that was why he was sitting so close to her, to sense the way her body tightened when she was trying to control her pain.

He knew she wouldn't agree to any painkiller, not when Laney had said Cassie wanted to leave pronto to return to the forest. As agitated as Cassie had been, she meant business. Which was the reason Alice and Sarah had kept her "company" until Laney had returned with a set of clothes. He had meant to have Fergus or Elgin keep an eye on her. The girls were so crestfallen that he figured they wouldn't let Cassie escape under their watch. It had worked out well for all concerned.

No matter what, he wasn't going to allow Cassie to suffer through the pain all night.

"Will she sleep through the night?" Elgin asked Leidolf as he carried her back to his bedroom.

"Hopefully."

"You want me to post a guard?"

Leidolf glanced back at Elgin as he tightened his hold on Cassie. "It won't be necessary."

Elgin raised his brows a bit and smiled a little. "Will you be needing me for anything else tonight?"

"I didn't see any sign of Irving or Tynan at the meal. Did they leave again?"

Elgin shook his head in an annoyed way. "No one's seen them since you spoke to them earlier. When they return, they'll be placed under house arrest for disobeying you without notifying anyone where they're off to again. In the meantime, we've got a couple of men searching for clues of what they've been up to. One thing, Fergus said he had a man check the bunkhouse, and their rifles are gone. Maybe they went hunting again for the cougar?"

Leidolf didn't like the news, worried that the two of them might get into some real trouble with all the hunters most likely searching for the red wolves. Leaving the pack behind without any word to the others and neglecting their ranching duties wouldn't be tolerated though.

"All right. Take Laney home. If Felicity needs anything, her mate can take care of it. Everyone else can retire for the night. I've got everything here under control."

"Will do." Elgin gave him a knowing half smile, turned around, and headed back to the great room. Leidolf knew Elgin would clear the place out in an hour or two so he could have peace and quiet. Although for now, Fergus was staying with Sarge in one of the guest rooms and Pierce and Quincy in another until they learned to behave.

He imagined pack conversations would center on Cassie and Leidolf, while others would speculate about the other mystery female red wolf. If he didn't have some planned hunts to try and locate her soon, he knew his bachelor males would do so without him. Which could turn into fights between them or unsafe, frantic searches. So first thing in the morning, he'd schedule the searches and hoped they'd locate the other wolf without further incident. A hunt for the cougar was also in order. And for Irving and Tynan, if they didn't show up soon.

He looked down at Cassie's sleep-filled features as he walked her into his bedroom, her expression so peaceful that he almost could envision she was his already, but he knew the fight lurked just beneath the surface. He shut the door with his hip and strode toward the bed.

When he had overstepped his boundaries with her as they sat beside each other on the couch, as subtle as his actions had been, he had loved her response. He could tell from her expression that she would have dumped the wine on him too. She continually tried to hide the fact she desired him as much as he desired her, which triggered his interest in her even more.

He had wanted to sense if she was hurting during the meal; he was testing her also, to see her reaction, to learn whether she was willing or not. Just like a wolf would his mate—becoming more affectionate with nudges and kisses, with bodies pressed together when walking, with licking and nuzzling. His actions were as much instinctive as they were driven by need.

Now the feat was in convincing her that she wanted him for a mate, forever. He knew what it was like being a loner. If she truly was a loner, and he suspected she was, he understood her needs. And he would respect them. As much as he could.

After laying her on the mattress, he unbuckled the belt—
his belt—at her waist. He shook his head. He assumed only
the minx herself would have been bold enough to retrieve it
from his closet. Which further emphasized the fact that she
was an alpha and perfect as his mate.

He removed the belt and slipped Laney's gaudy shirt
off Cassie's shoulders. He ditched the pants next, the busy
pattern and brightness enough to keep him awake half the
night. He took the clothes and tossed them in a hamper.
He'd rather Laney or someone else give Cassie other clothes
to wear for tomorrow. Although Laney had asked him about
taking her shopping, Leidolf wouldn't allow it. Not until he
knew Cassie wouldn't take off.

He covered her with the comforter and considered the
bandage on her shoulder. Tomorrow, he'd take a look at her
injury. He touched her forehead with the palm of his hand.
She felt cool enough to the touch, so he didn't think she was
having any ill side effects, a fever, or chills. He hoped the
pain would soon subside.

Then he took off his clothes, laid them on the desk
chair, and turned to observe the redheaded beauty, her face
tranquil in sleep, her eyelashes fluttering, her breathing soft
and steady. To wake to such a dream the rest of his days
would make staying with the pack all the more rewarding.
He could even deal with the financial mess they were in
and Quincy, Pierce, and Sarge's shenanigans. And the other
two—Irving and Tynan, whatever they were up to.

He took a deep breath. Something about the girls had
disturbed Cassie though. At first, he thought his pack
members had unduly upset her, possibly because of their
enthusiastic interest in her being their pack leader's mate

when she wasn't ready to commit. And being a loner, she might have been overwhelmed with all the members of his pack greeting her at once, all excited to meet her.

He again regretted so many of them showing up to check her out without his express permission. But he didn't think it was that. She seemed to feel some connection to the girls. Which bothered him somewhat. Carver was looking to have a mate. What if the girls really did need a mother? And Cassie was right for him?

Leidolf shook his head. Cassie had the hots for Leidolf, not for anyone else. Carver could have the other red female if she was truly a *lupus garou* and they could locate her. And if she was free to mate and agreeable.

Without a doubt, at least to his way of thinking, Cassie was Leidolf's.

He climbed into the bed, pulled Cassie into his arms, and closed his eyes. She quickly snuggled against him, slipping her leg between his, her soft cheek against his chest, her silky hair caressing his skin, her arm resting over his chest as if she owned him. He groaned. Wanting to believe she was giving herself to him, he had to remind himself he knew better. He hadn't been with a human woman in a long time. Now to have a chance to mate with a female *lupus garou* who was perfect for him in every way... He took a deep breath and caressed her back with a light stroke. She was heaven sent.

To an extent, he didn't believe in fate, but after learning Cassie was a *lupus garou*, he was rethinking his beliefs. His sister would just smile with that expression that said she told him so. He'd probably have to agree with her.

After about an hour of mulling over everything that had happened from the first time he'd seen Cassie until now and thinking about how he was going to convince her to stay with him, he finally drifted off. And returned to the place he loved to go, to get away, to recapture the wildness, to enjoy the solitude, to gather his thoughts and meditate.

Snow-capped Mount Hood stretched heavenward as fluffy clouds embraced its peak, the scene majestic, monumental, so far away.

The chilled water lapped at his legs and at the stony beach as he observed the beauty. He considered running in his wolf coat all the way there, letting the wind ruffle his fur, stretching his legs in the wilderness, getting away from the pack for longer than he'd planned, when a branch snapped in the woods behind him.

Whipping around, he saw her watching him. Red hair struggling to break free of its confinement. Green eyes challenging him to come for her. To take her. To make her his.

Cassie.

His body grew taut with need. Her parted lips beckoned him, taunted him to kiss them. She took a step back. She wasn't running away. Her eyes took in every bit of his nakedness. He smiled. She wanted him. And he wanted her. He stalked toward her, intending to help her make a decision to stay. And then she was running. She was his. All his, and he took chase. He was faster. He'd catch her. He couldn't let her get away.

Then he was jerked from the dream as Cassie crawled on top of him, her soft mouth forming quiet words that didn't make any sense, whispered against his chest, and she shivered. She was cold. He wrapped his arms tight around her and wanted so much more, but until she healed, until she agreed to be his…as difficult as it was, he would wait. He wouldn't quit trying to help her make up her mind faster though.

He slipped into the dream again. *Saw the mountain, felt the cold of the lake, heard the snapping branch, and faced the woman who would be his own.*

Cassie slowly woke to the feel of a naked man beneath her. Not just any man. *Leidolf.* His heated body, hard beneath her, warmed her, comforted her. She breathed in his maleness, the woods, the sexy smell of him, of his wanting her. What a mess she'd gotten herself into. Somehow she had to leave these people. The she-wolf depended on her. She was afraid Alex did also. Yet already she was feeling torn about leaving the pack behind.

The way they wanted her to stay, to be part of their family, she couldn't help but feel something for them. Even the way the band members who had played the music at the Forest Club, some of whom she'd seen watching and smiling at her as they ate their meals, the twin girls who seemed to look up to her, Laney, who acted motherly toward her... She sighed. Leidolf wasn't the only one who was making her feel the need to stay.

She lay very still, half wanting to slip away into what was left of the night and take care of business, half wanting to stay here and entice the man beneath her to make love to her, to claim her for his very own as she would claim him.

Then again, she knew what she had to do. Set aside these crazy *lupus garou* feelings she had and concentrate on what was important. She had to move off Leidolf, dress, and get away, but she feared any movement would wake him and he'd stop her.

With a monumental effort at trying to create the least amount of friction between them, she attempted to disentangle herself from the possessive man who had both arms wrapped around her back and one leg hooked over hers. The same leg she had sandwiched between his. She'd never been in this sexy a position with a man she hadn't had sex with. And she was having a hard time not envisioning what it would be like to give herself to him.

As she tried to pull her leg free, her skin slid over his. He stirred, and she didn't move a muscle. And then she worried. She hadn't had sex with him last night by mistake, thinking in her dreamlike state that he was a human, had she? She wasn't sure he would have stopped her if she'd gotten too amorous, and he'd been in an aroused state, thinking she was willingly giving herself to him. She felt perfectly lubricated, as though she'd had sex.

She sighed softly. When she attempted to pull her leg the rest of the way free, his leg caged hers in again, his heel hooking over hers like a manacle. She stayed stock still. Was he awake? Her heartbeat quickened. She couldn't get caught. Not this time.

Then his hand drifted down her back, lower still to her butt, and he stroked for a few seconds. Even though she was perfectly still, her heart was beating way out of bounds, and she feared he'd open his eyes and realize she was awake and planning to escape.

His free hand drifted to her hair, and he sifted his fingers through the strands. Oh God, he was awake. Or half awake, because she was sure he would have noticed how rapid her heart was beating, as astute as he was. And probably come to the conclusion she was preparing to bolt. Finally, his hands settled down and stopped their heavenly caresses.

Forever, it seemed, she lay still, not moving a hair. She listened to his breathing and thought from the steady, slow rhythm that he was truly asleep. She again tried to extricate herself from his leg, which was pinning hers down. And pulled free. She paused, waiting for him to wake. His hand tightened on her ass again. Controlling alpha male!

Finally, he appeared to drift off again. She eased herself off his stomach. He shifted his hand to his chest, and she slipped the pillow next to his head onto his belly. To her relief, he seemed dead to the world.

She imagined that running a pack was exhausting work. Probably more so than studying wolves. Although trying to track her and his men down might have had something to do with how tired he was.

She hesitated, ensuring he truly was asleep. And then she slid out from under the comforter, trying not to tug it away from him too much. She finally scooted away from him and off the edge of the mattress, which shook to high heaven despite how gently she tried to leave the bed. As soon as her feet hit the carpeted floor, she raced to the double-wide closet.

Jeez, Leidolf would have looked destitute if it hadn't been for the size of his bedroom and its sumptuous features: velvet comforter, heavy, rich oak furniture, sitting area, and French doors leading out to a patio. But the walls were bare, the shadows of where paintings or pictures had once been the only evidence the place had at one time been decorated.

Cassie pulled the closet door open, cringing in case it creaked. It was quiet, thank goodness.

The thought unwillingly flitted across her mind that the

place needed a woman decorator's touch as she unbuttoned a shirt to pull it off the hanger. Yeah, as in Julia Wildthorn's sexy, romantic touch. If Julia got hold of the bedroom and redid it in her own theme, Cassie envisioned a gold-gilt mirror hanging on the ceiling over the bed, a hot tub in the bathroom, silky pale-blue sheets, and an indoor-outdoor shower with a view of the forest and Mount Hood beyond. She harrumphed at herself for thinking anything of the sort. Jealousy was not part of her psyche. Not professional, not personal. She attributed her annoyance with his interest in Ms. Wildthorn to the fact that he was attempting to seduce her and planning on seeing another woman on Saturday.

Cassie growled under her breath and yanked a blue-and-black plaid flannel shirt off a hanger. Immediately, a bolt of pain shot through her shoulder, and she stifled a moan. She didn't have time for gingerly movements and jerked her arms through the sleeves, clenching her teeth against the pain.

She considered the rest of his clothes, wondering what he'd done with Laney's floral pants. Not that they would have helped much. Although the walk-in closet was wide and deep, with four racks for clothes, only a handful of jeans hung from one of the rods along with maybe half a dozen flannel shirts, mixed in with some short-sleeved shirts for the one month of the year that was really warm enough. She slid a pair of pants off their hanger and held them up to her waist.

She'd have a devil of a time with the length, perfect for his long legs but way too long for her and sure to trip her. She abandoned the jeans on the closet floor. A glance at the shelf of shoes showed all that he owned: five well-worn pairs of cowboy boots, a couple of pairs of running shoes, two pairs of hiking boots, snow boots, and one pair of sandals. None of which she could wear. Giving up, she rushed back into the bedroom.

Carefully sliding open a drawer, she found one pair of boxers. Needed to do a wash? Or just a token pair for appearances' sake?

She pulled open several more drawers as quietly as she could before she found one full of wool sweaters. Big, large-cabled, warm wool. Not having time to button the shirt, she yanked a green sweater off the top of the pile and slipped it over her head. A sharp pain stabbed her in the shoulder again, and she gritted her teeth to stifle a groan.

She searched through another drawer, found socks, and shoved her feet into a black pair, the heel riding higher than her ankles. At least they'd keep her feet a little warmer until she could reach her own truck, dress in her own clothes, use the can of hunter's fragrance that would hide her scent, and move her vehicle to some other location away from where she'd have to abandon the vehicle that she planned to borrow from Leidolf.

Glancing around the room, she was looking for the jeans he'd been wearing, figuring he'd probably have his keys in the pocket, when she saw a set of keys sitting in a glass bowl on top of the dresser.

She snatched them up and then hurried for the glass patio doors, hoping she'd make her escape before she woke him.

Cautiously, she pulled the door open, and a blast of cold night air hit her. A steady wind hinted at rain, and she frowned as she slipped outside, closing the door behind her with a soft click. All she needed was to get drenched in a rainstorm as she searched for the she-wolf and Alex.

Then she raced around to the front of the house toward

the welcome sight of a huge black Suburban sitting in the circular drive. She pushed the button on the keyless remote entry and then yanked at the door handle. No response. She tried the remote again. The door was still locked. Hell, different vehicle. In case the keypad battery was dead, she tried to insert the key in the door, but it wouldn't allow her to insert even a tip of the metal. Her skin heated with anxiety.

She glanced back at the rambling ranch-style house. Several windows looked out over the front of the property, but all were pitch black. Still, she envisioned pack members sleeping in each of the bedrooms she'd passed on her way to dinner. She couldn't help worrying that someone might look out one of the windows any second and see her trying to steal away with one of Leidolf's vehicles.

No security cameras hung under the eaves, so at least it seemed no security force watched for intruders. Not that anyone in his right mind would try to steal from a *lupus garou* pack leader who had a whole pack of men at his beck and call. Then she saw a black Humvee and a bright yellow Jaguar sitting in a garage, the doors to the garage wide open. Six more pickups were parked at another long building nearby, and she suspected they belonged to some of the male bachelors sleeping in a barracks.

She dashed for the Humvee, her sock feet silently padding over the cement drive. When she tried the remote on the vehicle, she heard the faint click of the lock, but when she tried the door, it wouldn't open. She used the key in the Humvee's lock, but it didn't work. Exasperated, she looked around the Humvee and considered the seductive allure of the mustard-yellow Jaguar. The doe-eyed headlights, the sloping sleek grill. Too splashy. Too conspicuous. Too expensive. But it *was* a set of wheels.

Skirting completely around the Humvee, she thought maybe pushing the button on the remote had unlocked the Jag's door instead. She yanked at the door handle…and voilà! The door opened. She hoped her insurance would cover the damage if she wrecked the sports car, or she'd be handing her life savings over in bulk to the alpha leader. That was if he ever caught up with her again. She didn't plan for that to happen anytime soon.

She climbed in, took a deep breath of the sweet smell of new butternut leather, and admired the lightly polished maple wood. Her car's worn cloth seats were padded economy style, but she sank into the driver's seat of the Jaguar as if she were ready to lounge at home. She shoved the key in, turned on the ignition, and then stared at the manual shift. It wasn't an automatic? She hadn't driven a stick shift in forever.

Suddenly, a figure loomed next to the driver's door. Her heart did a triple beat, but before she could react, the blond from dinner, the one who was being guarded, jerked the door open, reached in, and pulled the key from the ignition.

"You're taking me with you," he said, his voice low and determined, his blue eyes piercing her with the promise that if she didn't agree, he would cause real trouble for her. And she didn't doubt that he would.

She considered her options. No way was she taking a troublesome, newly turned *lupus garou* with her. Yet she assumed that if she tried to leave without him, he'd tell the world. If she took him with her, she'd have to ditch him somewhere along the way, and that wouldn't be safe for any of their kind. Or for him either.

"Hurry up, Cassie," he said, his tone ominous. "You have a second to decide, or I sound the alarm that you're running away in *Leidolf's* sports car." He tilted his head to the side a little. "And I could use some good points with Leidolf about now."

Hell, no way did she want to take this guy with her. He couldn't cope in the least if she were to leave him on his own alone somewhere. She doubted she could trust him to help her or keep quiet or not get himself shot by accident.

When she still didn't decide, he tried a more coaxing approach. "You're like me, newly turned. And I know you don't want to stay here. They'll force you to. You know it. So we can work together."

"Get in," she growled. Why weren't this guy's keepers making sure he stayed put?

"Thanks, I owe you. Then again," he said, pausing as he rushed around to the other side of the car and yanked it open, "I figure you owe me because I can watch your back."

Yeah, right. She'd be doing all the work, trying to keep both their butts out of the fire. She held her hand out for the keys.

He hesitated to give them to her. "Don't try to pull anything. I'll be watching you."

"What in the world do you think I can do? Wreck the vehicle? Not on your life. The insurance cost would eat me alive." She started the engine and backed out of the garage.

The engine purred, and she thought how much she could get used to driving in luxury like this. When she tried to drive forward on the gravel road, the car bucked and stopped dead. She stared at the controls and then, figuring she'd put it in second gear instead of first, she planned to try again when the blond guy said, "Don't you know how to

drive a stick? Here, let me have the key, and I'll drive." He
grabbed for the keys, but she slapped his hand away hard,
showing him just who was in charge.

"*I'll* do it."

No way was she letting this guy have any control over
her, well, any more so than he did at this point. She put the
Jag into neutral, started the engine, and rolled along the
road, this time in first gear and inching along at a painfully
slow pace. As they passed the bunkhouse, she cringed to
think every last one of the bachelor males would come after
her for stealing the pack leader's sports car. She envisioned
a mad chase of trucks in hot pursuit if they heard the car
leaving the compound in the middle of the night. What she
saw next surprised the hell out of her.

Her headlights shined a spotlight on the barracks briefly,
catching a couple of teens kissing in the shadows of the
building near the road she had to take, and she held her
breath. Hell...Evan and Alice?

Alice's father would kill Evan, she suspected, if he
learned they were out here kissing in the dark. Worse, she
was about to be caught.

The teens turned to observe the Jag, their mouths parted
in surprise. The tinted windows would hide her and the
blond sufficiently. She just prayed they'd think their leader
was taking a spin. The teens remained frozen as she slowly
made her way past them, not wanting to alert the others if
all of a sudden she roared down the road.

As soon as she passed them, Evan dashed for the house.
Crap. Alice didn't move. Probably didn't want her father
knowing she'd been alone with Evan in the dark shadows
late at night.

"Shit," the blond said. "Evan will warn Leidolf, and we'll both be in a hell of a lot of trouble."

Evan—yep, the boy Alice and Sarah had a crush on. He was a teen heartthrob already. She wondered if Leidolf had been like that or a loner early on. Probably always a loner. Or not. She frowned and then glanced at the blond. She suspected this guy would be in much more trouble than she would with Leidolf, just for being alone with her and threatening her with exposure if she didn't take him with her. Or maybe not. It depended on how attached Leidolf was to his hot rod. Probably a lot.

Her skin peppered with perspiration, Cassie sped up a little, but the road was gravel, and the car slipped a couple of times. Why would Leidolf have such an impractical, low-slung vehicle for out here on gravel and dirt ranch roads? Rich-guy mentality, she guessed.

"What's your name?" she asked the blond as she headed for what she hoped would soon be a paved road, figuring he was the one the girls called Sarge but wanting to make sure.

"Sarge is what everyone calls me on account of I was a clerk in the army for a couple of years."

"Didn't like the army?"

The view of a valley, grass just beginning to green with the spring rains, appeared below the main house. She spotted several elk in the distance and, closer in, cows, yearlings, and horses on higher ground. Some of the lower-lying pasture lands were under water, most likely due to recent heavy rains.

Sarge stared out the window and then glanced at her. "Got into trouble."

Figured. She had a feeling the guy was trouble in a lot more ways than just this incident, which accounted for his having had a guard detail at dinner. What had happened to the men who were supposed to be watching him? They'd surely catch hell when Leidolf discovered Sarge was missing.

"What kind of trouble?" she asked, wanting to hear the truth in his own words.

He stared at her as if putting a hex on her, and her skin crawled. Not that she couldn't handle him if she needed to, but she didn't like getting mixed up with a troublesome *lupus garou* on top of everything else.

Cassie pressed the gas pedal a little harder and crawled a little faster along the ranch road beside the river. Then she looked up at the main house and two others that overlooked the view. No one was following her yet. As soon as the teen told Leidolf his car was going out for a drive—without him—they'd be after her. And someone was sure to alert Leidolf that his newly turned *lupus garou* was missing also. She figured that he really wouldn't like Sarge having come along with her. Not that she'd helped Sarge escape but that he'd be worried about her with the unpredictable guy.

Sarge shrugged and looked back out the window. "I was kicked out of the service because of drug use. Lots of guys were doing it. No big deal. It's just that I got caught."

Which didn't explain how he came to be here. "Right. So how did you end up in Leidolf's pack?"

"I was a werewolf hunter."

Catching her breath in her throat, Cassie didn't say anything. She felt that Sarge was watching her, waiting for her response. Everything the girls had said was true. No wonder he was being treated like an omega, someone no one wanted to be friends with. A werewolf killer? Great, just great. She glanced at his arm, but she couldn't see the scar from where the tattoo had been removed. Probably on the other arm.

"You don't kill us anymore, right?"

"I didn't kill the others."

Relieved, she let out her breath. She wasn't afraid of him. She could take care of herself. But taking someone like him away from Leidolf's pack was a real mistake when he needed heavy supervision. "Those two men who were with you, were they serving as your guards?"

"Pierce and Quincy? Hell, they've been in nearly as much trouble as me. They joined a week before I did, although they were born *lupus garous*. Fergus…he's like Elgin, a subleader… he's supposed to be watching all three of us. And then Pierce and Quincy are supposed to be keeping an eye on me. They were busy watching a game, so that was the end of guarding me.

"And Fergus was looking for his son. Evan? The kid who was kissing the girl out by the building back there? My kind of kid." Sarge gave an evil smile. "So where are we running off to?"

If they caught her before she reached her destination, she'd never manage to sneak away again, she was certain. And alpha leaders ruled their territories, so if she wanted to stay here, she had to obey Leidolf's pack rules. Or at least those were the unwritten laws of any *lupus garou* pack. Taking this knucklehead with her complicated everything.

"I have business to take care of in Mount Hood National Forest. So when we reach the place I need to go, you can stay in the car and wait for me."

"And give me the slip? And Leidolf too? Not on your life, lady. How dumb do I look? If I stayed in this bucket, it'd be like having a neon sign plastered to it saying, 'Here they are. Right here.' Why didn't you take the Humvee? Less noticeable." He shook his head like she was some kind of idiot.

No other keys had been on the dresser top. Probably Leidolf didn't use the Jag as much.

She imagined Leidolf would drive it to the book signing at Powell's on Saturday, though, to take little Miss Julia Wildthorn for a spin. Show off his hot rod and even hotter aspects that were all his.

"So no thank you," Sarge said, jerking her from her thoughts about Leidolf and his planned romantic liaison with the romance author. "I'm sticking with you. I know I need guidance to get through this nightmare. I'd rather have yours than Leidolf's. A gentler woman's touch. Maybe we could even…you know, get to like one another." He grinned.

She refrained from rolling her eyes. If she had to confront him in her wolf form, bearing her very wicked canines, she'd have no difficulty. And he'd soon learn that she could be just as rough on him as any male.

"So…who turned you?"

"Leidolf. It was either that or kill me, he said, since I learned what he was."

She wondered if Leidolf would be rethinking having turned him instead of choosing the other option after Sarge pulled this stunt. *Probably.*

Then she spied what looked like the main road, and as soon as she reached it, she turned south and sped up. At least she thought that was the right direction. Hell, was it the right direction? She'd been asleep when they had taken her to the ranch house.

"Do you know which way they took me to reach the ranch house after Leidolf picked me up?"

Sarge shook his head. "They left me at home, well guarded. Pierce and Quincy got into trouble that time, looking for you in their wolf coats."

Great. This clown couldn't even help with navigation.

She continued to head south, figuring if she was going the wrong way and Leidolf thought she'd go the right way, he wouldn't find her. She could always stop somewhere and get directions. If she was going the right way, so much the better.

She didn't have a clue what she'd do with Sarge when she reached her vehicle though. She just *couldn't* take him with her.

He drummed his fingers on the armrest, and she was about to tell him to quit it when he asked, "Do you know the guys named Irving and Tynan?"

Cassie shook her head. "I've never met any of the pack members in this area before now."

"They're worried about you."

She glanced at Sarge.

He shrugged. "I overheard them talking. Said that you could be trouble."

"How so?"

"I don't know, and I wasn't about to let them know I overheard them. They were turned against their will a long time ago, Fergus told me. They still hold a grudge. Plan to kill whoever bit them. That's all I know. You're newly turned. You didn't bite them, did you?"

"No. I've never bitten anyone to change them."

"I've thought of it."

Cassie frowned at him. "Better not."

He shook his head. "I wouldn't. I just said I've thought of it. Jeez. Give me a break. Haven't you ever considered it? Some guy gets fresh with you? You shift and bite?"

"I have a little more control than that."

"Yeah, well, live a long time like this, and some day, you might just feel like it."

She shook her head. Sarge was the one who was a real problem.

Only a few miles down the road, a vehicle's headlights closed in on her from behind. Maybe her fate was already decided for her. Cassie's skin chilled in anticipation.

CHAPTER 16

BEFORE LEIDOLF COULD FULLY AWAKE FROM HIS DEEP sleep, a better sleep than he'd enjoyed in months, Fergus barged into the bedroom, his face red, his heart pounding, his breath short, and Leidolf knew something had happened to someone in the pack.

Before Fergus could tell him what was wrong, his son hollered from the great room, "Dad? Where are you?"

Fergus shouted from Leidolf's bedroom, "I'll be with you in a minute, son."

"But...did Leidolf take off in the Jag?" Evan asked, moving down the hall toward the bedroom.

Leidolf glanced at the empty mattress. That was when the realization that Cassie hadn't been a dream finally struck him. "Hell." He jerked the covers aside and climbed out of bed.

With every minute counting, Leidolf noticed the dresser drawers pulled out, a missing sweater and pair of socks, and discarded jeans dumped on the closet floor. He glanced at the glass where he kept his Jaguar's spare key and swore under his breath. He'd give her points for tenacity.

Turning, he nearly collided with Fergus, Evan not far behind. "She's got my Jag. She's probably headed for the location where we found her initially. Gather ten of our ranch hands to look for her, Fergus. Call Elgin and tell him to have Laney let us know if, by some miracle, she only went out for a spin and returns here before we locate her." As if the woman just took his Jag out for a joyride.

Leidolf began jerking on his discarded clothes. What the hell was so important in the damned woods that the woman would risk returning there in the dark to where she'd already been shot once? The female red wolf?

"Can I go?" Evan asked, racing alongside Leidolf as he stalked out of his bedroom and down the hall toward the great room, giving his father a backward glance for approval while Fergus spoke on the phone to Elgin.

Giving teens more responsibility was always a pack leader's goal, and Leidolf suspected that had been Pierce and Quincy's problem. They hadn't been allowed to make mistakes when they were younger. He gave Evan a curt nod. Although at a time like this, in the event hunters were targeting anything that moved, he preferred Evan staying behind. "When Elgin gets here, you can go with him."

Evan gave a long face, and Leidolf knew the teen wanted to go with him. He looked back at Pierce and Quincy as they hurried out of one of the guest rooms where he hoped to keep better track of them, both buttoning up their shirts. "No wolf coats this time."

They wore stern frowns as they nodded, but they looked as though something else was troubling them.

Leidolf didn't have time for this, but Quincy took a deep breath and said, "We lost him. We don't want to leave the pack, but we...well, we were watching a game and didn't realize the little weasel took off without us knowing."

"Sarge," Leidolf growled under his breath. And then he narrowed his eyes at them. "Hell, he had better not have gone with Cassie. She wouldn't have taken him willingly. If he threatened her in any way, he's a dead man."

Pierce and Quincy headed outside to their pickup, but

both looked like their necks were on the chopping block. Leidolf knew the only way he was going to get them on the right track was by giving them another chance…which in their case would most likely be many more chances, the way they were going.

He turned to Fergus. "Have every man who's available and staying behind look for Sarge, in case he's not with Cassie. If anyone locates him, let me know. And put a guard on him! If he's found, I want someone to watch him at all times."

Fergus was on the phone already, calling their people and issuing orders. He paused on the phone and said to Leidolf, "Will do."

For his pack members' sakes, Leidolf managed to keep his cool despite being angered that the woman would get herself into a hell of a lot more trouble the way she was going. Ditto for Sarge.

As soon as he stalked outside, he met several of his men waiting for his word, keys in hand. "You three head north, just in case she went in the opposite direction from the one I suspect to try and lose us. The others follow me."

With five pickups on the road, Leidolf drove his Humvee and headed in the most obvious direction, back to where Cassie had been found, and hoped she wouldn't run into any further difficulty before he caught up with her. He couldn't help worrying that Sarge might be with Cassie. Not that he figured she couldn't handle herself with him. He just didn't like the idea that she might be forced to.

As he drove toward the woods ten miles away, ones his people normally didn't hunt in—too close to home, but good when a pack member had to have a quick run to get it out of his or her system—he kept thinking he'd catch up to her. When he saw no sign of the Jag, he began to lose hope she'd come this way. Which made him realize how truly devious the woman was.

Despite being both angered and worried, he gave a small smile.

—∾∾—

The vehicle followed Cassie mile after mile, although she slowed down enough for the driver to pass. He wouldn't take the bait. So she sped up and he sped up, reminding her of the problem she'd had with a creepy, stalker boyfriend. Which was another reason for not getting hooked up with another one anytime soon. If the gray *lupus garou* hadn't finally found a mate, she was sure he'd still be stalking her. No stalking laws for *lupus garous*, unfortunately.

She glanced in the rearview mirror and narrowed her eyes at the bright headlights. At first, she worried that the driver might be a police officer, but she didn't see a rack of lights on the roof of the sports utility vehicle.

"Who is it?" Sarge asked, his voice agitated as he looked over the passenger's seat.

"Can't tell. He won't pass. Maybe just someone who's tired and mesmerized with our taillights as he follows us."

Although it could be an unmarked vehicle, and the fact that she was driving a Jag didn't help. If it had been any other make of car, she probably could have slipped away without anyone knowing anything different. Unless Leidolf's pack had a police officer, she suspected he wouldn't report that she'd stolen his vehicle. At least she hoped he wouldn't.

"I don't see a rack of lights on the top of the vehicle. Why the hell couldn't you have stolen a less conspicuous car?"

"Leidolf didn't leave all his keys out for me to steal," she grumbled. Although as soon as she said it, she was mad at herself for explaining. She didn't owe Sarge any kind of explanation for anything.

She looked back at the road. A twisted tree caught her eye, and she recalled driving past it before. Heart lifting, she realized her car was only a couple of miles south of here.

That was when the blue lights on the grill of the vehicle behind her flashed, and her worst fears were realized. She was in a hell of a lot of hot water.

"Hell," Sarge said. "What were you doing that you got the cops on our tail? I should have been driving."

"Just be quiet and let me do the talking," she calmly said, but her voice had bite, and if he said another thing...

She slowed down and pulled off onto the shoulder, but she kept her foot on the brake due to the slight decline in the hill. The mini-SUV stopped some distance behind her, but no one got out of the vehicle. Her palms grew sweaty as she clutched the steering wheel. He had to be calling in the plates, maybe checking with Leidolf to see if she'd stolen the Jag if he was suspicious of her driving. She knew she should have been driving faster.

So what would Leidolf say? If the guy wasn't a *lupus garou*, Leidolf probably wouldn't have her arrested. Or maybe he would.

Pack leaders whose pack members tested them could be totally unpredictable, even if she wasn't one of his members. Sarge could be another real problem. She didn't trust him to keep his mouth shut in front of the police officer.

The vehicle behind her continued to idle. *Come on, come on. Get it over with.* She slipped her foot off the brake, and the car rolled forward, but then she figured he might think she would try to make a break. She would, but not the way he probably would expect. Maybe nothing would happen. He'd say, "Hi, false alarm" and let her go on her way. *Fat chance.*

"What's he doing now?" Sarge asked.

"Just sitting in his car. Probably checking the license plate to see who owns it and if anyone has reported it stolen. If the guy is a *lupus garou*, he'll just 'arrest' us, so to speak. If he's not, Leidolf might have enough influence to have the guy detain us until he gets here. Either way, it's not good."

She applied the brake again and tapped her other foot on the floor. *Come on, come on. Do something.*

"Make a run for it. The Jag's got to be fast enough that we could outrun his vehicle."

She gave him a get-real look. As noticeable as the car was, even if they could outrun the police vehicle, helicopters would soon see the yellow Jag anywhere along the winding, hilly road.

Maybe the officer had contacted Leidolf and was waiting for him to arrive to confiscate his vehicle *and her* and Sarge. She just hoped the officer would hurry up and greet her at the Jag. Then she'd make her move.

Leidolf hadn't gotten far down the road when his cell phone rang. Jerking it off his belt, he flipped it open and recognized the sheriff's number. Good news hopefully. "Yeah, Sheriff?"

"Mr. Wildhaven, I stopped a Jag that was driving slower

than normal, brakes kept being applied, and the vehicle was weaving a bit. So I ran the license plates and found it was yours. We didn't have any others in the area, and you said you never drive it, so I just wanted to make sure the Jag hadn't been stolen."

Thank God for small miracles. Donating to the local sheriff's department, which didn't have a *lupus garou* on staff, sure had gotten his butt out of a sling a few times. Not his exactly, but a couple of his pack members' rather.

"Thanks, Sheriff. We're engaged to be married, but we had a bit of a disagreement. She's never driven the Jag before, so she's probably not real familiar with it. Where are you exactly?"

The sheriff gave him directions, and Leidolf said, "Just hold her for me, will you? We'll be right there."

"You got it, Mr. Wildhaven. And congratulations."

"Thanks. Anyone else with her?"

"I'm headed to the vehicle now. It's hard to tell who's in the car since the windows are so darkly tinted and with it being night and all."

"All right. Thanks. Be there shortly."

Leidolf passed the word along to his men and couldn't have pushed his Humvee any faster on the curving road after getting word that the sheriff had caught up with his little runaway wolf and maybe that idiot Sarge. Didn't she realize how conspicuous she would be in the Jag?

Good thing for him. This time, she wasn't getting away from him. And he was going to learn the truth about her. All of it. One way or another. As for Sarge, if he was with her and had coerced her in any way, Leidolf wouldn't be responsible for his actions.

Cassie watched in the rearview mirror, her skin perspiring lightly in Leidolf's flannel shirt and wool sweater that smelled musky and—if she was willing to be honest with herself—heavenly.

Sarge smelled of sweat and fear. She'd strangle him if he said anything that gave them away.

The driver's door of the police car opened slowly. Police had the market on giving good guys—well, normally good guys—a case of nerves. *Can you move any more slowly than that?* she wanted to scream.

Her eyes glued on the rearview mirror, she anticipated his every move like a wolf would.

He slapped a notebook against his leg, his look fierce, sure to put the fear of the law into her. And she would spill all her secrets as soon as he opened his mouth and began questioning her. *Right.*

Sarge shifted again in his seat. "Now would be a good time to make a run for it."

She ignored him but moved her foot to the gas pedal. Outrunning the police wasn't really in the plans. If she continued on this road in the direction she was headed, she'd drive right by her car. And if she tried to make a quick stop and switch cars at the trailhead, the police officer would catch her at it and could run her plates and know exactly who she was.

He drew closer, and although he carried a few extra pounds, he looked too fit to walk so darned slowly.

At least he hadn't drawn a weapon yet.

"Hell," Sarge said, folding his arms across his chest. "We could have left him choking in the dust."

As if this place ever got dusty, as rainy as it was. Muddy was more like it.

She opened the car window and tried to look cool and collected.

When the police officer reached her door, she let out her breath, not even realizing she'd been holding it.

"Ma'am, can you open your door for me? And turn off the ignition, please." The dark-haired man peered into the vehicle, his brown eyes darkening as he saw Sarge.

Now he had his hand near his revolver. As much as she didn't want to, she opened the door and pushed it wide, but she didn't turn off the engine, while she still rested her foot on the brake. His gaze went from her face downward to her bare legs. The shirt and sweater pooled over her lap, but they only reached about thigh-high. Socks, no shoes. For a minute, her appearance distracted him, and he didn't say anything about the fact that she hadn't cut the engine.

His brows arched a little, and he said, "Turn off the vehicle, miss."

Last chance to peel some rubber and take off. She turned off the ignition. The silence seemed deafening.

"Have you got some ID?"

Yep, but the driver's license was in *her* car.

"It was stolen," she said in a small voice, designed to earn her some sympathy.

The man's mouth curved up slightly, but his eyes didn't reflect any humor. "Like the car?"

"Leidolf loaned it to me."

"Ah, and his clothes also?"

She took a deep breath, but she couldn't smell any hint that he was a *lupus garou*. Leidolf must have told the sheriff that she took both his clothes and the Jag. Or he assumed it. The clothes were definitely too big for her, and menswear.

"Your name?"

"Cassie Robbins." Might as well use a different one since she didn't have any ID anyway. "Are you going to arrest me or what?" She was past trying to get his sympathy. Lost cause.

"Who are you?" the sheriff asked Sarge, ignoring her question.

"Sarge...uhm...Elmer Rowlington."

Cassie glanced at Sarge, thinking of Elmer Fudd of cartoon fame. Sarge gave her a dark look in return.

"From around here?" the officer asked.

"I'm originally from Millinocket, Maine. But now I'm one of Leidolf Wildhaven's ranch hands." He tried to sound tough, like a ranch hand might, but his voice hitched, and he fell far short of the role he tried to play.

She wondered how he could have gotten mixed up with a group who made it their business to kill werewolves.

"And you're with Ms. Robbins for what reason?" The sheriff spoke in a rough tone with both of them, but his voice got a whole lot darker when he talked to Sarge.

Sarge wasn't holding up well, not the way he swallowed hard, his Adam's apple bobbing, or the way he squeaked out the words. "She wanted me to make sure she drove the stick shift okay. She hasn't driven one in a long time."

The sheriff stared hard at Sarge as if he was trying to intimidate him into revealing the correct answer. The guy was easily intimidated and looked like he was about to crawl under the seat, head bowed, eyes lowered. Which meant? Cassie was the brains and muscle behind the operation, while Sarge was just a tag-along. Hell, the way he acted, the sheriff might conclude that she was the one who coerced Sarge to come along with her…because she hadn't driven a stick shift in so long.

The sheriff shifted his attention to Cassie. "No driver's license, half-dressed, driving a borrowed car that you didn't have permission to take… You're in a bit of trouble, miss. But Mr. Wildhaven said you and he had a tiff and that you were down on your luck, so he's coming to retrieve his Jag and take you home." He shrugged. "The thought of marriage can be overwhelming at times, but I've been married for twenty-seven years, and, young lady, you'll do just fine."

Marriage? She felt her face heat. Leidolf better not have said he and she were getting married. Did the sheriff think Leidolf meant to take her to her own home? She knew that wasn't going to happen.

"Who's the guy with you?" the sheriff asked as if confirming Sarge's story, and she wondered if he was worried that maybe Sarge was playacting, pretending to be a really subservient guy while, in reality, he had forced her to take him for a ride in the Jag.

"One of Leidolf's ranch hands, Elmer, like he said." She smiled. Teach Sarge to coerce her to take him along with her.

"All right. I'll let Mr. Wildhaven know you're both here. He should be joining us in just a few minutes."

That would be the end of her chance to take care of the she-wolf and the pups and locate Alex. Wait, if Alex made the 911 call, the sheriff would probably know, and she could possibly learn if he was all right. Then she would only have to search for the mother and her pups.

She cleared her throat. "I heard about the men found tranquilized in the woods. Did Alex Wellington call it in?"

The sheriff's eyes widened. "What do you know about any of that?"

Her lips parted. Not good. If the sheriff discovered she'd been there, he might assume she knew about the murderers too. What if he put her under some kind of house arrest? At the very least, if Leidolf learned about it, *he* probably would. Well, more so than she was already.

She attempted to appear nonchalant with a shrug. "Just sounds like something he might have done. I think he was supposed to be conducting some wolf biologist studies in the area."

"We don't...well, we *didn't* have any wolves out here." He narrowed his eyes at her. "At least I'd never heard of any before. What makes you suspect he was here?"

"He's always looking for them. How would I know?"

"You just said..." The sheriff shook his head. "The guy who called the 911 operator gave us the location and took off. We figured he was afraid the ones he said had murdered someone might locate him and kill him. Do you think he might be this guy named Alex Wellington?"

Hell, she really had thought Alex had stayed to ensure the zoo men were safe until the police arrived. That way, when the police showed up, they would have known who Alex was. "Uh, no. Come to think of it, he was working on a project in the Canadian Arctic."

"Canadian Arctic?" The sheriff didn't sound like he believed her. She wouldn't have either. "You can't be his girlfriend if you're marrying Leidolf."

She laughed and hoped the sound wasn't too faked. "He doesn't have regular girlfriends. I'm just a friend." She was getting them both in a deeper and deeper hole. Now she was afraid that if the sheriff began searching for Alex, word might get out to the murderers that he was the one who had been out in the woods listening to their conversation.

"Do you have a number or place of employment for him so I can verify where he is currently?"

She began to climb out of the car. "No. He's self-employed. I don't have his number, and he moves around a lot."

Sarge reached out and touched her arm as if to deter her, but she gave him a look that said if he tried to stop her, he'd be in real trouble. He quickly pulled his hand back.

The sheriff frowned and looked again at her bare legs. "You don't have to get out of the car. It's cold, and the way you're dressed—"

That was the last he said as she pulled her foot off the brake and hopped out of the car, and the Jag began to roll down the hill. She hoped the sheriff would catch it before it ran into anything, that he didn't try to stop her instead, and that Sarge wasn't injured in the runaway vehicle. It was the break she needed, and it served Sarge right for forcing her to take him with her. Besides, Leidolf would soon be here to take the guy back into custody. Not her though.

"Hell!" The sheriff tore off down the road, too busy trying to reach the car as it picked up speed to give her a second glance.

She thought Sarge might try to get into the driver's seat and take off in the car. As soon as the sheriff raced after the Jag, she couldn't worry about anything else while she ran for the woods, knowing Leidolf would soon take care of Sarge and the Jag.

She contemplated heading for the pups, but getting

her clothes and a good pair of hiking boots from her truck seemed a better choice. So in Leidolf's socks that were way too big, she dashed through the underbrush, the twigs and branches scratching her bare legs while she wished she could run along the road instead. Would have been much faster. She just hoped the sheriff would catch the Jag and stop Sarge from going anywhere until Leidolf arrived.

Normally, her wolf's sense of self-preservation would have forced her to slow down, to make the least amount of noise, but another part of her hoped that if she made enough of a racket, if hunters were looking for all the feral red wolves roaming the woods, they'd realize she couldn't be a wolf, as noisy as she was.

She smelled the faint odor of a mountain lion and cursed under her breath. Still, she thought it was quite a way off. But what if that meant the lion might locate the pups' den?

She stopped and stood still, her heart pounding hard, the blood rushing in her ears, trying to muffle any other sound. *Change,* her mind screamed at her. Shift and go back to find the pups. She'd be warmer and could run a hell of a lot faster, more quietly, and less conspicuously.

Then from a distance, the sound of something tromping through the brush in her direction gave her more of a worry. Hunters? Reporters? The zoo men? The murderers? Alex? The sheriff would have been coming in the opposite direction. She doubted he'd race through the woods in the dark after her or that he would have had time to stop the car and then chase after her. And it sounded like two people, not one.

She dropped low, crouching, hiding herself in the undergrowth, but her movement must have caught their attention, as both swiveled their heads in her direction. Hell, they were outfitted with those night-vision goggles attached to their headgear, their breaths coming hard as they shoved away branches and looked straight at her. One hundred fifty yards and closing. But their pace was slower now, as if they were afraid to scare away their newly found prey.

She lifted her nose slightly and smelled. Her heart beating frantically, her blood ran cold. Both were hunters, both wearing scruffy beards, camouflage gear, and olive-drab caps. For a second, she feared they would shoot her, thinking she was a wolf, being as paranoid as anyone else looking to kill a bunch of feral predators and expecting anything that moved to be one of them.

At first, the hunters stared at her slack-jawed and moved toward her even more slowly. She imagined that because of the lack of moon or stars on the overcast night and the shadows of the woods, they hadn't seen her until she'd moved. That was what had given her away.

Suddenly, they stopped cold and observed her. As if they were seeing a ghost, unsure of what they were actually observing. Thankfully. So they weren't going to just shoot her without checking her out further.

But did they recognize she was a woman, hiding in the woods and not doing a very good job of it? They wouldn't know she could see them too, but they had to realize she would have heard their approach. Maybe they figured she got scared then and stopped dead in her tracks. If they had been wolves, *lupus garou*, or those who studied wolves like she did, they'd know she was ready to bolt. She doubted they'd recognize that. And she didn't think they'd catch her if they gave chase.

"Holy moly, Ben. She's not one of those red wolves," the

man whispered to the other. "What would she be doing out here?"

Ben responded in a hushed voice, shouldering his rifle. "Hell, if I didn't know better, I'd say she was that wolf biologist I told you about that talked real pretty about wolves."

Crap, it couldn't be the man who hounded her when she lectured at the town hall.

"I dunno, but she's got to be in some kinda trouble. You move around that way, really quiet like so's not to spook her."

Ben gave a thumbs-up and began to circle slightly to Cassie's left.

She let out her breath in exasperation. Then she had another thought. What if she could get hold of the men's goggles and ditch them? The men wouldn't be able to see in the dark without them and follow her, and they couldn't look for the female wolf or her pups either. Cassie kept a smile to herself. Then how in the hell was she going to get the goggles away from the men?

"Are you...Dr. Roux, miss?" Ben asked, drawing a couple of steps closer. "Are you hurt?"

She stood up: no sense in pretending she couldn't be seen.

He lowered his binoculars as he looked down her legs to her feet where the socks rested in a puddle at her ankles.

She hadn't expected wolf killers to express concern for her safety, as normal humans would. But even though they seemed human in that respect, the hunters still were dangerous for the *lupus garous* and the wolves she'd made it her calling to study. She dashed for the cover of the forest, figuring she could outrun them. Ben took a couple of hefty strides and snagged her wrist.

CHAPTER 17

LEIDOLF'S CELL PHONE JINGLED, AND HE JERKED IT OFF his belt, flipped it open, and saw Sheriff Whittaker was calling again.

"Yeah?" Leidolf said, wholeheartedly expecting that the sheriff had Cassie and the Jag, that he'd learn if Sarge was with her, and that everything was well under control.

That misconception was instantly shattered when the sheriff spoke over the phone, huffing and puffing, half-winded. "Got the Jag in good condition, Mr. Wildhaven."

Hell, Leidolf didn't care anything about the Jag. It was the former pack leader's chick magnet. Leidolf didn't need anything that flashy, and the car was the next item on his agenda to get rid of.

"The woman?" That was all he cared about. Well, and Sarge. But Cassie was his first priority.

"The little lady nearly wrecked your car after jumping out of it while the brake wasn't set, and the Jag drifted down a hill. I dashed for the car, never thinking she'd run into the woods, but that's exactly what she did.

"At least I think. I was too busy saving your Jag. And the guy with her? Sarge? He was trying madly to get into the driver's seat. I figured he'd planned to tear off, but I managed to jerk the keys out of the ignition. When I finally returned the Jag and him to the scene, she had vanished. Unless someone picked her up."

Leidolf swore to himself. He didn't figure anyone would

have picked her up along the isolated road without the sheriff noticing it, even as busy as he was trying to stop the runaway Jag. The way she was dressed in this cold, she'd never make it far. And changing into the wolf and running on all four legs with an injured shoulder? She'd never manage that way for very long either.

He jammed the gas pedal down even more. "I'll be there shortly."

"I've got this guy in bracelets. He wasn't very cooperative."

"He's a friend's cousin who needed a good job and someone to watch over him to keep him out of trouble. He'll adjust eventually to life on the ranch. I'll be there in a few." But in truth, he was ready to terminate Sarge for taking Cassie hostage, because he knew she wouldn't have permitted him to leave with her any other way.

Minutes later, Leidolf saw the lights flashing on the sheriff's vehicle, his Jag parked in front of it. The sheriff was waving a flashlight into the woods, but it was too dark to find anything. As soon as Leidolf pulled in behind the sheriff's vehicle, the sheriff rushed out of the shelter of trees and waved at him.

"I'm so sorry, Mr. Wildhaven. I wouldn't have thought in a million years she would have run off like that."

Several pickups parked behind Leidolf's. "We'll take care of it," he said, climbing out of his Humvee.

"She mentioned someone named Alex Wellington. Know the man?"

Leidolf frowned. "A friend of hers." Although from what Leidolf had seen, the wolf biologist was more of a nuisance than a friend.

His men and Evan gathered around them.

"All right if we take Sarge with us?" Leidolf asked.

"Yeah. As long as you don't want to press charges, he can run along with you."

Leidolf nodded to Elgin, who hurried to the sheriff's vehicle to move Sarge to his truck.

"She said Alex was a friend, and at first she thought he might have reported the murderers' whereabouts in the 911 call. She changed her story, protecting the guy, I'm sure, once she learned none of us knew his name. We need to know what he heard exactly and what he might have seen," the sheriff said.

Leidolf ground his teeth. Hell, what if she'd been with this Alex Wellington and one of the murderers had shot her when she was in her wolf form? All along, Leidolf had thought a hunter had shot her. "We'll find her, Sheriff."

"Are you sure? I could arrange a search-and-rescue mission."

"No. I've got enough men with me. I'll take care of it." Not wanting Evan out in the woods on a mission like this, Leidolf waved at the teen. "Take the Jag back to the ranch, will you, Evan?"

Evan's whole face lit up. "Sure thing!" He hurried toward the sports car.

"Drive safely," Evan's father said, coming up behind Leidolf. "No speeding."

"I'll follow him back to the ranch," the sheriff assured him. "Let me know when you have the girl safely back, will you?"

"Yeah, I'll do that, Sheriff." Leidolf waited until Evan was behind the wheel of the Jag and headed back to the ranch with the sheriff following him. Then Leidolf turned to his men to give orders. "No wolf coats. It's much too dangerous. Create enough noise so that if any hunters are out here, they'll know you're just a bunch of men like them. And, Fergus, make sure one of our men takes Sarge back to the ranch—and sits on him if he has to."

"Yes, sir." Fergus motioned to one of the men and spoke to him in private.

"What if we don't find her?" Elgin asked Leidolf.

"We'll find her, if it takes all night. Spread out, men. One little redheaded lady isn't about to give us the slip for long." Leidolf noticed Satros stiffly climbing out of Carver's mini-SUV. He gave Leidolf a small smile. Leidolf acknowledged Satros's finding Cassie with a return smile, even though Leidolf hadn't gotten word until he'd found her himself. He still appreciated that Satros had tried so hard to find Leidolf a mate to ensure he stayed with the pack.

"Good thing you had spotted her at the river fishing earlier, Satros. Now, the trick is to keep her." Which Leidolf was bound and determined to do, the more he got to know the little lady. Everything in his life had been a challenge. Cassie would be the ultimate challenge this time around. "Let's go."

"This way." Elgin pointed at the ground as he followed her trail. "She's moving fast."

"Spread out," Leidolf said, quickening his own pace.

They rushed through the trees, stopping only long enough to listen, sniff the air, and catch her scent.

"Do you think one of the men who murdered the woman was the same one who shot Cassie?" Elgin asked from several feet away in the darkened woods. "And she was with this guy named Alex?"

"Yeah, that's exactly what I think," Leidolf growled.

"Think he's a *lupus garou* too, and that's why he didn't hang around and tell the police who he was?"

"No. He listened to her lecture at the town hall. He's a wolf biologist also, only of the human variety." Leidolf ground his teeth. What the hell had Alex been doing with her in the woods? Had he pushed himself on her when she hadn't wanted him around? Or maybe the reason she was so desperate to get back here had nothing to do with a female red wolf but rather with a human wolf biologist. Which meant even though he could usually read his people's actions, he was clueless about Cassie. And that he didn't like.

Leidolf strode forth, trying to get another location on his would-be mate.

—◆—

Cassie was determined to break the hunter's grip on her arm and run free while the other man punched in numbers on his cell phone.

"Sheriff Whittaker?" the man said. "This is Everett Hollis. My brother, Ben, and I found a woman in the woods half naked, and we're about half a mile from—" He looked down at her and then nodded. "A pretty redhead." He smiled.

"Yeah, she's the one. Ben said she spoke at the town hall. She's that wolf biologist from California. We'll bring her to the road to hand her over to Mr. Wildhaven. Sure, Sheriff. She's not going anywhere."

He snapped his phone shut and said to Ben, "The little

lady borrowed that rich rancher's Jag." He looked down at her clothes. "Looks like she took a little more than that."

Ben furrowed his brow at her. "I always thought rich folks didn't have any troubles." Then he gave her an evil smile. "Here I thought you were one of those stuck-up educated women, and come to find out you're down-to-earth like the rest of us." His grin broadened.

"You're hurting my wrist," she complained, frowning at him. He did have an ironclad hold on her, and it was cutting off the circulation, although her complaint was a little more devious than wanting to protest about the pressure on her wrist.

When Ben loosened his grip a little, Cassie twisted around and down, breaking his hold on her, and dashed south again for her vehicle.

"Damn it, Ben. How could you let a slip of a woman get away?"

They tromped after her in rabid pursuit. If she could just reach the truck before these men caught up to her, she could move it. Then she could return to the area where she'd left the salmon and locate the mother wolf and her den. Alex would most likely have left the area already.

She frowned as she plowed through tree branches and underbrush. Unless he worried about the wounded wolf—her—and was searching for her. Damn. Once she got to her truck, she could call Alex on her cell phone, if the cell-phone signal could reach him, and let him know she'd taken the wolf to a vet so he wouldn't worry about it—her. The lies would soon strangle her.

Leaving the hunters far behind where she didn't think they'd ever catch up, she kept running until she saw the narrow turnout where she'd parked her vehicle. When she reached the location, she found Alex's truck parked behind hers, blocking her in. She could scream. But the fact that he hadn't left set her to worrying about his safety again.

She didn't have any other choice. She used the keypad to unlock her truck, then tossed her clothes—Leidolf's clothes rather—inside and yanked off the bandage over her shoulder. Sharp pain streaked through the muscle and radiated down her back, and she let out a sorrowful groan. She shoved his garments and the bandage under the passenger seat, relocked the door, and shifted.

The shifting hurt. Landing on her front paws in her wolf form hurt. Everything hurt. But if Alex's truck was still here, he wasn't safe. Neither was she. For now, she had a couple of frantic rescue missions to accomplish, and she wasn't stopping until she did.

Leidolf's cell phone jingled again, and he quit walking through the woods to glance at the number while his men stopped to hear the news. *The sheriff.* Leidolf jerked the phone to his ear. "Yeah?"

"Just got the word two hunters came across a woman dressed like the one driving your Jag. Ben and Everett Hollis worried she was a runaway or had been traumatized, the way she was dressed, but then realized she was that wolf biologist who gave the lecture on wolves the other night. Ben said he's got her in tow, headed toward the road to hand her over to you."

Leidolf breathed a tentative sigh of relief. "Good news."

He didn't think the sheepherders would do anything but keep her safe, even if they wouldn't like her wolf politics.

But before he could sign off, the sheriff said, "Wait, got another message coming in." He seemed to pause forever before he spoke again to Leidolf, and the suspense was killing him. "They lost her. She shook loose of Ben's grip and headed south again, but they're in pursuit of her."

"Wearing nighttime goggles?" Had to be if they could see like wolves in the gloom of night.

"Yeah. You want them to keep after her?"

"Sure. I'll give you an update in a while." Leidolf didn't want to make it sound as though he needed to keep the whole thing secret from the sheriff's office. Not at this point. He figured Cassie wouldn't allow the brothers to catch her again anyway. "We're headed in that direction." Leidolf signed off with the sheriff. He wanted Cassie under his protection and didn't like the idea the men would be manhandling her.

"She's headed this way," Elgin said, a little way away. "A turnout is just ahead."

"She's probably parked there," Leidolf responded. "Hell, if she gets into her vehicle, that's the last we'll see of her." He started running. He wasn't letting her go until he knew her story. Well, that wasn't exactly true. He didn't intend to let her go ever, although convincing her he had her best interests at heart was going to be some task.

Elgin and the others began to run in their spread-out configuration. Hunting the female made the wolfish side of him want her all the more.

Then they broke into the clearing for the turnout. They saw two pickups, both dark, no one in either, one blocking the other in at the trailhead.

"The green one's hers. The black one is Alex's." He turned to Pierce. "Pick the lock, and wait for her in the cab in the event she returns. Quincy, you take the truck behind it. If she returns with Alex, she might try to leave with him. We need to make sure that neither takes off before I can question them further."

"Yes, sir," both of his men said.

Elgin motioned toward the Willamette River. "She's headed this way, Leidolf."

A good half hour later, he heard the rush of the river and saw her in her red wolf form near the edge of the water, limping as she paced, sniffing and searching in the area... for what? And what the hell was she doing in her wolf form, risking getting shot again? Trying to locate Alex? Although a sense of relief washed over Leidolf to see her there, unharmed except for the old injury.

When Cassie heard them approach, she stopped and narrowed her eyes. Their fluorescent color shimmered in the still dark, early-morning hour, but she seemed tired, her body, tail, and head sagging. Her shoulder had to be giving her fits.

"Are you looking for Alex Wellington?" Leidolf asked, motioning for his men to surround her but keeping her attention. He wasn't letting her go, not the way she was injured. She wouldn't make it anywhere safe when the sun shone in a few hours.

His expression told her she'd better not even *think* of crossing the river. He didn't believe she'd mind him if she wasn't hurting so much. "We'll find him, but you need to return to the ranch for your own safety." He hadn't meant to sound so irritated, but the notion of her risking her life and exposing their kind to be with Alex annoyed the hell out of him.

Suddenly, Elgin and Fergus came out of the brush from behind a Douglas fir, both gripping a man's arms. The man's blue eyes were bloodshot, but he couldn't see in the dark like they could.

Alex Wellington.

"What the hell are you doing out here? And who are these guys?" Alex tugged to free himself, but Leidolf's men would hold him tight until Leidolf said otherwise.

Had Alex been Cassie's human lover? If so, Leidolf planned to quickly remedy the situation. He frowned. "Did the men you overheard say they'd murdered a woman also shoot the red wolf?"

Alex didn't say anything, but he turned a little pale.

Leidolf didn't like having to repeat himself, and he figured that if Alex could have seen the look he was being given for his disobedience, he would have taken more heed. Leidolf tried again. This time, he growled: "Did one of them?"

Elgin sounded equally ferocious as he shook Alex's arm, "Answer the question."

"All right, all right. It's none of your concern. Hell, all you are is a damned rancher."

In response, Elgin smirked. Carver shook his head. Satros studied the wolf biologist but didn't say a word, his expression hard. He didn't have much to do with humans, as old as he was. And he didn't tolerate them well when he had to deal with them. Fergus cleared his throat as if he was going to speak but then didn't.

"Was that your truck across the creek on the turnout south of here?" Leidolf asked, even though he knew it was.

"Yeah. What's it to you?" Alex finally shook loose of Elgin and Fergus as Leidolf gave them the go-ahead to release him.

Leidolf growled, "What are you doing out here still?"

"If it's any of your business, I was looking for Cassie and an injured wolf. Instead of my locating the wolf, she found me again. But I haven't discovered any signs of Cassie."

None of which explained what Cassie was doing at the river's edge. Why didn't she lead Alex back to his truck? No, she was restless, pacing near the water like she was searching for something else. "We have a vet at the ranch. We'll take her with us and get her medical attention," Leidolf explained, trying to curb his irritation with both her and this friend of hers.

"If you're a rancher, why the hell would you want to take care of a wolf?"

"She's not a problem. We're having trouble with a cougar though. Killed a couple of our calves. Even so, we're turning the cat over to the zoo once we tranquilize it."

Alex's eyes rounded. "You didn't shoot those zoo men with tranquilizers, did you?"

Leidolf smiled, knowing the man couldn't see his expression in the dark. "We're only out to get the wolf medical attention and put the cougar in the zoo."

Alex's expression indicated that he thought Leidolf had shot the men and taken off with the wolf to protect her. Alex's face brightened, but then he frowned. "You tranquilized the men and took her home with you, didn't you? She must have run away again and come looking for me." He rubbed his stubbly chin and stared at the ground.

"Or she came back because of something else. I don't

understand though. She seems anxious, like she was looking for something but was afraid to leave me alone. She's wounded still too. Limping pretty badly. Why didn't you keep her safely at home? I mean, I'm grateful she found me and then you did, but you should have locked her up for her own safety."

"Just what I intend to do." Leidolf gave Cassie a look that meant he was going to back up his words.

"Let me go with you," Alex said.

"We can't. Fergus can escort you back to your truck. Sheriff wants to talk to you about what you saw as far as the men are concerned."

"You think he could protect me? She knocked the one down but didn't bite him even. She was protecting me. She's got to have been your pet. Was she?"

"Yeah, she's *mine*. She got loose. We'll take it from here." Hell, Cassie. How could she have gotten so involved with a human? Leidolf gave her an annoyed look.

"Have you guys got night-vision goggles? I can't see a blamed thing out here with just this flashlight of mine," Alex said, waving the small light around, highlighting a few needles of the Douglas fir straight ahead of him with a pinprick of light. "I figured I'd have to wait it out until morning to locate Cassie, when here comes the wolf. What's her name, by the way?"

"Red," Leidolf said.

Fergus turned on a penlight. "We're from around here and know the woods forward and backward…blindfolded. Come on. I'll take you to your truck."

"But Cassie is somewhere out here also."

Leidolf stalked toward him, ready to learn the truth about her relationship with him. "Who is she to you?"

The guy's eyes widened. Hell, Leidolf meant to ask more about her, not sound like a jealous damn lover.

His men smirked at him. Cassie growled softly in her wolf form, now lying on her stomach, nose on her paws, her eyes focused on Leidolf. He continued to scowl, and Alex frowned. "The woman I'm going to marry. We'll make a damned good team."

The guy couldn't have surprised Leidolf any more with the news. His men looked just as stunned, their mouths gaping.

"Marriage?" He swore she gave him a what-of-it look, although she appeared worn out from her ordeal.

"Yeah, we'll make a terrific husband-and-wife team. Really go places once we make a pact. It's not safe for her to be running around in the wilderness alone."

"She's engaged to you?" Leidolf asked, not bothering to hide the skepticism in his tone of voice.

Alex shoved his hands in his jacket pockets. "As soon as I can propose properly to her. I figured once I'd made the wolf find," he said, motioning to Cassie, "and hooked up with Cassie, I'd share the good news with her, and that would be what did it. Hell, if the wolf is just a pet, that won't interest her."

"If you ask her to marry you, she won't say yes." Leidolf couldn't tell what Cassie was thinking, but she was staring at Alex, waiting for a response. Leidolf could sure as hell tell her what *he* was thinking. No unmated red female was changing some human to be her mate.

"Sure she'll say yes. As soon as she realizes how perfect we'll be for each other."

"Are you lovers?"

Everyone was rabidly watching Alex for his response. Leidolf thought he heard Cassie emit a very low growl, directed at him, not at Alex.

"None of your damn business."

Leidolf smiled. Just the answer he wanted. *No, they weren't lovers.*

Leidolf folded his arms across his chest and stood taller. "I can tell you right now that she won't marry you. *We're* engaged to be married. Couple of weeks, and the knot will be tied."

Cassie shook her head and narrowed her eyes at Leidolf.

Elgin smiled broadly. "Yeah, I'll be best man at the wedding."

Motioning to the other men, Carver spoke up, "We're all Leidolf's groomsmen."

Alex closed his gaping mouth. Poor bastard was outnumbered and outmaneuvered. It paid at times like this to be a member of a wolf pack.

"Cassie's at home in bed where she ought to be, safe and sound. But now I need to get Red to the vet to take care of her injury. And lock her up so that she doesn't get loose and hurt herself further." Leidolf gave her a pointed look. "Fergus, take Alex to his truck, will you?"

Alex looked back at Cassie. "I'd like to drop by and tell Cassie congratulations on her upcoming marriage and see Red when she's healed up. Where did you say they'd be staying?"

"Fergus?" Leidolf said, not about to let this guy get anywhere near Cassie again if he could help it.

"Come on," Fergus said, leading the way with his small penlight.

Alex walked behind him in the direction of the turnout, muttering under his breath, "I don't know how you could see anything in this dark. Your light is even smaller than mine." Suddenly, he stopped and turned. "What about the other wolves?"

Leidolf felt the tension in the air renew among his pack members. "What other wolves?" He tried to curb his agitation that the guy would continue to question him.

Alex stiffened and gave Leidolf a look like he wasn't that dumb. "I'm a wolf biologist by trade. At least two other wolves were in the vicinity where the men from the zoo were tranquilized. As evidenced by the tracks they left behind, the wolves ran beside the men, who most likely drugged the guys from the zoo. So where are the other wolves?"

"Take him back to his vehicle, Fergus." Hell, what else could Leidolf say? He had a pack of wolves at the ranch—but he didn't have a license to keep wild animals on the premises? He didn't have any other wolves—and Alex would know he was lying? At least he assumed the man would know the difference between wolf tracks and dog's or even hybrid wolf-dog tracks. Unless the animals were more wolf than dog.

Besides, he would be damned if he'd explain anything to a wannabe lover of Cassie's.

Alex snorted. "All right." He turned and headed off with Fergus in the direction of his truck.

Once they were beyond earshot, Elgin warned, "He believes we have a whole pack of wolves back at the ranch."

Leidolf frowned at Elgin. "I'm not changing another damn human and taking him into the pack. Sure as hell not when the guy has the hots for Cassie."

"You don't think he'll learn too much, do you?" Carver asked, and the dark expression on his face said he'd take care of the guy one way or another.

"Tell everyone to be on the alert for a black pickup truck with California license plates. If he comes to the ranch, make sure no one is in their wolf coats and direct him to me."

"He knows we tranquilized the zoo men. He seemed to approve, most likely because he wants to study wolves in the wild and not have them penned up in the zoo, but he could still tell the authorities we were the ones who knocked out Thompson and his buddy," Elgin said.

Leidolf gave Cassie a stern look. This was what happened when werewolves got involved in human affairs. "We'll cross that bridge when we have to. Call Quincy and Pierce, if you can get hold of them on their cell phones. If not, send someone to run ahead and warn them to vacate Alex and Cassie's vehicles and lie low. Once Alex has driven off, have them take Cassie's truck to the ranch."

He turned to Cassie. "And *you* are returning with me to the ranch *now*." He stalked toward her. "You're welcome to shift." He smiled a little. "Easier to carry that way." More than that, he wanted to claim her as a woman, hold her tight, enjoy the feel of her close all over again, but he figured she already knew how he felt about her. Although he did want to know if she was keen on mating with a human and turning him. He had every intention of setting her straight on that matter.

Carver pointed to the river. "Hell, Leidolf, it's another one of them."

Leidolf stopped next to Cassie and looked across the river. A red wolf watched them. Smaller than a male, it had to be a female. Cassie was on her feet in an instant, as if she'd drawn on a pocket of energy. Before he could stop what she was about to do, she dove into the river.

"Hell and damnation, woman!"

CHAPTER 18

"YOU CAN'T FOLLOW HER DRESSED LIKE YOU ARE," Carver warned Leidolf. Carver looked as if he was ready to dive into the river himself to go after Cassie.

Leidolf was already stripping out of his clothes while he kept Cassie in sight. The water had swiftly swept her downstream as he was having a hell of a time fumbling to untie his wet bootlaces. "Tell the rest of the men where I've gone. Elgin, you're in charge while I'm away. I'll take her to the cabin until she's well enough to return. Just leave my clothes hidden nearby."

Carver frowned at him. "You sure you don't want me to come with you?"

"You have your girls to look after." But Leidolf thought Carver was interested in the other red wolf, in the event she was a *lupus garou* also, and wanted to have first chance at her before the other bachelor males did.

"What are you going to do about this Alex character?" Carver asked, staring off in the direction Cassie was headed farther downstream and struggling against the current to reach the opposite shore.

Leidolf let out his breath and ditched his jeans and then his shirt. "He can see Cassie once I've returned her to the ranch and she's feeling better. And then she can tell him to take a hike."

He quickly shifted and, as a wolf, raced down the rocky

riverbank to reach the location where Cassie had drifted. Then he dove into the cold river, sending the water flying, and swam toward her. By then, she'd reached the halfway point across the river.

Was the other wolf Cassie's sister, which would explain why Cassie had been so hell-bent on returning here? But why hadn't she just told him the truth? All his men would have been searching for the woman. Which maybe was the reason she hadn't told him the truth.

As a wolf, Leidolf paddled across the river, swearing it was growing wider as he traversed it. He sure as hell could run faster as a wolf than he could swim as one. Even with her having a head start, he was catching up to Cassie as she fought against the current to reach the other side. Then, she suddenly went under. His heart flipped.

His men shouted on the beach near where he had jumped into the water. "Hell, Leidolf!" Elgin said, his voice rife with concern.

"Do you want us to come in?" Carver shouted.

But Leidolf kept swimming to reach the last place he'd seen her, his gaze searching for any sign of her, his heart beating spastically. *God, Cassie, I can't lose you now.*

Then Cassie's head bobbed up, her ears perked high, her swim slow and plodding. She was getting closer to shore. Hell, he wished he could wolf paddle faster. If he could reach her in time, he'd grab her by the scruff of the neck and pull her in. Or swiftly shift to his human form and carry her the rest of the way to the shore.

She finally reached the beach and stumbled, landing on her stomach. *Cassie.*

Stay! Just stay there! he wanted to shout at her. He wanted to pin her down, like a wolf in charge would another, to make her obey.

Her chest heaving, she sat on the shore. He thought he might reach her in time before she could run off. Until she looked back and saw how close to shore he was. *Damn.* Her ears twitched, her eyes widened, and she closed her panting mouth.

He gave her the best steely-eyed, you'd-better-obey-me look that an alpha pack leader could convey. And hell, she took off running for the woods with a heavy limp.

When he reached the other side of the river, he glanced back at Carver and the rest of his men, all watching him to see that he made it. Then he bowed his head to them to acknowledge he was fine and to ask them to abide by his wishes. After shaking off the excess water dripping from his coat, he whipped around and took off in the direction the little red wolf had gone—his little red wolf. The other... well, if one of his men could convince her to stay with the pack also, so much the better. But Cassie was his. Like Alex had stated, Leidolf just had to convince her of that fact. Only he'd be the winner, not some lame human wolf biologist.

After racing through the forest for about a mile, Leidolf came upon Cassie sitting in ferns shielded by Douglas firs, panting and staring off into the distance, her energy totally spent. As soon as she smelled him coming, she whipped her head around, her gaze riveting to his. *Yeah, here's the big, bad wolf coming to take you safely home, young lady.*

Cassie's face looked ragged with pain. Warily, he approached her, not wanting to chase her off and cause her any more pain but wanting to ensure she didn't run away again either. He saw no sign of the other female and assumed Cassie just couldn't go any farther with her shoulder so injured.

She didn't make any move to leave. In fact, she lay down on her side, taking the pressure off her injured shoulder.

He drew close and nuzzled her face. She didn't growl at him, like she would have if she hadn't wanted his attention. She didn't lick him back either, though, as if she was too tired to make the effort or had given up and wasn't happy about it. Deciding she was just too worn out, he planned to carry her to his cabin by the creek where she could rest until she was able to return with him.

Leidolf nudged Cassie's nose, trying to get her to stir, but she'd closed her eyes and appeared to be sleeping or just ignoring him. He hoped they could reach the cabin without running into anyone in the woods—and soon.

Not liking what he had to do next, he shifted, and in his naked, chilled form, he leaned down and lifted Cassie as gently as he could. She yelped. "I'm so sorry, Cassie."

He figured his apology would have garnered a couple of chuckles from his men, had they witnessed it. He hated hearing the pain in her yelp, and he tried to carry her as carefully as he could. At least it would be dark for several more hours, and if all went as planned, she could heal while she rested. Then again, without clothing, they would have to remain there until darkness fell again so they could return to his Humvee in their wolf suits.

As he began hiking, he worried about the other wolf. She would be in as much danger as he and Cassie were in their wolf forms if hunters located them and wanted to eliminate the wolf threat. As soon as Cassie was safe in the cabin, he'd take a look for the other wolf. In his wolf coat.

Faster to travel, but he wasn't sure whether it would scare off the wolf or not.

For half an hour, Leidolf carried a sleeping Cassie tight against his chest, surprised—considering how much he cursed when he stepped on blackberry bramble thorns or stumbled over exposed tree roots he couldn't see for carrying her—that she hadn't awakened.

She'd been really still in his arms, but all of a sudden, she began to wiggle as if she didn't care for being confined.

"I'll drop you if you don't mind," Leidolf warned, tightening his hold on her and trying not to lose the squirming wolf. She tried to jerk away from him, but he squeezed tighter. "Behave yourself," he said in a hushed voice close to her ear as if he were whispering sweet sentiments to her.

Her subtle feminine fragrance stirred his senses, made him long for her, and all he could think of was how he was going to convince her she was staying with his pack—with him.

He reconsidered that maybe as a newly turned *lupus garou*, she wanted to change a human male for a mate so that he would be the same as her. Which made him think of the new Arctic werewolves he'd had to deal with in Maine. He wasn't going along with Cassie taking a human for a mate.

Then Cassie struggled harder, and before he could prepare himself, she was shifting again. Either she didn't have control over the shifting, which meant it was tantamount that she stay with a pack, *his* pack. Or she preferred his holding her tight in his hard embrace as a woman instead of as a wolf. Carrying a woman would be easier to manage, but he didn't like that she'd be as chilled as him.

Still, when she shifted and he was holding the silky-skinned nymph in his arms, he gave her a devilish smile as she frowned up at him, and he said, "Much better." He readjusted his hold on her and pressed her hot little body closer, trying to ensure she didn't get too cold.

He had every intention of setting the rules. "So let's get some things straight between us, Cassie Roux, little wolf biologist. You're a loner, don't have a pack, and have the hots for me." He grinned at the last.

She closed her eyes and groaned. She could pretend all she wanted that she wasn't interested in him the way he desired having her. She snuggled closer to him and breathed deeply. Enjoying the way his pheromones revealed how much he craved having her? Hers were driving him insane.

"And you're not going to take some lame wolf biologist for a mate."

She let out her breath in a painful sigh, her gaze staring up at him, beautiful, eyes narrowed a little in confrontation… and he loved it. "I have no intention of mating with Alex. It's all his idea, and truthfully? He couldn't make a commitment to one woman if his life depended on it. But I have a job to do, for which I'm getting paid, and no one's stopping me."

"You're not running through the woods on your own, Cassie. Not wounded like you are and not when those murderers could still be out here searching for that woman's body."

Ignoring him, she growled, "And furthermore, *quit* telling everyone we're engaged."

Then she scrunched up her face in pain, shivered in his arms, and started to move again. Before he could warn her he was about to drop her again, his hold tightening on her already, she shifted once more. She had to be *really* newly turned. Which made him wonder if some wolf had turned her and she'd run away before he mated her.

He ground his teeth, figuring that although he didn't want her exploring the woods further, he ought to at least ask her what job was so blamed important. The female wolf? What had she intended to do with her? "So what is the reason you had to return here?"

She appeared to be sleeping and didn't shift back to her human form or seem to have heard his question. He growled under his breath. As soon as he could, he was learning the truth.

And then a breath of relief gave him hope as he saw the log cabin nestled in between trees, about five hundred square feet in size, a full rock wall on one side, rounded logs for the other three walls, grimy unwashed windows in the three wooden walls, and a mortared stone extension on one end. All the materials but the glass looked to have been salvaged from the surrounding countryside. The roof was covered in moss, tall grass and ferns brushed the sides of the building, and a hemlock's branches poked at one wall. A human's version of a wolf's den. Perfect for Cassie's recuperation.

He shoved open the door with his hip and stared into the gloom. A couple of rough-hewn wooden chairs sat at a small table next to one wall. A fireplace was built into the rock wall, blackened with soot from years of use. A deflated velour mattress lay on the dusty wooden floor. As a wolf, Cassie wouldn't mind. Although as soon as he had the time, he'd try to inflate the mattress or make up some other kind of bed.

He laid her down next to the fireplace. She opened her eyes and looked up at him, her wolf's expression tired.

"I'll be back, Cassie. I'll get some wood and build a fire. Just stay here."

She closed her eyes, and he worried she might get sicker before she was better, as lethargic as she was.

"Cassie?" He crouched in front of her and touched her nose. It was wet and cool. He knew that a warm, dry nose didn't immediately signify illness. Lethargy, in addition to it, and loss of appetite could be more serious. "I'll…I'll be right back."

He headed for the door and turned to look at her, but she didn't open her eyes or acknowledge in any way that she knew he was leaving. The thought did go through his mind that she was only faking it, and that as soon as he left her, she'd run off again. Hell. He hated second-guessing her.

He walked outside, shut the door, and sniffed the air, trying to smell any sign of another wolf or humans that had been in the area while he waited to ensure Cassie wasn't planning to leave. He smelled nothing but the hemlocks and the water from the creek nearby, pines and pinesap, and a rabbit that had been in the area recently. He peered in through one of the dusty windows. Cassie hadn't moved a muscle.

He sighed and went to gather wood, which wasn't much fun naked. Chill bumps covered every inch of his skin, but he didn't have any choice. When he returned to the cabin with an armload of firewood, he found Cassie still dead to the world. He loaded the wood into the fireplace and found a cache of waterproof matches on the mantel. After a fire began to really catch, he watched Cassie's chest rise and fall, rise and fall. Her legs kicked a little as if she was running in a dream, and she whimpered.

Forever it seemed he watched her, not wanting to leave her alone, but he had to look for the other wolf in case she was in trouble. He leaned down and scratched between Cassie's ears. "I'll be back, Cassie, after I look for the other wolf. Just sleep. I'll be right back."

She didn't wake or at least didn't react to his attentions.

The cabin was so small that it was heating up nicely, making it even harder for him to leave the place. He went outside, closed the door, and welcomed the shift. Not that he wanted to run around in the daylight as a wolf, but the fur coat was welcome in the chilly breeze.

As a wolf, he ran back to the river where they'd crossed, where they'd seen the other wolf, and began searching for her trail. His men were gone, and he hoped they weren't off looking for the wolf on their own.

But the wolf was a female for sure. Her footpads had left a scent, and he ran along the trail until he came to a creek. And then that was the odd thing. The wolf had entered the creek, but when he traversed the fast-running water over the slippery stones, he didn't find her scent on the opposite bank. He followed the creek for some time downstream and then tried again upstream. Nothing. Hell, it was as if she just vanished. Or she'd stayed in the creek for a much longer time than he'd imagined. He wondered if Cassie had pulled the same thing when he'd tried to find her and then gotten shot by the zoo men.

Leidolf recrossed the creek and hurried downstream, figuring maybe the red female wolf had entered the creek, walked along it farther than he imagined she would, trying to catch a fish, and then exited it. He still couldn't find her scent that way, or upstream either. Which was more than bizarre. Then again, she was beginning to sound like she might truly be a *lupus garou* trying to avoid him, just like Cassie, and not a *lupus* who wouldn't think like a human.

Following the trail again, he tried to see if she'd backtracked her path as wolves would do and then went across the river. He couldn't tell. If she had backtracked, she'd just remarked her scent. Frustrated with not getting anywhere with the search, he shook his head. Time to return to Cassie and take care of her.

He raced back toward the cabin, hoping he might still catch a glimpse of the other wolf, but no luck. When he saw the smoke coming out of the chimney of the little square cabin, he felt an inkling of truly being home despite how austere it was. He'd never needed much of a place to feel at home. And if he had the woman of his dreams with him, that was all he could ask for. If he could convince her of it.

Without his whole pack watching his every move, this was as good a place as any for the conflict of wills to unfold.

CHAPTER 19

THE WATER LAPPED AT THE SHORE OF THE LAKE, THE soothing sound lulling Cassie into a sense of security as she watched the bronzed Poseidon wade out of the water, every muscle moving with powerful urgency, his green-eyed gaze focused on hers. The look in his expression said it all. She was his. But what he didn't know was he was hers. And he didn't have any choice in the matter.

She cast him a coy smile. *God of the sea, I am the huntress who has ensnared you, not the other way around.*

He strode up the bank, his skin glistening with droplets of water, his expression tight with need. Somehow, her Indiana Jones hat and backpack, her shorts, tunic top, shirt, socks, and boots all had vanished, and she stood among the trees as a goddess of the hunt, naked, ready to take her prey. *Come to me, Poseidon. Show me what you've got.*

In slow motion, he approached, as if afraid she'd attempt to escape him. She had no intention of running away like a rabbit bound for a bunny hole.

Suddenly, she was falling, tumbling down into darkness, the smell earthy, the landing soft as she arrived inside the rabbit's burrow. Only the world opened up again, and a giant rabbit greeted her, wearing her hat, backpack, and tunic.

Desperately, she clawed at the hole, trying to get out, attempting to reach Poseidon, to show the god she wasn't running away from him, had no intention of hiding, and Poseidon shushed her. "Cassie, quiet. Be still. You're safe."

He lifted her into his arms and kissed her too sweetly, when she craved being ravished by his touch. She tried to open her lips to him, to kiss him back, to spear her tongue into his mouth, to invite him in, and take his pleasure in her, as she would take pleasure from him.

"Cassie, you keep this up, and I will be forced to be less than honorable."

His smile was devilishly predictable, wolfish, not in the least bit honorable looking, and she loved it.

She licked her lips, moistening them before she kissed him and squirmed against his firm embrace, eliciting a moan from deep within his chest. She couldn't seem to lift her head to look at him again and instead gave a tired sigh.

His fingers combed through her hair as she listened to his heart beating hard, as if he'd been running all day. And his skin was wet, smelling fresh and clean, wild and free. His raging hormones, the sexy smell caught her attention. Her phero-mones... and his. The telltale sign they were ready to take the relationship further.

With a horrendous effort, she managed to lick his chest, tasted salty skin and water droplets, and again Poseidon groaned. "Vixen."

Cassie jerked awake, only she was no longer a wolf but a woman, lying against a very naked and hot-bodied man. Not Poseidon. *Leidolf.* He had wrapped his arms around her, resting against a bed of pine needles in a small log cabin, his own body serving as her mattress as he lay still, his eyes closed, droplets of water on his skin, his hair wet, a velvet-covered, limp air mattress rolled up beneath his head for a pillow. Outside it was gloomy, cloudy, the scent of rain heavy in the air, and still daylight. She guessed it was about midday or later.

She sighed and closed her eyes, resting her head against his chest again. If she had desired having a mate, she would want him to be just like Leidolf, protective and powerful.

Yet even as self-assured as he was, she saw the flaws in his character. The way he ordered his people around, how he was totally in charge, yet a vulnerable side kept appearing. The way he apologized when he'd lifted her while she was in her wolf form and she'd yelped. She hadn't meant to, but the pain had shot through her shoulder, and she couldn't help it. She thought he might drop her, he appeared so concerned. And then the way he brought her to this cabin, started a fire, even searched for the wolf they'd seen across the river, yet she'd sensed he hadn't wanted to leave her—even for a minute.

Although she knew that was due, in part, to his controlling nature, maybe worry that she might take off, she also knew he was concerned that someone might find her and try to eliminate her. She looked at the scratches on his arms that probably came from carrying the firewood. And listened to the steady beat of his heart, the blood whooshing through his veins, his body hot and his skin pure tactile delight. Like this, she could almost desire having him for a mate.

Almost. The problem with mates was that they had a lot of requirements. Lots of needs that had to be met. Especially when a mate was the alpha leader of a pack. And she'd have to be the alpha female. Not that she didn't have it in her. She could never be a beta. She'd bet her last paycheck he wouldn't like it if she continued her work studying wolves wherever she could locate the *lupus* kind. And never in a million years was she giving up her life work. Not when wolves had saved her life. Although no matter how hard she worked at it, she could never repay the pack that had taken her in.

Then a plan began to formulate. What if she did mate with Leidolf? No more having to deal with males who wanted an unmated female. What if he wanted her so badly that he'd negotiate for terms?

She mulled that over for a few seconds. She envisioned packing her gear for a trip to North Carolina to study the red wolves there, but when she reached the front door at the ranch, she would find Leidolf standing in the doorway, his arms folded across his broad chest, legs spread apart in battle stance, his expression an emphatic *no*.

So no, it would be an awful mistake. He wouldn't agree with her working, she was certain, and she would be stuck leading beside him, never fulfilling her own destiny.

Leidolf's fingers swept down her back in a tender caress, and she looked up to see him watching her. "How long have you been awake?" he asked, the timbre of his voice darkly seductive.

"Hmm," she said and burrowed her head against his chest, closing her eyes again. "Just woke. How long ago did I shift?"

He swept his hands lower, down her back until he reached her buttocks and made small circular swirls across her sensitive cheeks. "Hours ago. I tried to inflate the mattress, but it was hopeless. So I made a bed of pine needles and then pulled you off the cold floor so we could share some body heat."

She opened her eyes and looked at the fire, the flames stretching upward in little curlicues, sending out the steady heat still warming the small cabin. "Hmm. You made a nice fire, and *you* make an awfully nice mattress."

"You make a terrific blanket." And the way he said it made her think he believed they fit together in perfect harmony.

She knew better. Perfect meant making sure the wolf kind got a fair break. Although the way Leidolf was touching her made her desire something more.

His fingers continued their leisurely caress against her skin, heating her blood. She didn't want to feel anything for him, but already he was hot-wiring her pheromones, triggering her need to have him, to stay with him, to fulfill her sexual fantasies. But more than that. She still envisioned seeing the pups with Felicity, and that triggered Cassie's own mothering needs. She stifled a sigh. Everything and everyone were ganging up on her, trying to coerce her to take another path.

"How is your shoulder?" Leidolf asked, breaking into the dreamlike state she was still enjoying.

"It's really bad." She lied, knowing just where this dialogue was going.

His fingers stilled at her waist. Then he began the slow, methodical stroking again. "So being on top like you are now is less comfortable?"

"For what?" She knew what he was getting at. The alpha leader had a job to do. Take a mate. Create his offspring. Secure the future of his *lupus garou* pack. Similar to the wolf packs' existence, only the human element did come into play. He seemed to be leaving that part out.

He sighed heavily and then moved his hands up her waist, his thumbs touching the curve of the undersides of her breasts. "You know what we both need. What we both want. We're right for each other. You'd make a capable pack-leader's mate."

At first, she didn't say anything in response, her ire instantly stoked. Hell, of course she would make a capable pack-leader's mate. What happened to: I want you... I need you... I can't live without you? The human element, buster?

Then again, alpha males didn't wear their feelings on their sleeves, and if she had to guess what this was all about, she'd say he couldn't reveal his feelings until she said I *do* in a wolf way. Or maybe it was all about sex with him. That and the possessiveness. Conquering a mate who seemed uncon-querable. Laying claim to a female when there were fewer of them to be had. Maybe he would never be able to say he truly loved her.

Still, she felt as if she was sliding down a slippery mountain of negative responses, and when she reached the bottom, she'd ultimately end up saying yes.

Despite her mind saying he was wrong, that she didn't need to have a mate, her body kept telling her that, in one aspect, he was so right, and she had to reconsider. She'd been a loner for too long. And she had a job to do. It was what made her whole. Not the idea of running some pack with an alpha male. Even if he was as delicious as Leidolf.

Leidolf moved his hands to either side of her head and turned it so she was resting her chin on his chest, his green eyes challenging her to be honest with him. "Tell me the truth, Cassie. You don't belong to a pack."

She turned her head away and laid it back down on his chest again. "So what gave me away?"

He chuckled lightly. "Every inch of your skin blushed

when I looked at you—from your cheeks to your toes. You were embarrassed. Which told me you weren't with a pack and haven't been for a very long time. How long ago did you lose your family, Cassie?" His voice was soothing, like she envisioned a psychiatrist's voice would be as he made her lie down on a couch and reveal the guilt she felt that she alone had survived the humans' brutality to her family.

She swallowed hard and blinked away tears. She could live another two hundred years, but the images—the smoke, the blazing heat, the fires reaching for the sun as if to join it in one unholy blaze—would never fade completely from her mind.

"Cassie, how long ago?"

"Since I was a teen. Thirteen. I lost them when I was thirteen."

"Mother, father?"

"My parents, sister, three uncles, two aunts, and a cousin. It was a pretty summer day, and I'd been searching for a *lupus* pack in a forest near a river where I'd discovered them the previous spring. My father kept warning me to stay away from them, counseling me that we weren't like them. That without our human disposition, they could be dangerous. But I didn't believe it.

"They played like we play, hunted, and protected one another, just like we did. They even let me get close to the alpha female's pups and play with them. When I smelled the pack's scent in the area again, I was curious how differ-ent they would be from our own kind and if they'd accept me like a pack member, even if they hadn't seen me for over a year. Just for fun." She let out her breath in a sigh of frustration.

Leidolf stroked her hair, his fingers gently caressing the strands, making her feel wanted again, which terrified her. What if she got too close to him and he was killed also?

"Cassie?"

She ground her teeth, wishing she had done something more, wishing she'd taken revenge. "We were hunters, traders, sold skins. Not farmers, sheepherders, or ranchers like our neighbors. We never had anything to do with any of them. They didn't care for us, and we didn't want them to learn what we truly were. So we stayed clear of them and all was fine. But that day, I smelled fires burning from the direction where our homes were, the three cabins not far from one another in the woods. I worried the forest was on fire. I raced home in my wolf suit to reach our homes more quickly. That's when I saw the men, a ranch family, the father, two of his brothers, and a couple of his nephews watching the houses burning."

She took another deep breath and could smell the acrid smoke, the heated air burning her lungs as if it were happening now, saw the flames stretching upward as she watched the fire in the fireplace.

Leidolf kissed the top of her head.

"I thought they'd come to rescue my family. I thought they'd arrived too late, the fire crackling, the heat from the flame like Hades as the houses crumbled and fell. I'd hoped my family had made it out in time. Then one of the men said something to the effect of, 'Their deaths won't bring my sons or nephew back, but at least I won't have to know they're living while my own kinfolk are dead.'"

Leidolf rubbed Cassie's arm. "Sounds like a revenge killing."

"But for what, Leidolf? My dad never liked Wheeler or his family. None of my family did. The boys were always stealing from the mercantile or other farms around. Half the time, the old man was at the local saloon gambling and drinking. Whoring too, when he had the money. More than likely, his sons got into trouble over something and somebody killed them. But not my family. They wouldn't have had anything to do with murder."

Leidolf remained silent, but she didn't care if he didn't believe her. *She* knew the truth.

"I hated the Wheelers, stalked them for months, one by one. I wanted to kill every last one of them like they had killed my family."

"But you didn't, did you, Cassie?"

She swallowed hard. "I was too much of a coward."

He let out his breath. "You couldn't have killed them in cold blood."

She gave a haughty laugh. "After losing my whole family, you bet I could have."

Again, he didn't respond.

"I could have," she reiterated, wishing she hadn't let them live. Then she sighed deeply again. "I couldn't live on my own. Not that young. Not as a girl. My choices were limited. Either I had to move to the nearest California town and live as a human, attempting to hide the wolf side of me, and hope that someone I didn't know would take me in as a maid or something. I could have ended up with some really bad sorts. I just couldn't imagine life like that. Or I could live with"—her eyes grew misty—"the wolves. They didn't mind that I was half human. They accepted me as one of the pack."

"A wolf pack. That's why you study them? Hell, it's a good thing the alpha leader didn't try to take you as his mate."

Cassie cast him a tearful smile. "He had a mate. I just had to make sure I wasn't treated as the omega, lowest wolf on the totem pole."

"You'll be the highest one on the totem pole in my pack."

She stroked his muscular arm. "Hmm, well, I'm not joining a *lupus garou* pack. Not anytime soon. I have a job to do. And as soon as I take care of it, I'll have another, and another. The wolves need me as their advocate."

"I need you. *Our* kind needs you." He renewed his sensual strokes, every action designed to get her to capitulate.

And if she wasn't so dead set on not joining a pack, she might have given in. His declaration that he needed her might have done it, but that was followed too closely by "our kind needs you," and that was what brought her back to her senses. For the good of their kind. But what of the good of the *lupus* kind? They weren't as important in the scheme of things, as far as *lupus garous* were concerned. But they were to Cassie.

She sighed and closed her eyes, loving the way he touched her, wanting what he was offering but not about to go there. From the way he spoke, he would have no interest in the regular *lupus* and her pups. Only in the one *lupus garou* he wanted to make his mate.

"The truth is that my shoulder's feeling much better." She looked up at him. "And I need to get back to work."

He wrapped his arms around her and frowned. "You can't go anywhere right now. Not *dressed* as you are. And not until nightfall in your wolf coat."

"You have to let me go," Cassie said, her voice verging on a growl. She would risk anything to locate the mother and her pups and ensure they were fed and protected.

"Why? What's so important about your research that you gambled running as a wolf and getting shot over it?"

She could hear his attempt at keeping his voice even, but the testiness gave him away.

She had no choice but to tell him. Hell, he might even be reasonable about it. She doubted it. "What's important is the survival of a she-wolf and her pups. They have no one to protect them. No alpha male. No pack."

He didn't say anything for quite a while. Anything would be better than the silence. Then as though he knew she was still lying to him, he quietly said, "The wolf is a *lupus garou*."

She narrowed her eyes at him. "I heard the pups. She's strictly a *lupus*, not a *lupus garou*. A *lupus garou* wouldn't have pups in the wild."

"She behaved like one of our kind. I found her trail and followed it to a creek, but then she lost me. And believe me, no female wolf that had been in the area that recently would have evaded me. Except for a *lupus garou* like you. It was as though she had human thought processes, that she knew just how I'd look for her, and she did the unexpected."

An odd sensation tingled through her spine. Long ago, her sister and her cousin would evade each other using the water trick. Not that the ploy would be exclusively known to work for them, but still it gave her a ghostly chill of recognition. That she and her sister, Rhoda, and cousin, Aimée, had used the same device in games of escape and evasion.

Trying to ignore the eerie sensation slipping through her bones, Cassie thought about the times they had chased each other across the river, had made up spooky stories, and—she took a deep breath—talked about the kind of mate they wanted when they were older.

It didn't feel right that she would be the only one of the three girls to ever have a mate. She clenched and unclenched her teeth, then reiterated, "The female I encountered has pups."

"All right," he said, but he didn't sound like he agreed with her. "What if two of them are out there? One, a *lupus* with pups, and the other, a *lupus garou*."

Despite hating herself for it, tears collected in her eyes. She quickly blinked them away, but he took notice, like he seemed to about everything she did or said. "Maybe." She didn't think it could be possible that another *lupus garou* was running around the woods who wasn't part of Leidolf's pack already.

"Unless you're brand new at this business, you have to know that protecting our own kind takes priority over taking care of a feral wolf." His voice had an edge to it, and he was back to being his domineering rather than his accommodating self.

She narrowed her eyes at him. "Not just a feral wolf, damn it." She was unable to see how he couldn't realize how important this was to her. "A mother and her pups."

"Feral wolves still. What were you thinking?"

She fisted her hands against his chest. "Of saving them! What do *you* think?"

Leidolf let out his breath in exasperation. She laughed at herself. Here she was thinking that being with one of her kind, with his pack too, might even be vaguely viable, if he agreed to her conditions. Now she figured he'd just laugh at what she'd propose, and so she wasn't about to mention it.

And then he said the unexpected. "You do realize that your need to save the wolf and her pups has to do with a deeper desire to have babies of your own."

Surprised as hell that he would think that, she sat back for a second. Sure, she'd thought about having her own babies. All of which she attributed to spring and the she-wolf and her litter and Leidolf's pheromones triggering her own, but she didn't need some alpha male reminding her of it, damn it. She didn't even want to think along those lines. Ever. Babies meant settling down permanently. And she *really* wasn't ready for that.

She rose, her knees on the pine-needle bed, straddling him in a provocative way, her head above the king's, and if she had been sporting a tail about now, she'd have it raised high too, showing her dominance rather than subordination to the mighty pack leader.

He took his fill of her, his gaze settling on her breasts, the way she had her legs spread over him as if inviting him in, and she felt her skin blush again. He smiled and then folded his arms behind his head. "Another problem though that I wasn't thinking of. No moon for a while."

"New moon," she said under her breath. Hell, if he saw her shift when the new moon was out, he'd realize at once she was a royal since only they could shift during that phase of the moon. Then he would want her all the more.

She never paid any attention to the cycles of the moon—since, as a royal, she wasn't affected by them one way or another—so she hadn't realized it was that time already. "Fine. Then you look for the *lupus garou* and mate with her. I'll take care of the other wolf and her pups in the meantime."

"Without any clothes to wear?" He shook his head.

"Okay, then I'll stay here while you find the wolves. Just remember to come back for me within a reasonable amount of time with a set of clothes for me."

"As tenacious as you are, I wouldn't put it past you to run off as a naked woman in search of the wolf and her pups." He reached forward and put his hands on her thighs and stroked her skin.

His touch made her wet for him, and she fought lining herself up over his erection and just plain giving in to her sexual needs. "If the other wolf is a *lupus garou*, she's going to be changing back to her human form too. I mean, she probably already has. Then she will be freezing and need our help."

"If she's not a royal." His hands stopped at the juncture of her thighs, his thumbs seductively caressing her inner thighs.

"See? If she is, your problem is solved. She'd be a royal. You're one too. Perfect match." Then she thought of another sticking point. "Oh, except for one problem. You already have another female red lined up." She shrugged, attempting nonchalance when it really ticked her off in a jealous sort of way. "If this new one you're going to search for doesn't work out, you'll have the other choice."

She meant to climb off him, but he grabbed her wrist and frowned. "What other female?"

"The romance writer? Julia Wildthorn?" Cassie rolled her eyes. "Don't tell me you've already forgotten your date with her."

"Julia…" Leidolf's brows lifted in recognition. "Hell, that's Laney and Elgin's doing. Matchmakers, the both of them. How would you..." He gave an evil little grin. "You were snooping at my desk?"

She felt her face heat with embarrassment and tried to recover without showing too much annoyance. "I had to go by your desk when I escaped your bedroom and just happened to see her book open to her very photogenic picture and the note on your calendar. And you had no other books in sight. So what do you think I made of it?"

As soon as she spoke the words, she was mad at herself for explaining any of her actions to him, even if what she said was in part a fabrication. Then she asked the question she was dying to know the answer to and immediately could have kicked herself for asking. "What do you think of her romance books?" She sure as hell didn't want him thinking she cared. Even if she did.

A brief flash of amusement crossed his face.

Then he grew serious. "I don't agree with her that she should be writing them. Too easy to accidentally give real clues about us away. And you never know when people might think she's basing them on real *lupus garous*. That we truly exist."

Cassie smiled, glad he didn't think much of Julia's occupation. Then she frowned. He probably didn't think much of hers either. "Let me go, Leidolf. I'm not in your pack, and I'm not looking for a mate."

"I'm not searching for any other woman. Not when I've already found my mate." Then he released her, and she quickly moved off him.

He was on his feet so swiftly that he reminded her of a wolf getting ready to take down its prey. "You know what I like about you, Cassie?"

"No, but I suspect you're going to tell me," she said, stepping away from him as he stalked toward her. She suddenly realized he was backing her into a corner of the cabin.

"You're quick on your feet, compassionate about a cause—despite my not agreeing with it—sensitive to my needs..." He smiled when she did.

He was sooo arrogant.

"I love how you challenge me with those sensual green eyes of yours, never backing down, not even when you're embarrassed, not even when you know you'll lose."

"You think I'll lose if I become your mate?" she asked as her back bumped against the wall.

He smiled slyly. "We'll both be winners then." He caged her in, his hands against the wall beside her head, his gaze focused on hers, his body close, the woodsy outdoors smell of him tantalizing her, the feel of his body heat welcome. "No, I'm talking about losing...as in arguments. I'll always win."

"Always?"

He threaded his fingers through her hair and then grabbed handfuls as he lowered his face to meet hers. "Always," he whispered, and she thought she would melt right under him, agreeing to anything.

He was going to kiss her, and even as much as she knew she shouldn't allow it, that nothing good would come of it, she closed her eyes and tilted her head up, anticipating his kiss, the hunger, the drive, the fierceness of it. When nothing happened, she looked up at him, a little surprised and a lot disappointed.

He wore the same bigheaded smirk he'd worn before, and she shoved the palms of her hands flat against his chest, meaning to push him out of her way. As muscular as he was, she couldn't budge him. He smiled a little more though. Was he amused that she had revealed how much she wanted him when she had been saying *no* all along?

And then he cradled her face between his hands and kissed her. A whisper of a kiss, so light it was like the feathery touch of butterfly wings fluttering against her sensitive lips, but it was enough to start a slow burn building inside her. Making her want so much more.

That was when she curled her hands around his muscular arms and reached up to kiss him harder. Not really hard, but just enough to remember him by until she had a chance to meet a cute human guy and have a fling for a night. Because after being with Mister Totally Hot and Tempting, she'd have to have her needs met somehow or she was going to burst into flames with unfulfilled desire.

Her kiss against his lips went unanswered. And she felt a little more than disappointment again. Although she figured he was holding back unless she agreed to be his mate. Ransoming his affection. Still, she only wanted a kiss. So she reached her hands up quickly and rested them at the back of his head, holding him just where she wanted him. This time, she kissed him. Only he responded way too much, slipping his arms behind her back between her and the wall, and pressing her against his arousal, throbbing with need.

His lips were still noncommittal, even if the rest of him advocated wanting a whole lot more. And then as she touched her tongue to his lips, he devoured her as if the dam holding back the storm waters broke. Fierce and determined, hot and demanding. And she shamelessly responded, falling under the alpha leader's spell, her tongue tasting, touching, and teasing his, her fingers winding through his satiny hair, her body melting against his—awakened, alive, wanting.

But suddenly Leidolf pulled away, his eyes darkened and clouded with lust. "Hell, woman. If you're not ready to accept me as a mate, don't kiss me like that."

She nearly groaned when he gave her up. "I just wondered what it would feel like to be kissed by someone like you."

He reached for her shoulders, took hold, and rubbed them with his thumbs, his action possessive but loving. "You didn't want to be kissed by just anyone, Cassie. Just by me." His voice was husky and ragged with need, and he leaned his head against hers. "Is your shoulder really all right?"

"Better." This time, she didn't tell a tale. The wound was healing and her shoulder felt better, but even so, she didn't relish using it any time soon. "What if..." She hesitated to ask him the question. She was dying to have him but not willing to go all the way. "What if we just fool around?"

CHAPTER 20

LEIDOLF ARCHED A BROW, HIS HANDS STILLING ON Cassie's narrow waist, not believing what she had just proposed. Fooling around? Nothing more? He fought giving her a satisfied smirk. Hell, she wanted him, and she was willing to go partway. She wouldn't be able to stop at that for long. She had given him just the opening he was waiting for.

"No mating. We could get awfully close to the real thing. Just to fulfill some...primal need," she said, sounding a little unsure of herself.

"Sex without intercourse." He had to know what she desired, not wanting to go too far if that hadn't been her intention. It was killing him not to just lift her up and carry her back to their primitive bed and make her his mate.

"Or not. Just an idea."

Already she was distancing herself. Which he couldn't have.

He slipped his fingers between her legs and stroked her wet feminine lips. "Just this," he said and licked her earlobe. His free hand cupped her breast, his thumb and fingers caressing with a circular motion over the fleshy mound.

"Is this what you want?" He spoke with a seductive hush designed to solicit her surrender. His fingers rubbed her sensitive nub, already swollen; every nerve ending had to be screaming for more. She was ready for him, had to have been for a long damn time, as wet and primed as she was.

She reached down to cup his cock, but he stayed her hand. "I want all of you, Cassie. The sex, the mating, the mate who'll stand with me...waking up with you in the mornings, having lazy wolfish naps with you midday. But for now, I'll give you only what you want."

He wasn't sure he could hold back. Not the way he felt about her. Her hardened nipples, the drenched curls between her legs, and her erogenous fragrance all clued him in that he was the one for her. No other.

He truly craved having her for more than the sex. With Cassie, he wanted to settle down, and he thought he could finally have what he'd been searching for—something that would dissolve his need to find excuses to get away from the pack for his own solitude. He wouldn't need that if he had her with him always.

She reached again for him, but he wouldn't let her touch him. He was ready to burst he was so ready. But forestalling the pleasure made it all the more erotic.

"Here I thought you were so bad," she murmured against his cheek, her hands sweeping down his arms in a tantalizing caress.

"I am," he whispered into her hair, his breath touching her ear, his hands cupping her face. He leaned down to take a nipple between his lips, his tongue quickly teasing the firm tip.

She would have slid down the wall if he hadn't lifted her in his arms and carried her back to their makeshift bedding. "Which is better for your shoulder, Cassie?"

Her voice breathy with lust, she said, "Any way you want to do this."

He cast her a small smile. The way he wanted to do this

was to bury himself deeply inside her and take her for his mate for now and always. But he was fairly sure that wasn't what she meant—although he couldn't help but feel he could push her into wanting him for the long term if he played the game of seduction right.

He meant to have her on her back, resting her shoulder so he could show her just how he could give her maximum pleasure. She quickly changed his plans. She made him get on his back and then she climbed on top of him, her wet feminine lips pressed erotically against his throbbing cock. He knew then that she meant to tease him to death with her seductive charms. He was willing to have her any way he could too.

"Like to be on top, do we?" He reached for her hands, grabbed hold, and pulled her closer.

"I like to be in control of my destiny, since so many times in the past..." She quit speaking, and a painful shadow of her past seemed to haunt her expression.

He wondered what other difficulties she'd encountered to make her distrust a pack so, and he had every intention of dispelling every one of her concerns. "It's hard for me to really get close to you like this, Cassie, without...getting closer."

She twisted her mouth in thought. Her legs remained spread to him, her sweet opening begging for him to fill her, if she'd just agree to the commitment.

She wasn't buying his suggestion, though, so he rested his hands on her legs, his thumbs stroking the flesh of her inner thighs. She spread her legs further, her feminine lips pressing heavier against his erection. He moaned low.

She smiled wickedly. Vixen.

He brushed his thumbs against the feminine cleft between her legs, and she gave a start. He craved having her beneath him where he could suck her sweet nipples and kiss her tantalizing mouth. He wanted to be on top, in control, possessing her, for now. Until she agreed to be his. And then she could have her way with him in any way or at any time she wished.

He dipped his fingers in her wetness and then circled her swollen nub with a teasing touch. She closed her eyes, her mouth open, and a throaty groan escaped her lips. She arched her back and slid against his cock. Then she opened her eyes and gave a little devilish smile. Leaning down, she kissed his forehead, and as soon as she did, he held two generous breasts in his greedy grasp.

But his attention shifted to her soft lips brushing against his cheek, lowering still until she captured his mouth with hers.

Then her hands were on his nipples, her fingertips cajoling them into submission. And her tongue. Sweet God, her tongue pushed his lips open and then thrust inside his mouth like he wanted to do with his cock between her legs.

That was when he took charge and gently moved Cassie onto her back. Her eyes were dark with desire, and she seemed embroiled in the passion of the moment, almost willing to capitulate. At least she appeared that way. Or it might have been a case of desperate wishfulness on his part.

But seeing her on her back, her knees bent, her legs parted for him, her gaze saying she wanted him as much as he wanted her, he hated not fulfilling his primal needs. Still, he settled between her legs and covered her mouth with his. His tongue swept around hers in an erotic, ravaging dance.

His fingers molded around her breasts while his thumbs stroked her swollen nipples, and his heavy arousal pressed against her opening. And then he separated her feminine lips with his fingers and pressed the length of his penis between them like a hot dog sandwiched in a slick bun, sliding against her nub, the eroticism of the friction between them fulfilling his raw need. Although he still wanted to be deep inside her.

Faster, more vigorously he moved, adding fuel to the fire already heating his blood. She gripped his hair and parted her lips. His mouth took advantage of her open invitation. Tempestuous kisses added to the building climax, until her lips wrapped around his tongue and she began sucking. Gently at first, then harder, more rapidly, and he couldn't hold out any longer, his breath coming rapidly, his heart beating at a frantic pace. Slipping his fingers to her nub, he stroked until she cried out, a sheen of light perspiration and a look of sinful wonderment on her face.

He felt the world explode all around him as he came, spilling his seed on top of her. The fault was her own for not allowing him to take the desperate plunge deep inside her where he belonged.

She gave him a wickedly delicious smile, her hands grasping his arms and pulling him down on top of her stomach. "Hmm, you're good."

"Could have been better." He kissed her lips, heard her heart still beating overtime, took a deep breath of the way she smelled fully aroused.

"Nothing could be better," she said and wrapped her arms around him.

Because there was no commitment. But there would

be. He sifted his fingers through her silky hair and kissed her cheek. He thought she'd say something more about searching for the she-wolf, but she didn't say anything else. Instead, she gave a broken sigh and closed her eyes.

"Ahh, Cassie, you are a wonder." He rolled off her and pulled her gently into his arms, still concerned about her shoulder. Another couple of hours of rest would do her a world of good. And him too. Until the matter of two red female wolves running loose in the wilderness could be settled.

When they woke, Leidolf tightened his hold on Cassie. The fire was still blazing in the fireplace, and the cabin still toasty warm. He kissed her forehead and she sighed, a sexy, well-satisfied sigh. He let out his own breath, not liking the options that faced them.

"I'd search for the pair of wolves on my own, but I don't want to leave you here alone."

She didn't say anything, just toyed with his nipple, stirring his compulsion to want her again. It was midday, not the best time for him to be out in his wolf coat searching for the other wolves anyway. And if she wanted to play again...

She slipped her hands behind his head and looked into his eyes. This wasn't about sex, he figured. Something deeper. Another secret?

He ran his hands down her back in a gentle motion, hoping she'd tell him what was on her mind. Then she laid her head back down on his chest, and he feared she'd

decided not to talk about whatever was bothering her. With
his pack members, he often let them speak to him when
they were ready. But with Cassie, he worried that whatever
was eating at her would come between them and she would
never divulge her secret.

"Cassie?"

~~~

Cassie knew she shouldn't reveal the truth to Leidolf, but
she had no choice. If she was to leave this place to search for
the wolf and her pups, she had to be honest, since her previous plan of trying to locate them after Leidolf left her alone
didn't seem to be in the works. She was afraid he'd want her
even more than he did now. She lifted her head again and
gazed into his worried eyes.

"I can change into a wolf despite there being a new
moon out."

He stared at her for a minute as if he was trying to determine whether she was being honest with him this time.
"You're *not* newly turned." He didn't ask a question, but he
sounded incredulous.

She shrugged. "I figured you already had guessed that."

He smiled broadly and ran his hands through her hair
again and nuzzled his face against the strands. "Hell, you're
a royal. That's another thing I like about you. You're almost
as devious as I am when it suits me."

"You left me no choice."

"Good. I would have discovered the truth before long,
make no mistake about it. So we change and run together as
long as you can manage all right with that shoulder of yours."

Sooo arrogant. "With two of us as a target? Wouldn't it be better if we split forces?" Part of her thought it was the best idea, although she really wanted him with her this time. And that scared her. Was she already relying too much on him to be her champion?

"No. I'm not letting you out of my sight. Remember what happened the last time you were out here on your own? It won't be dark for a couple of hours. I'll catch us some fish, and we can cook it over the fire. When it gets dark, we'll search for the wolves."

Which should have been a good thing. The one wolf, yes, with her pups and all. But already, Cassie didn't like that he wanted to find the other wolf so bad. And here she'd never been jealous in her life.

"What about your men? Won't they come looking for us?" she asked, licking his nipple. She swore he groaned a little in response.

"Not anytime soon."

She frowned at him. "You wanted me alone."

"You're the one who ran off. Couldn't have had the royals in my pack shifting, then swimming across the river, and running through the woods after you."

She smiled coyly. "You wanted me alone."

He smiled back and cupped her ass with his large, capable hands. "Any reason would do. Stay here while I catch some fish."

"I need to wash up."

He touched the skin below her wound. "You need to rest a little more before you shift again. You'll be overexerting yourself as is. So after you wash up, I want you to come straight back here and rest further."

Then he kissed her long and deep and hard, his hands on her waist, his body pressed lightly against hers, touching, questing for release. "Let's go." Yet it took him longer than necessary to release her, as if he was trying to think of a way of convincing her to give in to him now. To become his mate. Then he cast her a devious smile, kissed her forehead, and rose from their bed of pine needles to help her to stand.

But something had changed in their relationship, despite her thinking it wouldn't with a hot morning of sex, strictly a one-night-stand kind of affair. He looked at her more tenderly now as he pulled a couple of pine needles from her hair. As if she'd become his mate even though they hadn't mated. As if the pressure was off.

"Afraid the water will be too cold?" He motioned to an old metal bucket. "I could fill it with water and warm it over the stove and you could wash up that way."

"Or I could shift."

Before he could say another word, she shifted. His mouth dropped a little in surprise. No way was she going to bathe in the melting snow run-off in her human form.

He shook his head and opened the door. "No fortitude at all."

She had fortitude but brains too. She dashed for the swiftly flowing creek and bounded in, splashing water all about her and snapping at the droplets with her powerful jaws, unable to control that part of her that came so naturally to wolves—the urge to play when no threat of danger existed.

Leidolf laughed from the shoreline, and she turned to see him watching her, his arms folded across his naked chest, his eyes sparkling with delight.

In that instant, she wondered again if somehow they

could compromise. She could become his mate and experience the best sex she'd ever had as long as he'd let her go to conduct her research unimpeded afterward.

Right. Once he mated her, he wouldn't allow her to leave him ever, just like he wouldn't let her out of his sight now, and they weren't even mated!

—∾—

Leidolf watched the emotions play across Cassie's face as she stood as a wolf in the creek and wondered what they meant. She had an intense way of looking when she was thinking deeply, and he knew it had to be about the two of them. Was it his laughing at her while she played like she was a wolf pup on her first adventure that caught her attention?

He strode forth, the chilly breeze whipping across his heated skin. The woman would be the death of him if he couldn't mate her soon. He'd finally found his royal match, and yet that wasn't all that appealed to him. She could have been newly turned for all he cared.

All he knew was he wanted her like he'd wanted no other woman. His twin sister had been right. Lelandi had said someday he'd find the woman of his dreams and no other woman would do. Despite believing what she had said was utter nonsense, he could see now that Darien, the gray wolf she'd chosen for her mate, could have been her one and only choice.

He took a deep breath of the cold air.

Cassie was every bit of that to him. He wondered what Lelandi would say about it. His mother would be here in a heartbeat, welcoming Cassie to the family before the little red wolf even agreed to be his mate. His wheelchair-bound father would undoubtedly give him a stern look and command that he behave himself where Cassie was concerned or he'd lose her.

Leidolf shook his head. He didn't believe Cassie would want him to be any other way. The problem was more her past, how she'd been living as a loner for so long, certainly not anything to do with him not appealing to her.

He stalked into the creek, headed straight for Cassie. For the moment, he planned to forget the fish. Her gaze remained locked on his, trying to figure him out, to determine what he was up to. He was ready to play with his little red wolf. That was what he was up to.

As soon as he dove for her, she darted away, splashing through the creek. He laughed as he ended up on his hands and knees, the icy water up to his whiskery chin. "You'll never get away from me, Cassie."

And that was a promise. He only had to devise a plan to convince her that what he already knew in his heart was true for both of them. They were destined to be mates.

Warily, she came up behind him and poked him in the ass with her nose. He grinned. "You'll regret that, darlin.'"

He swung around and grabbed for her furred neck, but she dashed out of his path again, and he took a nosedive into the cold water. The chase was half the fun. He scrambled to his feet and ran through the shallower water after her. She grinned at him as she stood waiting for him to close in.

Soon, he hoped, he'd catch his mate and win the game.

—◊◊◊—

Near the river where Leidolf had crossed, Elgin and Fergus talked close by, while Satros sat down on a tree stump a hundred yards away, and Carver stared across the river-bank, watching for any signs of Leidolf's return. He hoped Leidolf would have Cassie under his control and bring her back to the pack soon. The woman was just what Leidolf needed. Too many times in the last several months that Leidolf had been leader, he had run off to take care of pack business miles away. But Carver knew Leidolf had done so in part hoping to discover a mate located somewhere else and return her to the pack to start a family.

Carver sighed. He knew the feeling, the longing, the wanting. He should have been satisfied to have had a mate he'd loved with all his heart who gave him two beautiful daughters. He craved what he'd had with her until the car accident, and he wanted the girls to have a mother.

He narrowed his eyes as he stared in the vicinity of where the red wolf had run through the forest across the river. He wanted to go after her in the worst way, to learn if she was a *lupus garou* also, and to bring her safely back to the pack if she was.

"What are you thinking?" Elgin asked, coming up beside Carver.

"I want to go after them. Leidolf, Cassie, the unknown red."

"The unknown red mostly," Elgin observed.

"All of them," Carver said, not caring if he sounded on edge.

"Leidolf wants to do this alone. He was a loner before he came to us to take over the pack. He needs time away from the pack sometimes to get his sense of balance. Not to mention the little lady is probably a loner also. He needs to be with the woman alone."

Carver walked over to the river, the tips of his boots poking at the water's edge. "What about the other?"

"She may just be a feral wolf."

"Or she might be a *lupus garou*. We won't know until we find her."

Elgin shook his head and folded his arms. "Leidolf wanted us to let the others know where he was. Nothing else. Fergus got that Alex wolf-biologist character off to a motel, two hours farther away than he needed to go, letting him think there were no other ones available due to an antique-car show in the area. So he's taken care of for the time being. We've taken Cassie's truck back to Leidolf's house."

Elgin looked out across the river at the forest on the other side. "The Jag's in the garage again where it will continue to collect more dust until Leidolf tells us to sell it. Evan's there, safe and sound. Sarge is under heavy guard. Not only are Pierce and Quincy watching him, but two other men are also, and they've left the sheriff's bracelets on him until Leidolf returns. So we've done what he asked us to do. And now we either return to the ranch and wait further word, or we stay here and wait for him."

Elgin let out his breath. "Another matter too. Irving and Tynan returned. Irving said they'd speak only to Leidolf about what they had been doing."

Carver spared him a glance. "And you asked, of course."

"You know how they are. They could do no wrong where the former leader was concerned. They don't believe they owe anyone any explanations. I suspect they were up to no good, but I have no way to prove it. They seemed damned rattled that we'd had a wounded *lupus garou* female at the house though."

"Why?"

"Hell if I know. They seemed even more concerned that she'd run away and that Leidolf went after her."

Carver frowned as he stared across the river. He'd never liked the two men, who were always breaking the rules Leidolf had established since he'd arrived. Both had been favorites of Alfred's, and anyone in his circle of friends was to be watched. But Leidolf wanted to give everyone from the old pack a chance if they hadn't done anything like Alfred and his thugs had.

"Hell. Leidolf's the best man we've got for the leadership position. Well, you and Fergus do an excellent job backing him up, but if this Tynan and Irving intend to stab Leidolf in the back, they'll have me to contend with."

"Ditto for us, Carver."

"What about Leidolf? If he needs our help, how can he get word to us?"

"He'll howl."

Carver rubbed his hand over his cheek. "All right, we wait. If he doesn't come back with her by first light, we're searching for them." He didn't care if he wasn't a subleader and not authorized to take charge of the situation. He hadn't wanted the responsibility because of raising his daughters on his own. But he wasn't waiting to search for his leader and the women any longer than he had said. Not when he finally had a decent pack to live with.

CHAPTER 21

NOT BEING ABLE TO CATCH CASSIE AS A WOLF IN THE ICY creek and his skin half frozen, Leidolf shifted. In wolf form, he eyed her with interest, his little red wolf. She stood panting, lifted her head, and snapped her jaws closed, her gaze commanding him to catch her now, as a wolf would.

He gave her his best big-bad-wolf smile back. *Ready or not, here I come.* He ran toward her, sending water splashing out of his path. As if playing chicken, she waited. He was afraid he'd plow right into her, and with his heftier size, he'd knock her over. *Right or left, Cassie? Which way are you going to dodge?*

He watched her eyes, the way she observed him, challenging, willing him to come for her, the subtle way she shifted her body, giving her plans away. Left, he figured. As soon as he anticipated her twisting her body that way in an attempt to escape, she turned to the right. And he missed her. He wanted to laugh. She was his...*all* his.

He nipped at her hindquarter as she dashed out of his path. If she'd been in her human form, he swore she'd be laughing her head off. Then she totally threw him off his stride as she swung around and pounced on him, feet up on his back, head turned to nip at his neck. *Ah, Cassie, darling, you're mine.*

He whirled around and planned a frontal assault, intending to place his forepaws around her neck and challenge her muzzle to muzzle. She dropped her front quarters down in a crouching position, wagged her tail, and smiled.

He smiled right back. Then he sat down in the creek. She had won...his heart, his pack, everything. She rose to stand and then trotted over to where he was sitting and nuzzled his face. He licked hers back. Even though she still might not be able to commit to him forever, he felt the subtle change in their relationship again. Before, he'd felt he no longer had to compete for her affections. She was his. But now, there was a stronger tie. She had enjoyed playing with him as part of the wolf courtship phase, and he didn't think she'd want to totally give him up.

Although he had thought she wanted him to get on with the business of catching fish, he wasn't quite ready to quit playing with her. He rose and she watched him, waiting for what he planned to do next. He walked over to the dry shore and lay down. She still observed him, probably wondering what he was up to. And then he rolled onto his back, feet up in the air, waiting for her to respond. She didn't at first. Maybe a little too intimate for her at this point? Maybe not willing to concede he was baring his throat and underbelly in a way that said he trusted her completely.

Then she dashed out of the water, and it took every nerve he possessed not to get up and ready himself for the onslaught. He wasn't used to baring his vulnerabilities to another wolf. Not as an alpha.

She pounced on his chest and bit at his mouth in a mock fight, and he loved it. He growled and snarled as much as she did, their teeth clashing, her body pinning him down. Or he should say he let her pin him down, because if he'd wanted to get up, she didn't have enough weight to keep him on his back. After a vigorous workout, she lay beside him, and they watched the creek rumble by and the breeze rustling the leaves of the forest around them. Leaving the pack to get away would never be the same if he didn't have Cassie by his side.

She leaned against him and laid her head on her paws and then closed her eyes. He licked her ear but continued to watch their surroundings, ever watchful. And when Cassie woke, she rose, a little stiffly, he thought, and stretched. Then they both raced into the creek to hunt fish for dinner.

He was so busy observing her and the way she focused on the water, watching for a chance to catch her prey, that when she caught one, he realized he should have been fishing too. He loved to observe her in everything she did. She grabbed the fish and raised it up out of the water. The expression on her face said it all. *I have mine... Where's yours?*

Then she trotted back to the cabin, tail and head raised high, ears perked up, fish in mouth. After dinner, he knew exactly what he was having for dessert.

Cassie knew playing with Leidolf in the creek was a very bad mistake. Yet after having the best sex ever, she'd felt on a runner's high. What better way to extend that feeling of power than to play a little? The trouble was that the play had sexual connotations, not innocent in the least.

And the worst of it? She loved Leidolf for participating with her. Since she'd lost her family, she hadn't engaged in recreation with another *lupus garou* in wolf form. She hadn't remembered how much fun it could be. She glanced back at Leidolf still trying to catch his fish in the creek. He looked at her and gave her a wolf smile.

She laughed to herself. Then she headed inside the cabin and set *her* fish in the pot.

After a few minutes, Leidolf headed inside with his fish between his wolf's teeth, the trout smaller than hers. She felt like a lazybones, though, as she rested next to the fire, drying her fur, hoping to give her shoulder a break. She shouldn't have played so hard. Not giving it her all when challenging the alpha male was not her way, but now the injury was coming back to haunt her.

Leidolf dropped his fish in the pot, then came over and nuzzled her face with his own.

Then he shifted into his gorgeous hunk of a human self, water droplets sliding down his smooth skin and clinging to his hair and the shadow of a beard.

"We did too much," he said, frowning as he crouched next to her and ran his hand over her head. "I'm sorry, Cassie. I should have given more thought to—"

Cassie shifted into her human form and rolled onto her back on the pine-needle bed. "Hurry and cook the fish, Leidolf." She ran a finger over his muscular thigh. "I'm ravenous."

A slow, hungry smile appeared on his lips. "Are we still just at the fooling-around stage, Cassie?" He sifted his fingers through her wet hair. "Not ready for the real thing?"

She glanced at his crotch. Already the "real thing" was swelling with interest.

"We'd have to make a deal," she said softly, her eyes focused on his.

"A deal."

She knew he wouldn't like what she had to offer. Already his tone was aloof and his posture stiffened. One didn't make deals with alpha males.

"Like what, Cassie?" He shifted his fingers down her arm in a sweeping, tender caress.

"If I become your mate, I continue to do what I'm doing. Anytime, anywhere, without anyone's interference." Meaning, of course, Leidolf's.

He took a deep breath and let it out in a dissatisfied way. He didn't say anything right away, just continued to meet her gaze. Then he said, "I have a pack to run, Cassie." He continued to touch her in a loving way.

"Yes, I know. And that's why I have to have your assurance that if I was to become your mate, I would continue to do my research."

"And when you're pregnant?"

She twisted her mouth.

"We don't use birth control."

"All right, if I became pregnant, I would stay at home. Only once I begin showing. Not early on."

His fingers stilled on her arm, and he ground his teeth.

"All right?"

"What about after our children come?"

She let out her breath in exasperation. "Leidolf, when they're little, I'll be there for them. When they get older…"

"You're not taking them on hunting expeditions."

She raised a brow.

"Only when they're old enough," he said.

"What age? I want everything ironed out now. I don't want you telling me later that I can't take them with me on my research until they're eighteen or some such nonsense."

Leidolf rose to his full height and folded his arms. "What age then?"

She shrugged and winced.

His brows furrowed, he crouched back at her side. "Cassie, you shouldn't have played so hard. Now you're hurting, aren't you?" He touched her cheek so tenderly she wanted to cry.

No one had cared about her hurting anywhere since her own family had shown concern for her so many years ago. But she couldn't let him sidetrack her on the important issues. "Ten."

"Ten years old? No way. They'd get into all kinds of mischief at that age."

"Why? Because you did?"

He smiled coyly. "Yeah, and since they would be of my blood, I could just imagine the trouble they might get into. Not to mention you probably pulled your fair share of shenanigans when you were that age."

She had, but she wasn't about to let on. She scowled at him. "Twelve then."

He harrumphed. "Sixteen."

"Sixteen? You've got to be kidding. They'd be ready to run the ranch by then. Thirteen."

"Fourteen."

She narrowed her eyes at him. "Thirteen."

"What will our pack members say if they see their alpha female always leaving the pack?"

"Your pack members will live. Just like they've done fine without me before this. And don't you dare take it out on your pack when I leave you in charge by yourself," Cassie warned.

Leidolf sighed darkly and took Cassie's hand and rubbed his cheek against the top. "When you came to rescue me after I'd been tranquilized, you had already claimed me,

Cassie. You rubbed your scent against my face, declaring we were a match, that I was yours. And I declare it back. But a female alpha doesn't set the rules for the alpha male."

Cassie licked her dry lips. Although Leidolf was right, she wouldn't exactly concede his point. "A pregnant one does. Just think of me as being perpetually pregnant."

His lips lifted in an arrogant smile.

"I mean, envision it, not make it true."

He hesitated as if giving the matter serious thought, but he was so tense she figured he wanted to jump in and agree with all his heart right away.

"All right," he finally said, "we have a deal."

His expression was way too satisfied, and she was sure she'd fallen into that rabbit's hole with no way out. She felt as though she were making a deal with the devil, that he wouldn't make the concessions he had agreed to a reality, and an inkling of fear streaked through her. Her freedom was at stake. The oral contract was binding. She'd set out the rules...hell, had she left any important ones out? And he had agreed. Now they only had to consummate the relationship, and it was a done deal.

"You agreed, Cassie. Do you want to eat first or..."

"There can't be any stipulation—"

Leidolf smiled again. "No more clauses. I agreed. Now, eat first or...hell, I'm not risking you changing your mind."

He winked, and she managed a small smile. She'd definitely made a deal with the devil. Whatever happened, she hoped they could work things out to both their satisfaction.

She grabbed his arm and pulled him toward her. This was her fantasy. She was the huntress, and she'd caught her sea god. She licked a droplet of water off his nipple.

He smiled and ran his hands through her hair, his hot, hard body pressed against hers, his legs between hers, just working up to the moment to make her his.

She momentarily forgot about the way his arousal poked against her mound as he covered her mouth with his, tongue thrusting, ravishing, conquering, all-consuming. Like a man who'd been love-deprived for eons. And she craved his rabid touch, enjoyed responding back just as passionately, her tongue teasing and tasting his, her teeth nipping at his lips, her mouth sucking on his tongue. He groaned low, a sound that said she was pushing him beyond the outer limits.

He shifted a hand to her side, his thumb brushing the side of her breast, and his mouth moved lower, sweeping over her throat, her breastbone, and then lower to her breast. His tongue licked the rigid nipple, his heated breath making it even more sensitive as the cool air in the cabin mixed with the wetness. She swept her hands down his back, lower, taking hold of his buttocks and squeezing, thinking back to the way she'd first seen him swimming in the lake. What a great ass. And now? The sea god was all hers. She'd captured him on the hunt, just as she'd intended.

With his mouth latching onto her other nipple, he reached between them and began to rub her sensitive nub, slowly at first. Yet she felt as though he was holding back, as taut as his whole body was, wanting to get on with the real business but wanting to pleasure her first. And it was killing him to do so, his heavy arousal drumming against her body with need.

"Hmm, Leidolf," she whispered, not able to say much else the way he was stroking her, his wicked fingers quickening, rubbing her nub harder, his tongue encircling her nipple, his lips grasping and pulling gently. But his actions propelled her to arch against him, wanting more of his touch, just as she frantically caressed the skin of his muscled arms and back to his delectable ass, wanting to touch every part of him too.

This time, *she* moaned, spreading her legs farther, wanting him inside her...now. The ache between her legs begged for release, for satisfaction, the sexy smell of him, their pheromones mixing like a sensuous wolfish aphrodisiac spurring them on, compelling them to finish what they'd begun. Her actions spurred him on as well; every time she squeezed his buttocks, his arousal jumped. When she licked his shoulder, nipped it, and kissed and then twisted again, arching into him, wanting to scream at him to take her now, he nearly entered her. Almost. He wasn't through torturing her yet with his exquisitely masculine touch.

He reached up and held her face with such loving care and looked into her eyes, his own cloudy with lust, as if asking her one last time if she wanted this, and she knew then that she loved him. She smiled. "If you don't hurry, I'm canceling the contract," she whispered, her voice strangely husky.

"That won't do, Cassie. I told you that you were all mine."

"Then..."

She didn't have time to tell him to do it before he centered himself between her legs, her knees spread and readied, and eased himself inside her. Then he was thrusting fully into her, their bodies joined like two primal beings as one, horny, without reservation or regret, and destined to be. The feeling of exultation filled her as his deep thrusts enhanced the climax rippling through her, a heated wave washing over her again and again. He kept his gaze on hers, watching her expression, the awe, the buildup, the culmination, only leaning down once to kiss her lips.

There was a ragged cry from him and a gasp from her as he came and warmed her inside with the heat of his seed, thrusting still with the last of his power, her own orgasm filling her with aftershocks, and she swore she had to be glowing like the full moon on a clear, cold night, as glorious as she felt.

Still inside her, he slowly moved onto his back and pulled her with him at the same time so she was on top of him, his penis still connecting them like a steel lifeline. She was his, but he was hers also. For the first time in a century, she felt at home. Not here in a cabin with pine needles for a bed. But with Leidolf, her mate and her lover. Who looked to have the kind of stamina she needed in a man.

He was already stroking her back, and she folded her arms over his chest and rested her chin on her arms, looking down at him. His eyes and lips smiled like the devil. "Don't tell me you want to eat now." His voice was still husky with need.

"Something tells me you have something else in mind." Her voice sounded just as intrigued.

"Yeah, Cassie, and I'm not easily dissuaded."

She grinned. "So…what are you waiting for?"

The sexual festivities lasted only another hour when they heard something moving about the forest beyond the cabin. The dark had enveloped the woods, and it would have been time for them to shift and search for the two female reds, but the untimely arrival of unwanted guests gave Cassie's heart a start.

Leidolf pointed to the corner of the cabin where she guessed he wanted her to wait for him.

She wouldn't leave him.

"Cassie," he whispered, "if they're hunters, we don't dare shift. Wrap the mattress around you, and stay out of sight in the corner over there on the other side of the fireplace. If they're trouble, whoever they are, we can always shift and take care of them."

"You can't face hunters alone, Leidolf."

His face dark, Leidolf escorted Cassie to the other side of the fireplace. "Stay," he whispered, and she scowled back at him.

She was *not* a wilting damn wallflower.

Whoever moved around outside the cabin grunted, and Leidolf looked back at Cassie with raised brows. "Bear?" she whispered.

Little squeals of mild distress followed, and Cassie smiled. "Bear cubs and the mother," she whispered. But a mother being protective of her cubs could be dangerous if Leidolf or Cassie ventured outside in either their wolf or human forms.

"Probably smell our fish. I'll cook it once she moves away," Leidolf said, moving away from the door. "After we eat, we can track the female wolves."

"And then?" Cassie asked, tossing some more twigs on the fire.

"I'll need to let our pack know we're fine." He glanced at Cassie. "Your shoulder, is it all right?"

She smiled. "After ravishing me for hours, now you ask?"

His eyes sparkled, and he gave her a devious smile back. But now their relationship had truly changed, Cassie realized. She'd have to meet his family, and even though she didn't intend to stay with the pack always, they were also her new family with problems like all families had. But worse, the niggling fear that Leidolf couldn't give her up when it was time for her to go on her next mission…that was what really bothered her.

Look at what happened when the bear came around.

She watched Leidolf poking at the fish in the pot over the fire and feared the worst-case scenario—he'd use every excuse he could to always keep her at his side.

CHAPTER 22

WHEN THE DAY HAD TURNED COMPLETELY TO DARKNESS, the clouds blocking any hint of stars, Leidolf and Cassie left the relative security of their timber cabin and headed out on their mission of searching for the two female reds.

Leidolf tried really hard not to watch every move Cassie made as she raced through the woods, while she continually stopped to smell for the red wolves and then ran off again. He loved to observe her in her wolf form, the way she moved so fluidly, darting one way and then the other. The way she held her head and tail high, alert, alphalike. The way she concentrated on the mission as if nothing or nobody else existed. He was searching also, but he loved watching her pursuit of the two reds.

She suddenly turned her head toward him, her ears twisting back and forth as she listened for...

Hell, he heard it too. Pups whimpering for their mother. Cassie dug around in a bunch of leaves, sniffed, and then turned. She headed for a thicket of blackberries and shoved her nose into a hole. Pulling her snout out of the hole, she wagged her tail and made a little woofing sound. Tinier woofs responded.

Leidolf joined her and then nudged her face in greeting. He'd catch some fish for the mother. But what he hadn't expected to see was Cassie with a full-blown case of empathy for a mother wolf and her brood. Seeing her excitement at finding the pups made him desire having children with Cassie even more.

With a final glance back at her as she sat near the den in guard mode, he took off toward the river.

Cassie lay near the den, watching over the pups and hoping to see the mother soon. When Leidolf left, she couldn't have been more proud of him. She knew he was getting food for the mother, and for now, he'd let her do what she needed to do, provide protection.

But that was when the real trouble began. She thought she smelled a human. She lifted her nose and breathed in the air. No, two. She froze in place. No, no, no. The zoo men were somewhere close by. She prayed they hadn't seen her or Leidolf. That they hadn't spied the mother wolf.

Then a shot sounded in the woods nearby, and a familiar twinge of pain went through her shoulder as a reminder of the past, even though she hadn't been shot this time. She wanted to make sure Leidolf was all right, but she couldn't leave the pups alone. No matter what, she couldn't abandon them.

Everything was really quiet, way too quiet, and she feared the zoo men were watching her in the woods. She couldn't see them, but she still smelled them. If she took off running and they tranquilized her, they might not ever know the pups existed.

It was a standoff. Her not moving. Them not revealing themselves. Another shot rang out in another direction. Her heart drummed in panic. *Leidolf.* Where was Leidolf?

Before she made out the rest of him blending with the forest, she saw Thompson's blue eyes. He had his rifle readied. He planned to shoot her. She rose. He shouldered his rifle. She turned and pulled a pup from its hastily dug den.

"Holy cow," Joe said, emerging from the trees. "She has a litter of pups."

Thompson lowered the rifle, pointed it at the ground, and smiled. "We're going to take care of you, Rosa. You and the other wolves and your pups." He raised the rifle again and fired a shot.

Cassie cursed Thompson as the dart struck her in the flank. She collapsed and dropped the pup.

"Think there are any more of them?" Joe asked, hurrying with Thompson to check on Cassie, who was lying prone on the ground, the damned tranquilizer quickly zipping through her body.

If she could have, she would have bitten the bastard. She wanted the pups and their mother taken care of, not her!

"No. From the looks of the tracks where we were tranquilized, there were three wolves. Two others besides Rosa."

"Wait," Joe said, lifting her back leg. "She's not nursing. We'd checked her before and found she hadn't had pups."

"Then she's the babysitter. Maybe the sister of the other. Okay, well, let's get them to the cages, take them back to Portland, and have the vet check them out." Thompson poked his hand into the den. "Man, look at this. One, two... three...and four. Two males and two females."

"Hey, so the male we got was the mate of the one who had the pups, don't you suspect? So Rosa still needs a mate."

"Big Red will be happy to learn of it," Thompson agreed.

Cassie groaned.

Then out of the corner of her eye, she saw another red

female and blinked. Aimée? The drug was making her hallucinate if she was now seeing her long-dead cousin.

Thompson turned around to see what she was looking at so hard, but the wolf flipped around and disappeared into the trees, the branches she brushed against swaying slightly. Cassie blinked and dropped her head to the ground. The wolf couldn't be real.

When Leidolf woke still in his wolf form, he smelled dozens of animal smells and realized he was in a cage in some kind of room full of medical supplies and metal exam tables. *Shit.*

He looked around the room and saw a ragged-looking red wolf sleeping off the tranquilizer inside another cage. The mother wolf. No sign of the pups though. Farther over, he saw Cassie in a cage. She was sound asleep too. *Hell.* Were they at the zoo? Probably a holding room of some sort to check them out. Make sure they didn't have worms or other medical problems.

An elephant trumpeted in the distance, the sound muffled. Yeah, they were at the zoo. Damn it.

He sat up and woofed at Cassie, trying to get her attention. Instead, the mother wolf lifted her head, but she was too groggy, and she dropped her head down and blinked at him.

"The female that had the pups was treated for worms," a man said, shoving the door aside as Thompson walked inside with him. "And she had a bad case of ear mites."

"You're awake," Thompson said, observing Leidolf.

"He's a good-looking red wolf for living in the wild, don't you think, Dr. Chavez?"

"Healthy, good weight," the doctor agreed. "Good-looking teeth." He waved a hand at Cassie. "Same with the female. The mother wolf's half-starved though. Can't figure it out. Her mate would have been bringing her and the pups food."

"What if he's not the mother's mate?"

"You said they're the only red wolves you've found. The male and female have to be the alpha pair."

"It would seem so. What about the other? She's of breeding age. Health-wise, can we mate her to Big Red soon?"

"We'll have to put them together and see how they take to each other. In the wild, she wouldn't have had a chance to mate, unless she'd started a pack of her own. Here, if she's agreeable, he's all hers." The veterinarian smiled.

"I think this one's Rosa," Thompson said, peering into Cassie's cage at a crouch. "She didn't want Big Red before. But maybe now that she's a little older, she'll be more interested in him." Thompson stood. "She wouldn't find another red male in the wilderness. She's lucky to have Big Red as a mate."

Leidolf rose to his feet. Hell, they planned on giving Cassie to a real red wolf? And Leidolf was joining the mother and her pups? When his people learned of his being paired off with a regular *lupus*, accused of being the father of the pups…

He shook his head, irritated with himself. He didn't even want to think of what they would say. Not to his face, of course.

"When are you going to let her see Big Red again? Maybe since she's been away from him for a while, she'll be pleased to see a familiar face." Thompson glanced back at Leidolf. "He looks anxious. Maybe we should let him go to his mate."

"As soon as she wakes, we'll move them to a holding pen."

Cassie lifted her head, and Leidolf saw the look of disbelief in her eyes. He felt the same way, only he was responsible for her. How did he get himself and her in such a bind? More importantly, how was he going to get them out of it?

Cassie rose to a sitting position in her cage as Leidolf desperately wanted to go to her, to comfort and protect her.

Thompson rubbed his whiskered chin as he looked her over. "She looks in as good a shape as when we found her last year, despite getting shot."

Someone knocked on the door to the room. A young woman poked her head in. "Pups need their mom. Can they join her?"

As if on cue, the she-wolf sat up. She still looked a little groggy, her eyes a little dazed.

"Let's move them to the holding pen," the doctor said. "Rosa looks ready enough to pay Big Red a visit. Have you got a name for the alpha pair, Henry?"

Thompson rubbed the beard on his chin and then folded his arms as he looked at the she-wolf. "I'll think on it." He turned and observed Leidolf. "Same with him."

The woman had disappeared and suddenly reappeared with a bunch of men. They loaded the cages on carts and pushed them out of the room, down a long hallway, and then to a metal door.

"She goes into the next holding area," Thompson said, motioning to Cassie. "We'll have Big Red join her here once she's settled."

Leidolf thought for the first time since he'd laid eyes on Cassie that she looked really stricken. He wanted to tear anyone to shreds who took his mate away from him, but his human half warned of the consequences. Instead, although it killed him to do so, he behaved himself and held her gaze as long as he could to reassure her, until his cage and hers were rolled into their respective pens.

Inside the room, the walls were metal, the floor concrete. A trough of water sat against one wall. There were no windows, no bars, just a room to get to know his "mate," the supposed mother of his pups, who was already there. And a viewing door, with a nice-sized window.

The men opened the cage doors, and a couple more men brought in the she-wolf's pups, leaving them next to her, and then the men all stood back, watching the reunion. The she-wolf checked out her pups, inspecting them as they eagerly stepped on each other, trying to get to her teats for supper. She was so absorbed in the return of her brood that she ignored the men in the room and the alpha male who stood far away, watching her.

"Something isn't right," Thompson said, his voice low as if to avoid disturbing the wolf family reunion.

Joe shoved his hands in his pockets. "The male should have greeted her and the pups."

If Leidolf had, he'd risk the female tearing into him and upsetting her pups. Best to be standoffish and let the zoo staff sort it all out by themselves.

"Maybe we're upsetting him," Joe said. "Maybe if we leave them alone, he'll join her. Notice the way he keeps watching us? Not her. He doesn't like it that we're in here with her and the pups."

Thompson folded his arms. "Something more isn't right. I can't put a finger on it…but, well, if I were to put it in human terms, it is almost as though he has something going on with Rosa."

Joe's brows shot up. "Well, hell, if that's the case, maybe we should put the two of them together."

Thompson shook his head. "He has to be the alpha male, and the female wouldn't have had pups if she wasn't the alpha female. Look at his stance. Tail high, ears perked up, back rigid, gaze focused on…me. In fact, the whole time we've been speaking, he's been watching me. Even when you spoke, he continued to stare me down."

Joe chuckled. "He knows you're always in charge."

Thompson smiled at Leidolf. "All right. Let's check on Rosa and see how she's getting along with Big Red." Thompson turned, and one of the staff members opened the door. Then the four of them filed out, and Thompson closed the door.

Leidolf didn't take his eyes off the door, and sure enough, Thompson soon looked through the window. Thompson grinned as Joe took a peek also. "See, he's still watching me, almost as if he thought I'd check on him."

"Yeah, we'll have to give them some privacy for a while and then come back later and check on them. But I halfway suspect he'll still be watching the door for danger, or maybe an escape route. Eventually, he'll let down his guard and join his mate."

Not in this lifetime. But Joe was right. Leidolf continued to watch the door. And knew just what he had to do next.

—◊◊◊—

Cassie shook off the tranquilizer's effects and stared at the wolf observing her in an enclosed room. She sniffed the air. He was a male and a red, but because of their genetics, he smelled just like a wolf, as much as she did to him. Which wasn't good. A few times when she'd been with a real wolf pack in her wolf form, some over-rambunctious male had thought to mate her. If it hadn't been for the alpha leader of the pack discouraging the junior males— only one litter per alpha couple in the pack—she might have been in trouble.

For now, she was on her own, which she'd never been before when facing a situation like this. Big Red looked awfully interested. Still, he held back and sniffed the air.

She stood her ground, her back to the door. It was definitely a standoff. Neither moving an inch in any direction, their gazes locked, hers saying stay away, his saying he was already love-struck.

Footfalls headed in the direction of her cell, but she continued to watch Big Red. Whoever was approaching wasn't half the problem the wolf could be.

She wondered how Bella Wilder had handled Big Red. Probably snarled at him to back off. A male wolf wouldn't usually attempt to take advantage of a female if she wasn't willing. That didn't mean he wouldn't keep trying if she was ripe for the action.

The door opened, and Thompson and Joe stood in the opening watching her.

"She doesn't look like she's any more interested in Big Red than she was earlier," Thompson said, sounding disappointed.

Joe added, "She's still wearing the pants in the family."

"Let's switch them and see what happens."

"Are you sure?"

Thompson nodded. "If it doesn't work, we'll switch them back."

―⁓―

As soon as the men took Leidolf in a cage into the hall, he overheard their plans to move him in with Cassie. Even though he didn't want to be on exhibit for the zoo staff, he had to show them Cassie was his mate, not the mother with her pups.

When they rolled Leidolf's cage into the room, Big Red's ears perked up. Leidolf exited the cage and hurried for Cassie. But Big Red made a move toward her, and Leidolf growled low and got in between them.

Big Red bared his teeth, but Leidolf advanced so suddenly, Thompson said, "Holy shit, get one of the males out of here, now!"

Brandishing tranquilizer guns, the men stalked into the room. Leidolf backed off and corralled Cassie against the wall. Hell, he didn't want the men to shoot him and make the mistake of keeping Big Red with her.

She quickly licked Leidolf's face in a show of affection. And again.

"Him. Take Big Red out. These two are together." Thompson smiled. "Hot damn, looks like we'll have more wolf pups soon—if not this year, next for sure."

Joe slapped him on the back. "I swear the way they gaze into each other's eyes, they're speaking volumes in wolf language."

"They are." Thompson motioned to one of the men. "They've been checked out. You can move them into their exhibit."

—⁓—

The earlier nightmare Cassie had worried about when Thompson and Joe first tranquilized her and talked about putting her in the zoo had now come true. A lion roared in the distance, and Cassie snuggled next to Leidolf, sleeping on a bed of straw. How in the world were they going to get out of this mess?

At least they had a pen free of other wolves, and she had Leidolf to cuddle up to. In Bella Wilder's case, her hero had come to her rescue. In Cassie's? Her hero needed rescuing just as much as she did!

Cassie rose to her feet and stretched. Sleeping on a bed of straw was not her idea of fun, even in her wolf form. She'd have much preferred having a dog bed.

As she walked through the faux rock tunnel leading from their cement cave to the outdoor part of the wolves' exhibit, she noted a fingerprint-smudged window for zoo visitors to watch the poor wolves in their cave. It was almost closing time at the zoo, and soon no one would be poking their noses at the window, spying on Leidolf and her. She hoped.

At the end of the tunnel, she peered out. She looked above and all around the opening. And took a relieved breath. No cameras. Thompson must not have had the clout to have them installed in such short order.

Shade trees covered some of the sloping terrain, while

other areas were exposed to the elements. Boulders and mounds were dotted all over the place.

She jumped on top of a boulder and leapt to an even higher one to have a better vantage point to see the layout of the exhibits and plan how they might make their escape.

Behind them, elk were sleeping on sloping terrain covered in grass and other plants. A barn and paddock were located at one end. A chain-link fence between them was the only thing that separated the wolves from their natural prey.

Across the moat, a raised platform, covered to protect visitors from the rain and sun, would provide a view of Elk Meadow and all its inhabitants. That platform, the key to freedom, was where she'd love to be.

She lifted her nose and smelled. Next door, more wolves lived. She stretched her neck, trying to see what she could. Two juvenile gray wolves, both lying on their grassy terrain, watched her.

She headed across the exhibit to an eight-foot wall with a fence on top to keep the visitors to the zoo out of the pen. And to keep the animals in.

From an author's account of the story, Bella had slipped into a moat and then tried to climb out. But once she was in the moat, she couldn't crawl out, no matter how hard she tried. So they must have changed the exhibit since then. Cassie looked back at the elk exhibit. Surely she and Leidolf could leap over the fence in their wolf forms. The height was…about twelve feet. Or…was it taller?

So now what? Cassie glanced back at the den. Leidolf was standing in the opening, watching her. He stretched and then loped across the exhibit to her, hopped up on the one boulder, then higher onto the one she stood on. He licked her face, and the way his fur lay flat, his ears perked up, his tail raised high, he didn't seem in the least anxious or concerned.

She wasn't either. Yet.

Leidolf nuzzled her face as if reassuring her, and she nuzzled him back, letting him know that if *he* needed reassuring, she could handle it. She swore he smiled back at her.

He lifted his snout high, and she knew he intended to call for help. He howled.

How would that aid them? His own people were at Mount Hood National Forest, way too far away.

The gray wolves stood and watched Leidolf. Then the two of them lifted their heads and howled. If she could, she would laugh. Not only did Leidolf have a magnetic personality where she and his people were concerned, but he could draw real wolves to his aid.

Inside, wherever they were keeping Big Red and the she-wolf and her pups, a new pair of howls erupted.

What the heck. Cassie might as well join in the chorus. Throwing her head back, she released her own special one. Leidolf joined in again.

Footfalls ran in their direction. Rescuers? She doubted it. More likely visitors to the zoo who wanted to see the wolves howling and find out why.

Leidolf nudged her to leave the boulder. She leaped down to the lower rock and again to the grassy slope. Leidolf joined her and licked her face, then pointed with his nose toward the cave. He had something in mind.

As soon as they made their way through the tunnel

where a couple of kids raced to see them through the viewing window, Leidolf encouraged Cassie to return to their straw bed. Between the window in the tunnel and another in the "bedroom," she noted a small area where no one could view them.

In the worst way, she wanted to communicate with Leidolf, present an escape plan, and hear what his was. But no way did she want to shift and be caught as the second naked woman found in the wolves' exhibit at the zoo, the wolf long gone, just like before.

Leidolf nestled beside her on the straw and put his head over her back, but from the way his heart continued to beat with steady, strong thumps, it didn't sound like he was going into sleep mode.

He was waiting for the zoo visitors and staff to leave, and then? She was sure he had a plan.

CHAPTER 23

As soon as Alice heard Leidolf howling in the distance, she raced, heart pounding, into her sister's bedroom where Sarah was lying on the bed, reading *Romancing the Wolf* by Julia Wildthorn, headphones piping music into her ears. "Sarah! I was standing on the back porch watching a squirrel scurry up a tree when I heard Leidolf howling. And another wolf too. Then more. Lots more, only I'd never heard the other wolves' howls before."

She slipped backpack straps over her shoulders, prepared for any eventuality. Clothes for Cassie from her wardrobe and clothes for Leidolf from Dad's. Just in case they needed them.

"What?" Sarah asked, her eyes round as she bolted upright and yanked off the headphones.

"Cassie. Maybe it was her howling also. I don't know about the other wolves."

"What are you talking about? Dad said Leidolf went after Cassie in the woods at Mount Hood National Forest. They wouldn't be here."

"I heard them! They were howling for help."

"From nearby? Which direction?" Sarah's mouth gaped. "The zoo," she whispered.

"Yes, the zoo. Come on. We've got to go."

Sarah jumped from her bed and tossed the book aside. "Did you try calling Dad?"

"He's still deep in the forest along with most of the

other men. No phone reception. The women are tending to Felicity's babies. A couple of the men are watching Sarge and those twin brothers who keep causing so much trouble. So we're it. Evan said so."

"What?"

"He's on his way here. Since we live next to Forest Park and the zoo is here, we're the closest ones to the scene of the crime."

"This is not one of your mystery novels," Sarah warned.

"No, it's worse. We're to go to the zoo, sneak around to the wolf exhibit, and scope out the situation." Pulling on a sweater, Alice headed down the hall.

"You've got to be kidding. Dad will kill us."

Alice ignored her sister's prediction of impending doom. They didn't have any choice. "Evan's pickup isn't working, and the only vehicle he still had keys for was the Jag."

Sarah stopped halfway down the hall. "Which means?"

"He's driving Leidolf's Jag. It was the only way."

Sarah groaned.

"He drove it already. He knows to be careful."

"Yeah, and he'll speed all the way here, have a wreck, and be charged with stealing Leidolf's car…" Sarah shook her head and hurried after Alice. "Where are you going? Dad said for us to stay here while he was away."

"When Leidolf is calling for us to come rescue him and we're it, we have to do something." Alice jerked open the kitchen door, hurried outside, and stalked through the backyard. When she reached the rock wall that separated their property on the dead-end street from Forest Park, she climbed over it and slipped through the Douglas firs.

Sarah raced after her. "Forest Park is closed at this hour."

She chewed on her lip and then looked at Alice. "Why did you call Evan?"

Alice smiled.

Sarah groaned again. "I supposed you've been seeing him without any of us knowing."

"He's nice."

"He's trouble. Dad said we weren't to get near him. Besides, the zoo is closed at this hour. We'd never be able to…oh, yeah. We haven't sneaked in there since we first moved here, afraid if Dad caught us… What if the zoo staff catches us?"

"If we get caught, we get caught. We'll just be two teens having a little adventure. Nothing bad."

"Unless we get… How in the world did the zoo people catch them? Leidolf will really be mad. Maybe we can sneak them out without the pack ever knowing." Sarah rushed after Alice. "Aren't we waiting for Evan?"

"He'll park at our house and join us. He knows where to meet us."

"We're not allowed to shift without an adult being present, you know. I mean, we can't shift around a boy when we're not supervised." Sarah blushed. "You know what can happen."

"We're not shifting, Sarah. Just going as humans."

"Promise?"

"Listen, of course I know what can happen." Frowning, Alice stopped and faced her sister. "How do you think Mom got pregnant?"

Sarah's jaw dropped.

Alice began stalking through the woods again, staying away from the human trails and headed straight for the zoo.

"That's not true," Sarah said, her voice rising. "Take it back."

Alice let out her breath. "Sarah, you have to know why they kicked us out of Dad's pack. His uncle was furious that Dad and Mom went off on a hike when they were teens, got lost, stripped, but before they shifted, they got...distracted. After they found their way home, everything was fine, for a while. When Mom started showing..." Alice shrugged and started walking, slower this time.

Sarah didn't say anything for a long time. Then she asked, "That's why we weren't accepted at three other packs? They learned we were a mistake?"

Alice raised her brows. "Don't ever say that to Dad. Of course, we weren't a mistake. We just came...a little earlier than we should have. And it all worked out. Now we're in a pack that accepts us just like we are."

Sarah harrumphed. "How come I didn't know?"

Alice rolled her eyes. "You don't make it a habit to eaves-drop on others' conversations."

"No wonder Dad doesn't want us around Evan. He's afraid we'll end up like Mom." Sarah's eyes grew big. "Has Evan kissed you?"

Alice smiled.

"If Dad finds out..."

"Sarah, I already told you, we won't say anything, and neither will Leidolf. No one ever has to know."

"If we don't get caught. And what about Evan? What if he wants to tell everyone how he helped rescue our pack leader?"

"He won't." But Alice didn't sound as sure of herself as she wanted. What if Evan *did* tell the rest of the pack how he rescued Leidolf? He might. He'd leave Sarah and her out of his rescue version if she asked him to, she was fairly sure. "He won't tell anyone," Alice said with a little more conviction.

"Yeah. Whenever you're unsure of a situation, you repeat yourself."

Alice ignored Sarah, hating when she was right.

They stalked through the woods toward the zoo with another mile to go before they reached the perimeter. What next? They'd have to sit tight until Evan arrived.

"How long do you think it will take until Evan gets here?" Sarah asked.

"Two hours. That's how long the drive is from Portland to Leidolf's ranch. Zoo closes at seven, and probably not much staff will be here after that."

"I wonder how Leidolf got caught," Sarah said again.

"Rescuing Cassie." Alice put her hands to her chest in a dramatic gesture. "True love. Nothing will separate them. The zoo men took her hostage. He came to rescue her, and he got zapped with tranquilizers. That's what had to have happened."

Sarah chewed on her bottom lip. "What if Leidolf got shot first, and Cassie came to his rescue instead? Julia Wildthorn writes how her heroines save pack leaders sometimes. So maybe Cassie was trying to rescue Leidolf and then she got shot."

Alice tried to envision the scenario. "She did try to aid him the first time he was tranquilized."

Sarah nodded.

Alice shook her head. "Nah. Got to be the other way around this time. This time, Leidolf was rescuing her when…"

A branch snapped several feet away, and the girls came

to a dead stop. Her heart racing, Alice listened, trying to identify what had made the noise.

—⁓—

"There," Carver said, catching sight of the red wolf watching them from across the river. Half hidden in the dark woods, her fluorescent eyes shined like a welcoming beacon in the night. It wasn't Leidolf or Cassie but the one they had chased after initially. He stalked back into the woods.

Elgin and Fergus ran after him.

"I'm shifting. She's here for a reason." Carver unbuttoned his shirt.

"I'm going with you," Elgin said.

Carver grabbed his arm before he could begin to strip. "You're in charge while Leidolf's not here. You and Fergus. If I drown, no problem."

"Your daughters," Fergus said quietly, always the voice of reason whether it was wanted or not.

Carver jerked off his shirt. "Right. So I won't drown. Just think of this as delegating responsibility."

"Yeah, but we're supposed to be the ones giving the orders," Elgin said, casting Fergus a wink.

Fergus nodded as Carver paused, his hands on his bootlaces. "What are you waiting for, Carver? Get to it," Fergus commanded.

Carver gave a half smile, jerked off the rest of his clothes, and shifted in the dark woods. Then faster than he'd ever moved before, he raced for the river in wolf form. Although he wasn't sure what he was going to do once he reached the red wolf.

"How come he gets to go after the girl?" one of the other bachelor males complained. Since many of them weren't royals, having had too many human influences in their genetic backgrounds, they had no way to shift anyway during the new moon and would have had to track her down in human form.

"Because I said so," Elgin explained, his voice hard. "While Leidolf's gone, that's all you need to know."

That was all that Carver heard before the sound of the rush of the river filled his ears. He sure as hell wished he could wolf paddle faster than this. He hadn't realized how slow he was at swimming as a wolf, not ever having needed the feat in an emergency. He kept his eyes on the female as she stayed where she was in the woods. Occasionally, she'd look over at the other men as if wondering if they'd come too, but she didn't seem afraid of him. However, once he made it to shore, he suspected she might change her mind and run.

In that case, he would just have to change it back.

As soon as he reached the shore, he shook the excess water off his coat and looked back at the men, who all watched him with great expectancy. Fergus motioned to Carver to fetch her. Then he turned to observe the female. She stayed motionless, her gaze on his. Yet something about her expression told him she was going to make a run for it, her ears slightly flattened, her tail down.

He trotted toward her, sure that if she ran, he'd catch her soon enough.

She dashed deeper into the woods, and he heard the men shouting across the river. "Go get her, Carver. You can do it!"

"She's yours once you catch her!"

"Good luck!"

He smiled, but only because he was catching up, or she was already slowing down. He'd reach her soon.

―――∿∿―――

The last of the zoo visitors were gone, lights were off, and Leidolf lifted his head and then stood. None of his pack members had shown up to rescue them, so it was nearly time for him to set Plan B into motion.

He walked to the area hidden from the viewing windows, only he'd have to stoop once he shifted. Cassie watched him, and he thought she looked a little hopeful that he'd get them out of this bind. He had hoped that Carver's daughters might send word to other pack members about the mess they were in. He and Cassie couldn't wait for dawn to come, which meant the arrival of new visitors to the zoo. And the nuisance of having to wait until dark fell and the zoo closed again.

He shifted and sat down on the rough concrete. Cassie hurried over to join him, licked his cheek, and then stretched before she shifted. As soon as she changed into her human form, he admired her beauty. He would never get enough of it, from her red curls to her milky skin. Silky, sensuous delight. He pulled her naked body into his arms, and she sat on his lap and wrapped her arms around his neck.

"Now what, hero of mine?" she whispered.

He smiled and kissed her nose. "Now it's time to rescue the damsel in distress."

"Hmm, seems you're in the same predicament as me. Your

people are probably in Mount Hood National Forest still, don't you think? Waiting for your return? And the location of your ranch isn't that close to the Oregon Zoo, is it?"

"Carver's girls should be home. They live on the perimeter of Forest Park, close to the zoo. About two miles from here."

"Would he have left his girls home alone?" Cassie asked, cuddling with Leidolf in the cold, damp cement wolves' den.

"Maybe. We'll give it a shot. If the girls were home and heard us, they'll know to call my ranch house and alert whoever is left there, maybe Laney or one of the men. They'll know what to do."

"And if they don't?"

"It'll take them two hours or so to reach us. It's been nearly that long. If we have no word from anyone in a few minutes, we'll do it our way."

"Which is?"

"We'll climb over the fence, although I hadn't wanted us to be exposed in that manner. Too much speculation if we get caught—two more naked people in the zoo? Two more red wolves vanish?" He shook his head. "I had hoped some of our people could have gotten us out while we remained in our wolf forms in the event someone spotted us trying to escape."

"Couldn't we just jump the fence as wolves?"

"Too high."

Cassie sighed. "Bella couldn't manage either."

"The exhibit was different back then. The moat and the wall were such that she couldn't make it out. An elk exhibit didn't border the wolf exhibit at the time with just a fence in between either."

"If we make it out of this all right, I have a question to ask you."

Leidolf tightened his hold on Cassie. "You might as well just ask now. We have nothing better to do to kill time."

She sat quietly for some time, her fingers stroking his arm, the silence killing him.

He finally let out his breath and said what he had to say, even if she couldn't find the nerve to ask her question. "Cassie, you're not a lone wolf at heart."

"I've been one forever."

He dragged his fingers through her hair and held on tight. "You did what you had to do in the beginning as a necessity. But later…" He looked into her green gaze, her spirit drawing him in. "Later, you did so because you were used to being alone."

"I didn't want to lose anyone else I cared about."

"You can't stop that part of yourself from being." He leaned down and kissed her lips, her mouth softening against his. "You can't hide what your heart is truly telling you. That you want babies. You want to be part of a pack. You want to have a family. A mate. Physically, you're very aware of your needs. Psychologically, I feel you're still in part holding back."

"You can't understand. I know you said your sister died, but you can't feel that it was your fault, not like in my situation. I did want to ask you how you came to be a loner though."

He touched his thumb to her bottom lip and briefly caressed it. "I left my family back in Colorado to keep from getting myself killed tangling with the leader who had taken over when my father had become injured. I traveled all over the States until I settled in a cabin in the mountains, far from civilization. But I missed my family and having a pack, their idiosyncrasies, the good and the bad. My father…" He took a deep breath.

"He was injured in an avalanche. His entire pack died. When I arrived here, I saw the troubles the pack was having, but I couldn't fight the ones in charge. Not all of them. It was like living the whole horrible scenario all over again. At first, I fought the notion that this pack needed me. Then I realized they were just what I needed to live again."

He stroked her cheek. "I still love to get away, but pack business takes priority, and I needed that focus again in my life. You study wolf packs because you want what they have—the pack dynamics, the closeness, the loyalties." He smiled and kissed her forehead. "Playing games. You've just been afraid to be part of a *lupus garou* pack. Now that you've found me, you have to realize this is where you belong."

When she didn't say anything, he lifted her chin and looked into her eyes. "Cassie?"

"I'm a wolf biologist."

"Of that I'm well aware." He kissed the top of her head.

"I wouldn't give up my job for anything. The wolf pack that took me in saved my life. Then hunters killed them. Every last one of them. For a price. They were paid to kill them! The pups too. I only escaped by turning into my human form, and then the men caught me. They believed I was a wild child raised by wolves. I was, but not in the way they thought. I escaped them and moved farther south."

She leaned her head against his chest. "I have to show that wolves are not monsters, just survivors like everyone else." She gritted her teeth. "All I could think of was how I could have saved them. They were my second family, and I lost them too."

"I promise you won't lose us also. And I can't afford to give you up either."

"But I'm a wolf biologist."

Which he still wasn't happy about, but he schooled his reaction.

She gently pulled the hair on his arm and looked up at him with tears in her eyes. "I won't give up studying them and sharing what I learn with the world."

He dropped the subject. He didn't want her studying wild wolves and putting herself in danger, despite promising her he'd allow it. "The feral wolves are the only ones you intend to care for?"

She twisted her mouth and then gave a little ladylike snort. "As if you truly believe that."

"I have a pack to run."

"So run it. Nothing will change. Only I'll return and we'll have mind-blowing sex, and then I'll leave to do my studies again."

He sighed darkly. "I have a question for *you*. Did Sarge force you to take him with you?"

Cassie smiled. "Yeah, or he'd rat me out. He wasn't hurt, was he? What about your Jag?"

"The Jag's the former leader's sports car. Nothing mattered to me but that you were safe."

"And Sarge."

Leidolf grunted.

Cassie ran her fingers over Leidolf's chest in a teasing caress, stirring him up. "You talk tough, but if you'd really felt he needed to be terminated, you would have done it. Admit it. You have a soft spot for the guy."

"I would have killed him if he'd harmed you in any way. Or if he'd killed anyone when he was a werewolf hunter. But for his cooperation, he got off a lot easier than the rest of the Dark Angels. You sure he didn't threaten you?"

"If he had, he'd have seen some wicked wolf's teeth. He'll come around. And I suspect you believe he will also."

"Maybe you can help to influence him to settle down."

She laughed softly. "When I left him in the car by himself, headed down the hill? Don't think he'd be happy with me in the least."

"Served him right to mess with my mate." Leidolf tightened his hold on Cassie. "I believe it's time to find our way out of the zoo on our own."

Aimée hoped she wasn't making a mistake, taking the man chasing her as a wolf into her confidence as she leapt over another fallen tree in her own wolf form. She had to let someone know that her cousin had been captured and taken to the zoo. The mother wolf and her pups would be well taken care of. But the man who had been with Cassie needed rescuing too. And this was way over her head. She just prayed the man in hot pursuit of her wasn't one of the villains' friends who had planned to kill her.

"Wait! I won't hurt you," the man shouted from the woods, having changed to his human form. "Are you a *lupus garou*?"

She stopped among a stand of hemlocks as the feathery

leaves brushed her fur and waited for the man to catch up. He appeared in his very naked form, covered in water droplets from the river, his hair dripping wet. His breathing came hard and fast, and he blinked a couple of times as if not believing she was real. He was cute in a hard sort of way. A sturdy jaw, amber eyes that hinted at a stormy past, no scowl, but no smile either.

He definitely appealed on a basic physical level. The way he came after her…she liked that he had guts. His voice too, deep and commanding yet expectant, similar to his expression, intrigued her. She was a lost cause when it came to strong men with needs.

He waited nervously, like a guy on a first date, his hands clenched until he folded his arms around his body. "Are you looking for a pack?"

How she wished she had some clothes to wear. Not that shifting in front of *lupus garous* was a problem when she was a member of the pack, but when not, it was a bit uncomfortable. Plus it was damn cold out.

Hell, she didn't have a choice if she was to solicit help for Cassie. She took a deep breath and shifted.

The man stared at her, stupefied at first, and then finally he said, "You're one of us. I'm Carver."

She kept her arms wrapped around her and shivered. "I'm Aimée Roux."

"Cassie's sister!" Carver hurried forth, and before she could react, he pulled her into his heated embrace, warming her chilled skin.

"I'm Cassie's cousin. Her sister died many years ago. The…the men from the zoo took Cassie hostage. And one…of your men too."

"Leidolf?"

"Whoever was with Cassie."

"Leidolf. Our pack leader. *Hell*. Will you return with me?"

"One of your men planned to kill me," she said. Carver squeezed tighter, and she sure could get awfully used to his heated embrace. "Irving. Tynan was with him," she explained further. "Can you protect me? Keep me safe from them?"

He knew the bastards were up to something, but he'd never suspected anything like this. "Hell, yeah. Shift, and we'll return to the rest of the pack. Looks like we're bound for a trip to the zoo. Not our favorite place."

Aimée shifted from a silky-skinned beauty to an equally majestic red-furred beauty.

Then he shifted. She darted back into the woods toward the river. He took off after her, and when they reached the trees near the river, the men all drew close to the shore, expectant. Elgin wore a worried frown, and so did Fergus. But Aimée held back at the tree line. Carver licked her face and nuzzled her cheek, encouraging her to come. He would protect her at all costs.

Then he trotted toward the river, hoping to hell she would follow his lead. He didn't look back. His pack members all watched her. Then he heard her footfalls on the slippery rocks, and she bumped his left flank, assuring him she was with him on this, that she trusted him to keep her safe. He wouldn't let her down.

"Did you hear that?" Sarah whispered as she and Alice froze among the hemlocks.

Alice breathed deeply, trying to smell who was out here. "Tynan," she responded, her voice hushed.

Their father had warned them that he and Irving were up to no good. But what if he could help them get Leidolf out of the zoo? If she and her sister and Evan botched this, they could be in real trouble. *With everyone.* But if an adult like Tynan was with them, he would be at fault, being the eldest.

Still, Alice was hesitant to call out to him, a sixth sense warning her he was not to be trusted.

Then everything was decided. She smelled a whiff of Irving, the leader of the two men. Tromping at a run in the brush, the two men headed straight for her and Sarah.

CHAPTER 24

TRYING NOT TO RUSH CASSIE ON THE CONCRETE AS THEY crawled out of the wolves' tunnel, Leidolf led the way on his hands and knees and prayed they wouldn't get caught.

She grabbed his foot and wiggled it. "Hurry, Leidolf. I want out of this place." Her voice wasn't panicky or scared; she spoke in a teasing way as if trying to reduce the tension between them.

Loving the way she dealt with their dilemma, he chuckled. "This concrete is rough on my knees. You must have more padding."

She snorted. "I thought you were tougher than that. I'll have to remember you have delicate knees."

"You can kiss them when we're out of here."

"Hmm, and lots more than that. If we make it, someday we ought to revisit that lake I found you swimming in."

"Ready to take me up on my offer?" He hesitated and glanced back to see her expression.

"Maybe. I heard the soil made for a good comfy bed." She smiled at him as he raised a brow at her.

"Or ferns to lie down in, Douglas firs serving as our walls and canopy. Sounds good to me."

"And the Forest Club. I want to go back and dance. But this time, I want to order the plate of roast tenderloin."

"Didn't get enough the last time?"

"You were such a gentleman. Thanks for sharing with me."

He paused. "I had to. If you licked your lips one more

time while salivating over my roast, I would have had to join you on your side of the table and kiss you, right then and there. I didn't think you were quite ready for that. So I shared my roast with you instead."

She chuckled softly. He smiled again.

He reached the end of the tunnel and moved over so Cassie could kneel beside him. "We'll climb out there," he said, pointing to the fence on the north side of the wolves' exhibit. "Looks like one or two more fences beyond that. Once we've crossed all the fences, we'll shift back into our wolf forms, and traverse Forest Park, which is closed now. We can reach Carver's house in a short while."

He took Cassie's face and kissed her mouth long and hard. "We can't get caught, Cassie. No matter what, we can't get caught."

She sighed. "I don't plan on it. All right. Let's do it." Cassie climbed out of the tunnel first and sprinted next to a building and through a group of trees, and then dove at the fence.

Intent on protecting her, Leidolf kept up with her, watching for any signs of trouble, sampling the air for human smells, listening for anyone's approach. At this time of night, Leidolf figured no one would be roaming around the grounds, unless someone thought the red wolves were in danger of being freed again. He smiled wryly.

When he joined Cassie in attempting to climb the high fence, he reached up and gave her ass a boost.

"Thanks," she whispered, struggling to get over the top. "We'll have to bring wire cutters next time."

"Won't be a next time." He dropped on the other side, and then he reached up and helped her to the ground.

They dashed for the next fence and the promise of deep woods and the security of Forest Park, the bugs cricketing in a chorus as if cheering them on. As long as no park rangers caught them running in the park after it was officially closed for the night, they'd make it just fine.

"How are your knees?" Cassie asked, trying to reach the top of the next fence.

"Need some tender loving care."

She shook her head. He gave her another boost. "Ahh," she said. "Watch where you put your fingers."

"Sorry, hand slipped, but someone seems ready for me again."

"Yeah, but this isn't a really good time." She glanced back at the first fence. The gray wolves were watching them from their enclosure. "Hope nobody sees them watching this way and comes to inspect."

They'd made it over the second fence when Leidolf grabbed Cassie's hand and ran full speed for the safety of the forest.

Footfalls hurried toward the wolf exhibit, and Thompson's deep voice said, "I know, Joe. I'm not happy about it, either. The crew to install security cameras won't be here for another couple of weeks. They have to get funding approved, work orders, you name it."

"That means we'll have to do some surveillance. But the word's not going out until tomorrow. If anyone's going to steal them, it'll take some planning and…"

Leidolf continued to race with Cassie through the woods and then pulled her to a stop. "Let's shift. You okay?"

She nodded, her face flushed, her breathing fast. "I get to do a lot of running when I'm around you."

He shook his head. "Running away from me, you mean. This time, we're running together." He kissed her lips again, rubbed her chilled arms, and said, "Let's shift."

"Any second, Thompson and Joe are going to know we've escaped," Cassie said.

"Where are they?" Joe asked.

Cassie shifted and then waited for Leidolf. "Stick close to me, Cassie." Then he shifted and ran off in the direction of Carver's home, his wolf mate by his side.

But this time he meant to keep her safe.

Tynan stood a little way away, while Irving tilted his head to the side and smiled, but the look was pure maliciousness as he faced Alice and her sister. "Your father wouldn't want you girls running around in a closed park at night, now would he?"

Tynan shook his head. "Nope. You belong in bed. Run along now."

"Leidolf's—" Sarah said.

Alice bumped her arm as if she lost her balance. She didn't trust the men, and the girls were supposed to be quiet about Leidolf and his confinement in the zoo.

"We were just taking a walk. Guess we lost track of time," Alice coolly said.

"We won't tell your dad. Run along home now." Irving wasn't much taller than Alice, and the way he considered her—like he'd finally noticed she was not just a kid—gave her the creeps.

She didn't like it that he thought he could boss her

around either. Her father, yes. Leidolf, certainly. One of the other subleaders, of course. But not these men who broke Leidolf's rules all the time.

"Thanks," Alice said, then grabbed Sarah's hand and hurried her back in the direction of the house.

"What about Leidolf?" Sarah whispered to her, trying to keep up with Alice's quickened pace.

"We'll have to go farther around, maybe by the elk exhibit." Alice's phone vibrated, and she jerked it out of her pocket. "Evan, where are you?" she asked, her voice hushed.

"I'm right outside the fence for the wolves' exhibit. But I smelled Leidolf and Cassie beyond the fence. I think they've already escaped. If they did slip out, they'll be headed for your house," he said, his voice low.

"Irving and Tynan are out here."

Silence.

"Evan?"

"Go home. I'm headed that way. Don't stop for anything. Just go."

"Evan, what's wrong?"

"Trust me...just go."

Alice's heart was beating spastically as she shoved her phone back in her pocket. She grabbed her sister's hand and rushed for the house.

"What's wrong?" Sarah whispered.

"I don't know. Evan knows something about Irving and Tynan, but he wouldn't say. It's not good. The good news is Leidolf and Cassie freed themselves and are on their way to our home."

That was when gunshots rang out. Alice and Sarah froze and then dropped to the ground.

"Where is the shooting coming from?" Sarah whispered.

"Directly behind us."

"From where we just left Irving and Tynan," Sarah added.

"But neither was carrying a rifle." Alice listened for any sounds to indicate the men were headed in their direction, but except for the bugs making all their ruckus and the breeze tossing the branches about, no other sounds intruded.

"Then someone's shooting at them."

—◆◆◆—

"I want you to stay in the Humvee," Carver told Aimée as they pulled up along a street near the zoo, with five other pickups owned by pack members parking behind them as they arrived in rescue mode to free Leidolf and Cassie from the zoo.

But Aimée wasn't staying behind. If she could save her cousin this time, she'd be there for her. "What's the plan?" She climbed out of the vehicle wearing Carver's shirt and jacket and his boxers, while he was left wearing his sweater and jeans.

"You're not dressed for this kind of weather, no shoes even," he scolded, trying to convince her to stay behind.

Elgin, Fergus, and the other men gathered around. Elgin offered, "I'll leave a couple of my men with you."

"I'm not worried about Irving if I stay with you," she said, tugging at Carver's sweater.

Elgin sniffed the air. In a hushed voice, he said, "Leidolf and Cassie have already broken out on their own. But Evan's out here too."

Fergus growled under his breath, "He'll be grounded for a year."

Carver hurried to join them with Aimée in tow, joining in on the conversation but keeping his voice low in the event that zoo personnel were in the vicinity. "They'll be headed for my place. Come on. Let's go."

That was when they heard men rushing out of the wolf's pen. Carver and the rest of Leidolf's people stood in the woods quietly listening.

"I can't believe they're really not there," Joe said. "How in the hell did they know the wolves were here already? And free them so quickly? No fences cut that I could see. Just a man and woman's bare footprints. Hell, how could anyone be running around in bare feet in this cold, and why?"

"We'll stop them this time," Thompson said. "They can't have freed the wolf with pups and Big Red too." He paused at the next exhibit. "Gray wolves are still here. The thieves were only after the red wolves. Come on."

"You know what this reminds me of?"

"What, Joe?"

"That Bella Wilder found naked here last year. You don't think they're some kind of cult that runs around naked with wolves, do you?"

Thompson laughed. "Hell if I know. Maybe they didn't think we could track them if they left footprints instead of boot treads. Who knows?"

Carver and the others returned to the vehicles and drove to Carver's home just up the road. The house had large enclosed porches and five bedrooms. It was perfect for pack gatherings when members were in Portland because the house backed up on Forest Park. For once,

Carver felt a pang of sympathy for Fergus having to deal with a son who was too busy kissing the girls to do any real ranching—and now was in as much trouble as their new pack members. Although he remembered being the same way when he was a teen, and he sure as hell didn't want Evan around his daughters because of it.

When he arrived at his home, he did a double take when he spied Leidolf's yellow Jag sitting in the driveway, and immediately he thought of...Evan.

But what was he doing at *his* house? No, they'd smelled his scent at the zoo. He had to have gone to rescue Leidolf.

His girls!

A sickening dread filled him. He'd kill Evan if the girls went with him and anything bad happened to them.

"Did your bullets hit Leidolf?" Tynan whispered, somewhere several yards away from where Alice and Sarah lay still in the ferns.

Terrified, Alice reached for her sister's hand and held on tight.

"I don't think so. He would have yelped," Irving whispered back.

They meant to kill Leidolf?

Sarah shivered, and a chill ran up Alice's spine. They had to warn Cassie and Leidolf. They had to warn Evan.

Alice's phone vibrated in her pocket, but she didn't dare open it for fear Irving and Tynan would see the light from it.

"We've got to reach them before they get to Carver's

house. The pack will gather there as soon as the rest get word Leidolf's thought to be in the zoo," Irving warned.

"I think we should just get out of here. Leave well enough alone. We couldn't find that woman's body, and if Leidolf or any of their men discover it, we're in big trouble. We missed killing Leidolf again. We're going to end up just like Alfred, feeding the worms beneath the earth," Tynan said.

"He took us in, damn it. When no other pack wanted us, Alfred gave us a home and taught us what we needed to know about being wolves. He appreciated us for all that we did for him. That damn Leidolf took over, and if he learns what we've done...hell, once we get rid of him permanently, we can take over. Elgin and the others will never be able to run the pack on their own without having to look to someone else for guidance. And they'll get it. From me. Come on. We're wasting time."

They moved away from the girls, and Alice's phone vibrated again. But the men were still too close for Alice to risk opening it.

Once the men's footfalls completely faded away, Alice opened her phone and looked at her missed calls. "One from Dad and the other from Evan," she whispered to Sarah.

Since Evan was in the woods and in more danger, she called him first. "Evan," she whispered, "Irving's trying to kill Leidolf."

"Lock all the doors. Deadbolt them. You're home, right?"

Tears in her eyes, she shook her head. "No, we didn't make it. Irving started shooting, and we dropped to the ground."

A significant pause followed. "All right. Stay where you are. I'm tracking them."

"No, Evan. Stay away from them."

"My dad called to check up on me when they headed back to town and he could get reception again. He told me Irving and Tynan are to be taken into custody and held at the ranch. They tried to kill Cassie's cousin."

"Cassie's cousin?"

"Yeah, Aimée is her name. Just stay there. I'll call you later."

"Did you tell him about Leidolf and Cassie being at the zoo?"

"No. I figured since they're headed into town, he probably already knew. I didn't mention I was here. Figured I'd get an earful. Especially when he learns I drove the Jag here. I've got to go. Just stay quiet."

"Irving is armed, Evan. You can't risk going after him."

"He might be armed, but not the way he thinks. Keep yourself safe, Alice. I'll call you." Then he clicked the phone off, and the deafening silence stirred her into action.

She called her father. He immediately answered.

"Dad—," she said.

"Where—"

Alice broke in before she got a big lecture. "Irving and Tynan are trying to kill Leidolf. We're in the woods about a mile from home. Sarah and I are keeping still, but you need to save Leidolf and Cassie! Evan's trying to track Irving and Tynan down, but he's going to get himself killed." Unwelcome tears spilled down her cheeks.

"Are you safe?"

"Yes, we're fine. But the others aren't."

Her dad's voice an order, he said, "We're on our way. Stay put."

But staying put wasn't at all what Alice had in mind.

—〰—

As soon as the gunshots sounded in Forest Park, Leidolf's heart leaped, and he prompted Cassie in their wolf forms as he bumped her shoulder to run in a more westerly direction. How did the zoo men locate them so quickly? He didn't think it could be hunters. But no matter what, whoever was shooting at them couldn't keep up at a wolf's pace. Police sirens soon wailed as they headed in the direction of the zoo.

His heart thundering, all Leidolf cared about was getting Cassie safely to Carver's place. The idea that she would get shot again made his blood run cold.

The sirens wailed louder as they drew closer. Thompson and Joe must have discovered that Cassie and he had escaped from the red wolf exhibit. Or maybe the police were after whoever was shooting unlawfully in the closed park.

Leidolf and Cassie were less than a quarter of a mile from Carver's house when the forest came alive with his men—Elgin, Fergus, Carver, armed with a rifle, and at least fifteen others—and a redheaded woman who resembled Cassie, her eyes wide when she spied Cassie. Her sister? Astounded that she had family still, he couldn't be more thrilled for Cassie.

"Omigod, Cassie! It really is you!" the woman said, hurrying toward Cassie with her arms wide open.

Cassie hesitated and then dashed to greet her, jumping at her like she was at play and nearly knocking the woman down.

But while the woman was hugging Cassie, Carver quickly spoke to Leidolf, "My girls are out there. Irving and Tynan were planning to kill you, but my girls are still out there."

"And Evan," Fergus said, his expression both worried and angry.

Leidolf quickly shifted to speak with his men. "Police are on their way. I'll grab a change of clothes. Cassie can stay at the house, and you too," he said to her relative.

"Aimée Roux," she said. "Cassie's cousin."

"Welcome to the pack, Aimée. Carver, lose the gun. If the police catch you with it, they'll suspect you've been doing the illegal shooting." Leidolf shifted back to his wolf form, nuzzled Cassie's face, and then encouraged her to race with him the rest of the way to the house. He hoped she'd be sensible and not want to come with them.

At the house, Carver hurried to get a change of clothes for both Cassie and Leidolf, and once they had shifted and dressed, they met the men in the living room.

"The women will stay here and call us if the girls reach the house before we locate them," Leidolf said. He preferred chasing Irving and Tynan down as a wolf, but he didn't want to get caught that way if the police descended on the area in droves.

Cassie was fighting tears as she hugged her cousin again, but then she released her and gave Leidolf a tight embrace. "Don't get injured. Promise."

He smiled and kissed her lips. "Can't afford to. If the men come this way, don't let them in. Just call us." Then he kissed her again, squeezed her one more time, and hurried outside with his men. Irving and Tynan were dead men.

As soon as Leidolf and the others left, Aimée took Cassie's

hand and led her to the couch. Although she was more filled out, more womanly, she was just as pretty and the way Cassie remembered her. Same light smattering of freckles bridging her nose that made her impish-looking in a sweet way. With her hair curled down about her shoulders, her eyes bright and moist, she was Aimée. Her cousin, as close to her as her sister had been.

"What…what happened to our family was all my fault," Aimée said. Tears filled her eyes as she sat down with Cassie and held her hand as if she never wanted to let go.

Cassie hugged her again, not accepting that their family's deaths were Aimée's fault, but still she couldn't believe that Aimée was really here, not dead as Cassie had thought all those years. "I…I can't believe you're all right. Better than all right, Aimée. But you're wrong about our families."

"No, you don't know what happened. I saw two of the rancher's sons, the Wheelers, stealing from your home while your father was fishing. Your mother was washing clothes at the river with your sister, and I thought you were with them. I heard noises coming from your house, believed it was that pesky raccoon that kept breaking into our places, and went to investigate. I caught the men red-handed, carrying a feed sack bulging with stuff—your mother's treasured silver candleholders and a silver tray that I could see.

"I should have gotten out of there before they saw me. But I was so shocked it wasn't the raccoon that I hesitated. They shot me a couple of times, and I cried out." She looked down at the floor and brushed away more tears.

Tears streaked Cassie's face too. She hadn't known what had preceded the fire, only what she'd seen at the end.

"I shouldn't have made a sound. I should have played

dead. Instead, because of my stupid screaming, your family came running from the river. Your father killed both boys at once, no hesitation, as he found them in the house and me bleeding on the floor. Old man Wheeler must have been in the woods nearby with his other two sons. Probably sent the first two to do his bidding.

"He and his remaining sons ambushed our families. I managed to crawl out of the house and into the woods. My only thought was to escape. I believed we'd all be all right. That we'd heal from our wounds. But later when I came to, I found the houses all burned to the ground, still smoldering."

"It wasn't your fault, Aimée. It was theirs! They were always robbing from all the neighboring houses. They caused our families' deaths. They should have been dealt with long before that. You couldn't have known how it would play out."

Aimée shook her head and hastily wiped away more tears dribbling down her cheeks. "I could barely get around because of my own injuries, but I tore off my clothes and shifted. That was the only way I figured I had a chance to survive. I thought you must have died in the fire too."

"I was with the wolves," Cassie said, swallowing hard. "I was with them when I should have been with my family."

"You would have been dead too." Aimée patted Cassie's shoulder. "We're all that's left of the family. Will you forgive me?"

"There's nothing to forgive, Aimée. God, I'm glad you're here with me now." Cassie hugged her again. "You did nothing wrong."

"When I healed up, I planned to kill our families' murderers. But Wheeler cheated over cards, got into a confrontation with the sheriff, and was shot and killed in the street. His remaining sons got into a brawl with a couple of drunken cowboys later that night. I planned to kill them after they were bodily thrown out of the saloon and began to stumble home in a drunken stupor." Aimée hesitated and took a deep breath. "But I...I lost my nerve."

Recalling how she'd moved silently as a wolf, carefully staying in the shadows of the buildings night after night, following them, Cassie said, "I stalked them for several days right after they killed our family. Then like you, I couldn't do it. I gave up, left the town, and joined the wolf pack. The wolves I lived with were killed later that year. I vowed to help people realize that the wolves deserved to live in the wilderness like we did."

"I should have guessed that if you had survived, you'd go to live with them. But I was sure no one in our family had lived. Then again..."

"What if...?" both Cassie and Aimée said at the same time.

"What if our families didn't all die?" Cassie finished for them both. "You and I didn't. What if some of the rest of our family survived?"

Aimée took her hands and squeezed. "They might not have. We might get our hopes up for nothing."

Excited to think of the possibility, Cassie stood up from the couch and paced. "But what if any of them are alive?"

Aimée didn't say anything right away as if she was mulling over the possibility. Finally, she asked, "How could we hope to locate them?"

Cassie shook her head. "I don't know. I've been published in several magazines. Wouldn't they have heard of me and then contacted me?"

"Science types? Nature magazines? Regional? Would our families have read them?"

Cassie had to agree with her cousin. "The chances would be slim."

"Wait." Aimée stood. "Your mother and mine were always researching genealogy, curious if they could discover how far back our royal lines go. They found a relative in France and two in England, corresponded with them even. Remember? Of course, back then, it took a year to hear from them."

"You…you think maybe if they were still living, they might be researching genealogy roots? They probably have stuff like that online now. Come on."

Cassie and Aimée rushed through Carver's house until they found a computer in an office, but when she turned it on, the access was locked. The same with the computers in the girls' rooms.

Exasperated, Cassie said, "We'll have to do this later." She led her cousin back to the living room, still hopeful they might locate some of their family. "How did you end up here?"

"I teach botany at Portland Community College." She shrugged. "I went from climbing trees when we were young to teaching about them. Well, and other kinds of plants. The nature lover in me, I guess…except I concentrated on plants rather than animals."

"Did you ever run through Forest Park in your wolf form?"

Aimée sighed. "Yeah. I hadn't shifted in eons, but the moon was full, and I'd broken up with a geology professor, and I just had to run as a wolf to get back on track. You know how it is for us."

"He wasn't one of our kind, was he?"

"No, just a lover and friend. *Was* a friend. Then he got the hots for a biology teacher at a high school." Aimée growled at the last.

Not wanting to upset her cousin further with the discussion of her former lover, Cassie asked, "Didn't you know about the pack living here?"

"No. I never ran across them. Not as big as Portland is. And many of them live outside the city limits."

Cassie nodded. "Here I thought it was the she-wolf whose scent Carver and Leidolf had run across in Forest Park."

"No, probably me. But I'd run into Irving and Tynan at a convenience store and overheard them talking about taking over a pack and how they'd picked up a woman who wasn't pliable. They'd murdered her, Cassie. Left her body in the woods. That's when they saw me in a security mirror, listening to them from another aisle. I got out of there as fast as I could, but they followed me. Tried to shoot me, but I shifted and tore off into the woods. After Irving tried to kill me and I saw you, I couldn't leave. Not before I knew the truth. That you were indeed my cousin." She leaned back on the couch and smiled at Cassie. "You took Leidolf as your mate, didn't you?"

"Yes, but only with the agreement that I would continue to do my wolf studies."

"And he agreed?"

"Sure, he had to." Cassie turned to listen to the back door. She swore she heard a noise.

"I believe you've finally met your match." Aimée glanced at the kitchen. "Did you hear someone using a key on the back door?"

CHAPTER 25

LEIDOLF AND HIS MEN COMBED THE WOODS, CAREFUL not to alert Irving and Tynan that they were looking for them.

Carver had tried calling his daughters' cell phones several times, but neither was answering. Fergus had tried Evan's phone also, but his son didn't respond either. Everyone was tense and silent as they continued the search through the forest.

No more gunfire had sounded. Had Irving and Tynan aborted their mission?

Then lights suddenly appeared like specters, filtering through the thick woodland landscape, bobbing here and there and everywhere. And noisy footfalls. Men approaching. Several. No conversation though. Silent.

Leidolf motioned for his men to stop. Either they were police or zoo officials, Leidolf assumed. He figured Irving and Tynan would head out of the area pronto before the police caught them carrying rifles.

"Police!" a man shouted, identifying himself to someone deeper in the woods. "Put your hands up where I can see them."

Hell, one of Leidolf's men was in trouble. Leidolf hurried in the direction of the police officer's voice. "We're searching for three teens, Officer," he called out, hoping he wouldn't alarm the man and get shot himself. "Two men are shooting in these woods, and three of our kids got lost.

When they called to tell us, they heard gunshots and are hunkered down somewhere."

"And you are?" the officer asked, tall, focused, his brows knit in a frown, gun in hand.

"Leidolf Wildhaven. Own a ranch out of the city, but Carver's house is located right next to the park. His twin sixteen-year-old daughters went for a walk, and Evan, Fergus's seventeen-year-old son, went to find them. They may be separated. We don't know. They're not answering their cell phones now though."

"All right." The man called the specifics in to someone else and gave his location, and the place was soon swarming with police.

"We found them," a policeman said, hurrying through the trees, bringing the girls with him.

They broke free and ran to hug their father, their eyes filled with tears.

"Where's Evan?" Fergus quickly asked.

"We couldn't find him," Alice said. "He went..." She glanced at the police officers and hesitated. "We don't know."

"If it's all right with you, Officer, we'll take the girls back to their father's house in case the shooters are still out here," Leidolf said.

After verifying names and addresses, the police officers released them with a warning. "Until the woods are secured, stay at the house."

"Hell, Leidolf, I've got to locate Evan." Fergus tromped back through the woods to Carver's house, looking like he was ready to kill anyone if they said anything more to him.

"You know he'll be all right—" Leidolf said, but then something made the hairs on the back of his neck stand at attention. He wasn't sure what it was—a noise in the distance or just something that set him on edge. "I'm shifting. Take my clothes, Elgin, would you?"

Leidolf quickly stripped and shifted and took off running as if his life depended on it. It wasn't his life he was worried about.

—∿∿—

"They're here," Cassie whispered, smelling the men she assumed were Irving and Tynan. Fear and anger cloaked them, and she and Aimée were in trouble. She pointed to Carver's rifle. "Ammo?"

"Tranquilizer darts."

Cassie frowned.

"He didn't have time to get anything else," she whispered back. Aimée grabbed the sweater she was wearing and started to lift it, but Cassie stopped her.

"I'll shift. You use the rifle."

"But…"

"I could always pin you down, even though you were a little taller than me. You were always a better shot than me. No time to argue." Cassie jerked off the borrowed jeans and shirt she was wearing and shifted.

Aimée turned the TV on in the den, and then they waited to ambush their prey.

Aimée moved to the couch and said out loud, "I love this movie. *Romancing the Wolf*? Julia Wildthorn sure knows how to write werewolves with just the right touch."

Standing next to the door, ready to pounce, Cassie wanted to growl at Aimée's comment. Aimée silently moved to the other side of the door frame, the rifle ready as the movie progressed.

"You're only a half-blood," the man in the movie was saying with an arrogant air.

"So you're a blue blood. Who says you're any better than me?"

A wolf growled nearby, and the man said, "I can shift and fight the threat. You?"

She chuckled. "They won't like my kind of bullets, so lead on."

"You, remain here, where you can look pretty and stay safe."

"I'm a bounty hunter, Seth. I'm paid to look pretty and take risks." She shoved past him and—

Cassie heard the soft footfalls of two people headed down the hall. The floor creaked a little, and the footfalls died instantly.

Growls erupted in the movie, shattering Cassie's wire-tight nerves.

"No!" the woman screamed on the television.

More growling in the movie erupted, and then the footsteps in the hall hurried toward the den again, faster this time, as if the men thought the noise from the movie would drown them out.

Cassie tensed, never having felt this ready to kill but never so afraid, not for herself this time but for her cousin. She couldn't lose her a second time. Only this time could be for good.

The wrong man started through the doorway. The one without the rifle. "She's a wolf!" Blackbeard warned his cousin.

The redheaded man started to come into the room, his rifle ready to shoot, when growling in the movie seemed to echo down the hall. Fierce, angry growling like she'd never heard before.

"Holy shit!" the redhead said, swinging around to shoot at the new threat.

The perfect ambush. Leidolf to the rescue.

Blackbeard grabbed Aimée's rifle, and it would only be a matter of seconds before the much bigger guy would wrest it away from her. Cassie lunged and bit him in the arm, and he immediately let go. He cried out and sank to the floor, his eyes watering, his arm bleeding.

Aimée shot him in the chest and knocked him out, and then Cassie raced into the hall to help Leidolf. He was still growling, his eyes on fire, wickedly large canines fully bared, his hackles raised.

Behind him was Carver, wearing his fur coat too and appearing calm, but she recognized under that controlled exterior, he was ready to continue the fight if Leidolf faltered.

Leidolf's eyes shimmered with contempt as he continued to stare the threat down. Cassie expected him to kill the bastard. He nodded his head in Cassie's direction. Did he mean for her to kill the man?

A gunshot blasted next to her. Aimée had fired the shot. A dart struck the man, and he went down.

It was decided then. Trial between wolves. As soon as the men could shift, when the waxing crescent moon again shone in the night sky and all *lupus garous* could shift between forms.

"We have new problems," Leidolf said to Cassie as they returned to his bedroom at the ranch, but all she could think of was doing more of a search for her family, freeing the red wolf from the zoo, and—she wrinkled her nose—taking a shower to get rid of the smell of the bed of straw that she'd rested on at the zoo.

Aimée was staying in one of the guest rooms until the issue was resolved with Irving and Tynan, who were incarcerated in Fergus's cellar. Fergus scheduled his son, Evan, extra ranching duty first thing the next morning for taking Leidolf's Jag out without permission, for not making sure his elders knew what he was up to, and for taking matters into his own hands.

"Besides the myriad of other problems we have—financial problems and the difficulty with Pierce, Quincy, and Sarge, not to mention Irving and Tynan—we don't have a nurse or an accountant." Leidolf glanced at Cassie hopefully.

"Don't look at me. I'm neither a nurse, nor do I have a head for figures." She started stripping out of her borrowed clothes, glad that the men had brought her truck to Leidolf's ranch so she had the two bags of clothes she'd stashed in there. She still needed to return to the woods to reclaim her backpack and favorite safari gear though. "Do you have internet access?"

He raised his brows at her and began taking off his clothes. "Already planning to leave to study more wolves?" He sounded a trifle annoyed.

She tilted her chin down and gave him a condemning look. He'd better not have a problem with her leaving every time she suggested it. "I might be able to locate some more of my family."

"Oh, sorry, Cassie. I thought…you were getting ready to leave me already."

For an instant, she felt guilty. But on the other hand, she was a touch peeved that he'd try to make her feel guilty. She sighed. Maybe she could hang around for a few days until the situation with Irving and Tynan was resolved and she had time to visit her cousin before she took off. Although she had to meet her deadline with the magazine for the article she was supposed to write, and with the red wolf incarcerated in the zoo, that wasn't happening.

"I'll have everyone working on it to see if we can locate your family," Leidolf added.

She smiled up at him, but before she could kiss him to show her appreciation, he slipped his hand around hers and led her into the bathroom.

She'd expected to find elegance, but nothing like this. White marble everywhere, floors, countertops, and a big, big whirlpool tub. Brass and porcelain fixtures, tile mosaics on the wall of wolves lounging at a lake, and a painting of blue skies and puffs of white clouds on the ceiling.

But the shower really caught her eye. She opened the clear glass door to the shower stall, where the whole back half opened up to take in the cliff-side view of the surrounding woods. A privacy glass door was all that stood between them and the wilderness. Her lips parted as she thought of what Julia Wildthorn's take would have been on this for one of her wild romance books.

"Hmm," Cassie said, leaving the door open to the wild open spaces, and reached down to turn on the hot water.

Leidolf moved in close behind her, placed his hands on her hips, and pressed his arousal against her butt. "Hmm is right, Cassie." He rubbed against her, and she chuckled.

"You ready for something?" She was fairly sure that no matter how hot the sex was, he wasn't going along with her next plan of action—freeing the wild wolf and her pups. But that was her next goal anyway.

The water sluiced over her shoulders and breasts, pouring down her waist and lower as he grabbed a bottle of sweet-smelling soft soap, the refreshing fragrance of tanger-ines and limes heavenly.

He began soaping her up, while she went straight for his package, thick, curved, and ready for action. His member jumped in her hands, and he sucked in a deep breath. He cupped her face with his slippery hands and kissed her mouth roughly, as if he'd been deprived of her affections for way too long, as if he was afraid he'd lose her again soon.

His kiss was anything but gentle—demanding, pressur-ing, conquering. She nibbled at his lips, his tongue, her hands sliding all over his hardened planes, his chest, his waist, his hips. God, he was perfection. Her sea god. Poseidon. Seducer of women, only she was seducing him instead.

Raw passion blazed through her as she wrapped a leg around his, hooking her heel around his own, and rubbed her sex against his thigh.

"You're so wet for me, Cassie, aren't you?" he murmured against her lips, his eyes glazed with desire, his voice rough-hewn, the baritone quality sending shimmers of need racing through her.

"Always," she whispered back, pressing her body tightly against his, rubbing, making every bit of her so much more sensitive to his touch, her nipples teasing the light hair of his chest, her feminine lips caressing his taut thigh, her hip playing with his rigid sex.

He groaned and gave her a roguish grin. She had hunted and captured him and he was hers, for all eternity. He leaned down and slid his hand around her backside, lower until he'd found her feminine lips and slipped his fingers inside. "Warm, wet, and willing."

Her skin felt feverish between his touching her and the heat of the water. Only the cool air from outside kept her from burning up on the spot. He dipped his fingers in deeper, priming her even more for his penetration.

Or maybe *he* had captured her! She meant to prolong the exquisite way he was touching her, stroking her with wild abandon until the slow burn built into a bonfire, the flames flickering heavenward as she neared the peak. Arching away from him, she concentrated on the wicked way he touched her until she exploded with fiery sensations of exquisite bliss. Her body trembling with spent pleasure, she wanted him inside her now. She spread her legs farther apart, rubbed harder against him, and whispered, "If you're done torturing me…"

He chuckled tightly. "*You* are the one who is making me suffer." He lifted her legs around him, pressed her back against the shower stall, and entered her with one swift move.

Heavens above, she was in ecstasy! Her own body still convulsing with orgasm, she tightened her hold on his thrusting cock. Deep inside he plunged, his hands holding her tight against him, penetrating with savage urgency.

With a frenzy not his usual style, Leidolf drove again and again, coupling with the woman he loved, expressing the yearning he had for her that could never be extinguished. With every thrust, he took her for his own, his mate forever.

Her silky skin rode against his, every curve of her body a tactile delight. He tackled her mouth again as she breathed hard, her eyes half-closed with desire. He thought again about boosting her over the fence at the zoo, his fingers slipping into her wet cleft and how hard that had made him, despite their predicament.

The woman was an aphrodisiac for him, no matter where they were or what they were doing. She moaned just as his seed spilled inside her, and for a second, a wicked thought flashed through his mind. Her pregnant, her belly growing with their babies. He groaned as he released the rest of his seed, loving her and wishing she'd never want to leave him.

After letting her down and gently washing her off, he grabbed a towel and began to dry her sweet body, flushed with arousal.

"I wanted you from the moment I saw you," he said, taking a deep breath, his gaze fixed on hers.

She smiled and lifted another towel off the hook and began drying his skin. "You thought I was human."

He smiled. "You loved wolves. That's all I needed to know. If I'd learned what you were, you'd never have gotten away from me." He lifted her into his arms and carried her to the bed, figuring on sleeping for a while, or not. Depended on whether Cassie could handle more loving tonight. The way she was teasing his taut nipple, he suspected she wasn't quite ready for sleep.

Until he heard someone rushing toward his bedroom door. Hell.

CHAPTER 26

HEAVY KNOCKING AT LEIDOLF'S BEDROOM DOOR WAS followed by Pierce saying, "Elgin sent me to tell you that Thompson is here. Elgin told him to come back at a decent hour, but the man insists that if you don't speak with him, he'll get a judge's order to have the place searched."

Leidolf cursed under his breath and set Cassie on the bed. "Stay. I'll be back shortly." Then he yanked on a pair of jeans and tugged a shirt on. Buttoning it, he left the bedroom, shut the door none too gently, and stalked toward the great room with Pierce at his side.

"Sorry, Leidolf. I know you didn't want to be disturbed, but Elgin said if we didn't handle this right, you'd really be pissed."

"It's not your fault. I knew this would eventually come back to bite us in the butt one way or another."

Elgin hurried to meet Leidolf before he reached the great room. "I've got him waiting in the den. But Thompson is here to see you about the red wolves. And that wolf biologist? Alex Wellington? He's with him."

"Hell. That's probably how Thompson knew about us. All right. Warn Felicity and everyone else at the ranch."

Leidolf met Thompson standing in the den and stretched out a hand, giving a firm handshake. Thompson's blue eyes studied him in return, measuring him, categorizing him. Like a wolf would analyze his potential enemy. Leidolf offered a small smile. Despite the guy tranquilizing him, he admired him for wanting to protect the wolf kind. "Leidolf Wildhaven."

"Henry Thompson." The man looked over at Alex.

"We've met. I'm Alex Wellington. Where's Cassie? You said you'd tell me when you located her." Alex sounded irritated, but he would realize he'd lost whatever chance he thought he'd had with Cassie, once he'd learned of Leidolf's claim to her.

"She's sleeping." Leidolf motioned for Thompson and Alex to take a seat on a sofa in the den. "What can I do for you?" he asked Thompson.

"I was told you have some wolves on the premises. *Rare* red wolves." Thompson glanced at Alex, confirming where he'd learned of this.

Leidolf gave Alex a look like he was not surprised.

When Thompson and Alex had settled in place, Leidolf sat down on his recliner, the only piece of furniture Laney had talked him into selecting. As if it was his throne, he was the only one who ever sat on it, even if he offered for others to sit there. They didn't dare.

Pierce and Quincy joined Leidolf as if they were his backup, along with Sarge, who they were still guarding. He'd better keep his mouth shut. Fergus soon joined them also.

Thompson eyed them briefly, probably wondering why Leidolf seemed to need so much muscle. But pack dynamics being what they were, he wouldn't keep his people in the dark about a potential problem. If he had to turn Henry Thompson and the wolf biologist, he would. And his people had to know the reason.

Thompson leaned forward. "Let's get down to why I'm really here."

Leidolf seized the opportunity to turn the scenario around to suit his pack. "You learned we could use your help, right?"

Thompson closed his gaping mouth and sat up a little straighter.

Leidolf shrugged. "A cougar's been killing our newborn calves. Three of them already. We could just take it down ourselves, but we'd heard you were interested in preserving wildlife whenever possible. Elgin was supposed to have gotten hold of you before this, but we've been trying to track down the cougar without success in the meantime."

"A cougar." Thompson was clearly thrown off the wolf trail momentarily. "Elgin didn't say anything to me about a cougar. But I did tell him I wanted to talk to you about the red wolves you have on your ranch."

Well, hell, guess the wolf tracker wasn't so easily misled.

"You're not interested in the cougar?" Leidolf sighed dramatically for effect. "I'd hoped you might find a home for it. I'd rather not have to…" He shuddered. "…kill it."

"So you own rifles, Mr. Wildhaven."

"Of course. Living on a ranch way out here makes it a necessity."

"You wouldn't happen to have tranquilizer darts, would you?"

"Yes. We hoped to take down the cougar ourselves. Peaceably, if possible." Leidolf stretched out his legs. "Who mentioned we had red wolves out here?"

Thompson hesitated to say, as if drawing out the suspense. Then he leaned against the sofa back and waved at Alex. "He finally came forth and said he was the one who found my friend and me tranquilized in Mount Hood National Forest.

Do any hunting out there recently? Maybe searching for the cougar? But hit something else by accident?" He raised a brow.

"Can't say that I have."

"Mr. Wellington said you were out there looking for your red wolf. Called her Red. Said she protected him from two men, and since he's a wolf biologist, he knew it wasn't natural for a feral wolf, so he figured she had to have been someone's pet. As much as wild wolves can be pets. But two other wolves were with her. So where did you say your wolves are on the ranch?"

To Leidolf's surprise, Cassie stalked into the den. He hadn't wanted Alex to see her ever again. And he didn't want her exposed to Thompson's grilling.

She smiled at Thompson, bowed her head at Alex in greeting, and then headed straight to Leidolf's chair and leaned over and kissed him on the cheek. "Did you tell Mr. Thompson about the cougar, darling? How he's killing our poor little calves? I think it's a mother feeding her young. So it would be horrible if she was hunted down and her kits not cared for."

Leidolf pulled Cassie into his lap and wrapped his arms around her.

The look on Thompson's face was strange, as if their actions had revealed something important to him. He rubbed his whiskered chin. "Are you that wolf biologist Alex had been looking for?"

"Cassie Roux, yes. He wasn't searching for me as much as he was wolves for his study."

"From what Alex says, you're from California. Been here long?"

"For a while."

Immediately, Leidolf didn't like Thompson's questioning of his mate. When he gave her body a squeeze to let her know so, she leaned back against him and relaxed, indicating she wasn't concerned about the questions, so Leidolf shouldn't worry. He did worry. Any wrong answer could prove disastrous.

"You wouldn't happen to have known Bella Wilder, would you?" Thompson asked.

She smiled. "I heard about the case. Anything concerning wolves catches my attention."

"You wouldn't have wanted to remove a wolf from the zoo, would you have?"

Still relaxed, she shook her head. "I study wolves in the wild. Caged and human-owned wolf 'pets' don't qualify for the kind of research I do. I study wolf pack dynamics, how they hunt together, act toward one another, the family unit. In a zoo environment, it's not the same."

"So you wouldn't want to see them in a zoo."

She didn't respond.

"She didn't say that at all," Leidolf said, sounding perturbed. She looked annoyed at him for responding on her behalf. He didn't like that she hesitated to respond. It made her sound guiltier than sin. Which he suspected she was when it came to not wanting wolves incarcerated in the zoo.

Thompson cleared his throat, sat taller and folded his arms across his broad chest, and directed his comment to Leidolf. "I believe you tranquilized me and my friend, Joe, when we discovered Rosa injured in Mount Hood National Forest. I suspect that you took off with Rosa, which you refer to as Red. Not only was she one of your pets, but you have a couple more wolves here at the ranch.

And I assume that you freed Rosa and her mate from the zoo more recently."

Cassie stiffened her back, and Leidolf tightened his hold on her, worried she was going to punch Thompson or say something she ought not to.

"Did you know that a wolf daughter killed her mother and a son killed his father while in captivity, Mr. Thompson?" Cassie asked.

Thompson opened his mouth to speak but clamped his lips shut before he said anything, but he seemed clearly surprised.

Cassie continued, "In the wild, wolves live in family units. Eventually, the children move on, start their own packs, become the pack leaders, and start their own families in their very own territories. When they're forced to live in a captive environment, the natural order isn't natural any longer."

She waved her finger at him in a scolding manner. "Let me tell you of yet another scenario, Mr. Thompson. In the wild, the alpha male and alpha female mate. They're affectionate beforehand during the courtship phase. And then she is treated like the queen when she has her pups." She glanced at Leidolf and smiled.

He gave her a smug smile back. "She has to be pregnant first." And getting Cassie that way would only be half the fun.

"I was observing wolves in captivity, Mr. Thompson, where the pack behavior was all askew. A male was trying to mate a female in heat. He mounted her, and she snapped at him, not wanting his attention. His tail and hers were down the whole time. He wasn't the alpha male. Just a horny wolf. The alpha male stood nearby and put his head over the female's back at one point, ears perked up, his tail up, his gaze focused on the troublemaker.

"When the beta male tried to mate with the female again, what did the alpha do? She was trying to get as close to him as she could for protection. The alpha male scooted his rump around her backside some, and the alpha male and female stood side by side while he attempted to protect her. Do you think the alpha male would have accepted that behavior from a beta when they're in the wild? He would have bared his teeth, snapped, and snarled. He probably would have bitten him, pinned him down, forced him to accept his leadership."

Thompson opened his mouth but then shut it again without commenting.

"So you see, they're better off in the wild."

"But that doesn't mean we're taking the female and her litter of pups out of the zoo," Leidolf hastily said.

"I suspect that, deep down, you realize how dangerous it would be for the mother wolf and her pups in the wild without a mate." Thompson almost looked sympathetic about the whole mess.

Cassie sighed. "I agree. She couldn't have lasted without another wolf to help her raise the pups."

"So where's her mate then? The father of the pups? Here? At the ranch?" Thompson asked, and this time, he sounded like he might have goofed and separated a family.

"She's strictly wild," Cassie said. "I imagine hunters killed her mate."

Thompson switched tactics. "How long have you known Mr. Wildhaven?"

"Why all the questions, Mr. Thompson?" Cassie asked, sounding a little taken aback.

"We've never been able to piece together how Bella was left naked in freezing weather in the zoo. And then the red wolf we placed in the zoo pen with a male wolf disappears. But not the male. Just the female. Anyone who likes wolves might have had an interest in removing her from the pen. Particularly if she'd been a pet and had run off."

"And got in your way?"

"She's a rare red wolf." Thompson looked at Leidolf. "Can I see Rosa…Red?"

"She's not here right now." Leidolf stood, through with the interrogation that he should have ended once it began.

"At least whoever stole the two wolves had enough sense to leave the mother wolf with her pups at the zoo for their own safety." Thompson cast Leidolf a searing look. "But what I don't understand is why no one wants to steal Big Red. Why only Rosa and now her mate?" Thompson drummed his thumbs on the arms of the chair and then rose. "Plenty of safeguards will be in place, in other words, lots of security at the zoo, in the event you're planning on taking her and the pups out."

Alex rose from the couch too, the look on his face as he studied Cassie one of admiration and a little longing.

—◆—

Leidolf pulled Cassie close again. She distinctly got the impression he wanted her to leave the situation well enough alone. But the more Cassie thought of the wolf in the zoo, the more she wanted to free her. Not here where there were no red wolves, but why couldn't she live in Alligator River National Wildlife Refuge in northeastern North Carolina where other red wolves had been reintroduced and now lived in family packs?

She wasn't sure if Big Red could handle being out in the wilderness with a bunch of wild wolves, but she hated to leave him alone in the zoo. Besides, just the way Thompson talked about Big Red, the man sounded concerned that the male wolf would be left alone if they didn't steal him also. Or maybe that was just wishful thinking on her part.

"Was Big Red originally a wild wolf or bred in captivity?" Cassie asked.

Thompson's brows shot up, and a small smile touched his lips as if he knew she'd ask and he knew just why too. "Wild, brought in a year ago, shortly before Rosa was captured."

Good. He would most likely adjust back to living in the wild.

"If you're through," Leidolf said, motioning for Thompson and Alex to leave.

"Thank you for your time," Thompson said curtly. When he and Alex headed for the front door as Leidolf walked with Cassie to see their guests off, they heard Felicity's wolf pups whining and woofing.

Hell.

Immediately, Thompson switched direction and headed down the hall toward the guest bedroom she was staying in while Leidolf stalked after him. "You can't go down there."

"I hear...pups, damn it. How could you have stolen the wolf and her pups that quickly?" Thompson glanced over his shoulder at Leidolf, while Alex hurried after them.

"This is private property, and you can't disturb a mother and her newborns."

Thompson laughed. "Newborns? Right." He jerked

open the door to the bedroom where Felicity was staying and stood stock-still in the entryway to the room. Cassie peeked around Leidolf, hoping Felicity and her litter had enough time to shift. With one baby suckling on each breast, Felicity looked tired and annoyed at the interruption.

Harvey held a baby in each arm and scowled. "Who the hell are you? Get the hell out of our bedroom."

"I…I thought I…" Thompson's face was crimson. "Sorry, my mistake." He pulled the door shut and faced a furious Leidolf.

"Should I call the police about an invasion of privacy, or can we settle this right here?" Leidolf asked.

Thompson glanced back at the door. "I could have sworn…" He shook his head and looked at Alex for confirmation, but the wolf biologist looked just as shocked. "Just remember what I said about the surveillance and alarms. They'll be up by tomorrow morning after what happened there tonight," Thompson warned. He gave Cassie a stern look, and she swore he was telling her to take the wolves before she lost the chance to free them.

She smiled. "It's good the wolves have an advocate in you." She took his arm and walked him down the hall, ignoring the way her mate looked like he was about to have a conniption. "I hope you catch that cougar. If you need any help in catching him, I'm sure Leidolf or his ranch hands would be happy to help."

Thompson paused at the front door. "No room for cougars here too, eh?"

"You know how it is. Dog and cat fights." She shrugged.

"You know, Cassie, you sure remind me of Bella Wilder. You're not related to her, are you?"

"Never know. You just never know."

"Yeah, that's what I was thinking." He glanced back at Leidolf. "Thanks for your time. I'll let you know if I learn anything about the cougar."

But Alex finally broke his silence. "Cassie, are you looking for wolves anytime soon?"

"Soon, yes. If you didn't know, Leidolf and I got married."

"Already? It wasn't supposed to be—"

"We couldn't wait," Leidolf said, pulling Cassie into his hard embrace, protecting her from the outsider.

Another strange hint of recognition flashed across Thompson's face. As if it was déjà vu. Someone else, Bella and Devlyn maybe, had acted in a similar manner and made Thompson see the similarity.

"Goodbye, Alex, Mr. Thompson," Cassie said.

"Remember what I said about the security." Thompson headed out the door as Alex gave Cassie one last look of longing.

Fergus hurried to shut the door, while several others joined them.

"Everything all right?" Elgin asked, wearing a worried frown.

"Everything's fine." Leidolf said to Cassie, "We can't free her. She and her pups are safe where they are."

Leidolf slipped his arm around his waist, while Cassie's thoughts switched to just how they could steal her away.

"What if we—" Quincy started to say.

Leidolf's glower shut him up.

Pierce shoved his hands in his pockets, looking like he wanted to offer a piece of advice but thought better of it.

Elgin appeared uneasy. Cassie thought it might be

because he figured this could cause a big rift between her and Leidolf. He was right.

She began to pull away. Leidolf tightened his hold around her waist. "It's late."

She wasn't in the mood.

Laney folded her arms and looked crossly at Leidolf.

If Cassie hadn't been so irritated with him, she would have smiled to see his people's reactions. At least she had their vote of confidence.

"She doesn't belong in the zoo. You know it, and I know it," Cassie said to Leidolf.

"Even if you remove her and take her somewhere that red wolves are, she might not be accepted. She needs a mate and territory of her own."

"Just what I was thinking."

Leidolf let out his breath. "Cassie, if you're thinking of Big Red…"

"I am."

"They need time to get to know each other."

"Here. With all our other red wolves." She gave him a quick smile.

He shook his head. "I just got you out of the zoo. And now you want to go back? They'll be waiting for you, Cassie, and then I'll have to find a way to get you out of jail."

"That sheriff was a friend of yours, wasn't he? You can get him to let me out."

Leidolf ran his hand down her arm, then took her hand and squeezed. "I take it we're not going to get any sleep tonight until we try this crazy scheme of yours."

She took a deep breath. "It's my life work to study wolves.

She doesn't belong there. They breed many of the animals in captivity to keep the zoo's exhibits full, and the animals never know anything else but a life of captivity. She's feral, not the same thing."

"All right, Cassie Roux, little wolf biologist. You are bound to get us into a whole lot of hot water, but what the hell." He looked at Elgin. "You're in charge while I'm... we're gone."

Elgin frowned. "You can't go alone."

"Pierce and Quincy can come along," Leidolf said.

Sarge looked hopeful, but Leidolf shook his head at him. "When you learn to behave, and I don't mean taking my mate hostage when she slips away in my Jag, then you can go on missions like this."

Cassie bit her tongue. She thought maybe Sarge would finally fit in if he could do something positive. Even if in doing so, it was something illegal. Probably the reason he wanted to go along in the first place. But she'd finally gotten Leidolf's okay, and she didn't want to go against his ruling on this. *Choose your battles wisely* rattled around in her brain.

"I'll join you," Fergus said.

"All right. That makes five of us. Let's go, because I want to get some sleep tonight." He gave Cassie one of his devil-ish winks that said he didn't intend to sleep in the least, and she'd better damn well make this up to him.

She was totally ready to, but after they completed their mission.

CHAPTER 27

WHEN CASSIE AND HER TEAM OF SHE-WOLF RESCUERS arrived in the dark outside the second fence barrier to the wolves' exhibit three hours later, she felt both excitement and apprehension. It hadn't been that long ago that she and Leidolf were escaping the place and now, all dressed in black, the five of them—Fergus, Quincy, Pierce, Leidolf, and she—made a motley group.

Everything was so quiet that she suspected a trap. Fergus, Pierce, and Quincy were ready with cages for the wolves, one for each of the adults and one for the pups, while Leidolf was getting ready to cut the wire on one of the fences.

"Wait," Thompson shouted, coming out from behind the wolves' building with Joe trailing behind. "I'll make this easy for you."

Leidolf moved Cassie behind him. "Go, Cassie. Go home. I'll deal with this. Fergus, go with her."

"No, I'm staying with you. I'm just as guilty, and I'm staying with my mate," she said.

Thompson stood at the first fence and took a deep breath. "I knew you'd try to steal her. You'll move her and the pups and Big Red to your ranch first, and then where to?"

Dumbfounded, Cassie stared at him.

"We don't have long. The security team will be here in an hour or so," Thompson warned. "They called and said they're coming early because of other priority jobs they have to complete due to thefts."

Leidolf gave him a wry smile. "You're serious."

"What the hell?" Thompson said, his hands spread, palms up. "You're going to steal them anyway. Might as well do it right. And safely for all concerned. But I want Big Red to go with the family. And I don't want them released out there where hunters might take potshots at them."

"No. We'll move them when the pups are older. To a place where others of their kind live," Cassie said as Thompson opened a secured gate.

They hurried to get the cages to the indoor enclosure where the she-wolf, her pups, and Big Red were staying. Everyone helped to get the wolves into the cages as quickly as possible.

"Joe and I will help you get them to the gate."

"But what if you get caught?" Cassie asked.

Thompson waved a piece of paper. "Forged transfer documents."

"Thank you, Mr. Thompson."

He raised his brows at her. "You made a pretty persuasive argument back at Leidolf's ranch, young lady. We still have the gray wolves for the exhibit, and they came from another zoo, so they're zoo inhabitants through and through. I hope you don't plan to move them. Maybe some day we'll have reds in an exhibit that were born in captivity."

She squeezed his hand, her eyes blurry with tears. "Thanks again."

Then they pulled the cages through the gate, and Thompson locked it again. "Keep them safe. Oh, and we caught the cougar. Litter of five. All of them are happy and healthy and well fed, sleeping in the big-cats exhibit. Seems like a fair trade."

Leidolf thanked him this time, and they all headed out across the woods toward the street where they'd parked a van. After loading their precious cargo, they drove back to the ranch. Cassie finally caught her breath, when Leidolf said, "I don't know how you talked me into this."

Cassie lifted her chin. "She's like one of the pack."

"Just how long are we to keep the mother and her pups and Big Red at the ranch?"

"Until they're ready to begin life all over in North Carolina. Won't the park rangers there be surprised to see the new additions all of a sudden?"

"You're not babysitting them tonight."

"They'll be fine left to their own devices. Do you have a secure place to keep them?"

Leidolf snorted. "Now you ask."

"Yeah," Fergus said. "We have an enclosed building with an outdoor run that'll be perfect. Pierce and Quincy and I can make some straw beds for them for the night."

"Anything else you have in mind to do with what's left of the night?" Leidolf asked Cassie.

"Just collapse in bed and sleep, unless my mate has something else in mind."

"Just what I'd hoped you would say, Cassie."

Once they were home, they didn't sleep at all except for a few catnaps. Cassie felt she was close to being in heaven. The way Leidolf was so attuned to her needs, the way she could turn him on and prime him to such an extent that she drove him right over the edge.

She sighed, loving how he couldn't get enough of her any more than she could of him, and cuddled next to him while he slept soundly once again.

For three days, she tried to fight her compulsion to leave and do her job. She hadn't seen Aimée, but she and Carver and the girls were getting to know one another, and she was happy with that. But the looming deadline for a contracted magazine article was setting Cassie's nerves on edge. She'd never missed a deadline…ever. And she couldn't quit thinking about it.

Somehow, she managed to sleep in between love fests with Leidolf, but after sharing a bite to eat with him and returning to the bedroom where he began mulling over the financial mess the ranch was in, she paced.

"Don't worry about it, Cassie. They'll use someone else's article, and you can send them yours later." Leidolf looked up at her. "Unless you're here to distract me from this so that we can return to that." He motioned to the bed.

She'd quickly learned that when he was trying to figure out finances, it was better to let him stew in private. She knew if she mentioned leaving to him again, he'd stop what he was doing and give her another excuse why she couldn't leave yet. She had to get away.

She folded her arms. "I could just run over to Idaho and do a story on the wolves there."

"No. My mother and father and sister are coming soon to meet you."

"Soon. It could be weeks."

Leidolf shuffled more papers, poked at an adding machine, and watched as the paper rolled out with more numbers on it.

"I could be back long before they showed up."

"We need to take care of Irving and Tynan. Since the new moon has given way to the waxing crescent moon, they can now shift, so we can take care of this business once and for all. Tonight. You need to see that justice prevails."

She sighed deeply. "Fine." And paced some more. She stopped suddenly. "My backpack. I need to return to where I stowed it. It's my favorite outfit for observing wolves in."

Leidolf was frowning as he stared hard at the papers, muttering numbers to himself.

"Shouldn't take long. I'll see you late tonight. Earlier if I find my backpack sooner." She walked out of the room.

She had nearly made it to the front door when Leidolf stalked out of the bedroom. "Where are you going?"

She turned around and gave him an exasperated look. "To the place where I stashed my backpack."

"Alone?" He acted like she was going to take a trip to the moon, solo.

"Yes, alone. Everyone's got work to do. I'm just going to the forest. I'll grab my backpack and return. You're busy with your financial reports and—"

"I'll go with you." He yelled for Elgin. "Cassie and I are going to Mount Hood National Forest."

Elgin came out of the kitchen holding a glass of milk and an oatmeal bun. Fergus appeared with Evan, who was hastily finishing a piece of toast before he had to do his extra ranching duties.

"You're in charge, Elgin. We'll decide Irving and Tynan's fate tonight."

"We've got everything under control here," Elgin said with a very commanding presence, the connotation being that Leidolf and Cassie could stay at the lake as long as they liked.

"Thanks, Elgin." Leidolf took Cassie's hand and headed

outside as Fergus, Elgin, and Evan saw them off. "Do you want to go fishing?" Leidolf asked Cassie.

"Fishing?"

"I saw a huntress at my lake dressed in safari gear, and before I could make her mine, she vanished in a sea of green."

"I saw a sea god dripping with water, but before I could take advantage of him, I smelled my prey, the mother wolf."

Leidolf pulled out the keys to his Humvee. "Sea god? I like that. Much more impressive than pack leader."

"Hmm," she said as he tucked her under his arm, "then I must be a goddess."

"Beyond a doubt." He glanced at Elgin and Fergus. "I shall return, but make sure no one takes my Jag out for a ride without my express permission." He gave Evan a hard look.

"Guess there's no chance of me taking it out for a spin on a date." The alpha teen grinned and bowed his head.

Leidolf shook his head at him. Shades of himself at that age, except Jags hadn't been invented back then.

Inside the garage, Leidolf grabbed a sleeping bag and another bag of camping gear. "Creature comforts I usually don't bother with when I go to the lake, but for my nymph..."

"I get royal treatment?"

He chuckled. "Here I thought you were newly turned, and instead you were a royal."

"Yeah, well, sometimes it's a good idea to play down our heritage."

They climbed into the Humvee and, with as much fanfare as royalty would get on short notice, several of Leidolf's people stopped working to wave at them.

"When the cat's away, the mice will play," Cassie remarked and smiled, getting comfortable in the seat. She definitely hadn't had enough sleep. She glanced at the cloud-filled sky. She couldn't see it, but she knew the waxing crescent moon was headed on its way into the night sky. "Do you think Irving and Tynan are equally guilty in the crimes they've committed?"

"Yes. Even though Tynan's the follower, he's participated just as much as Irving has."

"I've, well, I've never witnessed a wolf fight to the death like that."

Leidolf reached over and rubbed her thigh. "You don't have to watch if you don't want to."

"It's different when the wolf is attacking you. Then I wouldn't have any qualms."

"They'll be attacking, rest assured."

"You won't be fighting both at once, will you?"

"It's the only fair thing to do."

She scowled at Leidolf. "So what will you be trying to prove? How macho you are?"

Leidolf didn't respond, and she realized she'd hit a nerve. "Why would you have to prove anything? You're the pack leader. Everyone looks up to you and respects you."

Then she recalled what Alice and Sarah had told her. That Leidolf hadn't fought Alfred or the others in the pack leadership to free them of the evil. That he'd been too injured even to show up. She bit her lip, hating to have brought it up. Yet if he couldn't fight four of the wolves at once, could he manage two? The other he'd fought had been a big gray. Irving and Tynan were reds, and although they had lived long lives, they still hadn't been born *lupus garous*.

Cassie ground her teeth. Damn.

"You're grinding your teeth, Cassie. Why?"

She clenched and unclenched her hands, trying to alleviate the tension. "You don't have to prove anything to anyone. Least of all your pack. And certainly not to me."

Leidolf didn't say anything. She was about to tell him that she wouldn't stay to watch then. That she'd take off for North Carolina and get to know the packs there before she introduced Big Red and the she-wolf and her pups into the area.

Leidolf reached over and took her hand and squeezed. "Not for the pack, or you even, Cassie. I have to do this for me."

She bit her tongue. Despite his saying that it wasn't to prove anything to anyone but himself, she knew better. He was bound to be top wolf, and settling a matter like this would prove it. Despite desperately wanting to leave so that she couldn't see him injured, she knew he'd want her there, supporting him, cheering him on.

She tried to enjoy the scenery as they reached the turnout where Leidolf parked the Humvee. She attempted to enjoy his hand on hers, the way he brushed his body against hers as they hiked through the woods. Breathing in deeply, she tried to concentrate on the way the earth smelled so rich and full of minerals, the trees fragrant with pinesap, a hint of rain on the breeze. But the impending fight continued to clutter her thoughts.

After a brief search, they found her backpack, and she smiled to see his clothes wadded inside too. "Looks like you planned on making a permanent residence with me a long time ago."

"Yep, suitcase, backpack, home, even zoo pen, any varia-tion." He gave her a quick smile, and she returned it.

When they finally reached the lake, he dropped the camping gear, pulled her back against his chest, wrapped his arms securely around her, and stared at the vista of Mount Hood in the distance. "When I was here last, I wanted to change into the wolf and run all the way to Mount Hood, just for the fun of it."

"But you didn't."

"I got distracted."

She smiled. "I was searching for the red wolf and then found this naked hunk standing in the lake. Totally distracted me from my mission too."

"But in a good way. I only wished I'd distracted you enough that you wouldn't have left. Want to swim?"

"In that cold stuff? As a human?" She shook her head.

"Want to fish?"

"I envisioned something a little more...*intimate*."

"In the woods?" He rubbed her arms. "Or here, by the lake?"

She pulled free, grabbed the sleeping bag, and headed for the woods. "Intimate." She smiled back at Leidolf. "Out here by the lake is more...*exhibitionistic*."

"It's nature, as natural as being here with only wild animals as our witnesses." He pulled the sleeping bag from her grasp and slid his arm around her shoulders. "You have to experiment a little."

"I've never had sex with a man in a shower open to the whole wide world."

He smiled. "See what a little experimenting can do?" He dropped the sleeping bag on the ground, but when she crouched down to roll it out, he crouched behind her, knees spread, caging her backside with his body, his ramrod-stiff penis pressed against her.

She looked back and smiled up at him. "Did you not want to use the sleeping bag?"

He reached in front of her and began to unbutton her shirt. "Whatever you want, Cassie." She could tell by the tone of his voice, thick with desire, he was ready to take her in the ferns, the sleeping bag be damned.

And she loved him for it, for wanting her with such passion that he couldn't control his needs, for wanting only her and no other. "Hmm, well, I'll just roll the sleeping bag out then."

No sense in having to lie on damp earth. But his fingers were stripping away her shirt, and then they were reaching around to cop a feel of her breasts still confined in the tank top and bra. The way he pressed his package against her ass, showing her just how much he wanted her and now, really got her attention. Well, his fingers stroking her nipples through the cotton fabric of her shirt and lace bra did too.

She was already wet with need, the ache building between her legs, her knees spread as she tried to maintain her balance while she attempted to unroll the bag. Even dressed, she still felt exposed and sexy and wild.

Somehow, he managed to slip her tank top over her head and then he lifted her bra, not bothering to unfasten it. He just pulled it up, freeing her breasts, and slid the lacy bra farther until he'd pulled it over her head too and dropped it on the ferns beside them.

"Hmm," she said, ready to forget the sleeping bag, strip

off her shorts, and flop on her back, opening herself up to the sexy sea god.

Leidolf's heavy breathing caressed her neck as his thumbs stroked her nipples, making them peak with his tantalizing touch. She was frozen in time and place, unable to move as she felt him stir against her butt.

"Hmm, Cassie, you would make me give up the world just to have you with me always."

She stiffened a little at his words but then sighed. She wasn't going to change him overnight about this issue. Let him get used to the fact that she had to leave him sometimes to do work. Lifting her butt slightly, she rubbed against his crotch.

He groaned out loud. "Hell, woman, I'm trying to go slower this time."

She chuckled darkly, loving how she could manipulate the poor wolf into having to take her faster and not torture her to death with his slow, seductive strokes. And that was all it took.

Quickly, he lifted her and laid her out on the sleeping bag as if preparing for the final assault. And she was ready.

She lay on her back on the comfy, soft sleeping bag, tugged at her hiking-boot laces, and tossed the boots aside. She reached down to unfasten her shorts zipper while one big, bad wolf tore off his own clothes, his lustful gaze latched onto hers. Before she could wriggle out of her shorts, his large hands were skimming them down her legs and tossing them aside.

He pushed her knees open, gave her one of his more roguish grins, and knelt before her. She grabbed his hand and pulled him against her needy body, loved the feel of his hardness, his warmth, as the cool breeze circulated around them.

His mouth was fully on hers, his tongue plunging between her parted lips, his hands on her breasts, fondling and caressing her into submission. She combed her fingers through his hair, teased his tongue with hers, and grinned when he did.

"My sister said she knew when I allowed Elgin to drive me to Mount Hood National Forest that it had to have been over a woman. Not over any woman, but the one who had captured my heart." He ran his fingers through her hair and looked at her with such longing that she knew he loved her without even saying so.

"She knew I had to be in a bad way, injured, medicated, to allow Elgin to drive and still be insistent about returning to the forest in my condition." He kissed Cassie's lips gently now, not so rushed, his package pressed against her mound, stirring with need. "I always wanted what other men had found in a woman, admired them for winning their heart's desire, and now…" He sighed deeply. "Cassie, you're it. The one who makes me whole."

She didn't. Not really. Not if he still felt he had to fight two wolves tonight. That was when it really hit her. He said he was doing it for himself, but he wasn't. He was doing it to avenge her family. To settle a score with Alfred and his henchmen. To make things right with Cassie. He was doing it for everyone else. Always taking care of the pack, of her. Maybe deep down, he had to settle his own need to be top wolf, but she figured his other needs always would take priority over his own.

She tugged on his hair and smiled. "You really are a big, bad wolf. And all mine."

He grinned again, and she wasn't sure if he liked being her sea god or her big, bad wolf more. She seemed to have lit his fire again, and driven, he reached between them and began stroking her already primed nub, until all she could concentrate on was the way her heart beat hard and his did too, the way they barely breathed as she stroked his skin, slipping her hands lower, until she could feel his tensed buttocks, the way he eagerly licked her nipples, the breeze caressing the wet tips...oh, sweet eroticism.

"Here, let me," she said, wanting to do the same to him, her tongue tickling his nipples, wetting them, the cool air sweeping across them, a wicked grin stretching across his face.

And then his fingers stroked her nub faster, as if the poor man could take no more, and she arched under his ministrations, forgetting all but the pleasure of his touch. The slip of a moon was in reach, so close, so very, very close that she felt she could touch it with her fingertips, when the tidal wave hit her, propelled by the moon and the wolf, filling her with luscious tremors of climax. But before she could sink into exhaustion, he filled her with his thick shaft, thrusting deeply.

Their kisses renewed, she probed his mouth and then sucked on his tongue, making him moan low. So now who was the big, bad wolf?

And then he came, her actions making him capitulate so much faster. She loved making him lose control. Showing him who really was in charge when it mattered.

The warm seed filled her inside, carried by the wave of climax still trembling through her. He sank against her, spent, satiated, totally satisfied. He rolled onto his back into the ferns and dragged her with him. She cuddled against his body, pulling the sleeping bag over to cover them. On the spring day drifting toward night, they slept, a man and a woman, two wolves mated for life, enjoying the beauty of nature.

Except that the threat of the fight later that night still loomed.

―――

When Leidolf managed to open his eyes much later, he yawned and stroked Cassie's silky back. He imagined she'd want to swim as a wolf to clean up, and that was the best way for them to fish. Getting in some wolf play at the same time appealed.

What he didn't want to think about right now was returning to the ranch and dealing with Irving and Tynan. But the time was coming, and if he wanted to spend more time with Cassie, he needed to get the ball rolling.

"Cassie?"

"Hmm," she said and swept her fingers down his waist.

"Hungry?"

"Hmm-hmm. Go fetch us some fish."

He chuckled. "You catch bigger ones than I do."

She groaned and pushed the hair out of her face. "You're only saying that because you want me to work also."

"As wolves, right?"

"You're not getting me in that water unless I'm in my fur coat." She slid off him and smiled.

God, she was beautiful. He rose to his feet and kissed her lips. "I thought we could play a bit as wolves, but if you'd rather do something else…"

She chuckled. "I'd never get fed at that rate." She pulled

away and stretched her arms over her head, and before he could blink twice, she was a wolf, racing off to the lake.

He soon followed, figuring to skip dinner. He was ready to play first. They splashed through the water, nipping at the spray, chasing each other back and forth until Cassie suddenly stopped and stared at the woods.

Her hackles instantly raised. Leidolf jerked around to see what concerned her, expecting the bear with cubs or another cougar. He never expected to see the wolves, one red and one black, loping toward them, their eyes hard, their ears slightly flattened.

Irving and Tynan. How in the hell had they gotten loose? That meant someone was either dead or injured back at the ranch.

CHAPTER 28

IRVING WAS THE LEADER WHERE TYNAN WAS concerned, so Leidolf leapt at him out of the lake, no running, no hesitation, no warning. With two of them to face, he couldn't allow either of them to get the best of him and kill Cassie.

As soon as he pounced on a startled Irving, who attempted to scurry out of Leidolf's path to no avail, Tynan raced after Cassie. A distraction, Leidolf thought. To attempt to get him to stop the assault on his cousin. Shit, Irving was by far the smaller wolf. The leader, yes, but Tynan was bigger and could easily kill Cassie.

After knocking Irving down, Leidolf whipped around and chased after Tynan, who was still trying to catch Cassie. She was smart, knowing that the wolf would kill her if he caught her. And she was quick. Damn quick. He couldn't be more proud of her.

But for all Tynan's bulk and the injury Cassie had inflicted on his arm at Carver's house, the black wolf was fast too. And he was catching up to Cassie. Before Leidolf could reach Tynan, Irving attacked his back, biting hard. Leidolf stumbled. If he'd been prepared for Irving's attack from the rear, he could have handled it better. But his action put Cassie at further risk.

Furious, Leidolf lashed out at Irving, teeth flashing, hair standing on end, all his actions making him appear bigger and more threatening. He didn't need appearances.

Standing on his back legs, his front legs landed on Irving's shoulders as the shorter wolf struggled to stand and fight against Leidolf's fury.

Their teeth clashed. Leidolf tasted blood, his and the other wolf's. But before he could swing his head around Irving's to get a good grip on the other wolf's throat as the feisty wolf twisted his head back and forth to prevent Leidolf, Cassie yelped.

His heart in his throat, Leidolf gave up on Irving and whipped around to take care of the threat to his mate. He wouldn't let Irving distract him again.

Cassie was cornered among a cluster of rocks, baring her teeth and snarling, but no matter how bravely she postured, she couldn't win against the bigger wolf.

Leidolf lunged at the black wolf as Irving dove for Leidolf. Cassie ducked her head, rather than attempt a futile stand to fight Tynan, and bit him in the chest as Leidolf jumped at his back.

Tynan turned in the confined space and tried to defend himself against a wolf his own size, although Leidolf had much more experience fighting a man, wolf to wolf. Nothing like Tynan's usual fare, beating up on a female wolf or killing with a gun.

That was Leidolf's advantage. Age-old experience in wolf fighting.

Cassie was squished up against the rocks as Leidolf struggled to get a fatal hold on the black wolf. At least neither of the wolves could attack her for now.

She wasn't passively watching either. As Leidolf and Tynan's killer canines snapped at each other while they did their deadly waltz, front legs on each other's shoulders, prancing back and forth, Cassie bit Tynan. Hard. Had to have hurt, the way he howled. The way he pulled away from Leidolf. The way he attempted to whip around to kill Cassie for whatever she'd done.

In the meantime, Irving had mysteriously disappeared behind Leidolf, who'd been expecting another cowardly rear assault when he heard snarling from close by. Irving's and...hell, Evan's.

Irving yelped, and then Evan did.

Leidolf bit Tynan's backside, once, twice as the black wolf kept trying to bite Cassie. She was crouched low now, unable to move in any direction, her eyes flashing with anger, probably more at herself than at Tynan for getting herself in such a predicament.

Leidolf bit into Tynan's butt again, and the black wolf flipped around, too angry to watch his throat. Leidolf grabbed hold and crushed it, letting go to see the wolf draw his last breaths.

For a split second, Leidolf looked at Cassie, who was standing straighter now that she had some room to maneuver, but her shoulder was bloodied. Then he whipped around to take care of Irving before he killed Evan.

Evan was a wiry kid and taller than Irving. But he didn't have the stockiness that Irving did. As soon as Irving saw Leidolf coming, Evan fatally attacked him. The kill quick and painless, Irving collapsed and expired.

That was when the wound on Leidolf's back stung as the breeze whipped across it, and Cassie limped to join him. He nuzzled her face. They joined Evan, who looked proud with his ears perked and tail raised high but quickly lowered them to show his contriteness for being here without anyone's permission.

Cassie walked over and licked his face, praising him for a job well done. Evan's ears perked a bit until he looked at Leidolf, and then they drooped a little again.

Leidolf joined them, nudged Cassie to follow his lead, and the two returned to their clothes in the woods. After shifting, they helped each other to dress. Cassie's shoulder was bloodied, and Leidolf's back hurt like the devil. So much for making love for a little while.

They returned to Evan, and Cassie checked him over. "His ear's torn, but I'd say he got away without too much of a scrape."

They heard movement in the woods and then shouts. "It's Elgin, Leidolf! Are you all right?" Elgin shouted, still at some distance before they could see him.

"We're all right!"

Elgin, Carver, Fergus, and a handful of other men rushed out of the forest with rifles. Fergus's mouth dropped when he saw Evan in his wolf coat, bloodied, and Irving at his feet. "Damn, Evan, didn't Leidolf tell you not to take that Jag out for another spin?"

"He had another really important date," Cassie said, slipping underneath Leidolf's arm.

Elgin motioned to the other men. "Get their bodies. Bury them in the woods. Are you all right? Hell, Fergus went to take the last meal down to Irving and Tynan and had a two-man guard escort, Pierce and Quincy. Irving and Tynan had shifted. They tore up our other men and knocked Fergus out. By the time Fergus came to and raised the alarm, it had been several hours."

"Are Pierce and Quincy going to be all right?" Cassie asked.

"Yeah. They wanted to come, but we didn't need any more injured men out here."

"How in the hell did you get here so fast?" Fergus asked his son. "Forget it. I know how. You raced that Jag here, didn't you?"

Carver shook his head and patted Fergus's shoulder. "At least he got away with it. The sheriff gave us a ticket, which is why we're so late getting here. You have a son to be proud of. And Leidolf? Watch out. The kid may be taking your place one day."

Leidolf shook his head. "Just took over and already someone's trying to best me."

"Is Aimée all right?" Cassie asked.

"She's worried about you. I persuaded her to stay with the girls and make sure they remain behind. She wanted to tell you that she hasn't had any luck with finding any sign your family still exists," Carver warned.

"We'll keep looking then," Cassie said, but Leidolf could tell the news was not something she wished to hear.

"Let's go." Leidolf was glad that this business with Irving and Tynan was behind them. Then he stopped. "Hell, if you're here, Fergus, and Quincy and Pierce have been injured, who's watching Sarge?"

Elgin turned a little pale. Fergus did too. Just what Leidolf thought. *No one.*

Hell. He took Cassie's hand. "Are you all right, Cassie?"

"My bite doesn't look half as nasty as yours. I guess I won't be going anywhere for a while." Cassie sighed. "That means I'll miss my magazine deadline."

"Where were you planning to go, Cassie?"

"North Carolina."

"We'll stop over in Colorado. See my family. They have a hospital there specifically set up to cater to injured werewolves. Then we'll continue on to North Carolina where we can extend our vacation. No mate of mine is taking a vacation without me."

She raised her brows at him. "I'll be working."

He kissed her forehead. "*I'll* be vacationing then."

She shook her head. "If I work, you have to work. You can hold the camera."

"You sure you trust me? I'm liable to focus on one subject only. A little red wolf, *lupus garou* variety, the love of my heart."

Some of the men chuckled behind them. Yeah, he was sure Cassie and he could work things out just fine with a little give-and-take now that his subleaders were almost ready to take the reins while he was away for an extended time.

When they reached their vehicles, Leidolf gave Fergus permission to drive the Jag while Evan slinked into the passenger's seat still in his wolf form. "No claw marks on the leather," Leidolf warned. "Have to sell the Jag one of these days. Maybe that will help us with the financial mess we're in."

The rest of the men got into an SUV, and Leidolf drove Cassie to the ranch in the Humvee while she slept soundly the whole way. As soon as they arrived home, Quincy and Pierce, their arms bandaged, most likely from defending themselves against Irving and his cousin, were waiting with most of his other people. They looked half relieved that Cassie and Leidolf were all right but half worried that Leidolf would be furious that they had let Tynan and Irving escape when he had entrusted the safety of the pack to his people.

As everyone piled out of the vehicles, Laney handed a

roll of medical tape to Leidolf for his and Cassie's wounds and then hurried to embrace Elgin. Alice and Sarah squealed to see Evan lope toward them, and both wrapped their arms around his furry wolf neck. Tears in her eyes, Aimée gave Cassie a careful hug. Satros sauntered out, the ancient old guy, casting Leidolf a nod as if he knew Leidolf had finally proved he had what it took to be the pack leader.

Sarge ran outside, and Leidolf was damned thankful they didn't have to chase him down for once. He was waving a stack of papers. "I figured out your mess!"

Several groaned at hearing Sarge's words.

Quincy strode forth. "Didn't I tell you to watch what you say to the boss?"

Sarge scowled back at him and then grinned at Leidolf. "We're not broke after all. Half of the receipts for cattle sales just hadn't been figured in. They were buried under a bunch of romance books in the bottom of one of your desk drawers. Looks like my being a finance clerk in the army was worth something after all."

"You were a finance clerk?" Leidolf asked, incredulous.

"Yeah."

"Why the hell didn't you say so in the first place?" Leidolf growled.

"You bit me. Figured you could muddle through it yourself for a while." Sarge's grin got even bigger, if that was possible. Then it faded. "When everything was in an uproar and no one was watching me, I thought, what the hell. If Leidolf lives to see another day, I'll prove to him I'm not an…what does everyone call me?"

No one said anything for a minute, then Sarah said, "An omega wolf."

"Yeah, one of them. So I'm not any longer. Am I?"

"You've got the job of chief accountant," Leidolf announced, hoping he wouldn't regret it.

Sarge's eyes widened. "No more ranching duties?"

"Not unless you need a physical workout to keep in shape." Leidolf led Cassie into the house.

"Romance books?" Cassie asked. "A whole drawer full of them?"

Leidolf smiled. "Yeah, but I'm not going to Julia Wildthorn's book signing. Laney, the girls, and Aimée are going if you want to tag along."

Cassie harrumphed. "A whole drawer full of her books? Don't tell me you never read any of them."

He guided her down the hall to their master bedroom where they'd clean up, tape up their wounds, and make arrangements for their trip to Colorado and North Carolina.

"She described several intriguing sexual positions that I'm not sure are physically possible. Want to try them out? When we're feeling better, of course." He closed the door to the bedroom.

Careful of Leidolf's back wound, Cassie wrapped her hands around his waist. "So what positions did Miss Julia Wildthorn describe exactly in these werewolf romance books of hers?"

He cast her a devilish smile. "I'll demonstrate later. If you don't mind being…tied up a bit."

She chuckled darkly and dragged a fingernail down his chest. "Not if you don't mind either."

―∾∾―

Leidolf might have proved he was the top wolf in the pack once and for all to himself, to her, and to the rest of the pack. But she finally realized nothing was more important than being part of a pack, Leidolf's mate, and finding her cousin again.

After being a loner for so long, she was glad she was no longer alone in the world.

"Come on, hero of mine. Let me take care of your wound. The faster you heal up..."

"Have any silk scarves?" He cupped her face and leaned down to give her a sizzling kiss.

Sounded like they needed to go shopping...

HUNTING
THE
RED WOLF

A HEART OF THE
WOLF NOVELLA

CHAPTER 1

Janice Langtry was searching for herself in a world of shadows and darkness, hearing her heartbeat and another, yet the heartbeat was in sync with hers, as if they were one and the same, and yet…not. Someone was out there with a connection to her. Or was it her, looking for her real self? She didn't know, felt cut off from the other, cut off from the world. She wasn't the same as anyone else, stripping off her clothes, feeling the heat invade her body, the wind in her fur, running as a wolf. She longed to howl, to reach out to someone like her, but especially to the one in the shadows—the one with the same heartbeat. The one like her.

Janice woke with a start and glanced at the clock, vaguely recalling her dream. It was always the same—the same one she'd shared with her parents, who had dismissed her silly dreams, and the one she'd shared with a fortune teller once, who had told her she had a twin.

It made her wonder.

On her never-ending mission to discover why she was a wolf sometimes, with no logical explanation for her condition, Janice had made a reservation to take a tour of the White Wolf Sanctuary located in a coastal mountain region of Oregon near Tidewater and was on her way there. Only another fifteen minutes and she'd reach the facility. She'd thought of volunteering to work with wolves at a sanctuary, hoping she might find another wolf like her at one of these places. Several times, she'd been to Wolf Haven

International, a wolf sanctuary an hour away in Tenino, Washington, but she'd had no luck in finding anyone like her. Her primary goal was to find a way to get rid of her disorder.

She was desperate to learn the truth about why she was what she was—before the full moon made its appearance in another two weeks and she was out of a job—again. And what if she had a sister? A twin even? She hadn't put a lot of stock in it to begin with, and maybe it was only wishful thinking. Her parents, now deceased, had vehemently denied it. But what if it was true? And she had the same affliction as Janice?

Usually, Janice could tell when someone was lying, but her olfactory senses hadn't picked up the smell of fear—so her parents weren't fearful that she'd catch them at lying. Stress, yes. Her parents had often been stressed out about her.

She couldn't help it that every time the phase of the full moon was upon her, she had this wickedly urgent need to turn into a wolf. And not just at night either. Calling in sick for a week every month hadn't gone over big with bosses while working at various jobs as a receptionist, the latest at a busy law firm. Hence, she kept getting fired. She needed to get a job that she could work at out of her home while making enough money to support herself. She'd started looking into editing works of fiction since she had a degree in English, but the two jobs she'd had weren't going to pay the bills.

She hadn't always had this affliction either. It had first started when she was fourteen. She had to get this curse under control or get rid of it before someone realized she wasn't like everyone else. And she had to discover she truly had a sister and if she was just like her. She had to know if there were others who had been cursed like her. People with superpowers who could run faster, were stronger, healed quicker, could hear better, see better, even at night. *And* had to turn into wolves around the appearance of the full moon at some point in time. Not for the whole week, and not for every waking hour and all night long. Thankfully. And not for hours on end, but just long enough to get it out of her system.

An hour or two and she was back to being normal. But predicting when it would occur was the problem. Talk about a shock when she'd had her first period and turned into a wolf. It wasn't until later that she realized the urge to shift always happened during the full moon!

Exasperated with herself for not just being happy for what she was, she let out her breath. She should probably get over it already. After all, she liked some of the powers.

She was tired of trying to figure this out on her own every minute of the day, desperately wanting to learn the truth.

She did love how fast she could heal. Even when everyone was practically dying from the flu, she was over it before it barely registered that she was sick with it. She'd always had exceptional hearing, so for the longest time, she just thought everyone else could hear like her. Except they didn't. And she did love that. Seeing at night? Now that was totally cool. It was the furry part that caused all kinds of trouble with her life. The other abilities she could hide. Not *that*. *Not* during the full moon.

She pulled into the parking lot of the White Wolf Sanctuary. Certain she wasn't going to find someone like her locked up in a wolf sanctuary, she didn't know where else to look. If people like her existed, they couldn't shift during the new moon. So if they were incarcerated in a cage, they wouldn't be able to hold their wolf shape. Once they turned human, they'd be in big trouble. If one *was* locked up at a zoo or wolf reserve that she visited, would he or she even recognize Janice was one too? Heck, would she even be able to tell if one was like her?

As soon as she made her way into the facility, she smelled the wolves and felt both happy and anxious to meet them. She felt a kinship to all wolves, but she knew they didn't feel a particular kinship with her. They were wild animals. She was very human, except for her little full moon shifting problem she had to deal with every month.

It was cold, and she smelled a hint of snow in the air. The eleven wolves were running free in their sanctuary filled with trees, meadows, shelters, and ponds, beautiful and picturesque. All the wolves were Arctic, except for one gray timber wolf.

Janice hadn't realized how much seeing wolves having fun would affect her. She was glad for them and sad for herself. She wished with all her heart she'd find more of her kind, if there were any more like her. Maybe she was an anomaly. Like Superman or Batman, she thought facetiously.

―⁓―

Brad Redding arrived to do his weekly volunteer work at the White Wolf Sanctuary. He usually fed the wolves, played with them, and helped clean up the grounds. Sometimes he picked up supplies for the facility. He often filled in holes where the wolves had been digging, cleared tree limbs, and checked for other hazards. Like many of his red wolf pack members, he volunteered to help here because they lived on a ranch about an hour away, and they loved to do what they could for their wild wolf cousins. There were other jobs at the facility—fundraising, computer work, assisting or conducting tours, which many of his packmates did—but he preferred being out-of-doors with the wolves. They trusted him as part of their extended wolf pack.

As soon as he walked inside the office, Sibley Struthers, the manager of the facility, smiled at him.

He knew that look and suspected she had a chore for him that he wouldn't like.

"Hey, Brad, the woman who was supposed to give the tour called in that she's got sick kids at home. Do you mind taking over the tour?"

Everyone knew that he much preferred any other chore than giving group tours, but he knew his stuff when it came to wolves, and since no one else was available, he reluctantly agreed. "Sure." He tried not to sound too resigned about it.

Her gray hair tied back in a ponytail, she just smiled at him. "You're a former Navy SEAL. You can handle a few visitors who need to mind you. In fact, you're one of the best at handling them. You have a group of seven adults and three teens. They've all signed the waivers and have been read the rules. You know what to do. If you have any trouble, just let me know." Her phone rang and she grabbed it. "Roadkill? Sure, bring it in. We can always use fresh meat."

Yeah, Brad knew what to do, but sometimes it was easier taking out the bad guys than trying to keep wolf sanctuary visitors in line.

Brad left the office and found the group of visitors looking through the fence at the wolves. Most of the visitors were middle-aged, a couple of them appearing to be parents to the three teens, all boys. One woman who was probably in her late twenties was standing farther away from the rest, looking like she was on her own. She was slight of build, wearing hiking boots, worn jeans, a parka, and a hat featuring wolves of another wolf reserve, and her red-gold hair was swept up in a hairclip. She appeared to be a fan of wolves, so she might not give him any trouble like being aggressive with the wolves, or calling out to the animals, trying to get their attention, or running to or away from the animals if she was used to obeying the rules set up for wolf sanctuaries.

She turned to look at him, her already large green eyes widening. She acted like she recognized him, but he was certain he would remember her. And he didn't.

He gathered the group together, but the pretty redhead still stood apart from the others, as if she didn't want him to believe she was part of the riffraff. "No flashy or dangling jewelry, no smoking, no food, no cameras, no sudden movement, no running, no yelling or shouting," he said, reiterating the rules.

He couldn't help but wonder what her story was. She'd come alone and seemed to have a fascination for wolves, but particularly, she seemed glued to his every word, her eyes holding his gaze whenever he glanced at her.

Breaking free from the hold she had on him, he led the group into the viewing area to see the wolves. He talked a little bit about each of them at the sanctuary. "We often pair up the wolves because most like companionship. They play together, chase each other around their enclosures, and sleep together.

"At night, they howl as if gathering the pack together, and in the morning, they howl to wake everyone up."

Several of the visitors laughed. The redhead was smiling as she watched the wolves.

"Everett and Nukka are enclosure mates and do everything together, including playing, napping, and even sharing food bowls. They love meeting visitors. Nukka also loves to give visitors kisses and gentle nibbles."

He gave the spiel about the rest of the wolves, and then everyone visited with them. He was watching everyone, making sure no one did anything to upset the wolves. He found himself moving in the direction of the redhead, not meaning to get into her space, but he couldn't help but be curious about her because of the wolf hat she was wearing. He wondered if she was considering volunteering here.

Then he got a whiff of her as the breeze shifted, and he was shocked to the marrow of his bones that she smelled like a red wolf. Two possibilities existed. She was one of them, or she worked with them. He suspected the former since wild red wolves were so rare, but he'd never seen her before. He vaguely heard one of his other tour guests asking him a question about the wolves, but for a moment, he was lost in the woman. "What is your name? Where are you from?" he asked her.

"You're…" She sounded choked up, tears filling her eyes.

He hadn't expected *that* kind of a reaction, and it had him wondering what was wrong. He couldn't say he was a red wolf, just like she couldn't. Not in front of the humans. "We'll talk after the tour."

"Janice Langtry." She offered her hand.

He shook it. "Brad Redding." Though he needn't have mentioned it again since he'd introduced himself in the beginning as their tour guide. "I need to answer some visitors' questions. Don't go away."

As if she were going to run off.

"How fast can a wolf run?" one of the teens asked.

"Up to forty miles per hour, top speed for a short distance when trying to catch prey quickly. They can run around twenty-five miles per hour for up to two miles." He noticed she wasn't watching the wolves any longer, even though Nukka was pushing at her hand to get some attention. Janice finally looked down, smiled, and stroked Nukka's head between her ears.

He was trying not to overthink the situation with Janice, but he could hardly concentrate on his job when all he wanted to do was talk to her and learn all he could about her.

Until the two brothers, Pierce and Quincy, who were known to break pack rules, arrived at the sanctuary, ready to work. They were supposed to be here tomorrow when more of their wolf pack was here so somebody could supervise them. Brad already had his hands full with the tour group and one mystery woman—and learning all about her was his new priority.

CHAPTER 2

BRAD FROWNED AT PIERCE AND QUINCY. THEIR PACK leader, Leidolf, would blow a gasket if he knew the twin brothers had come to work today. They meant well, but they had to follow the pack rules! The only time they were scheduled to work here was when they had another wolf who could supervise them the whole time they were there.

Pruners in hand, ready to trim back tree branches, they hadn't even looked to see who was leading the tour group when they saw Janice and immediately strayed from their mission—wolves that they were. If they'd seen Brad first, they would have known to turn around and head back home.

As soon as Brad answered another visitor's question, he said, "Excuse me," and headed for the troublesome brothers targeting Janice.

Janice's eyes grew just as big when she saw and smelled the men closing in on her. Hell. They had no sense of restraint when it came to she-wolves who might be unmated.

"Hey, we haven't seen you around before." Quincy smiled broadly at the woman, definitely intrigued with her.

"I'm Pierce." A smile stretched across his brother's face too.

"And you're out of here." Brad joined them and looked crossly at the brothers.

"We didn't know you were working here today," Quincy said. "I'm Quincy," he quickly added for Janice's benefit before Brad bounced him and his brother out of there.

"Go, before Leidolf hears you're here without supervision." It was part of their condition to stay with the pack, and they really needed a pack. They were still only twenty and hadn't had enough guidance during their formative years.

Usually, the brothers listened to him, since he was a former SEAL and he had the knowhow to back up his words, but the red she-wolf was just too appealing, and the brothers were slow about leaving right away. Maybe they thought Brad wouldn't bodily throw them out because it would make a bad impression on the woman, or that he didn't want to make a scene in front of his tour group.

Brad knew how to circumvent the situation right away. He pulled out his phone.

The brothers both let out their breaths in a huff and headed back to the tool shed, but Brad continued to observe them to make sure they actually left the facility after that. "Sorry about that," Brad said to Janice. "I've got to get back to the group." He didn't worry about watching Janice. She was one of them, and he figured she knew how to handle herself around the wolves.

One of the teens was trying to hide the fact that he was taking videos of the wolves with a small camera, and Brad quickly reminded him and the others, "No pictures and no videos. Park rules. We don't want to upset the wolves or make them feel threatened." Not to mention the center had professional photographers come here to photograph the wolves to sell online and at the gift center as a way to help support the wolves.

The dad said to the kid, "Hey, what did I tell you about that?"

The dad didn't sound like he was upset with his son for taking the video. He probably figured they'd paid enough to go on the tour that they should be able to take some pictures.

Brad had to give the tour group ample time to visit with the wolves, and it was good for the wolves too. The wolves needed the enrichment. It was great education for the visitors also, who helped to spread the word about the wolves, and their fees and purchases at the gift shop helped to support the wolves too. After the visitors left, the wolves would continue to smell the scents they left behind.

Even so, Brad was trying not to count the minutes going by, wanting the tour to end. He had work to do after the visitors finished their tour, and he knew he couldn't just take Janice with him while he did his chores. She'd have to be vetted, signed up, and trained to do the work.

He drifted back to Janice, unable to help himself. She was like a she-wolf magnet. An intriguing mystery wolf.

"Hey, have you ever worked as a volunteer at a wolf reserve? I couldn't help noticing your hat was from the wolf sanctuary in Tenino, Washington." He was half watching her while glancing back at his charges.

"No, and to answer your earlier question, I'm from Washington."

"State?"

"Yeah, Tacoma. What about you?"

"About an hour north of here. Most of us are from Oregon. I've been away—in the navy—so I just recently rejoined the group at a ranch closer to Portland, near the Willamette River by Salem, about an hour from Portland."

"Group," she said.

"Red wolves." She had to be a red wolf Brad figured. But she seemed awfully clueless about them, which made him wary. She had to have smelled that he and the brothers were red wolves. But then he worried. What if she'd been bitten recently? What if she was an even newer wolf than some of the ones they already had in the pack? Here he'd been interested in talking her into joining their pack, but he wasn't sure Leidolf and his mate, Cassie, would want to take in any more new wolves.

Then again, they always had a shortage of female wolves, and they really had to take in wolves who needed their help. It was safer for the new wolves and safer for the rest of them.

"I've got to get back to business." Reluctantly, he moved back to where the other visitors were and talked with some of them.

When they were finally finished with the tour, he thanked them for coming.

Except for Janice, who thankfully held back. Once everyone else had gone inside the gift shop or out to their cars, he took her back inside the enclosure so they could talk in private. "You're not with anyone, I take it?"

"You mean like with a boyfriend?"

"Right, but also you're not with a pack?" He grabbed the pruners out of the tool shed.

"No. I…didn't know if anyone else like me…existed." She paused and looked around at the wolves who were lying down and resting now after their big adventure with the tour group. "I didn't think I was supposed to be back here with you after the tour ended."

He couldn't believe she was a lone wolf on her own who didn't know about them. Had a wolf bitten her then?

"You're not supposed to be back here. But we need to talk, and I've got some work to do before I leave."

"Do you need me to do anything?" she asked.

"No, because of liability purposes, and we don't have a waiver for you to work here, just visit with me. I think they'll trust me to take care of you."

She smiled. "All right." Then she followed him around as he trimmed tree branches. "How did it happen?"

"How did *what* happen?" He sawed off a dead branch.

"You know. How did you become one?"

He stopped what he was doing and looked at her. She seemed so genuinely perplexed. That was what he was worried about. That she was totally new to this. And that wasn't good if she had no control over her shifting during the full moon. "Most of us were born into it. Not you? Were you bitten?"

Her jaw dropped. "Uh, no. I've always been this way. Strange. Cursed."

He chuckled but quickly grew serious when he saw she was serious. "What about your parents?"

"They were not like me."

"Hell. Okay, so you've been raised by humans."

Her eyes grew wide again.

"We're *lupus garou*, wolves who shapeshift. Werewolves, but not like the fiction you might have read. You know that much, right?"

"Yeah, and we can't shift during the new moon, and we don't have control over the shifting during the full moon."

He frowned at her. "You're a new wolf and you haven't had wolf roots for that many generations then."

She sat down hard on the ground, and he hurried over to her, undone by the tears in her eyes.

—m—

Janice wasn't the fainting type, but she came close when she realized she had found others like her. It wasn't a curse, but she still wasn't exactly like Brad and the others. What did that mean for her? She'd always have the shifting trouble? Here she thought she might be able to get rid of a curse.

She never was able to tell a soul about what she was, and it was like opening a gate and letting out all the memories and emotions at once.

"My parents knew about all my *other* strange oddities, which had distressed them to no end. When I was ten, I fell off my bicycle and landed wrong and broke my arm. My bone mended twice as fast as normal people's broken bones would. After all the fuss doctors made when they learned how fast I healed, my parents hid the truth from others."

"Right. We have to be careful about that."

"My parents told me not to tell anyone else I could see in the dark when they couldn't."

"And our hearing is better too."

"Right. They worried about my strange obsession with wolves and how I would take walks in the woods for hours at a time—alone in the woods where wolf packs were known to live—though I never told them I was looking for them in the wild. I couldn't tell my parents about the wolf business at all."

"Ahh, hell, Janice. No one should ever have to have gone through what you did alone," Brad said.

She let out her breath. "Yeah. I really wanted to meet others like me. When I was growing up, my dad killed wolves if they got anywhere near their sheep farm. And that distressed me something awful! What if one of them had been just like me?"

"I agree."

"Luckily, the sheep were used to me, so they didn't realize I was a wolf in human disguise. And I didn't have any urge to kill them. Not like a wolf might, which confused me, unless it was the human part of me that kept that urge in."

"It was," Brad said. "We're one and the same, the wolf and our human halves. But our human conscience controls our more primal urges."

"Good. I was concerned the wolf half of me would take over and I wouldn't have any control. Well, other than the shifting issues. Now at twenty-eight, my parents are gone, the farm is sold off, and I'm alone. I had no one I could talk to about my strange…affliction. At least Superman could hide what he was, if he hadn't wanted to be a hero all the time."

Brad smiled.

"Me? I just wanted to be normal. No superpowers, no wolf half. After all the years of searching, I had no more clue as to why I was what I was than I did when I started to delve into the mythology of werewolves. I wasn't one of *them*. Not a ferocious beast when I turned into a wolf. Not one who would lose his mind and kill anything in his path. I was my regular self—just furrier than usual, and a real wolf, not some made-up monster. My thoughts were still my own, though I saw things differently from my parents—feeling part of the woods, sensing so much more."

"Exactly. We're part of it because of our wild wolf halves. We are lower to the ground, so we sense so much more and we fit in."

"Good. Thanks for validating all I've been going

through, even if you haven't had to deal with exactly what I have. It's been driving me crazy. When I was in school, I read all about werewolf lore and joked about it with my friends, none of whom were cursed. They teasingly called me wolf-girl, and the name stuck."

"Now that would be hard—dealing with these issues when going to school."

"It was. And of course the fact that I had to always take off from school during the full moon? It just convinced everyone I was crazy and really thought I was a werewolf. I thought I was getting the hang of this—controlling when I have to shift. It used to be that I'd have more problems for a longer period of time. The time has shortened a bit. The wolf moon—the January full moon—will be here before I'm ready, and I'm already feeling the pull of the wolf."

"You're going with me to see the pack." Crouching beside her, Brad took her hand and didn't ask if she wanted to.

"All right. I'm a liability, aren't I?" But she also now knew her parents weren't really her own. They had to have adopted her, and they never told her the truth! After learning she was so different from them, why didn't they tell her she wasn't related to them so she could learn about her real family? A wolf family? But it also meant she might truly have a sister.

Brad didn't answer her right away.

She knew she would be a liability. Even to other wolves.

"You have to be careful about being out when the full moon is nearly here, during the full moon, and a couple of days afterward."

"Yeah, I know. I mean, I always have to take off work then. It's a real pain. And I've been let go from several jobs because of it. I don't blame them. It's like I have full-moon PMS and can't work."

Brad smiled at her.

She frowned back at him. "It's not funny. You don't ever have any trouble with the shifting?"

"No. I'm what we call a royal, with wolf roots going way back in the family history." Brad reached out and rubbed her shoulder. "Are you going to be okay?"

"Yeah, I can't believe I felt so faint all of a sudden."

"I can't believe you've been living with this for so long without knowing there are others like us." He helped her up, and she still felt lightheaded.

Before she expected it, he wrapped his arms around her and held her close. She breathed in his scent, red wolf, slightly different from the gray and white wolves, but maybe it was just that he smelled different from any other wolf— their kind or the wild wolf kind. Soap-washed skin, other wolves, the mountain air, and maleness.

"Wolves mate for life," he warned her. "And we take care of each other."

She hadn't expected their kind would mate for life. Real wolves, sure. But when the human equation was introduced, no. "What if the others don't want me around?"

"We take care of our own. Seriously. We take care of wild wolves too."

"Even though I can't always control my shifting?" She'd never considered she might find others like her and she would be the exception to the rule!

"*Especially* because you can't control your shifting. Hey, let me text my pack leaders to let them know I'm bringing you home with me."

"To give them a heads-up as to the kind of trouble I could be?"

He smiled down at her. "Because they're my pack leaders and they need to know about things that could have an effect on the pack."

"Because I can't control my shapeshifting."

"Uh, right." He looked like he wanted to kiss her.

She wouldn't have wanted him to. Not when she didn't know him. Not normally. But he had some kind of magnetic draw to her that she'd never felt toward the guys she'd dated. Not that Brad was interested in dating her. She was bad news, when he was a royal.

"Are you sure you're going to be okay?" he asked, one arm still wrapped around her, his free hand rubbing her other arm reassuringly.

Yeah, but she didn't want him to release her. What was wrong with her? She was never clingy with *any* guy. She didn't like the feeling. Well, not normally. But it was chilly out, he was hot and wolfish, and his blue eyes focused on her as if she was the only woman left in the whole wide world. *His* woman.

"Yes." She was sure her delayed response proved she wasn't okay.

"Okay, I'll text our leaders and get this work done and we'll go home. Can you drive okay?"

She laughed lightly. "Yes. You can't know what a shock this has been for me."

"You're right. I can't even imagine how you have survived all this time, not knowing there were more of us out there or having anyone to show you the way and having to keep your gifts secret." He released her then and texted on his phone. Afterward, he began trimming more branches.

Gifts. Right.

Despite him telling her not to do any work, she couldn't stand not doing something. She began stacking the twigs and branches in a pile for him.

He smiled at her.

"Wolves have multiple births, right?" she asked.

"Often, yes."

"And our kind?"

"Yes, definitely. I have a twin sister who will be joining the pack in a few weeks."

"I…I might have a sister. Maybe even a twin. Maybe. I've been mistaken for some other woman in Yakima. I don't live there, but the first time it happened, I was getting gas at a travel station. I went inside to use the bathroom, and this guy said, 'Hey, I haven't seen you in forever.' Then he frowned. 'Sorry, I thought you were someone else.'

"I'd never met him before. He was just some random dude. You know how people will mistake you for someone else. It didn't mean anything at the time. Just a mistaken identity. When I got home, I mentioned it to my parents as just a funny experience I'd had. They cast each other glances and seemed a little upset. I thought their reaction was odd at the time. I laughed and said, 'So I have a sister?' My mother said, 'Of course not.' She wasn't joking either, like I thought she would be. I felt like I'd hit a nerve, but I hate confrontation, so I let it go. Not only that, but I-I also have had strange dreams."

"About a sister? Twins can have them. I've had them about my sister."

"Ohmigod, so I could have one then!"

"You could, and we need to find her if you do. Do you

mind if I take a picture of you? I can share it with the rest of the pack so we can look for someone who looks like you."

"Sure, go ahead." She smiled.

He took the picture, then texted something to someone.

"I don't know her name or how to go about looking for her."

"We'll find her."

She let out her breath. "Yeah. But what if she isn't like me?"

"If she's your sister, she most likely would be. That leaves a couple of possibilities. Your birth parents raised her, and by some means, they lost you and you were put up for adoption, or they died and both of you were put up for adoption. Well, a third scenario would be that you were stolen, one or the both of you. We have a lot of resources available to us, so we can search for her."

"Me too. I want to help look for her."

"We're going to have to do this without getting ahold of the local police. If she exists and she's your twin, we can't have them involved. Also, we have the issue of the approach of the full moon phase."

"We only have a few days to find her then."

"That's one nice thing of having a pack to help you with issues like this." He cut off another tree branch.

Janice's eyes filled with tears, and they slipped down her cheeks. She quickly brushed them away, but not before Brad noticed. She felt like she was a bundle of emotions: hope, worry, disbelief, but mostly hope that she could find a sister who was just like her. Not that she'd wish her condition on anyone, but still, she'd have real family, and that meant everything to her.

Brad pulled her in for another hug. This time, he kissed

the top of her head. "Even if she's a twin, she could look very different from you but similar enough it confuses people. My grandmother and great-aunt were twins, but one had darker brown hair and was thinner than the other. If you have a sister, we'll find her. She might even be a cousin."

"I've tried looking for her in case she is real, but I haven't had any luck. I've been to the same gas station several times, but I haven't seen either the guy who thought I looked like someone else or anyone else who might. Thank you, from the bottom of my heart."

"You're welcome." He finally released her when she didn't look like she was going to cry again and started to cut more tree limbs.

She swore she wasn't going to shed another tear and delay him in his work again. "What was going on with those two men you told to leave?" She grabbed several more branches and added them to the growing pile.

"They are twin brothers we took into the pack a while back. They're both twenty years old, and after their parents died when they were teens, they hadn't had a lot of discipline. Other packs didn't want to put up with their shenanigans. Basically, they're good guys, and we want to make sure they stay that way."

"As opposed to…?"

"Rogue wolves. You should know if you bite someone, you could turn them."

"Oh."

He glanced back at her. "Have you? Bitten anyone?"

She shook her head. "Though it wouldn't have been my fault if I had. How would I have known I could turn someone?"

"True."

A couple more men came into the wolf enclosure to work, both outfitted in work gloves and carrying shovels.

"Brad," both men said in greeting, looking in Janice's direction.

Brad inclined his head. "I'm showing Janice the ropes."

"Welcome to the pack," one of the men said, and then he and the other man left to do some chores.

"They're part of the pack?" she whispered.

Brad smiled. "No. Just something most everyone says who volunteers here."

She was hoping she wouldn't get into any trouble being here with Brad when she wasn't supposed to be. Chewing on her lip, she glanced back toward the office, hoping Brad didn't get into any trouble for having her back here either.

She appreciated that he wanted her to stay with him. Again, she felt that annoying clinginess she'd felt toward him before. She kept feeling if she blinked her eyes, he would vanish, and she would be searching for wolves like her all over again. She still couldn't believe she'd run into honest-to-goodness wolf shifters here. That she could now get some answers. Yet she was nervous about meeting the others. She couldn't even imagine what it would be like to be with a whole pack of wolves—that shifted into humans. And to possibly find a sister too?

His cell phone pinging him, Brad paused in his work to pull it out. He read the message and smiled. He sent a message and slipped his phone into his pocket. "Cassie said the brothers already reported I was bringing you back to the pack for keeps."

She sure hadn't expected to find a whole pack of wolves that wanted her to be part of their family. Which would mean quitting her job and moving there? She wasn't sure she was ready for that. She was already feeling overwhelmed by the whole idea. Meeting a bunch of strangers. Them deciding everything for her. Pack leaders even. What if the pack leaders thought she was like the twin brothers? A problem that needed to be contained? Well, she *was* a problem when the full moon was well on its way. And she could use some help when that happened. But she wasn't sure she wanted her life to be totally regulated by anyone else. People she didn't even know. Not since she'd moved out of her parents' home had she had to abide by someone else's rules.

Brad bundled up all the branches and hauled them to another part of the compound. "Come on. It's lunchtime. Did you want to get something to eat on the way to the ranch?"

"Yeah, sure." She was torn between excitement about finding someone else like her and apprehension about meeting a whole pack.

"Does a seafood restaurant sound good to you?"

She smiled. She thought Brad was going to take her to a burger place. She loved burgers, but waitressing in one when she was younger meant fast-food burger places had lost their appeal.

"I'll lead the way. What's your phone number, by the way?"

She exchanged numbers with him. She halfway expected him to give her the pack leaders' numbers as if to say she was part of the pack already, but he didn't.

As soon as he was in his blue pickup truck and she was in her car, they left the facility and headed out to the main road, then drove north. He called her on her Bluetooth, and she smiled.

"Hello. I didn't want you to get the wrong impression that we're forcing you to join the pack or anything. Everyone will want you to, but it's entirely up to you and how you feel about it," Brad said. "There's no pressure to join. If you decide you need time to think about it, you can do that too. Return to Washington, come back to see us when you want. It's totally up to you."

"Thanks, I did worry about it. I didn't know if there was some kind of requirement for wolves to live in a pack or not. Or especially ones like me."

"No. Lone *lupus garous* exist. Some families just live as families and consider that their pack. Others are small, a couple of families living together. Some are larger like the red wolf pack, and the Silver Town pack where Leidolf's sister is a co-pack leader with a gray wolf, Darien Silver."

"Oh, so there are other kinds of wolves that can shift?"

He hesitated to answer, then said, "Uh, yes. Sorry. There are gray wolf shifters and Arctic wolves also. I forget how much you need to learn. We have some newly turned wolves in the pack, but they were bitten, and it's been a while since they joined us. There's an Arctic wolf pack Leidolf ran into in Maine. They were from Seattle, so I imagine they'll be returning there."

"Oh, I never went up there to check for wolves. What if people see me as being trouble for the pack like the twins are?"

"Uh, no, unless you purposefully run off during the day as a wolf to places where we shouldn't be seen."

"I've done that, but not on purpose."

"Right. The brothers have no excuse. I wanted to

mention to you that Cassie said that she and Leidolf are having a quiet dinner tonight and have invited us to eat with them."

She suspected they were worried they'd chase her off if too many of the pack members met up with her right away. "Is it always like that with them?" She envisioned a castle, the king, queen, and minions all eating in the great hall for all their meals. Some in furry coats, like her, if they couldn't control their wolf.

"Yeah. Even though we're a pack, we all have our own lives to live. Most of us help out with the wolf sanctuary, some work full time on the ranch, but others work in Portland or surrounding communities at various jobs. One family even owns a restaurant that has a dance floor. I work out at the ranch." Brad pulled into the parking lot of a seafood restaurant.

It was good to hear that some of the wolves could get on with their lives and fit in without the issues she had to face. Considering how nice the restaurant looked, she sure hoped Brad was paying for the meal or she'd probably only be able to afford an appetizer.

CHAPTER 3

As soon as they were seated in a booth, Janice and Brad looked over their menus. Nearby, a rowboat served as a salad bar. Seashells, glass balls, lifesaver rings, and fishnets covered the walls, while old-looking brass lanterns added a seafarer's touch. He hoped she liked the restaurant. He loved the food and the atmosphere.

She was looking over the menu and then settled on the appetizers. Unless she'd had a big breakfast or often ate light lunches, he suspected she might have money issues. Particularly if she couldn't hold a job because of her shifting trouble.

"Lunch is on me," Brad told her.

"Thanks," she said.

He was afraid she'd still stick to the less expensive appetizers, but she finally began looking at the lunch meals, and he picked out salmon for himself and she chose the same.

"I won't deny Leidolf and Cassie will want you to stay with them while we look for a sister of yours," he said.

The waitress came back with glasses of ice water and rolls and took their orders, then left.

Folding her arms, Janice sat back in her chair and tilted her chin down, looking annoyed. "She's my sister."

"I know, but as we get closer to the full moon, you're going to have more of an issue with it. If we don't find her before then, you can help us search afterward. We'll keep looking for her in the meantime."

"And I'll help search for her before the phase of the full moon has too strong a pull."

Brad looked at her skeptically.

"All right. We'll do it your way. I'll go with whoever's searching for her, and then if I feel I'm losing it—"

He raised a brow.

"Getting ready to...well, you know. I'll return to...well, go wherever no one will catch me at it."

"Okay. You'll be with me."

"Don't you have any other work to do?" She sounded surprised he could just do whatever he wanted to without having to get time off from the job.

"Our kind take priority over other jobs, and since I was the first one to...*discover* you, so to speak, it rests with me to...watch out for you." He was afraid she didn't like the sudden idea of everyone watching over her. For someone who had been on her own until now, it would be under-standable. But it was also up to him to make sure that, despite telling her she could leave and be on her own, she didn't choose that option. Not when she could get herself— and the rest of them—into deep trouble.

Yet he knew he had to tread carefully with this. He did wonder if she might be more comfortable with Cassie, or another woman in the pack, staying with her.

Before long, their salmon was delivered to their table, and they began to eat their meal.

"If you would feel better about having a woman stay with you, I'm sure any number would be willing to assist you. I know what it's like for our more newly turned wolves to have trouble shifting. We want to help you in whatever way you want so you won't feel like your whole world has been turned inside out." He cut into his salmon, hoping she'd decide to stay with him.

"Believe me, it already has, from the moment I shifted the first time when I was fourteen. I don't know that anyone else would make it any easier to deal with. Since I've already met you, I'll stick with you for the time being. Unless you think I'll be more trouble than it's worth."

He smiled. "I was a Navy SEAL. I'm used to dealing with trouble."

"And you're not seeing a wolf now?" She cut up one of her asparagus spears.

"Uh, no. I haven't been with the pack in eons. I just retired from the navy and was glad to learn we had new leadership. I hadn't known we'd had trouble with the former pack leader and his cronies until I visited last year and discovered Leidolf and Cassie were running things. They're good for the pack. I was happy to return here when I was done with the navy."

Janice finished eating her salmon, crispy potato wedges, and asparagus and sat back in her seat. "Okay, so you're a beta wolf. All of the wolves must be beta also, except for the pack leaders."

He nearly spit out a mouthful of water, quickly managing to choke it down. Clearing his throat, he shook his head. "We're not the same as wild wolf packs. We're human too. There can be several alphas in a pack at one time, as long as we follow the rules set by the pack leaders. Leidolf and Cassie are very democratic. They make the ultimate decisions about the pack, but they always listen to input from the rest of us if a decision impacts all of us."

"So you're an alpha."

"Yeah. I can take orders like anyone else, but if Leidolf or Cassie needs me to lead, I'm right there for them. Cassie's a wolf biologist, so she's often off lecturing about wolves somewhere when she's not at home with the pack."

"Is she a royal?" Janice asked.

"Yeah, so is Leidolf. That means they don't have to worry about shifting when they're out running around."

"That's good. Where will I stay?"

"While we're in Yakima looking for your sister, you'll stay with me. When we return to the ranch, you can stay with…well, me or anyone else who won't mind putting you up. I'm sure you'll have a ton of offers. The ranch has over thirty thousand acres—some of it is pastureland for cattle and horses, acreage for crops, and lots of it is forested. All of it is free for us to run as wolves and howl to our heart's content. It's not like living in a city. It's the perfect place for us wolves. We also have a river filled with rainbow trout and wild brown trout to fish from. The lake is perfect for swimming, both as humans in the summer and as wolves anytime. Occasionally, we see black bear near the river, fishing for meals."

"Oh, wow. Has anyone had any trouble with them?"

"No, we leave them alone and they leave us alone. We also have elk and deer, sandhill cranes, raptors, and migratory songbirds. Sometimes we have trouble with hunters, but we deal with them quickly. We have a couple of wolves on the police force, and a judge too. He always gives the maximum sentence for anyone caught trespassing on our land. We have no trespassing signs posted all over, and all the land is fenced in, so no one can use the excuse that they ended up there by accident. But of course the draw of hunting on the land will always attract a few humans. We can't allow it because we don't want anyone to see a red wolf pack roaming freely there when we have time off. Humans don't realize we can hear sounds from a great distance away—they only think they have to get far enough from the main ranch house and the other homes and working crews."

"Have they ever seen you as wolves and reported it?" Janice asked.

"So far, no. You'll have to see the land to really get a feel for it. With a lake and rivers and forests, it's perfect for us. Some of our people live in Portland, and they bring their families to the ranch to run as wolves whenever they want to."

"I've been praying for a miracle cure for this or a way to better control it. I guess if neither is possible, the ranch and your pack is the next best thing."

He smiled, and then he paid the bill. "We can find you a job at the ranch. You won't have to leave there when you're having trouble."

"All I've ever done is waitress and worked as a receptionist at various jobs of late because I could never go to college. Not with these issues."

"You can probably get a degree online, but it's not necessary unless there's something you really want to use a degree for. You can just get used to the pack. You won't need to earn your keep until you feel you're ready. We just want to make sure you're happy."

"Thank you. I feel like if I close my eyes, all this will disappear."

"Not on your life. We'll go to the ranch, and I'll show you around. If you can turn into your wolf, we'll go for a run."

"I can. I have full control over my shifting except for during the full moon."

"Okay, good. Then we'll have fun." He walked her out to her car. "Don't be surprised if folks just wave or smile and don't come and greet you right off. Cassie or Leidolf would have told them to give you a chance to see the place before you're overwhelmed by wolves wanting to welcome you to the pack. Especially if you're unsure if you want to join us."

She smiled. "Okay, thanks for letting me know. Otherwise, I might be worried they thought I was more of a problem than anything else."

He hoped not, but he was willing to help her in any way he could.

A half hour later, they arrived at the ranch, and Janice was surprised and impressed to see the acres of trees and meadows and mountains, a main ranch house and bunkhouse, and several other homes and barns. She imagined the bachelor males lived in the bunkhouse. She was excited and apprehensive about meeting all the wolves. A couple of ranch hands came out of the loafing barn and waved at her and Brad as they pulled up to one of the houses. He couldn't live in one of the larger homes, she didn't think. Not if he was a bachelor. Surely, it was for a family.

"I'm a subleader." Brad took her inside the house. "If you wondered why I have a home when I'm a bachelor male. They gave me one when I returned because of my military record and the help that I'd been before I left."

"Wow, okay. I did wonder."

"I have three bedrooms. Pick whichever you like, and you can stay here for as long as you want. I'll show you around the place, we'll go running as wolves, clean up, and go to the pack leaders' home for dinner. Then tomorrow morning, early, we'll drive up to Yakima. How do you feel about that?"

"It sounds like a great plan. I sure hope we can find her, if she truly exists."

"We will, with all of us assisting. Let me help you get your bags." They went back out to her car and grabbed the three bags she had, then carried them into the house.

He showed her one of the bedrooms next to the guest bath. "As soon as you're ready, just meet me at the back door. All the houses have wolf doors—another great thing about living in a wolf community."

"This will be great. Thanks." Her guest room was light and airy with a view of the forests and lake down below. A beautiful view, and she was already feeling at home.

The queen-size bed was centered on a wall, a bedside stand on either side, shelves rising to the ceiling and across, with books and blue glass jars interspersed.

"My mother's collection of books and glass jars." Brad set her bags down on the carpeted floor.

Janice perused the titles. "Romance author of wolf shifter books."

"Julia Wildthorn. Yes. She's one of us. A lot of our kind read her books."

"You?"

Brad smiled. "I haven't had the time."

Too macho? She would have to read them and check them out. "About us for real?"

"She changes things up a bit so she doesn't give our kind away."

"And you know this how?"

She swore Brad's ears were tinged a bit red with embarrassment. He cleared his throat. "That's what my mother said."

Mother. Right.

"Okay, I'll let you get undressed and shift."

"Thanks, for everything."

"You're welcome. See you in a few minutes."

She rarely willingly ran as a wolf because she was too afraid she'd get caught. She was glad she was going to be able to let down her wolf hair and really enjoy the run. She stripped out of her clothes and shifted, but then hesitated to leave the bedroom. She'd never shown off her wolf persona to anyone. She didn't know how to act around another wolf as a wolf. Trying to settle her unruly case of nerves, she left the bedroom and walked into the living room where she found Brad waiting for her by the back door. He was a beautiful coppery red wolf with a black splash of ink coloring the tip of his tail, warm golden eyes smiling at her.

Other than seeing herself in the mirror or the reflection in a pond while she wore her wolf coat, she hadn't seen another red wolf in person before, and it was hard to imagine he was the same person as the hot SEAL in his human form. His fur was lighter than hers by a couple of shades, and he had the most beautiful eyes, watchful, his tongue hanging out as if he had already gone for a run, his mouth smiling when he saw her.

She thought he liked what he saw, and she hadn't ever

considered how wonderful that would make her feel. She had always imagined that if anyone had seen her in her wolf coat, they'd be afraid of her, not *like* the way she looked.

He walked over to her, and she stood stock still, not sure how to react. Then he nuzzled her face, and she liked how his muzzle felt rubbing against hers. She smelled the way his masculine wolf scent was now clinging to her fur, just as her scent was on him. It was a way of showing she was part of their pack.

Then she wondered, was he claiming her too? Showing other male wolves that he was interested in her? Maybe. She certainly didn't know enough about this business to be sure. She felt, in a way, like she was a toddler, taking tentative steps among the wolves—her kind.

She nuzzled him back, and then he licked her cheek and she smiled. He woofed, and that was a shock too. A wolf talking to her who was just like her! Then he pushed open the wolf door, and she followed him outside.

Seeing the houses and the landscape was different as a wolf. She was lower to the ground, but she still couldn't shake loose of the fear of running as a wolf around other people. Even though she knew they had to be wolves too, they didn't look like wolves. They looked like ordinary humans—a couple of men riding horseback out to the pasture where other horses were corralled, a couple of kids playing chase beside the barn, a woman holding two toddlers' hands, with a third child following close behind as the woman entered one of the other houses.

None of them looked like anything but strictly humans.

Then Brad took off running down the road, and she raced after him. They finally reached the meadow and headed toward the forest beyond. But they were getting closer to a meandering river that cut across the acreage.

She felt like she was on an adventure and hoped she could run as long and as fast as him. She didn't often go running. And even when she couldn't contain her wolf, she would often end up pacing in her apartment. She couldn't do much else. Not when she didn't have land like this to run free in where animal control wouldn't be called to pick her up and take her to a pet rescue facility. What a surprise they'd be in for when they realized she wasn't a dog.

She and Brad scared some California quails that took off flying, startling her for an instant. She was supposed to chase them like a good wolf would, not be scared by the sudden movement of the wildlife. She was still thinking with her human brain.

They ran along the river where rainbow trout were jumping out of the water. Now she wanted to fish as a wolf, but she'd never done so, and she wasn't sure she could. She stopped on the rocky bank and watched the fish swimming beneath the surface of the water. She wanted to catch one, just to prove she could do it. That was when she saw a couple of men upstream fishing, their lines in the water, their folding chairs and two ice chests nearby. They waved at Brad and her. Brad woofed back in greeting.

Janice realized that was another thing she'd never done. Practiced using her wolf voice. She hadn't ever woofed, barked, or howled, afraid making any sound as a wolf would have drawn attention to her condition.

Brad licked her face and then stepped into the water, as if he knew just what she wanted to do—catch a fish with her wolf teeth—and he was going to show her how. She could see the advantage in having wolf teachers show her the way, and she appreciated him for it.

He suddenly hopped into the air and landed on a fish, then with his muzzle dipping into the water, he pulled the trout out of the river with his teeth and left it on the bank. It flopped around, and she realized even if she was able to catch a fish, what would they do with it?

One of the men fishing hollered, "Show off. We'll pick up your fish, store it in our extra ice chest, and deliver it home."

Ohmigod, how neat! Free pickup and delivery!

Well, she was good at trying new things, even if she felt way out of her comfort zone. She moved into the water and concentrated on where the trout were swimming beneath the currents. If Brad could do it, she could do it. They were both wolves after all.

She saw the rainbow trout she was going after and jumped, just like Brad had. She landed on mossy stones and slipped, the fish gone. Realizing this wasn't as easy as Brad had made it look, she stood quietly in the knee-deep water, keeping her tail still, her ears perked, her eyes focused on the water, watching for another trout to come to her. Getting the hang of catching fish as a wolf might take some time.

Then she saw one coming straight for her. She got ready, jumped, and missed him. Darn it! But she wasn't giving up. After three more tries, she finally caught one and pulled it out of the water with her teeth, so proud of herself. She did it! If she was ever lost in the wilderness, at least she knew she could survive if she was near a fish-filled water source.

She saw three more trout sitting on the bank that Brad had fished out in the meantime. She set her fish down with his and smiled at him. He *was* a showoff, but she was impressed. Then he nudged her to continue running with him. They ran along the river's edge for some time, and she saw some deer drinking at the water's edge. She thought they would take flight. Wolves usually would cause that reaction, but they didn't.

Wasn't she supposed to be a scary wolf? But then the wolves here probably never chased them, and the deer didn't realize the wolves were natural predators. She hoped that never changed.

She and Brad swam across the river and headed into the woods when she heard men talking. Figuring they were more of the red wolves, she didn't think anything of it until Brad detoured into her path and stopped her from going any further. Hunters? Illegal hunters?

Great. Just when she was feeling safe and secure here. But there would always be lawbreakers who felt it was their right to do as they pleased, assuming they wouldn't get caught at it.

She didn't know what to do. She wanted to stop the men from hunting on the pack's land, but she didn't want to get shot. Brad moved closer to her and nudged her to follow his lead. He moved her away from the sound of the men talking low, and then when she couldn't hear them anymore, they moved to the river, swam across, and reached the other side.

The men were still fishing, the fish she and Brad caught probably in their spare ice chest now. Brad ran toward them, and they immediately set down their poles, and one pulled out his cell phone. Brad shifted and said, "Hunters, two, in the direction we just came from."

She was shocked the hunky SEAL had shifted into his

human form out here in front of God and everyone, though she realized he had to in order to tell the fishermen what was going on with the hunters. He was spectacularly muscled, beautiful chest and arms and legs and…well, everything. He would definitely be a sculptor's perfect choice to recreate David. She shouldn't have been staring so hard at him, but when he shifted back, he nuzzled her face, and she thought he might have been amused about it.

She knew what she'd be envisioning when she closed her eyes tonight. The blurring form of a wolf shifting into his human—oh-so-beautiful human form—the image paused and paused and paused until he shifted back into his red wolf form.

He led her toward the homes on the hilltop. She would never be able to see him again while he was wearing clothes without thinking of what he looked like without them.

In the meantime, the man with the phone said, "Yeah, Leidolf. Two hunters are in the area. Brad and the new wolf found them while in their wolf coats." He gave Leidolf the coordinates. "We're going after them. Badges and guns. Yep. We're always prepared."

Now that surprised her. Were they the wolf police officers Brad had mentioned? She just hoped the hunters didn't shoot them.

As soon as Brad and she arrived at the top of the hill, she saw several men armed with rifles headed down the road in pickups to reach the river. Now that truly was a pack in action, each of them helping the others out. She really admired that they did that for one another. She'd figured just the two guys would deal with it. If the hunters knew they'd be facing so many men armed with rifles, maybe they'd think twice about pulling this stunt in the future.

Once Janice and Brad were inside his house, they slipped off to their respective bedrooms, and she shifted and dressed.

"Hey, are you all right?" Brad asked, bringing her a glass of ice water.

"Yeah, thanks," she said, coming out of the bedroom. "I didn't know what to do. I wanted to take the men down. I've never felt like that before. Well, maybe a few times when guys were bullying kids in school. I had to feign sickness every time it got close to being the phase of the full moon. My mother knew I was faking it, but what else could I do? She was afraid something else was wrong with me, but I couldn't tell her that there really was. But yeah, I'm fine."

"Good. I hope you don't feel you can't run out there with hunters being an issue."

"If they are, I'm sure you'll protect me."

CHAPTER 4

INTENDING TO TALK TO JANICE ABOUT BEING ONE OF their kind, Brad led her into the living room. She sat on his favorite brown, faux-suede recliner, and he took a seat on the matching sofa.

He didn't know if she wanted to discuss all the issues of being a wolf with someone else, but he felt like he was her mentor already. "I don't blame you about the school issue. We homeschool our kids even though they have control over their shifting. If they got mad at some bully in school, it could have disastrous consequences. Oh, and probably something you don't know, if you're running as a wolf and someone kills you, your body returns to its human form."

"Ohmigod, no."

"Right. Not something we want to advertise to the human population."

"What about our blood? When we see a doctor? Wouldn't he see something that didn't look right? I didn't worry about it for a long time, not until I was older and realized I might be in trouble if I had any bloodwork done. I never got checkups, afraid a blood test would show I was part wolf or something."

"No. You're good there. We're wolves through and through, from our fur to our blood, then when we shift, the same thing with our human half. All human, microscopically and otherwise."

"Oh good," she said, sounding relieved.

He thought he should touch on the subject of sexual relations between consenting wolf adults, and how it was different from humans. "Okay, you may not want me to discuss the birds and the bees with you, but…"

—∾∾—

Brad's masculine lips and beautiful blue eyes smiled warmly at her.

Janice felt her face heat with embarrassment. She hadn't considered having sex with another wolf. Well, maybe a little, but she hadn't expected to have a hot wolf telling her about the birds and the bees of wolf sex. "Yeah?"

"If you'd rather have someone else—"

"No. Go ahead." She smiled. She couldn't contain her amusement.

"Well, we normally don't have sex as wolves. It's not forbidden, and it's something we can do, but we like to have more…options with having sex as humans. It's just a lot more…intimate."

"Okay, I wondered about that."

"The courtship is enjoyable as wolves. The nuzzling, sharing scents with each other, licking each other's faces."

Just like he'd already done with her? Did that mean he was interested in "courting" her?

"We don't carry STDs. It's something we don't have to worry about."

"But you don't marry humans."

"No. And we don't normally turn them, though there have been some exceptions to the rule. Unconsummated sex with a wolf is fine, as long as neither of you is mated.

Once you have consummated sex, you're mated for life. As to babies, it's rare a union between a human and a wolf can create a child."

Thank God for that!

"If you have a wolf mate and become pregnant, after your babies are born, they won't shift until you do."

"It would happen only during the full moon or some other time I choose?"

"Right. They'll have more wolf roots if you mate someone like me, who's a royal. They may have more control over their shifting. But until they're older, they won't be able to shift on their own. Which means they can't shift if mom doesn't shift or is too far away from her children to cause the shift."

"Or dead?"

"Uh, yeah."

"Okay, so like me, I didn't shift until I was older. The first time for me was when I turned fourteen."

"Uh, usually around six or seven."

"Oh, wow, I'm glad I didn't turn into a wolf *that* young!"

"Without a family to help you, that's for sure. What have I left out?"

"Is...sex any different between wolves in their human form versus humans with humans?" She couldn't believe she asked the question, yet she was curious about it.

He smiled. "Okay, first of all, we're *lupus garous*. We can't know exactly what it's like as a human with a human. But we can *guess* because our senses are so much more acute. Our pheromones get jumpstarted, and we can sense them when humans can't. I'd say...it's better. *Lots* better. You do realize since I haven't had a mate, I haven't had consummated sex with a wolf. It's speculation on my part. You could ask a mated couple though."

As if she'd want to ask a mated couple about those kinds of intimate details! She couldn't even believe she was talking about this with a man she'd just met. Though everyone else who had been raised by wolves would already know all this, and it probably was a good thing to know something about it so she wouldn't get herself into trouble. What if she got really interested in two wolves? More than with just Mr. Hot Wolf Brad? What if she really let go of her cautious wolf nature and wanted to have sex with a couple of hot wolves just to see what it was like? And then learned what a no-no that was? She'd never realized there would be rules and consequences to all this.

Yep, it was better to know than to be clueless. She could see being drummed out of the pack before she'd even joined for making some really colossal mistake like that.

"Oh, and as for having your babies, it's your choice as to whether you would have your kids as a wolf or as a human," Brad said.

Her jaw dropped. She would never have imagined birthing kids as a wolf.

"I mean if you have your kids as a wolf, they would be wolf pups."

She laughed. "I wondered. I can't even imagine having them as a wolf giving birth to wolves, but the other notion came to mind too. That would be a nightmare."

He smiled. "With multiple births, some of the women just find it's easier to be a wolf."

"Multiple births. Right. How many?" She was thinking she might not want kids after all.

"As many as wolves have. But most of our kind only have a couple, some three, some only one. I think our human half comes into play to help keep us from going overboard. Statistically speaking, we do have more multiple births than the general human population. Can you think of any other questions?"

She shook her head. "I think I'm totally overwhelmed right now." Between finding wolves that were just like her, or almost just like her, and being able to run as a wolf without too much worry, and having help to locate her sister? If she had one? She was overwhelmed.

"It'll get a lot easier when you meet others in the pack and start to make friends. Everyone will know you haven't lived with wolves before so they won't hesitate to answer any questions you have. Are you ready to go to dinner?"

"Yeah, sure." She had purposefully dressed in a soft blue sweater, leggings, and boots for a little dressier look than when she was at the wolf sanctuary.

She didn't know what to expect from the pack leaders. She hoped she made a good impression. "What about your parents?"

"Cooper and Kelly Redding, retired military, living in San Antonio. I'm hoping they'll move here once my sister does. But she's still seeing a gray wolf back there, so we'll see."

"That's so nice." She wished she had parents that could settle down with the pack too.

As soon as Janice and Brad arrived at the pack leaders' ranch home, she was surprised at how beautifully decorated it was. She'd expected more ranch-style comfortable rather than elegant.

"The décor is mostly from the previous pack leader, but we kept it because it was so beautiful," Cassie said, giving Janice a hug.

She was a pretty redheaded red wolf, warm and friendly. Janice immediately liked her. Leidolf was smiling, a little more standoffish. Cassie cast him a look like he'd better get with the program. Janice suspected he didn't want to make her feel uncomfortable. But this was just what she needed. Wolf love. To be shown that others were fine with her being a wolf.

He was smiling rather wolfishly at his mate, and he looked like he was ready to eat her all up in wolfish fun. Then he gave Janice a hug. "Welcome to the pack. I'm sure Brad told you that you didn't have to join our pack, but I'm also sure he expressed how much we want you in the pack."

"He did. Thanks. I have a lot to learn about all this. I have such a time with controlling my shifting during the full-moon phase, it's nice to be around others like me where I'll be safe."

"You sure will be. We've already sent a group of men and women to Yakima to search for a woman who looks similar to you from the photo Brad sent us of you," Cassie said. "We're so glad you ran into Brad at the wolf sanctuary. It has to be providence." She set out a platter of chicken, potatoes, and carrots while Brad served the wine and Leidolf brought over glasses of water for everyone. "When I first met Leidolf, I was trying to stay clear of his type. I had important business to take care of—finding a mother wolf and her cubs and getting them to safety. I was afraid Leidolf and his pack would interfere in my business."

"I didn't know Cassie was a wolf right off. She was wearing hunter's spray." Leidolf smiled at his mate.

"Hunter's spray?" Janice asked.

"Concealment to keep deer and other prey from smelling the hunter. In her case, she was trying to keep the wild wolf from smelling her, and it meant I couldn't smell her either."

Liking the couple already, Janice smiled. "Did you find the wolf and her pups and take care of her?"

"Eventually," Cassie said.

"And I learned Cassie was a red wolf too, and that meant she was all mine." Leidolf served up the chicken for everyone.

"Do you think that was providence?" Janice asked.

"Certainly. She'd come into my territory to talk about wolves. I had to learn what she had to say, and some farmers were hassling her."

"He was my hero when I needed one, though I do my fair share of helping him out too."

"I'll say," Leidolf said. "Are you going to be staying with Brad, or would you like to stay with us or with another family?"

"I'm fine with staying with Brad as long as he has no problems with it." Janice didn't want to impose on him. "Do you have something on the ranch that I could do?"

"The wolf's moon will be here before we know it. Don't worry about a job just yet. You need to get settled in. Move your stuff down here from Tacoma. You'll have all the help you need to take care of it," Leidolf said.

"I helped raise sheep before my parents died," she said. "Otherwise, I was waitressing and then working as a receptionist for different jobs. I know how to sew and cook."

"What about kids? You could serve as a nanny," Cassie said. "Several of us who have jobs need to hire wolves to look after our little ones. We need to start a preschool also and will need a couple of preschool teachers."

"I don't have any training to being a teacher."

"We'll all help set it up if it sounds like something you might like doing. We're going to have to do it anyway. We just haven't had the time to organize it. We'll make sure you're trained also so you'll feel you know what you're doing."

"Okay. Kids and animals always seem to gravitate toward me." Janice was really thrilled she could help out with the wolf kids. She'd probably learn something from them too. "But when the full moon is out?"

Cassie served up another potato for herself. "We'll have someone else cover for you. There won't be any problem with it at all."

"And when I have time off, I can volunteer at the wolf sanctuary?"

"We'd be thrilled if you would," Cassie said. "See? It's providence. Brad will help you get moved, and we'll go from there."

"But I'm looking for my sister too, if I have one."

"Certainly. Hopefully, we'll find her anyway and convince her to move here also," Cassie said.

Janice was thrilled. Things were really looking up for her. Of course, everything would be a real learning curve, meeting all the other wolves, learning how to teach preschoolers, courting the hot wolf she was staying with. That part she might be able to fumble through without a lot of guidance. She just hoped he was agreeable. She smiled at Brad. He smiled back at her.

"Okay, that sounds good. We're leaving early tomorrow for Yakima. We can spend a couple of days looking for my sister, and then head to Tacoma to pack up my stuff. On the way back, we can check in at Yakima again."

"That will work," Cassie said. "Those from our pack who are in Yakima looking for her will continue to do so."

"Oh, and the hunters you two found were arrested and charged with trespassing, hunting without licenses, hunting off season, and I'm sure we can throw a bunch of other charges at them. They won't want to do that again anytime soon," Leidolf said.

"At least not in our territory," Brad said.

She hoped the same so they could run as wolves on the land without worrying.

After a delightful dinner and feeling much better about having met pack leaders and finding they were nice, normal people, she and Brad headed back to his house.

"You know we're courting each other," she said matter-of-factly. She half expected him to laugh at her, but he didn't. He just smiled. "I'm serious. I don't think any of the other male wolves will ever do."

"You haven't even met them yet."

"Are you going to introduce me to them?"

"No."

She laughed. "Okay then. That means we're courting. If that's how this is done."

He smiled and put his arm around her waist about the time they saw the twin brothers heading for the bunkhouse.

"He got the girl," Pierce said to his brother. "You saw the way he kicked us out of the sanctuary when we went to speak with her."

"Yeah, I know. I was thinking we need to become Navy SEALs like him," his brother said.

She chuckled. Brad laughed.

When they were inside the house, Brad pulled her in for a kiss. "We're courting, but that doesn't mean you're stuck with me if we decide we're really not compatible with each other."

Before she could agree with his comment, he was kissing her like this was the real deal. She was caught up in his hotness, feeling the heat through their clothes, the hardness of his erection pressing against her as he slipped his tongue into her willing mouth. She'd never been with a man who made her feel so alive, so desirable, and she realized some of the reason for the sexual craving she had for him had to do with their pheromones calling to each other, urging them to take this further.

She'd always been careful about getting into relationships with men because she'd have to disappear from their life every time the full moon appeared. She couldn't explain what was wrong with her, and she had given up trying to have a normal relationship with a guy when she wasn't normal.

With Brad, she could enjoy being with him to her heart's content. That made her feel freer with him, yet she had to remember they couldn't consummate the relationship, which was a downer. Not unless they really were meant to be together...forever.

She kissed and stroked his tongue with hers, rubbing her heated body against his. Without her express approval, it was like her out-of-control hormones were thinking for her, and she began pulling off her sweater.

He didn't stop kissing her until she pulled her sweater over her head and dropped it on the floor. His eyes were clouded with lust, his large, capable hands caressing her bare shoulders. Because of his hesitation, she was afraid he was putting on the brakes because she was too new at this to understand what was going on. Hell, she knew just what was going on, and she wanted this. Maybe not the whole tamale right now, but she sure wanted more of him.

She reached down and pulled his sweater over his head, tossing it on the carpeted floor. Then she ran her hands over his soft skin, his hard chest, the palms of her hands feeling the heat, his nipples already as erect as his cock, straining to be free of his jeans. She soaked in his masculine scent combined with wolf and the great outdoors and his wolfish pheromones in overdrive.

This was what she'd been missing in her life! Feeling normal with one of her own kind. Better than normal. Hotly needy.

She kissed his mouth again, tasting the delightful red-berry wine on his tongue and lips. Wanting to ravish him through and through, she kicked off her boots, and he quickly reached down to remove his. Then they were removing each other's pants, and he lifted her so she could wrap her legs around his hips. Wearing only their underwear, he carried her into his bedroom, as if he was going to share his whole abode with her, bed and all.

She couldn't believe she was so ready for this when she'd just met him, for heaven's sake! But she wanted this, needed this, craved this connection with a wolf like her.

His rigid cock was riding against her mound as he carried her into his bedroom and set her on the mattress.

She unfastened her bra while he removed her socks, his hands sliding up her calves in a seductive caress that had her wet and wanting. As soon as he reached her panties, he pulled them down slowly, his mouth pressing sizzling hot kisses down her thighs. It didn't seem to matter that she was wearing the most boring white panties and bra known to mankind. Note to self: shop for some more intriguing styles when she had a chance. Whoever would have thought that a trip to the wolf sanctuary would have meant baring her underwear to a male red wolf?

Brad was wearing black, form-fitting boxer briefs that were hugging his straining erection, and she reached out to free him. Once she pulled his boxer briefs down, his cock sprang free, and she wanted him pounding inside her now! She was aching for him, like she'd never felt with any other man. That had to mean something, right?

Then they were kissing again, his body rubbing up against hers, soft skin, hard muscles creating a friction that was driving her crazy. *Enough! Get it done already!*

He switched his attention to her breasts and began licking her nipples, the touch of his tongue sending tiny thrills through the nerve endings. She ran her hands over his backside and squeezed his firm buttocks. He was glorious. His touch, the feel of his warm breath against her sensitive nipples, his hand sweeping down to begin stroking her clit—all of it made her feel desirable.

He was a consummate lover, and she knew she couldn't last. Every stroke pushed the envelope, brought her closer to the bright side of the moon. A blast of heat and pleasure rocked her, ripples of delight climaxing through her. She wanted to just glory in the feelings, but she pushed him onto his back and straddled him, ready to help him come. He was smiling at her, his eyes still smoky with desire, his cock stretched out to her. She took hold of his cock and worked her way up and down the shaft, sliding her hand over the weeping tip, making him groan with the need to find release.

She was glad she could make him feel as wondrous as he had made her feel. Man, had she won the jackpot when she woke up this morning and decided to go to the White Wolf Sanctuary first and met the best tour guide ever.

Brad hadn't expected to be involved in bed play with a she-wolf who, from the moment he had set eyes on her, had turned his world inside out.

Every stroke she made on his arousal brought him that much closer to orgasm. The pressure of her hand gliding up and down his cock changed as she watched his face and sensed the tension in his body. He stroked her thighs, concentrating on the way she was making him feel, needy and wanting, his blood sizzling. He felt the surge of impending release, and he gripped her thighs when he came. He was satiated and invigorated all at once. He wanted to run with her as a wolf again in the dark of night, to howl, to let the pack know she was his. At least for now. But he hoped she would continue to be his.

No way would he ever have thought he'd be entangled with a woman who couldn't control her shifting at all times, but he was rethinking those ideas in a hurry. He had always imagined his mate would be a royal like him! Especially when the newly turned wolves presented such a problem in the pack. With her, she was *his* kind of trouble, and he was ready to do whatever it took to see she was happy with him and the pack.

She lay down on the bed beside him, her head lying on the crook of his arm, and he kissed her forehead.

"I hope you know what this all means." He hoped she hadn't done this out of a sense of need and still wasn't sure how all the wolf business worked.

"We're courting," she said, "and I'm not giving you up. If some other she-wolf wants you, she's going to have to fight me for the right."

He chuckled. "Hell, I've never had a she-wolf fight another over me. Sounds damn good to me." He ran his hand over her arm. "Okay, I'm going to take a shower, and if you'd like, we could go on a wolf sunset run. If you're not too tired. I'm sure there will be others out there, taking in the sunset too."

"Yeah, I'd love that."

"Okay, be out in a minute." He left the bed and smiled back at her as she closed her eyes and just stayed on the bed. She was beautiful, her skin creamy and soft, her nipples still dusky pink and erect, her red curly hairs dewy, the rest of her red hair draped across his pillow. He hoped she didn't fall asleep while he was in the shower, but if she did, he was climbing back into bed with her and sleeping the rest of the night away.

After he moved her bags to his room.

He quickly soaped up, rinsed off, and opened the fogged-up, glass shower door. Sitting on the tile floor was Janice in her red wolf coat, his towel in her mouth. He chuckled and reached out to take his towel from her. She released it to him, and he quickly dried off. "I'd say I could get used to that, but next time, we can shower together." He hung up the towel on the rack.

She woofed. It was the first time she'd made any sound as a wolf, and he was glad to hear her voice. He suspected she was feeling more comfortable around him and the others.

"You can howl with me, and I bet you anything, if the other wolves aren't already howling, they will join in." He wanted to hear her beautiful howl. It was a way for wolves to learn the sound of her voice also, and when they heard it coming from the same location as his, they'd know just who it was. It was important to recognize her wolf's voice if she was off on her own and ever needed help. And he wanted her to know she could sing away and be safe among wolves.

CHAPTER 5

TONIGHT, JANICE WOULD BE EXHAUSTED IN A GOOD way. She hadn't expected to run as a wolf with Brad at sunset, but tonight was spectacular, the pinks and oranges of the setting sun reflecting off the clouds and the water. It made her think of fishing earlier and how proud she was that she'd caught her very own fish as a wolf.

Now she was running with the wolf who made her dreams come true. She suspected he would want to move her into his master bedroom. She thought maybe she should slow down a bit as far as their relationship went. Still afraid she might be too clingy or needy because he was the first wolf to befriend her, she decided she wasn't going to give in to doubt. She wanted to be with him as long as that was what he wanted too.

As soon as they reached the riverbank, they stopped, and she lifted her head and howled. She truly had intended to follow Brad's lead and join in when he howled. Before he could howl along with her, others off in the distance answered her call. He smiled at her with a wolfish grin, then licked her cheek. He lifted his head, pointing his nose toward the heavens, and howled too.

He was beautiful, from his rock-solid body to his voice that could make a smitten she-wolf swoon. She howled again, and he joined in with her this time, the resonating howls echoing through the woods and meadows, older wolves, young wolves, and every age in between calling out in greeting. For wild wolves, she knew it meant a gathering of the pack for the night. But for the *lupus garous*, they had their safe human homes to live in, and no need to all be gathered together to protect the rest of the pack. They were just letting everyone know they were out here, having fun, running as wolves, enjoying the sunset. When she set out to look for her kind, she'd never in a million years imagined this.

What surprised her was when wolves up at the homes began to howl.

Did they all howl at night? Or was it for her benefit, so she'd know them if she heard them again? She'd be clueless since there were so many of them, and it would take time for her to begin to recognize their beautiful voices.

Because she was a wolf, she thought she might be able to run a lot more tonight, even though she wasn't used to it. He seemed to realize she wouldn't be able to run a great distance tonight and nudged her to head back to the house. Maybe he was just as tired, but she suspected he wasn't. Not when he was a Navy SEAL and used to running as a wolf.

When they arrived at the houses, several wolves were standing around and barked at her in greeting. She smiled and woofed back at them, thrilled to be accepted. Then she went in through the wolf door, and Brad followed her.

He loped down the hall to his bedroom, and she went into hers. She shifted and opened a suitcase to pull out a long T-shirt. She thought maybe she was still staying in the guest bedroom. Then she heard him moving down the hall, and she pulled the shirt over her head.

He poked his head into her room. "You're staying with me, right?"

"Yeah, sure."

"Good. Let me get your bags." He was wearing blue plaid, flannel pajama shorts.

She wanted to pump her fist in victory, but instead she smiled and grabbed one of her bags while he carried the other two to his bedroom. "Do the wolves all come out and howl at night like that?" she asked.

"Yeah, and in the morning when the sun rises. It's a way to say good morning out on the ranch. Now the rest of the wolves who live in town or elsewhere don't, of course."

"Does anybody ever hear the wolves and come to investigate?"

"Sometimes we have a wolf biologist snooping around, claiming he heard wolves out this way. We deny it and chase him off. Or reporters show up, looking for a story." Brad motioned to the mattress. "Which side of the bed do you want?"

She pulled out her toothbrush and toothpaste and shampoo. "Whichever side you're not used to sleeping on." She didn't want to totally uproot him from his routine.

"Okay, the left side can be yours."

"That works for me. Do you want to use the bathroom before I take a shower?" she asked.

"No, go ahead. I'm going to check my emails."

"All right." She went into the bathroom and shut the door. She supposed she hadn't needed too, but she felt more comfortable doing so and giving them both a bit of privacy. When she was done, she left the bathroom and found Brad stretched on top of the bedcovers, looking over his phone. Man, he was so buff.

She climbed into bed and saw him frowning at the phone, not appearing to even notice she had joined him. "Any news?"

"My sister, Sierra, is coming to see me later than expected. I was hoping she'd get to meet you sooner. She hasn't retired from the army yet, but she'll be staying here for a couple of weeks on leave."

"Well, I'll probably be here for a while."

He glanced at Janice and smiled. "I sure the hell hope so."

"Thank you for everything you've done for me."

"You're most welcome. If you need anything, don't hesitate to ask." He smiled and set his phone down on the bedside table, and then he pulled her into his arms for a kiss.

This was the only way to end what had turned out to be a beautiful day!

Early the next morning, before Janice was awake and before the sun began to rise, Brad called Leidolf while he made some coffee. He thought the pack could forgo their morning wolf wakeup call for once so she could sleep in a bit.

Leidolf chuckled. "I'll let the pack know. When are you leaving for Yakima?"

"As soon as we've had breakfast and can get on the road. Has anyone learned anything up there?"

"No, no word. Too bad we couldn't find her on YouTube videos. That's how one twin discovered her sister. She was in several videos, and her sister saw it. Once they got in touch, they realized they had the same birth dates and after they were born, they had been adopted by separate families. A law exists now that twins have to be placed with the same family. In any event, another person saw a photo of an identical clone of his friend on Facebook and it turned out to be his twin. Social media can really make a difference. DNA tests showed in each of the cases that they were indeed twins. Good luck with your search."

"Okay, thanks."

"We want to keep her here at all costs, for her safety and ours. If we have to suspend howl-and-greets in the morning, that's not a problem."

Brad could imagine several of their people waking up late this morning because they were so used to the morning routine. He packed a bag as quietly as he could. Janice had to really be tired not to wake, no matter how quiet he tried to be. Of course they'd fooled around a couple more times last night and that had helped to wear her out.

An hour later, he heard her in the bathroom. "Want some eggs, bacon, and toast?" he called out to her.

"Yes!" she called out from the bathroom. "Thanks! You should have woken me. What happened to the wolf howl?"

"Suspended until further notice."

She laughed. "I love your pack."

He was glad for that.

After breakfast, they drove to Yakima, and the first place Janice wanted to see was the travel station where she'd met the man who thought she was someone else. Brad understood her reasoning—this time if the man saw her, she could ask who the woman was. But they didn't see any sign of the woman or the man. Just in case the woman frequented the area, they hit up all the shops nearby with no luck. The woman might not even go to the travel station. It might have just been by chance that Janice met up with the man who knew the other woman.

For three days, they searched for the woman without success. They met up with others of the wolf pack doing the same thing there and had lunch with them, but at night, Brad and Janice went to a hotel nearby and were on their own.

It was getting close to the time Janice wouldn't be able to fight the pull of the moon.

That morning, Brad drove her to the travel station yet again. "Did you want to return to the ranch or go to your place and pack up your things so you can move? We can at least start that process."

Janice let her breath out in a huff. "Sure. Let's do that. Right after I stop to check out the station and you can get some gas."

He wanted to stay with her at all times. But he agreed to get gas while she went inside. He couldn't follow her every-where. He didn't want to drive her crazy. Nights were good, though he sensed the tension building in her. The stress of having to shift was clearly bothering her, and he wanted to do everything he could to help her get through every full moon by having fun with it, not feeling dejected because she couldn't control it.

He finally finished filling the tank and was about to head inside when he saw Janice standing next to the glass windows talking to a man Brad didn't know. He hurried to meet up with her in case this was the guy, or someone else, who knew her sister.

"Listen, the only one coming in here all the time who looks like you is you," the man said, who was wearing a blue shirt with the logo of the travel station on it.

Brad swiftly joined her, and the way he moved toward them, the guy quickly stepped away from Janice, looking and smelling like he thought he was about to get a knuckle sandwich.

"No luck, honey?" Brad asked Janice.

She shook her head.

"Are you ready to go?" he asked.

"Yeah, thanks. Wait, we've run out of bottled water. Let me grab a couple of them." She went to fetch them, and Brad eyed the employee with disdain.

"Hey, man, she's asked me the same question like twenty times."

"Really? That many times?" Brad had no use for the guy if he couldn't help her out, but since she was grabbing the water, he might as well talk to him.

"Yeah. Twice today already."

"Wait, today?" Brad's heart skipped a beat. He couldn't believe it. Had they really found someone who saw Janice's sister?

"Yeah, today, man."

"We haven't been in here today."

"No way."

"Yeah way. The woman is her sister. Did she give a name?"

"No. None of the times."

"But she was wearing something different?" Brad asked as Janice joined them. "He saw your sister. Unless you have a doppelganger who isn't related to you."

Janice nearly dropped the bottles of water she was holding, and Brad seized her arm to steady her.

"What did she look like?" Janice asked.

"Hell," the guy said, "like you."

CHAPTER 6

JANICE COULDN'T BELIEVE IT! ALL THIS TIME HER SISTER had been trying to find her too? She was thrilled, but she still couldn't believe it. "She asked about me?" she asked the employee.

"Well, like you, she didn't have a picture to share. She said she only had a picture of herself and you were supposed to look just like her. Just like you told us. So I figured you were the same woman every time you came in."

"What was she wearing? Was her hair fixed the same way?" Janice hoped she'd get a clue that would help find her faster.

"Her hair was down like yours is." The guy shrugged. "I don't remember what she was wearing. Jeans, I think. A parka. Boots, maybe? I don't know. I really wasn't paying much attention because she looked just like you."

Janice let her breath out in exasperation, but she couldn't fault the guy. She could see how she and her sister could confuse the employee when they were both coming here and asking about each other. "She didn't tell you her name?"

"You didn't tell me your name. I guess the two of you think alike."

"Uh, no, I did tell someone my name and gave them my number. Okay, listen, here's my phone number and my name again. I guess the other employee didn't share the information. If you see the other woman again, give her this note, okay?" Janice wrote it down for him. "Tell her we're eating dinner at El Rancho at six."

"Write down the place and the time. I won't remember it. She might not come in again today or tomorrow. She was here twice this morning already."

"Okay, thanks. What time did she *actually* come in?" Janice asked.

"How would I know? I get busy. I'm supposed to be stocking shelves." The employee raised his palms in a gesture of 'I don't know.'

"Early morning? Late morning?" Brad asked.

"Both, I guess."

"A long time apart?" Janice asked.

"Yeah, I guess."

"Does she come in here all the time?" Janice hoped she did so they could catch up to her soon, before the full moon caused trouble for the both of them.

"No. I don't know. I mean, you're in here all the time."

Okay, this wasn't going to work. "Please share that information with your coworkers again." Janice could just see her sister arriving and this guy would be gone, and her sister wouldn't get word that Janice had been here.

Then she noticed Brad was writing some information down on a card. "Let's let this guy get back to work. We can pay for the water and get out of here."

She agreed. They weren't getting anywhere with this. But then she had another thought. "Can we look at the security surveillance?" she asked the employee.

"Uh, someone already asked that. A police officer. But the owner has to approve it, and he won't unless there's been a crime committed," the employee said. "That's the law."

"Great," she said.

When they went to pay for the water, Brad handed the

card to the cashier. "Janice is searching for her twin sister. They appear identical. Apparently, her sister was hunting for her this morning, but everyone believes she's the same woman. So if you see her, please give her this card and let the other employees know they are trying to get in touch with each other."

"Oh, how cool," the girl said. "You came in here looking for her earlier."

"That was my sister." Janice felt all choked up. She couldn't believe they kept missing each other. They needed to do a stakeout on the place. She appreciated Brad for giving the other clerk a card too with Janice's information.

"Okay, sure, I'll give her the word," the clerk said.

Then Brad paid for the water, and they headed out to the car. "That's really good news. We're going to find her."

"I'm sure of it. I'm so glad she's trying to get in touch with me too. I feel like just parking here and not leaving until she shows up, but I know it's foolish. She might not come back for days."

"I'm texting the others here searching to concentrate on staying here to watch for her. Someone will always be here."

Janice sighed. "Thanks for everyone's help with this."

"You wouldn't believe how many bachelor males are up here, eager to meet your sister."

Janice laughed. "No wonder they're so willing to help."

"Yeah, that will do it. Well, of course they want to help you and your sister too, and the issue of your shifting is cause for concern among all of us wolves."

"Right."

They headed to the restaurant and ordered dinner, and Janice was hopeful her sister would call or show up soon. "I want to go to the travel station to see if she shows up first thing in the morning."

"I'll let everyone know we'll take the shift at eight."

"Okay, thanks."

They both had beef and cheese enchiladas, and after that, they returned to their hotel, and Brad checked in with his pack members. He shook his head at Janice. "She hasn't returned to the travel station, but it's open twenty-four hours. We'll have someone there at all times just in case she returns later. I let everyone know we'll be there at eight."

"Okay, great." Janice bolted the bedroom door and took hold of Brad's hand. "Let's think about something else for the time being."

After making unconsummated love with Janice that night, Brad sure hoped she would consider being his mate soon. He hadn't wanted to pop the question to her until she had been with him for a while, to give her a chance to know what she really wanted. But he didn't want anyone else courting her either.

They'd both fallen asleep, but sometime in the middle of the night, she kicked him with her wolf feet, and it woke him. He wondered how long she'd been a wolf.

Trying not to wake her and upset her, he gently rolled her over and wrapped his arms around her. She was still sound asleep, and he cuddled with her. It was the first time she had shifted without controlling it, and he hoped if she woke as a wolf, she wouldn't be mortified by it. He hadn't known how he'd feel about it if it happened while she was with him, but he was fine with it. He wanted her to know he was too. He worried she might have trouble tomorrow keeping her human form when they tried to find her sister. Her sister might be having the same trouble too.

They slept for a couple more hours, and then Janice looked back over her shoulder at him and stared at him for a moment. She licked his cheek, and he smiled at her.

"You're a beautiful wolf, you know?" He kissed the bridge of her nose, and she turned back around, letting him wrap his arms around her again. He already knew she was the one for him.

He sure hoped they'd find Janice's sister soon. He thought he might even propose a mating with Janice after they found her sister and could relocate her to the ranch, if she agreed to move there too.

Then, with the wolf wrapped in his arms, he fell asleep again and, much later, woke to find his sexy she-wolf in her human form, snuggling her cheek against his chest, her bare leg settled over his in a way that said, "Mine." He was all for it.

—∾—

After Janice woke that morning, they both showered and dressed, and Brad asked, "Do you want to order room service?"

"Yeah, sure." Janice couldn't believe she had shifted into her wolf in the middle of the night and Brad hadn't gotten upset about it. She wasn't sure how she would have felt if he'd been a wolf in bed with her. Then again, she'd slept with her Labrador retriever when she was young. Yet it wasn't exactly the same.

She figured he wanted to have room service because she shifted last night unexpectedly. "I could have stayed in bed." She stretched.

"You could have, but we slept in a little, and I know you want to get to the travel station by eight."

She had to get the business of her shifting out in the open with him. She'd been horrified when she'd kicked him as a wolf in the middle of the night. Not just shifted. Being awakened like that couldn't have been conducive to a good sleep for him. She was afraid he'd be worried about her now being out and about where she could be seen by humans until she was past the full moon phase.

From the breakfast menu, they decided on omelets, toast, ham, and coffee. Brad placed the order.

She began brushing out her hair. "Hey, about last night—"

"It was great." He took her hairbrush from her and began brushing her hair.

Boy, did that feel heavenly. Wait, he was talking about sex? "I mean about my shifting into a wolf in the middle of the night and kicking you while I was dreaming." *That* couldn't have been great.

"Yeah, no problem. You're soft and cuddly no matter which form you're in. Totally works for me."

"Are you sure? You can make me get off the bed to sleep on the floor if that happens again."

"Are you kidding? No way."

A half hour later, they heard the cart coming with their breakfast. At least she figured it was for them.

Brad headed for the door and opened it before the guy even knocked. Startled, the waiter jumped back. Once he delivered the food to their table, he left, and Brad and Janice sat down to eat.

She still couldn't believe how she'd turned into a wolf and kicked him. "If I start kicking you in bed again…"

"I'll cuddle with you until you stop kicking. Believe me, I'd much rather have you *in* my bed than not have you at all."

She smiled at him, loving how he seemed to always have the right words to make her feel more comfortable about being a shifter. She buttered her toast and spread on a thick layer of blackberry jam. "About this morning—"

"Yeah, I've been thinking about that. If you have the urge to shift, we'll leave and return to the hotel. At least it's only a few minutes away. We'll make sure someone is covering the travel station in the meantime."

"Okay, that works." Though she knew it was easier saying so than dealing with the issue if she had to suddenly strip off her clothes and shift in the truck. She could just imagine someone catching her, and what a disaster that would be. What if her sister showed up and had the same problem? And the two of them were scrambling to get out of sight?

It would be hard enough for one of them to hide fast enough without two of them being double the trouble. Then she wondered if both of them would shift at the same time, like women who worked and lived together who had their periods at the same time.

Still, she wanted to be there if her sister showed up. Janice planned to stay at the travel station until lunch, just to see if her sister ended up there. Then again, maybe her sister would be too worried about making an appearance because of the situation with the moon. She couldn't fault her. Janice was certainly on edge about it. She finished her breakfast in record time. "Are you ready?"

"Yeah, sure. Let's go."

They soon arrived at the travel station. To Janice's surprise, they found Leidolf and Cassie there, staking out the place. They got out of their respective vehicles and joined each other.

"How long are you going to be here for?" Cassie asked.

"Until lunch. We'll need coverage again then." Janice hadn't thought the pack leaders would take part in something like this.

"We're going home, and we'll have another team spell you before you leave," Leidolf said. "Good luck."

Janice thought Brad might tell them of her shifting problems last night, but he didn't. She wondered if she should, but she didn't want them to hang around when they wanted to return home. They must have a million things to do as pack leaders and wouldn't have time to babysit her and her sister.

"Thanks to you both and everyone who's helping with this," Janice said.

"We wouldn't have it any other way." Cassie gave her a hug, and Janice hugged her back.

Leidolf hugged Janice, and he and Cassie said goodbye to both of them, then got into a black Humvee and drove off.

Now it was just time to wait and see.

"I'll get some coffees for us. We can sit inside the restaurant or sit in the truck, whichever you feel more comfortable with," Brad said.

She hated to tell him she was feeling antsy about the shifting. Not that she was uptight about shifting, but she kept feeling like it could come on at any moment, her blood heating, and not in an amorous way. A rush of warmth would flood her body when she was shifting.

"I'll sit in the truck if you don't mind."

"Nope, not at all." He gave her a hug and a kiss. "I'll be out in a minute."

She climbed back into the truck and watched for anyone who pulled up at the station. Men, a couple, a teen, no one who looked like Janice's clone.

Brad finally left the station carrying a couple of hot coffees. The heat from the coffees mixed with the cold air, and steam rose from them. She was already getting cold from sitting in the truck. She hoped they could manage for a while out here, but if not, she'd have to chance sitting inside.

⁓

They finished their coffee and were talking about her moving her stuff from her place to his when Brad changed the subject to something he needed to say.

"I've dated a few wolves over the years," Brad said, not usually into talking about his past relationships or how he felt. But with Janice, he wanted to, felt compelled to, needed to.

She watched him, waiting to hear what he had to say.

Here he was a tough-as-nails alpha wolf, but he realized telling her his vulnerabilities wasn't really an easy thing to do, even though he felt comfortable with her and felt a trust with her he hadn't had with other women.

"I admire you for making it in life without exposing our kind all these years and having the fortitude to continue seeking us out in the event there were more of us. You stood out from the rest of the she-wolves I've met right from the beginning. Your strength, your vulnerability, hell, you had just been exposed to three of us wolves and were processing all that when you began to help me with my chores at the wolf reserve."

She smiled. "I like to keep busy, help out when I can. I enjoy it."

He smiled back, loving the way she smiled at him with genuine warmth. "When I was on active duty, I was there to protect and serve."

"And with me, you feel that need too?"

He chuckled. "Uh, yeah, but more than that. I love the outdoors, hiking, swimming, exploring new places. It sounds to me you do a lot of hiking too, while you were looking for our kind, and visiting new places."

"Oh, yeah. I could hike all day in the woods, and part of the fun of looking for the wolves was seeing other regions of the States. I'd planned on visiting all them in my search for the wolves."

"That's what I want to do too. I haven't seen half of what I want to, but visiting other locations with another wolf would be much more fun."

"I'd love to do that with you too."

"When I'm with you, I feel…good, inspired…"

"Protective?"

He laughed. "I hope not too overprotective."

"I haven't had anyone in my life like that in years. It feels comforting. Makes me feel safe when I need to. I'll let you know if it's too much though. I felt the same way when I met you, drawn to you, not just because I smelled you were a wolf but some deeper draw. The way you were so altogether, knew so much about wolves, were able to manage a couple of wayward *lupus garous* and keep the center visitors in line with the perfect touch of authority but with aplomb, and in a way that was persuasive, not dictatorial."

"I can be dictatorial when push comes to shove."

She laughed. "I bet you can." She sighed. "I feel the same way about you."

"Wanting to be protective of me?"

Smiling, she said, "You bet. If someone gave you trouble, I wouldn't be standing on the sidelines to see how you dealt with it. I could get really growly when anyone bullied my parents, believe me."

"Okay, then if you're up to it, we could plan some trips to some national parks closer by, for now, around the new moon. I'd love to take you to other countries too that I've been to and fell in love with. I'm retired from the navy, so I have the retirement income."

"That would be wonderful. A dream come true. Can you take off that much time from work?"

"Yeah, Leidolf's flexible about things like that. If it's important for a wolf's well-being, then it's a given."

"My well-being or yours?"

He smiled and gave her a hug. "Truthfully? I'm speaking for myself."

Chuckling, she hugged him back. "It's a deal. I..." She suddenly turned to look away from him, and he saw the woman too.

Janice's doppelganger in the flesh.

—◆◆◆—

Janice had been so wrapped up in Brad, forgetting for the moment about her mission here, when she saw a woman that was the spitting image of her heading for the door of the station. For a moment, Janice couldn't believe her eyes.

"That's her!" Brad said, startling Janice from her intense concentration.

"Yes!" Janice hurried to get out of the truck to intercept her. She was trying not to run and tackle the woman. What if, by some twist of fate, the woman looked just like her but wasn't related? Janice still hurried to reach her. "Excuse me." She breathed in the woman's scent, but she smelled just like Janice—wolf-wise!

"Ohmigod, I can't believe I really have a twin," Janice's sister said, both of them rushing forth to give each other a hug.

Their eyes were misty with tears, and they smiled at each other in amazement. Janice still couldn't believe it.

"I'm Dorinda. For days, I've been smelling…well, you know, our kind. It was like the whole population of Yakima had increased by a hundred wolves." Dorinda just shook her head, her hands now holding Janice's.

"I'm Janice Langtry. Yeah. I couldn't be certain you really existed. And I can't believe we kept missing each other here. When I came looking for you, they thought that you were me. So the same thing must have happened to you."

"Yeah, exactly. Even though I left my information with them like you probably did." Dorinda glanced at Brad, took a deep breath, and smiled broadly. "Wow."

"He's mine," Janice said, not meaning to say that, but the wolf's side of her nature came out in a vengeance.

Brad smiled, looking like he appreciated the comment,

not that he thought she shouldn't have said it. Janice was grateful for that.

Dorinda laughed. "Well, I just hope there are more like him around. I've been…smelling the others but I just couldn't ever seem to run into them. You smell identical to me. I've smelled a couple of women and several different men lately. I thought maybe one of the women was you, but your scent is just like mine."

"I know. That's why when the guy thought I was you a few years back, I didn't smell any others like us in the store. I thought it was just a case of mistaken identity."

"Oh, Richie? He called me to tell me he'd seen my looka-like in the store. When you didn't recognize him, he figured you couldn't be me. We dated for a time, which is probably why he knew we weren't the same person. I've been looking for you ever since."

"I lived in Tacoma. I'm moving to the ranch where more of Brad's people live." Janice realized she hadn't even intro-duced him. "Uhm, this is Brad Redding."

"Hmm," Dorinda said. "I'd shake your hand or give you a hug, but I think my sister would bite me. Speaking of which, I'm not feeling myself. I didn't even think I'd make it in to see if you showed up today."

"Oh, God, me either." Janice had been so excited about seeing her sister, she hadn't been paying attention to the signs that told her she was going to need to shift soon.

"I can drive you to the ranch, south of here," Brad said.

"Or you can come to my place. It's only a few minutes from here. Just follow me there." Dorinda headed for her car.

Janice and Brad started for their vehicle.

"Did you want to ride with me and we can talk, Janice?"

Dorinda asked. "If you can give up your hunky man for a few minutes?"

"Can you make it there without shifting?" Brad sounded worried.

"Yeah, it's only a few minutes from here. I usually walk, unless I need gas, but things are iffy for me now."

"Sure, I'll go with you." Janice was certain Brad wanted to hear everything they said too, but she could at least ask Dorinda about the boyfriend and tell her about the birds and the bees for wolves, if she didn't know about it. She suspected she didn't.

When she got into Dorinda's car, she noticed she was using the same air freshener Janice used, and she had a little wolf sitting on the dashboard similar to the one Janice had.

"So you were dating the human?" Janice asked.

Dorinda laughed. "It sounds funny calling him that, but yeah, I guess you're right. It was for a short while, but I couldn't share my greatest secret with him. I'm sure he would have run off screaming if he'd known."

"I felt the same way about dating humans."

"This is just too good to be true. You can't know how glad I am to meet you. So how many wolves like us are there?"

"In the pack? I'm not sure. I only ran into Brad a few days ago at White Wolf Sanctuary where he was volunteering and was our tour guide. But there are a lot of wolves. Red wolves. Just like us. And there are gray wolves and Arctic wolves too. The pack has a thirty-thousand-acre ranch where you can run wild any time you want."

"Sounds like a dream come true. Is it like a commune?"

"No. People work everywhere or on the ranch. But not

all the wolves are like us. Some don't have trouble with the full moon and shifting."

"Oh, wow. I wish I could be like that."

"Me too." Janice explained about the birds and the bees.

Dorinda's jaw dropped. "We can have babies as a wolf?"

"Wolf pups."

"Whew," Dorinda said. "I could just see delivering a human baby as a wolf."

The ladies both laughed, and then Dorinda was pulling into her modest-sized, wood-frame house.

"So what do you do for a living? I keep getting fired because I can't work during the phase of the full moon. I'm a receptionist at a law firm otherwise," Janice said.

"I teach online writing classes."

"Oh, that's so cool."

"Yeah, so I don't have issues with my shifting and my work."

"I was thinking I needed to come up with a job where I could work at home too. But now with working at the ranch, I won't have any problems. Would you like to work with me as a preschool teacher there?"

Dorinda smiled. "And when we shift?"

"They'll have us covered."

"Okay."

"I have to ask you something kind of weird. I-I have these dreams—" Janice said.

"Ohmigod, you too? Where you're looking for me, only you don't know if you're trying to find yourself or a twin?"

Janice couldn't believe it. "Ohmigod, yes!"

"Yes, absolutely. I looked it up, and researchers say through the use of ultrasound, they have discovered that twins' behavior and disposition is varied—they have both individual and interactive reactions in the womb. Probably one of us is the alpha. Hold that thought." Dorinda parked in the garage and jumped out of the car. "Your boyfriend can close the garage door if he doesn't mind." She rushed for the door to her house.

Janice hurried after her, feeling the same urgency to shift.

"Close the garage door, will you?" Janice asked Brad, feeling panicked. She hurried inside after her sister. She *had* a sister. Really truly had a sister! She hoped this didn't cause problems for her!

CHAPTER 7

BRAD COULDN'T BELIEVE HOW TERRITORIAL JANICE HAD become with her declaration that he was hers. He'd been both amused and honored. Would he have felt the same feelings toward Dorinda if he met her first? Maybe not. As identical twins, they might look just alike, but their personalities would be different.

He closed the garage door and waited for a few more minutes at the door to the house. When he heard a woof and another woof, he opened the door. Both ladies were wearing their wolf coats, looking at him, their clothes strewn about the floor.

Damn, if they didn't look alike as wolves too, though it shouldn't have surprised him. They had the same coppery fur, same black-tipped tails, same light-colored chests. And they smelled the same. He swore they used the same shampoo, a delightful tangerine fragrance. He could be in trouble if Dorinda joined the pack and he mistakenly thought she was Janice. But with both sisters having fewer wolf roots and the issue with shifting, Dorinda needed to be with the pack also. They did have a shortage of female wolves, so eligible females were always important to the pack.

To his surprise, Dorinda woofed at Janice and then took off for the back door. A large dog door had been installed, and she pushed through it. Janice didn't hesitate to join her. Brad hurried after them, worried neighbors would see the two wolves in the backyard. When he unlocked and opened the door, he saw the backyard was heavily treed and had a six-foot-tall wooden fence. All the adjoining properties had one-story homes, so no one could see over her fence and observe the wolves. He relaxed, pulled up a seat at the round wooden table outside, and watched as the two sisters played.

He wanted to play with them as a wolf too, but they needed this time for their own.

Smiling, he couldn't believe how much his world had changed. Here he'd thought it would with his sister's arrival and he'd have to fend off the other male wolves who wanted to court her if she needed his help. Now he would have two sisters and one mate if Janice was of the same mind, and he'd be just as protective of Janice's sister as his own.

The two she-wolves snarled and bit at each other in fun, racing after each other, one way, then the other. He swore each knew the other's moves before they made them, anticipating, charging, clashing.

He suspected Dorinda hadn't been able to use her wolf voice much either, except maybe to bark if she felt the urge. He just hoped she'd be agreeable to come home with him. That reminded him—he needed to call off the search for Janice's sister. He called Leidolf and gave him the good news.

"Have you convinced her to join us?" Leidolf asked.

"I hope to. They're in their wolf coats playing in the backyard."

"Do we need to send a van?"

"They can both ride in my truck. There's enough room, and I think they'll want to be together. In any case, I don't think it's possible for Dorinda to drive on her own down to the ranch at this time."

"I suspect not. Okay, let us know if you need a van. I'll

call off the search. Can they both stay with you at your house, or do we need to make other arrangements?"

"They can both stay with me." He suspected they'd want to have time to visit with each other. He hoped Janice wouldn't forget all about him. He hadn't really thought about that aspect of the reunion. But he was glad they were together.

They finally wore themselves out, sitting in the tall grass, panting. Then he heard someone pull up to the house out front. He thought maybe it was some of their people, but they wouldn't have Dorinda's address. Dorinda suddenly woofed and raced back to the house. Janice ran after her, and they both barged through the dog door, Dorinda first. Brad opened the door and closed it. Then he heard a mower start in the front yard. Dorinda must have a yard service, and he was glad the sisters had quickly entered the house.

The two wolves sat in the house panting.

Brad asked, "Do I need to pay the yardmen?"

Dorinda shook her head.

"Did you want to come with us, and we'll return to the ranch where you can meet others like us?"

Dorinda nodded and wagged her tail.

"Okay, why don't we wait until you can shift back to your human forms and then you can pack a bag. We have to grab our bags from the hotel room also. On second thought, I'll go and get them and check out of the hotel while you are both waiting to change back."

Janice woofed.

Dorinda woofed too.

"Okay, I'll be back shortly." Brad hated to leave the women alone, even though they were in the house safe and sound. But he still worried something could go wrong.

He left the house, unable to lock it without Dorinda's keys. He figured if anyone tried to enter the house while they were wolves, the uninvited guest would turn around in a hurry once he saw them.

Brad got into his truck and took off for the hotel, calling his sister on the Bluetooth. "When you arrive, you'll meet a couple of female wolves staying with me, Sierra."

She laughed. "Two now? I thought you said there was a shortage of she-wolves in the pack."

"There is. We had a new arrival about a week ago. But we got lucky with you coming here and the two sisters joining the pack. At least I hope her sister wants to."

"If they're staying with you, does that mean you're interested in one of them?"

"Yeah, Janice. Though I have to admit, they're identical twins, so they look and act a lot alike."

Sierra laughed again. "I hope they *both* don't want to be your mate then."

He was only interested in Janice.

"I may have to get in sooner than I planned, just to make sure you don't get yourself into trouble over the two women."

"I have to warn you, they aren't royals, and they're having trouble holding their human form right now."

"Oh."

"And they just found each other, so it means they're getting to know each other."

"All right. Well, then I can keep you company if you start to feel unloved."

He chuckled. "I'm proposing a mating to Janice as soon as she's human again."

"Oh, wow, you *are* serious."

"Yeah, I am."

"Okay, I'll be there soon."

He laughed. He knew Sierra wasn't coming home early to make sure he didn't mess things up with Janice but so she could meet her new sisters if things worked out between him and Janice.

"Yeah, so you don't screw anything up. I'm thrilled for you, Brother. I'll see you soon."

Maybe she was a little worried he'd mess things up on his end.

They ended the call, and Brad finally reached the hotel. He packed his and Janice's bags in a hurry, wanting to get back to Dorinda's house as quickly as possible. The whole time, he was thinking of when he could propose a mating to Janice—he wanted to elicit the right response. He checked out of the hotel, and on the way to the truck, he got a call from Dorinda. He assumed Janice had shifted back too. "Hey, yeah, Dorinda, I'm on my way."

"It's me, Janice. I'm helping my sister pack, and we can head to the ranch after that. She's eager to meet a wolf like you."

He smiled. "I'm headed over there now. I told my sister you two were staying with me."

"I hope she's okay with it."

"She's ecstatic."

"Oh, good. I was hoping it didn't cause problems between you and your sister."

"No. Sierra's good." He wanted in the worst way to tell Janice he wanted to mate her. But he didn't think asking her over the phone was the best way to go about it. And now he wouldn't have the privacy he'd like to have at the house. Ah, hell, screw propriety. His sister would give him grief when she learned how he did this, but he wasn't waiting. "Will you be my mate?"

Janice laughed.

He sure as hell hoped he was really talking to Janice and she was *only* laughing because of the way he proposed it to her. "Janice?"

"You...want...to...mate...me? Are you sure?"

"Yes, Janice. I love you. And I want you to know even if you want to wait on a mating. I have no interest in seeing anyone else. I've never felt this way about another wolf. Sorry for doing it this way, but we're going to have lots of company, and I didn't know when I could talk to you in relative privacy. If you're ready too, I don't want to wait."

"I guess wolves don't get down on bended knee."

He chuckled. "I'm sure some do. It's hard for me to do that when I'm driving the truck."

She laughed again. "Okay, yes, with all my heart, I'd love to be your mate. Uh, hold on."

In the background, he heard Dorinda say, "Are you sure you're not jumping the gun?"

"No. We're perfect for each other, and before you say it, I'm not afraid he'll want you instead."

"Are you sure he won't get us mixed up?"

"Of course he won't get us mixed up." Then Janice said, "Brad, will you?"

"I'll try damn hard not to."

Janice chuckled. "Okay, then yes, yes, I want to be your wolf lover."

Dorinda laughed in the background.

Brad smiled. "You made my whole year, Janice. I'm pulling into the driveway now."

Janice came outside, and as soon as he got out of the vehicle, she threw her arms around his neck. "You're one hot wolf and a half, and I'm so into you," she said. "I love you for being you. Being with you is mind-blowing."

Smiling, he pulled her against his body in a tight hug. "I feel the same way about you. I love you." He kissed her, letting her know just how much he cared about her, the passion igniting between them like it always did. "Let's get you ladies home." He was thrilled they would be part of the pack, enjoying the comradery of the other wolves.

As soon as they walked into the house, Dorinda gave Brad a hug. "I hope you both know what you're doing."

"I know this is right for me, and if Janice agrees, there's no sense in delaying." Brad carried Dorinda's bags out to the truck, and Dorinda and Janice brought out some of the more perishable food.

"And I totally agree," Janice said.

"If that's the case, I'll let you both have some privacy to get on with the business with the birds and the bees when we arrive at the ranch," Dorinda said.

Brad laughed. Janice must have told Dorinda about the little talk he'd had with her. But he didn't want Dorinda to feel like she needed to be somewhere else just so he and Janice could have some privacy. Even though he *did* want that.

"I'm sure there's someone else I can stay with overnight at least," Dorinda said as they got on the road.

"Are you sure?" Janice asked.

"Yeah. You know if you were me, you'd want to do the same thing."

"That's true."

"Our pack leaders would love to have lunch with you so

they can meet you. And I'm sure they'd love to have you stay with them. They offered that choice to Janice if she hadn't wanted to stay with me."

"As if that was going to happen," Dorinda said. "God, I feel like I know everything about you, Janice."

"You do. I can't believe we like the same TV shows and use the same shampoo, love the same chocolate, peppermint ice cream with chocolate syrup on top, and pickles with our grilled cheese sandwiches."

"I guess I need to get some more groceries," Brad said, amused.

"We'll give you a list," Dorinda said.

The two she-wolves were going to keep him on his toes.

When they finally arrived at the ranch, Dorinda's mouth gaped. "Ohmigod, this is fantastic. I want to run as a wolf. Thirty thousand acres? This is wolf heaven. I couldn't even imagine what it would be like when you talked about this. But it's beautiful."

"It is," Janice said. "I felt the same exact way."

"They've expanded it a lot since I was here, but with all that acreage, we shouldn't have any trouble." He drove to his house first to drop off their bags and the food.

"Except for illegal hunting," Janice said.

"Yeah, and reporters every once in a while." He called Leidolf to let him know Dorinda wanted to meet them, hopefully for lunch. "Janice and I agreed to a mating."

"Hot damn, Brad!" Leidolf said.

"Yeah."

"Cassie and I will love to have Dorinda come for lunch and stay with us too," Leidolf said.

"Thanks, she said she'd love to."

"Bring her on over. We're fixing spaghetti for lunch."

"All right. We're just dropping off some groceries." Brad ended the call. "Okay, we're all set. You'll have lunch with the Wildhavens and then stay with them tonight."

"That works for me," Dorinda said.

After they put the groceries away, they took Dorinda over to see the Wildhavens, but Janice and her sister had to hug each other again as if to reassure themselves they weren't going to be separated again.

Dorinda gave Brad a hug too. "Thanks for being my brother."

"You're so welcome. I'm sure with three females in the household, I'm going to have my work cut out for me."

Dorinda laughed.

Cassie and Leidolf came out to greet them.

"I understand you have a lot of bachelor males here," Dorinda said.

The pack leaders both smiled. "Yeah," Leidolf said. "You will be *very* welcome in the pack."

"You sure will be. Come in and have lunch with us," Cassie said, then she added for Janice's benefit, "Dorinda will be in good hands."

That was Brad's cue to take Janice home with him and officially make her his mate. They said goodbye, and he hurried Janice off to his place. "Are you ready?"

"You bet I am. But we might have to be quick about it. I didn't want to mention it in front of everyone. Heck, I hope Dorinda will be all right during lunch."

"She will be. One way or another. You also, if you have to shift. No matter what, everything will be right with the world."

CHAPTER 8

JANICE WOULD BE DISAPPOINTED IF SHE HAD TO SHIFT before or during their lovemaking. She just hoped Brad was being honest with her and himself that he was all right with it.

As soon as they were in his house, Brad swooped Janice up in his arms and carried her to the bedroom. "No wanting to wait on this?" he asked.

She loved how thoughtful he was. "No way. You are my world. Besides, everyone will expect us to be mated tonight. I know it seems like such a whirlwind affair, but I wouldn't want it any other way. Besides, what if I said I wanted to wait, and my sister made a play for you?"

"She wouldn't dare." He set Janice on the bed and shrugged out of his jacket and then pulled off hers.

But she began removing her clothes as fast as she could. Smiling, he did the same with his own clothes, tossing them aside as fast as she was.

She really was afraid she'd shift in the middle of making love to him! That would go over big, she was sure. And he might be having second thoughts about mating her if this was always the problem when the full moon was so close at hand. Maybe they should wait, but she didn't want to.

Both of them were soon naked, kissing, lying on the mattress. He paused to stroke her hair, as if they didn't have any urgency. "If we don't hurry…" she said.

"We can wait. I can wait. It won't kill me."

"It might kill me."

He smiled at her and kissed her again. "I'm not giving you up, no matter what."

She kissed his mouth, and he kissed her back, their tongues caressing and stroking, the feel of his touch making her body thrum with anticipation. She forgot about the worry of shifting then, she was so caught up in the moment with him, his body pressing against hers, so hot and aroused. His pheromones were doing a number on hers, and she was already wet with need. The musky scent of her, of him, were mixing and intermingling. He rubbed his body against hers, and she felt his arousal pressing against her.

She swore the stars had aligned perfectly when she met Brad. He was so powerful and exquisite.

She ran her hands down his muscular arms and kissed his broad shoulder. Impressive, not like a bodybuilder's bulkiness, but just perfect for hugging on. He nuzzled her throat, licking a path to her nipple, latching on, and tonguing it. She felt a tightening in her belly that reached lower, an ache of need filling her. She moved her hands to his waist and slid them over his lean hips. He traced kisses across her breasts and kissed and licked the other nipple, then pulled on it lightly.

Oh…my…God. She was practically undone. Then his hands swept down to her clit and began to stroke her nub. She'd never imagined being with a wolf would be this hot. Not with any wolf though. This one, who had taken her in to help her find her sister and given her a home and his heart. And was teaching her the way of the wolf. This was the best lesson ever.

Even now, her pheromones were sweeping around his in a way that said he was hers, delicious, enticing, pushing the sensory sensations to an all-time high.

Even when they were making unconsummated love, he knew all the right buttons to stroke and just how to use the perfect pressure and speed to make her arch her back and want more and more and more. Now. Just like he was doing with her right this instant.

He captured her mouth again, keeping up the strokes on her nub, making her world catch on fire. She could stay in bed with him the rest of the month and do just this!

She was so wet and needy for him and feeling like she was going to come any…second…now.

She felt her world tipping on end as he stroked her into the next world, his kisses peppered all over her body. Their pulses were beating rapidly, and she felt breathless as he continued to ply her with strokes.

She felt the end coming. He was so good at this, and she loved him for it. Then she was crying out, feeling her whole world come unglued.

"Ohmigod, I love you."

He smiled at her and kissed her. Then he spread her legs wider and pushed his cock into her, sliding all the way in.

She tightened her inner muscles around his cock, loving the way he stretched her and plunged inside her to her very core. All her attention was on the masculine wolfish smell of him, which intrigued her no end, the way he pressed inside her and on top of her, his compelling kisses—all making her feel well-loved.

It wasn't just the glorious sex between them but the uniting of two wolf souls, the love they shared, boundless. Nothing compared to the primal need she felt while being with him. Raw, passionate, instinctual love.

He slowed his thrusts, then pushed deeper, faster, harder.

She felt the explosion deep inside her, rallied his climax with another of her own, and cried out while he growled his release.

He pumped into her a few more times, then relaxed, their bodies still joined. His body rested comfortably on top of hers. They fit each other perfectly.

This was heaven. She was in heaven.

"I will never"—he kissed her cheek—"complain about"—he kissed her mouth—"taking over a tour"—he teased her tongue with his—"again."

Smiling, she wrapped her arms around his neck. "Because you met me?"

"You're damn right. What if I'd been off cutting branches and out of sight of the tour group like usual, and I hadn't met you?"

"Then I would have met Pierce and his brother, Quincy."

Brad groaned. She chuckled.

"It was providence. I'm sure if you hadn't been giving the tour group lecture, I would have run into you anyway. I would have met the brothers, and they would have told you that I was there—"

"No way."

She laughed. "They would have convinced me to see your pack but before we even went anywhere, you would have learned they were there, and so was I, and the same thing would have occurred. This. A blissful mating." She pushed him onto his back and lay down on top of him. "I love you. How did I get so lucky to meet you?"

"I wished upon a falling star the night before." Smiling at her, he rubbed her arms with his hands.

"Really. You wished for a mate?"

"No. I wished I could have a couple of days' vacation."

She laughed. "Well, looking for my sister wasn't much of a vacation."

"Being with you has been the best vacation ever," he said. "You would be every wolf's dream mate, but you're all mine. I love you."

"When I tried to imagine what my dream mate would be like, he wasn't like you."

Brad smiled. "No, eh?"

"No. He was some geeky guy without muscles and wearing a pair of black-rimmed glasses. But he'd be so smart, he could steer me to the truth. I didn't realize a buff male wolf could do that for me better than anyone else who was totally clueless about us could." She closed her eyes, the heat flowing through her body, signaling she was going to shift. "Great." At least she wasn't dressed.

She rolled off Brad in a hurry…and shifted. Staring at him in her wolf form, she was about to leap off the bed.

He reached out and petted her chest. "Come here, beautiful wolf of mine. Let's get some sleep."

What really surprised her was he turned into his wolf, and she and he curled up together on the bed. She loved him for being so caring when she had no control over her wolf. This…their mating…couldn't be better.

—∿—

When they finally woke, Brad realized Janice had shifted but he hadn't, and she was cuddling him anyway, as if it didn't bother her that he was a wolf in bed with her. He quickly shifted, rolled over, and wrapped his arms around her. "Do you want to get some lunch? Grilled cheese sandwiches and some chianti wine—medium-bodied with a hint of cherries?"

"And pickles."

Brad laughed. "And pickles. Will dill pickles work?"

"Yes. That's perfect."

He got out of bed, threw on his boxer briefs, and she got up and dressed in her panties and sweatshirt. He wasn't planning on getting fully dressed. Not when he intended to be back in bed, making love to her again after lunch.

When they were in the kitchen, he pulled out the cheese and butter. She wrapped her arms around his back and hugged him while he sliced the cheese. "You're exquisite. I never thought a wolf would be this...this..." She kissed his bare back.

"Hot?" he asked, loving her. He put the sliced cheese on buttered slices of bread, then started grilling them.

"Yeah, hot." She slid her hands down his chest, her body pressed against his back, then slipped her hands down his boxer briefs.

He chuckled, ready to take her back to bed in a heartbeat. "You're making it awful hard for me to be the chef."

"Okay." She slipped her hands out of his boxer briefs.

He quickly objected. He liked having her hands all over him.

She laughed.

He flipped the sandwiches, and she kissed his back again. Then she washed her hands and got the pickles out of the fridge.

"I was going to ask what you wanted to do after lunch, but I think I already know," Brad said.

"Yep. You don't have any peppermint ice cream and

chocolate syrup, so a trip back to bed will make up for it," she said.

"That works for me." He served up the sandwiches and the wine, and she set out the pickles and ice water. They sat down to eat.

"These are great sandwiches," she said after taking a bite.

"They're sharp cheddar, the best kind of cheese. Extra sharp is great too."

"I'll say. The wine tastes delicious too."

"It is. So where were you born?" he asked, realizing he should have asked about this before, but they'd been concentrating on finding her sister.

"MultiCare Tacoma General."

"And your birth date?"

"Fourth of July, twenty-eight years ago." Janice smiled.

"Fireworks baby." Brad got on his phone to call Leidolf, hoping they might be able to learn who Janice and her sister's parents were. Maybe even learn if they had any more wolf relatives. "Hey, can one of our police officers check hospital records for twin girls born on the Fourth of July at—"

"Already checking into it. We were discussing this with Dorinda, and I've got one of our police officers at Tacoma General now. If we need it, our judge will send him the necessary paperwork so he can have access to adoption records."

"Good. Maybe we can find their parents or more of their family."

"Just our thought on it too."

"Okay, thanks. I'll let Janice know. How's Dorinda doing?" Brad asked.

"She's loving it here."

"Oh, good. I'll tell Janice."

"How are you and Janice doing?"

"We're mated."

"Hallelujah! I'll let everyone in the pack know so no one will be hitting on your mate."

Brad laughed. "Thanks. Then I won't have to get all growly with anyone."

When they ended the call, Janice moved the dishes into the kitchen. "You can tell me all about it later."

It wasn't long before they were removing their clothes and getting back in bed to share mated bliss. He would never complain about being a tour guide at the wolf sanctuary again. Not when it meant meeting the love of his life and making her his mate.

Two days later, Brad's sister, Sierra, arrived at the ranch in time for dinner. She seemed just as excited to meet up with the sisters as she did her brother. "So where are you staying?" she asked Dorinda.

"In a home of my own. Did you want to stay with me? Bachelor males live in the male barracks, but I was the only single female, and the house has three bedrooms," Dorinda said.

"Uh, yeah, sure," Sierra said.

"Okay, great. It's better than having Brad always watching over us," Dorinda said.

He raised his glass of wine to Dorinda. "I will *still* be watching over you and my sister."

The ladies all laughed.

"Yeah. I'd like that," Sierra said.

Brad was glad he and Janice would have more time together alone.

"Okay, and the other thing is we're starting a preschool. Could you help us with that? Then when Janice and I *can't* do it, you could," Janice asked.

"By myself?"

"Cassie said we'd have other coverage whenever we needed it."

"Well, I could give it a try. I mean, I'm not retiring for a while, but when I do, I guess I can." Sierra turned her attention to Brad. "You and Janice—that was quick."

He smiled. "When you find the right wolf, there's no sense in waiting." He hoped she'd give up the wolf she was dating at Fort Hood, Texas and find a wolf who she was really meant to be with.

"Yeah, and when I showed a bit of interest in Brad, my sister declared he was hers right away," Dorinda said. "I didn't stand a chance, and I look just like her."

Janice chuckled. "I didn't want him thinking I wasn't interested."

"No chance of that," Brad said, having smelled the interest Janice had in him from the beginning. "We'll take you for a wolf run tonight to show you the ranch, Sierra and Dorinda."

"I'd love it," Dorinda said.

Sierra agreed.

"Because we can't turn into wolves during the new moon, we can work at the White Wolf Sanctuary on the weekends when we aren't running the preschool," Janice said.

"You bet." Brad got a call from Leidolf. "Yeah, Leidolf?"

"I just wanted to say we're glad your sister arrived and can't wait to meet her. But also, we have some really good news. The sisters' parents, Rhonda and Kirk Wild, are here, eager to meet their daughters."

"Here?" Brad was so stunned, he just couldn't believe it. And they were alive! He felt overjoyed, as if they were his own parents, which he hoped they'd be.

"Yeah, Brad. I thought you'd like to tell the sisters. Their mom and dad are here at our house, eagerly waiting to see them. I would have sent them over there, but they just got here, and I thought they could just meet them over here."

"Okay. We'll be over in a minute." Brad knew they wouldn't want to wait, and though he was dying to hear how their parents were alive and they'd lost the girls, he wanted them all to hear the story at the same time. Since he and his sister were part of the family now, they'd all go over. "Well, we have good news. Your parents are alive and well, and they're at Cassie and Leidolf's house, waiting to see you."

Janice and Dorinda didn't respond at first, their mouths open, appearing as shocked as he had been. He really hadn't believed they were still alive, and had they been, he'd expected to get an update that they'd located them before they arrived.

Then the sisters' eyes filled with tears, and they both jumped off their chairs, but before they could bolt out the door, Brad hugged them both. Sierra followed suit.

"Let's go see them, shall we?" he asked.

—◊◊◊—

Janice and Dorinda hugged each other and were crying as they all left the house to meet the twins' parents. Janice had never expected to see them alive, so she was as stunned as her sister.

When they arrived at the Wildhavens' house, Janice and Dorinda's mother and father were just as teary-eyed as they were, and they hurried outside to hug each other, crying, grateful.

"Cassie showed us a picture of you, Janice. They didn't have one of Dorinda, but they said she looked just like you," her mother said. "I-I can't believe how grown up you both are. I kept envisioning seeing you both as newborns, just as you were when I held you to my breast while I was nursing you." She choked on the words.

Janice and Dorinda hugged her again. "We're together now. It's time for us to start making new memories." Though Janice felt cheated that she hadn't been able to live with her birth family and had to deal with years of insecurity about what she was. Dorinda must have felt the same way.

Their mother and father both had red hair: his a darker red, her mother's more of a strawberry blond. Both had green eyes like Dorinda and Janice. "You definitely look like our parents," Janice said smiling.

"The girls' smiles are just the same." Their father hugged them again.

In all the enthusiasm to meet their parents, Janice had forgotten to introduce her mate and her sister-in-law. Brad and Sierra were standing off to the side, smiling, look pleased the family was together again. "This is Brad Redding, my mate. And his sister, Sierra, now our sister too."

"I can't believe one of our girls is already mated, but

we're thrilled to have you in our family," Rhonda said, giving Brad and Sierra a hug.

Kirk agreed. "I might have wanted to meet with you first. But given the circumstances, I'm just glad we have even more of a family to celebrate." He hugged them too.

Leidolf motioned to the house. "Why don't we take a seat in the living room, and Rhonda and Kirk can tell their story of how they lost you."

After they took their seats—Rhonda and Kirk sitting on a loveseat, and Janice, Dorinda, Brad, and Sierra all sitting on another sofa, with Leidolf and Cassie on another loveseat—Rhonda began. "Your father is a royal, but I was human, bitten and turned. He found me and took care of me, loved me, despite how growly I was when all this first happened." Rhonda smiled at him, and Kirk kissed her. "He wanted to kill the wolf who had bitten me and left me for dead, but a hunter had shot the wolf and killed him, luckily at the edge of a cliff. When the wolf fell, he shifted, but the hunter only found a dead human downstream and hadn't seen him shift in death."

Janice couldn't believe her mother had lived through such an awful ordeal, and she loved her father for taking her mother in when she had been a problem wolf like Janice and Dorinda were with the shapeshifting issues.

"I couldn't live without your mother. She easily became the love of my life," Kirk said. "Within the year, we were having the two of you, and we couldn't have been more ecstatic."

"We weren't with a pack though, and Kirk's parents had died, so we didn't have any support system. Kirk told me it would be easier for me to have the babies on our own as wolf pups. But you girls didn't cooperate. It was the time of the new moon, I couldn't shift into my wolf, and I didn't have any choice. We had been traveling, and you were coming. We had to go to the hospital in Tacoma. We knew we had to leave soon after, but before we could pack you up and slip out of there, you girls were taken from the hospital. A woman dressed in scrubs said you needed to be weighed and measured. And then she disappeared with the two of you."

"But she didn't keep either of us," Janice suspected.

"No. She was wearing hunter's spray, and I didn't see her," their dad said. "I had run to the bathroom. Otherwise, I would have known right away who took you girls. I was furious, devastated, just as much as your mother was."

"Who took us?" Janice and Dorinda both asked.

"An ex-girlfriend," Rhonda said. "She was a royal like your father, but he didn't feel anything for her. They'd already broken up, but she kept wanting to get back together with him. Then she learned that not only had he picked me up as his new girlfriend, but I was newly turned, and he mated me right away. She was livid and even angrier when she learned I was pregnant with twins."

Janice wanted to kill the woman!

"We didn't know who it was right away. The police were involved. We were devastated. Then we saw the security footage, and I knew it was my ex-girlfriend. Rhonda had never met her before. I would have rescued you girls and killed her if I could have. But she disappeared. We checked all the adoption agencies, no luck. We considered that she'd killed you but were hopeful she had adopted you out to good families, maybe through an agency that wasn't so reputable," Kirk said, clasping Rhonda's hand.

What a horrible thing to do to a new family! Though

Janice was glad at least the woman hadn't just murdered them.

"The problem was I couldn't control my shifting during most of the month. That put you girls in way too much danger. We had to move far enough away from the two of you, at least we hoped we were, so that my shifting wouldn't trigger your shifting."

"Ohmigod, Mom, I'm so sorry," Janice said, Dorinda nodding her head vigorously.

"We were just so worried about you girls," Kirk said. "Since you were born in Tacoma and we were from California where I was a bank president at a local bank, we moved to the East Coast, hoping no one had adopted you in Florida, where I became a bank president again."

"We got word from a police officer who had worked the case in Tacoma that a new cop was looking into it. We had always kept in touch with the officer who had originally handled our case. He gave us the cop's name and number. We contacted him, and he was thrilled. He told us in so many words that you were with a red wolf pack out here that he belonged to, and we immediately booked a flight." Rhonda wiped away her tears. "We've been invited to join the pack, but we can't tell you how many times we wished we could have found you over the years."

"Us too," Janice said, speaking for her sister also.

"What about the woman who stole us?" Dorinda asked, looking as angry as Janice felt.

"Once I identified her on the tape, I knew she couldn't go to prison. As a royal, she could manage her shifting, but still, there's always the fear that a wolf incarcerated might get so aggravated he or she might shift anyway. The police didn't hesitate to plaster her picture all over the States though, and she knew before long she'd get caught at it. When the police located her, she'd already taken an overdose of sleeping pills," Kirk said.

"And didn't leave a note?" Janice asked.

"Yeah, she left a note. All she said was I should have mated her," Kirk said.

Janice wiped away tears and gave her mom and dad a hug, Dorinda right beside her. "Thank you for taking our mom in."

"She was the only one for me," Kirk said. "And you girls were the joy in our lives for the brief time we had you."

"I felt it was all my fault I'd lost you girls," their mom said.

"I felt it was mine. If I hadn't gone to the bathroom, I would have seen her and called security."

"It was only her fault," Janice said.

"None of that matters now," Dorinda said. "You're here with us now. You're staying, right?"

"Yeah. We sure are, with Cassie and Leidolf's blessing, and yours," Rhonda said.

"We've got a lot of catching up to do," their father said. "But we have time to do it now. I retired from the bank in southern Florida, so we're looking forward to getting to know you girls and your new family and the pack and doing whatever we can to help our kind."

Their mother agreed. And so did Janice and her sister.

After hours talking, it was getting late, and Dorinda and Sierra called it a night and headed to what they were referring to as the bachelorette house. Dorinda and Janice's parents were staying with the Wildhavens until they could build a home there.

They all hugged and kissed before Brad took Janice home. She knew that look in his eye meant he was ready for some more loving.

He deserved it, and lots more, just like she did. She couldn't believe her father had fallen for a newly turned wolf, and Brad had been just as sweet to have fallen in love with her. She'd finally found not one but lots of wolves to be with: her mate, her sister, her parents, the whole wolf pack. She was right with the world, perfectly normal, no longer cursed, just one of the rest of her kind like all the others who couldn't hold their form during the full moon.

A trip to White Wolf Sanctuary had enriched Brad's life more than he could ever have imagined. His lovely mate and her family had expanded his world tenfold. The addition of his sister too made him feel as though this was Christmas in January, of love and hope and family. All that was needed to make it complete was his parents' arrival in a couple of weeks.

But for now?

Brad chased Janice into the bedroom, her squealing in delight, and he tackled her on the bed. Tonight and every night and whenever else they could squeeze it in, they were going to have lots of loving, any phase of moon, day or night. The sky was the limit.

ABOUT THE AUTHOR

USA Today bestselling author Terry Spear has written over sixty paranormal and medieval Highland romances. In 2008, *Heart of the Wolf* was named a *Publishers Weekly* Best Book of the Year. She has received a PNR Top Pick, a Best Book of the Month nomination by *Long and Short Reviews*, numerous *Night Owl Romance* Top Picks, and two Paranormal Excellence Awards for Romantic Literature (Finalist & Honorable Mention). In 2016, *Billionaire in Wolf's Clothing* was an *RT Book Reviews* top pick. A retired officer of the U.S. Army Reserves, Terry also creates award-winning teddy bears that have found homes all over the world, helps out with her grandbaby, and is raising two Havanese puppies. She lives in Spring, Texas.